CROSSHAIRS

Center Point
Large Print

Also by Patricia Bradley and available from
Center Point Large Print:

Justice Delayed
Justice Buried
Justice Betrayed
Justice Delivered
Standoff
Obsession

**This Large Print Book carries the
Seal of Approval of N.A.V.H.**

NATCHEZ TRACE PARK RANGERS
BOOK 3

CROSSHAIRS

PATRICIA BRADLEY

CENTER POINT LARGE PRINT
THORNDIKE, MAINE

This Center Point Large Print edition
is published in the year 2021 by arrangement with
Revell, a division of Baker Publishing Group.

The text of this Large Print edition is unabridged.
In other aspects, this book may vary
from the original edition.
Printed in the United States of America
on permanent paper.
Set in 16-point Times New Roman type.

ISBN: 978-1-63808-143-2

The Library of Congress has cataloged this record under
Library of Congress Control Number: 2021944096

In memory of my nephew,
Bradley Haynes.
Like I always said,
"Brad, you're my favorite nephew."
To which you replied,
"I'm your only nephew."
October 19, 1976–August 23, 2020

1

*C*ome on! It was almost midnight, and the light in Cora Chamberlain's bedroom blazed like a neon sign.

He ground his teeth as rain poured from the skies, running off his black slicker.

Tornado watches had been issued for the area, and while those were as common as mosquitoes in the springtime, he never remembered a June tornado in Natchez. Still, it'd be his luck for one to hit the town tonight. Especially since nothing else had gone right, starting with the phone call an hour ago from Miss Cora, when she only teased him about the journals she'd found. It was why he stood in a copse of trees outside her antebellum home.

"You'll never believe it, but I discovered two more diaries!" Miss Cora's voice wavered, but even at ninety-two, it had not lost its cultured tone. "I scanned the first few pages of the oldest one, and I believe it was written the summer before Zachary Elliott was killed. I'm certain I'll find proof my great-grandfather Chamberlain was innocent of murder. Do you know what that means, Sonny?"

Only his runners called him Sonny now. Well, except for the aging spinster and her sister who he'd known since he was a boy. "Of course I do," he said. "If it has the information you've been searching for, you'll be able to clear his name. Why don't you let me come over—you can read one, and I can read the other. You'd get your answer much quicker."

"It's too late tonight—maybe tomorrow. No. Ainsley is here . . . I do wish I knew where I put that first journal. Then I would have the complete set to finish my book."

He ground his teeth. Once again she was rambling.

"Maybe one day you'll find it." *Or not. Especially since it was in a safe in Sonny's apartment over the Blue Lantern.* "I can be there in ten minutes."

"You're a dear boy," Cora said, "but it's much too late. After Ainsley leaves will be soon enough."

And that was why he was waiting in the rain for her bedroom light to go out. He owed people money, and they were pressing him for payment. He had a week at most to come up with fifty grand.

He'd stolen the first journal, thinking a private collector might give him a few hundred dollars for the leather-bound book because of the historical value, but no takers. Last week, he'd stumbled over the diary again when he'd been looking for anything he could sell and remembered Cora mentioning Adele Kingston had threatened to sue if Cora published what was in it.

Sonny had always heard the devil was in the details, and details of the murder over 150 years ago had not been in the journal he already possessed. It stood to reason if the new diaries were written not long before the murder happened, the details he sought would be in them. Details Jack Kingston would pay to keep private.

Sonny caught his breath. What if Ainsley decided to stay with Cora tonight instead of with her grandmother? He immediately dismissed the thought. Cora would have mentioned it.

If he was a praying man, Sonny would pray the old woman wouldn't mention his name to her niece. She'd never liked him, and now Ainsley Beaumont was in some sort of law enforcement. She'd probably think he was taking advantage of her great-aunt. And she would be right.

His gaze darted to the house across the street where Cora's sister lived. Rose's house was already dark, and so were the houses on the opposite corners of the intersection. Good.

Stop worrying. Miss Cora had promised not to tell anyone she'd found the new journals, and she was old school. If she told you something, you could bank on it.

9

When he asked where she'd found them, she babbled some nonsense about showing him later. Well, he wasn't waiting for later.

He rubbed his hand over his eyes, wiping away the rain. The corner light on the first floor dimmed to black. Things were turning around. He'd give her thirty minutes to fall sound asleep before he entered through the cellar and crept up the secret passageway that opened into the library on the first floor where Cora worked at her computer.

The woman was remarkable to navigate computers the way she did at her age. Too bad she had to die. It shouldn't be too hard to make it look as though she'd died of natural causes in her sleep. A pillow should do the trick.

He flinched at a sudden pop of lightning followed almost instantly with thunder that shook the ground. As he looked up, more lightning revealed a thick wall cloud. He didn't have time for violent weather tonight.

However, maybe the noise of the storm would hide his breaking and entering, and he wouldn't have to wait thirty minutes. Sonny slipped away from the woods, then dashed to the cellar steps at the back of the two-story house and descended to the doorway. When another bolt of lightning lit up the sky, he thrust a fallen branch from the nearby magnolia tree through the glass pane above the handle just as the follow-up clap of thunder shook the windows.

Once inside the cellar, he eased behind the stairs and stood motionless, letting rain run off his slicker and listening for any sign he'd been heard. When no telltale footsteps sounded, he used the flashlight on his phone to illuminate the wall and find the small hole in the second panel of wood.

Once he triggered the latch, the door swung open noiselessly, and he quietly climbed the steep stairs. At the top, he unlatched the sliding door, pushed it to the side, and stepped into the library. He'd learned about the secret stairway as a young boy when his father replaced the door in the basement with a hidden panel for Miss Cora.

Once again, he stood perfectly still while the storm raged outside. So far, no tornado sirens sounded. When he was certain Cora hadn't heard him, he flicked on the light from his phone again and scanned the room, stopping at her desk.

He frowned. Where were the journals? They should have been on the cherry desk beside Miss Cora's laptop—that's where she put everything. They weren't on the table beside it either. Sweat beaded his face. He had to find them.

A thorough search of the desk revealed no journals. Could she have taken them to her bedroom? What if she had referenced them to someone in an email? He stood behind the desk and booted up her computer, relaxing after he found nothing pertaining to the journals in her sent box.

"What are you doing here this time of night?"

He whirled around. Miss Cora stood in the doorway, looking like an avenging angel with her white robe cinched around her and her finger pointed straight at him. "Sonny?"

"Where are they?" He took a step toward her. "The diaries. What have you done with them?"

She turned her head slightly toward the bedroom. He'd been right—she'd taken them to her bedroom. He rushed past her, knocking the old woman out of the way.

Sonny ignored the resounding crack her head made when it hit the floor. He found one diary on the table beside her bed. *Where is the other one?*

He quickly returned to the library and shook her. "Where is it?" he demanded, then frowned. She was so pale. He felt her wrist. No! She couldn't be dead. Not until she told him where it was. Maybe in a safe somewhere?

The front door banged open. He froze.

"Cora! Wake up! There's a tornado coming!"

Rose, Cora's sister. But he thought she'd gone to bed.

"Where are you?" Her voice, so like her sister's, rose to a high pitch. "We have to get in the cellar!"

Maybe he should kill her too. No. The police would assume Cora fell and hit her head, causing a brain bleed, but two deaths would cause suspicion. Ainsley was probably with Rose anyway.

12

He would find a way to return and tear the house apart if he had to in order to find that other diary. He could not take a chance on anyone else finding it. He dashed toward the secret passageway.

"Cora! Where are you?"

"You check her bedroom, and I'll check the library."

That had to be Ainsley. The door had barely closed behind him when he heard her cry out.

"Oh no! Gran, quick! The library!"

Seconds later he heard her say, "Siri, call 911!"

2

Ainsley Beaumont knelt beside her great-aunt as she identified herself and gave her location to the 911 dispatcher. "My aunt has fallen, and I'm not sure she's breathing!"

"Can you give CPR?"

"Yes." She'd applied the technique more than a few times, but never to a family member.

"Do I need to stay on the line with you?"

"No. Just get the ambulance here ASAP." A slight rise in Cora's chest sent relief washing through her. "She's breathing, although it's shallow."

Ainsley had no sooner disconnected from the call than the blaring wail of the tornado siren assaulted her ears. A tornado was the last thing they needed. She felt her aunt's wrist. Her heartbeat was too fast to count. When had she gotten so thin? And frail? She'd always been so strong.

Ainsley should have come home more often, but it'd always been easier to get her grandmother and aunt to come to her rather than for her to return to Natchez.

She was here now. *You could have been here this past week instead of on that Caribbean cruise.* Ainsley squelched the accusing voice in her head.

"Is she . . ." Gran's voice shook. Cora was her only sister.

"She's breathing." If only she had her first aid kit to check Cora's blood pressure. Where were those first responders?

Ainsley winced as the tornado siren raked her ears again. They needed to get to the basement, but Cora was as tall as Ainsley's five-nine. While she was thin, she would be too heavy for Ainsley to get down the steps by herself. It would take a gurney or stretcher for that. "Is the front door unlocked?"

"I'll check."

When her grandmother opened the front door, Ainsley barely distinguished the sound of the tornado siren from an approaching ambulance. Once again relief pulsed through her. The paramedics would have the equipment to get Cora to the basement, where they all needed to be.

Within minutes, the paramedics were kneeling beside Cora, and Ainsley recognized the lead medic. Kanesha Davis. They'd grown up together. "Is my aunt going to be all right?" she asked.

"It's too early to tell," her friend replied. "You need to get to the basement."

"I'm not going anywhere without Cora," Gran said. And that meant Ainsley wasn't going either.

The storm abated into an eerie quiet while the two medics worked on her aunt. From her nightgown and robe, it was obvious Cora had been in bed before she fell. Why had she come to the library? Ainsley paced in front of the desk, her gaze shifting from Cora to the carpeted floor and then to Gran, who sat on the edge of the leather sofa, watching their every move.

With storms predicted for the evening hours, her grandmother still wore her day clothes and had insisted Ainsley remain dressed, saying they weren't getting blown away in their pajamas. Ainsley's lips tugged upward as she imagined what Gran was thinking about Cora's robe and gown.

Her grandmother glanced toward her, and Ainsley ducked her head to hide the grin, her gaze landing on the floor again. The carpet was the kind that showed every footstep, and it looked as though some of the fibers might be wet. She knelt and ran her hand over the spot. Damp. Had she and her grandmother tracked in water? Definitely, but neither of them had stood in that particular spot. Had someone been in the room other than Cora?

"What do you think happened?" Gran whispered.

Ainsley stood, intending to search for more wet carpet. "I don't—"

Sudden, frantic pounding jerked her attention

to the front door, then the bell went crazy, and seconds later the door burst open. "There's a tornado crossing the river! Everyone needs to get into the basement!"

Ainsley froze. What was Lincoln Steele doing here? He was the last person she wanted to see tonight. Or ever. Linc appeared in the doorway just as the roar of the wind picked up again. All she needed now was for her dad to show up.

She found her voice. "What are you doing here?"

"I heard the call go out for this address," he said. "Is Miss Cora okay?"

Kanesha looked up. "She's in A-fib, but we can't transport her with a tornado bearing down on us. We have to move her downstairs until this blows over." She turned to Ainsley. "Where're the basement stairs?"

"Down the hall."

"I'll show you."

They'd both spoken at the same time. She jerked her head toward him, and their gazes collided. Ainsley's heart crashed against her ribs, and she found it hard to breathe. She'd hoped to avoid him while she was in Natchez, had in the past whenever she was in town. Or maybe he'd been avoiding her.

The gurney blocked her escape, and she had to wait while Linc helped the two medics gently lift Cora onto it. She and Gran followed behind as he guided them toward the basement door. With the wind now sounding like a jet taking off, Ainsley was glad to escape underground. Searching for evidence that someone may have been in the room with Cora would have to wait.

She was surprised when Linc flicked on the basement light switch practically hidden on the other side of the door. Why was he so familiar with Cora's house?

Another question for later. Ainsley helped her grandmother down the steps and settled her in one of the straight-backed chairs that had been placed in the basement for such a night as this, before sitting in the one beside it.

Her grandmother patted Ainsley's hand. "We will be fine."

Maybe from the tornado. She wasn't so sure about being safe from Linc. A quick glance at him sent her heart rate skyrocketing again. He hadn't even had the decency to go to pot. Instead, his form-fitting T-shirt revealed sculpted muscles as he slipped out of the black slicker.

He pulled off the rain hat and tossed it on top of the slicker, then ran his hand over black hair with a hint of wave in it. Heat flooded her face when Linc looked up and caught her watching him.

The wind shook the house and drowned out any conversation coming from across the room as the medics dropped the wheels on the gurney and parked the bed in the corner. She glanced at her grandmother. Her lips were moving, and Ainsley was certain she was praying since prayer was Gran's go-to. Used to be Ainsley's until she went to Nashville. She brushed the thought off and squeezed her grandmother's hand.

The paramedics continued to work on her aunt. Linc talked to Kanesha while she fitted an oxygen mask over Cora's nose and mouth, then he strode toward them. Ainsley averted her gaze and studied her clasped hands.

"How is Cora?" her grandmother asked. "Is she conscious?"

"In and out. Kanesha says she's stable for the moment," Linc said. "As soon as this lets up, they'll take her to Merit."

Merit was the hospital not far from their house, but then practically everything in Natchez was reachable in ten minutes.

She looked away from Linc. Her fingernails were turning white, and she relaxed her hands. This was crazy. She'd faced criminals with more courage.

Besides, he was the one who'd forced her to choose between him and her dream. Ainsley lifted her chin but almost faltered when she found herself gazing into Linc's hazel eyes, which had once looked at her with love.

"Does Kanesha know what's wrong with Cora?" Gran asked.

"If she does, she's not saying . . ." He glanced

toward the gurney. "From the knot and cut on her head, it could be a brain bleed caused from falling."

Her grandmother gasped. "No."

Ainsley's heart sank. Brain bleeds equaled strokes. Cora was ninety-two, and recovery would be iffy. "Do you think we could talk to her? In case on some level she can hear us?"

"I think that would be good." Linc held out his hand to help her grandmother stand.

Ainsley joined Gran at the side of the gurney. A small monitor beeped a rapid 120 beats a minute, and oxygen flowed through the mask. At least Cora's color was better. Now if she would just open those bright blue eyes and recognize them.

"You are going to be fine," her grandmother said, leaning near Cora's ear as she rubbed her sister's limp hand. "Just fine."

"We love you, Cora," Ainsley added softly, willing her to live. Gran would be lost if anything happened to her sister.

Suddenly her eyes fluttered open.

"Cora," Ainsley said, leaning toward her. "We're here."

"Charlotte's . . . diaries," she whispered.

Ainsley could barely hear the words through the face mask and leaned closer.

"New . . . find . . . them."

"What diaries?" Gran asked.

Cora stared at her briefly, then closed her eyes.

"Cora Jane Chamberlain," Gran said. "You better not die on me!"

"Don't . . . worry," she whispered. "Head hurts . . ."

"Was anyone here tonight when you fell?" Ainsley asked.

Her aunt turned her head slightly, her eyes opening. "I . . ." Her lips moved, but no words came.

"Shh," Gran said. "Just rest."

Ainsley's first instinct was to push Cora to remember, but pressing for answers could make her condition worse. Instead, she backed away from the bed to give the sisters privacy.

What diaries could she be talking about? Earlier in the day they'd discussed the one leather-bound diary Cora had found but then misplaced, which was not like her aunt at all. She might be past ninety, but she was still sharp. Gran too. Had Cora found more diaries? Who would care? Her questioning mind returned to the damp carpet.

"Nice tan you've got there," Linc said.

She jumped.

"Sorry, I thought you saw me standing here."

"Well, I didn't." He must've been watching her to notice her tan. She forced her thoughts back to the wet carpet upstairs. "Why was the carpet by Cora's desk wet?"

"What are you talking about?"

Ainsley usually worked alone, and sometimes

her habit of talking to herself could be embarrassing. "Nothing." Why did he rattle her so?

Linc crossed his arms. "Do you think someone was in the library with her?"

He sounded like a cop. Oh, wait. He was former FBI. "I don't know. I didn't have time to investigate or see if anything else was out of place," she said and explained what she'd found. "Pretty sure someone had been standing there with wet shoes, or water had run off their clothing, maybe a slicker like you had on. Then you arrived, and here we are. As soon as this storm passes over, I plan to check it out."

Linc chewed his bottom lip just like he had years ago when he was trying to solve a problem. "Could you have—"

"No. The wet carpet is behind her desk, where neither of us had walked."

"What do you mean, the carpet is wet?" Her grandmother had crossed the room to where they stood.

"It's probably nothing," she said, not wanting to worry her.

"I want to know why Cora got up from her bed and went to the library in her gown." Gran glanced back at her sister.

"If she thought someone was in the house, wouldn't she call 911?" Ainsley asked.

"You know better. Your great-aunt would have acted first and thought later."

"So that's where you get it from," Linc said with a chuckle.

He was trying to make it sound like he was teasing, but Ainsley knew better. In spite of what he thought, she hadn't jumped into breaking up with him without agonizing over it. *He* had been the one who'd sided with her father, and she would never forgive him for it. Or open her heart to him again.

3

Was he crazy or what? Trying to tease Ainsley like they were friends. She would more likely befriend one of the gators in the swamps around Natchez than him. A strand of her raven hair had come loose from the clip, and he clenched his hand to keep from tucking the loose curl behind her ear. Besides, given the glare he was getting, she would probably shove his hand off. Black hair and flashing blue eyes. A deadly combination. At least for him, anyway.

She narrowed her eyes. "How come you know your way around Cora's house? I don't remember you two being that close."

"I'm advising her about her book, and it's easier for me to come here."

"Why would she ask you—"

He palmed his hands. "Your aunt came to me and asked for my help. I presume because I'm the historian at Melrose, and Melrose's second owners, the Davises, were neighbors and friends of the Chamberlains."

"*You're* the historian at Melrose?" Her eyes

widened. "I mean, I knew you were a ranger, but you were a sharpshooter with the FBI. I thought . . ."

"That I was in law enforcement, like you?" So she kept up with him, but no one had told her he was an *interpretive* ranger. One that led tours and didn't carry a gun. "No. I've had my fill of killing." He wasn't about to tell her he couldn't even think about holding a gun without feeling sick.

Ainsley sagged into the chair she'd vacated earlier, and color flooded her face. "I'm sorry. I didn't mean to argue with you." She glanced toward Rose, who had returned to her sister's bedside. "I just want to understand what happened here tonight."

Linc released the breath trapped in his chest. He didn't want to argue with her either. They'd had enough of that in the past. He took her grandmother's chair and leaned toward her. "You really think someone was in the house with Cora when she fell?"

Instead of answering, she looked up as Kanesha approached them.

"I'm having trouble keeping her blood pressure from bottoming out, and the storm has abated enough for us to get to Merit," Kanesha said. "Is there another exit from the basement?"

"Over here," Ainsley said. She stood and hurried to a small hallway. Linc followed and saw the broken glass from the window in the door at the same time she gasped.

"Someone *was* here," she said.

"Maybe." A branch lay just inside the entrance. "Or the storm blew that in."

"Mighty convenient it only broke out the pane above the doorknob," she said.

Linc glanced at the water near the door. Could have blown in, or someone tracked it in.

"Does the driveway circle around to the back of the house?" Kanesha asked.

Ainsley nodded. "There's no shelter, but it's only a few steps from the basement to the drive."

"We're going to transport soon, then."

"Gran," Ainsley called to her grandmother, "I'm going to check out the library while they get Cora in the ambulance. I'll be back before they leave."

"Mind if I tag along?" Linc asked.

"Why? You're not in law enforcement."

No, and he never would be again. "Does it count that I'm a volunteer with SAR?" Search and Rescue didn't require a gun. "This could fall under the 'search' end."

She studied him a minute, then barely shrugged. "Sure."

Linc followed Ainsley up the stairs to the library and knelt beside her as she ran her hands over the short carpet near where Cora had fallen.

"Is it wet?"

"Somewhat, but it's probably what the para-medics tracked in. Or us." She held up a blade of grass. "But I doubt any of us brought this in."

She moved to the desk area and raked her fingers through the rug, frowning as she held up a fragment of a leaf and more blades of grass.

"Could've been there awhile," he said.

"No. I came over to Cora's this afternoon and couldn't believe she was trying to vacuum this room. She is so fiercely independent, she almost didn't turn the vacuum over to me. Someone tracked water and debris into the library since then."

Ainsley ran her hand over the carpet again.

"Will you be staying in Natchez long?" He'd been dying to ask that question since he arrived.

She looked up at him. "I don't know."

"What do you mean?"

Ainsley hesitated, then shrugged. "I'm here because of the girl who was killed. Sam Ryker called in ISB."

Everything fell into place. Ainsley was an Investigative Services Branch ranger. "The girl at Rocky Springs?"

She nodded, then turned her attention back to the carpet, and he took his cue from that. "Is the desk where you first noticed damp spots?"

"Yes." On her hands and knees now, she slowly felt the carpet, crawling as she followed what appeared to be a trail of damp carpet that led to the fireplace. Ainsley's phone dinged a text and she stood. "They're ready to leave," she said. "I'll have to come back later."

He cocked his head, listening. "Since the worst of the storm seems to be over, I should see if anyone needs help." Linc hesitated. "Would you keep me in the loop about Cora's condition? And if you discover that someone broke into her house."

Her shoulders stiffened, and she pressed her lips together in a thin line.

Before she could say no, he said, "I've gotten close to her since we've been working on the book. If someone hurt her . . ."

Her mouth relaxed, but the nod she gave him was curt. "I'll keep you informed as much as I can. However, if I determine someone was here, it'll be a matter for the police. I don't have jurisdiction in Natchez other than on the Trace and at the park service historical sites."

He could probably get more information from the chief of police than from Ainsley anyway.

"I'll make sure the doors are locked," he said as she brushed past him. A light lilac scent took him back to a time when they weren't on opposite sides of an argument that had destroyed their relationship. He'd been a fool to side with her dad back then, and he needed to make amends. "Ainsley . . ."

She stopped at the top of the basement stairs and looked toward him, her eyes questioning.

"I—"

"Ainsley! They're leaving with Cora!" Rose called from the basement.

Now was not the time or place. "Be careful," he said.

A flicker of annoyance crossed her face. "I'm always careful."

Yeah, right. He'd almost said the words before he caught them. "Just thought I'd remind you. And let me know what the doctors say about Cora."

"Sure." Then she disappeared down the stairs.

After they left, Linc descended the steps into the basement to repair the door. After examining the damage, he scanned the basement for a hammer and nails and found what he needed in a red toolbox. After he didn't readily see a board, Linc used the light on his phone to search the area. Was a piece of lumber sticking out under the steps leading upstairs? When he investigated, he stopped short. A puddle of water had accumulated on the floor behind the stairs.

Water didn't just accumulate in a basement unless there was a leak somewhere . . . or someone tracked it in. And, if someone had been in the basement, he would've had to come up the same steps they came down and he didn't remember any water on the steps when they brought Cora down. But then again, he hadn't been looking for any.

Linc snapped a photo to show Ainsley later. Warmth spread through his chest as he nailed the board over the broken glass. He had a legitimate reason to see her again.

Immediately reality slapped him. It was a fool's wish he harbored. A former FBI agent who couldn't touch a gun, let alone shoot one, didn't deserve her.

4

Sonny's fingers shook as he gripped the phone. The man wanted to argue about what Sonny was asking for the diary. "It's fifty grand. Take it or leave it." He had to have that much to pay his debts.

"Does it specifically state that Charlotte Elliott and her husband owned slaves?"

"Yes. And plenty more that your wife's society friends will find interesting. But that's all right. Your opponent is also interested in buying them." Sonny ended the call. Fifty thousand dollars was coffee change to his caller.

Adding another buyer had come to him out of nowhere. But it was a good idea. Beaumont would have a totally different reason to want the diaries. *If* Sonny could convince him that he needed the journals.

He calmed himself and dialed another number. The man answered on the third ring.

"Hello?"

"I have information your opponent is trying to buy from me."

"Who is this?"

"That's not important. I have diaries that depict your family most unfavorably."

"What are you talking about?"

"Slavery and how your ancestors were slave owners."

"That isn't relevant in this day and age."

"Your opponent seems to think it is. He's willing to give me fifty thousand for the two diaries I have. You think about it. I'll call you again in a couple of days."

"Wait! Where did you get the diaries?"

Sonny could hardly say he'd stolen them. "Found them in an antiques store this side of New Orleans."

"How do I know they're about my family?"

"Did you have a great-great-grandfather by the name of Robert Chamberlain?"

He didn't wait for a response but ended the call and pocketed his phone. It was all about perception. Until he'd approached them, neither man perceived that he needed what Sonny had to offer. And now they did. If he played his cards right, maybe he could get them to bid against one another.

Cora had said there were two diaries, and he'd only found one. While he looked for the missing journal, he would let both men stew a bit.

He scanned the area, then climbed out of the car. According to the radio, the tornado had hit the bluffs and skipped over much of Natchez, hitting the south part of the county. At least the police would be too busy with the aftermath to bother about a car parked a couple of streets over from Cora's house at one a.m. He pocketed his keys and struck out for the Chamberlain house. Hopefully, the broken window had not been discovered and he could easily access the house again.

Minutes later, Sonny swore when he found a board covering the broken pane. He should have made a duplicate key to the house—it would have been easy enough to lift the one hanging in the kitchen.

Most people kept a key hidden outside, but he scanned the area before he started searching. The house backed up to a wooded lot, and while it would be hard for anyone to see him, it was always a good idea to double-check.

If he were Cora, where would he hide a key? He used the light on his phone to search for an out-of-the-way place she might have hidden one and looked under every flowerpot and rock to no avail. Sonny was about to give up and break the board when he spied a concrete frog beside the basement wall. He felt inside the frog's belly, and his fingers closed on a key. Bingo! After using it to enter through the back door, he returned the key to the frog before slipping inside the house.

Someone had left a hallway light on, and he flicked off the flashlight on his phone. Amazing that even burner phones had them nowadays. He quick-timed it to Cora's bedroom and searched it from top to bottom, being careful to leave everything as he found it. No diary. He wondered if maybe he'd overlooked it earlier in the library, so he returned to the room.

When the diary wasn't in plain sight, he slowly scanned the room. Could there be another hidden space, other than the stairway, where she might have stashed it? He walked around the room, tapping on the walls.

Lights flashed in the drive. No! He'd only been searching for two hours. Sonny had anticipated the family would be at the hospital until morning, giving him plenty of time to find the diary. Had Cora died? That would solve at least one problem. When Sonny heard a car door slam, he quickly activated the sliding door and entered the hidden stairwell, then closed the door, making sure it closed properly inside the groove.

He waited quietly, straining to hear any conversation that might tell him who had entered the house and why. Footsteps approached the library.

"What do you need from the library?" He recognized Rose Beaumont's voice. "We have the medicines her doctor wanted us to get."

"Just want to check something out."

The granddaughter, and it sounded like she was poking around not six feet from him. What was she doing? If only whoever had built the stair-case had put in a peephole!

"Do you smell that?" The Beaumont girl again.

"No . . . what does it smell like?"

"I'm not sure . . . sandalwood, maybe."

Cold chills ran over him. Surely she didn't smell the cologne he'd put on this morning.

"I get a hint of it by the fireplace . . ."

He eased away from the wall.

"But it smells like cheap cologne."

Cheap cologne indeed. Sixty-five dollars an ounce was not cheap. But he would have to remember not to wear it again.

"I think you're imagining it," Rose said. "What are you doing on the floor?"

"Trying to see if there's more wet carpet."

He must have tracked water into the library.

"Do you really think someone was in here with Cora?"

"I do, but unless she remembers what happened, we won't know for sure. The doctors don't hold out much hope she'll remember anything around the time of the accident, especially if they have to do surgery." Minutes ticked by, then a sigh. "I can't find anything."

"Everything isn't a crime, Ainsley."

"Maybe not, but I won't be satisfied until Cora can tell us that no one else was here. Are you ready to go home?"

"We're not going back to the hospital?"

"We can go in the morning. Before we left, Cora made me promise to take you home and see to it you get a few hours' sleep."

Their voices faded as they left the library. He balled his hands. It was apparent that Ainsley Beaumont would keep digging into what happened here tonight. Maybe he should give her something else to worry about.

5

The Search and Rescue coordinator had sent Linc to the south side of the county, where other SAR volunteers were already working. By the time he arrived in the neighborhood that took the hit from the tornado, the power company had rigged up portable lights, enabling volunteers to see what they were doing as they dug through the rubble.

The SAR coordinator directed him to one of the hardest-hit homes, where the owner, an older woman, had taken refuge in an inner bathroom. As he helped move a beam that had blocked the bathroom door, Linc kept a steady stream of encouragement going to her. When he finally pulled the door open, he took her hand and said, "It's going to be okay."

"Thank you, young man," she said. Though her voice quivered, her soft brown eyes reflected strength. "Was anyone in the neighborhood hurt?"

Her house was destroyed, and she was worried about other people. "Not as far as I know. The funnel cloud lifted over the city, hit here, and then lifted again. Your house sustained the most damage."

Linc surveyed the row of homes. How did one

have a roof blown off while the house beside it appeared untouched? If someone told him a tornado could drive a straw through a tree trunk, he'd believe it. He'd seen too many weird things happen with twisters, and this one could have been worse.

She turned and surveyed what was left of her home, her breath catching.

"I'm sorry about your house," he said. All that remained were the four walls around the bathroom.

"Things can be replaced. I'm just thankful to be here. Not the first twister I've survived in my eighty years," she said, sighing. "What's your name, son?"

"Lincoln Steele."

"I'm Hattie Bell." She tilted her head, studying him. "You part of the Steeles over by the Junction?"

"Yes, ma'am. My grandparents," he said. "Do you have any family around here?"

She pulled her sweater tighter and shook her head. "Got no family left."

About all she had were the clothes on her back. Before he could ask any more questions, a woman in her midfifties approached them. "Miss Hattie! You're okay! When I heard your house was blowed away—"

"I'm fine, Wanda. This nice young man is helping me."

"Well, you're coming home with me. The storm purely missed us."

Linc breathed a sigh of relief. He hadn't known what he was going to do with Miss Hattie. He doubted she would go to the shelter being set up, and he couldn't leave her here by herself.

"She needs to be checked out by the paramedics. They're set up at the end of the street," Linc said.

He walked the two women to a waiting pickup and helped them in. As the driver drove toward the first aid station, he scanned the area for his Search and Rescue supervisor. Instead, Sarah Tolliver and her videographer came into view, and he returned her wave. He should have known the news reporter would be here. The woman never slept.

Sarah walked toward him. "Not surprised to see you helping out," she said, giving him a warm smile that reached all the way to her huge brown eyes. "Can I interview you?"

"Nah, find someone else."

"The lady you helped into the truck. Did one of the homes belong to her?" Her honeyed voice was one reason she was so popular with viewers.

"That one," he said, nodding toward the flattened house.

She turned. "Can't believe no one was injured. She just walked away unscathed?"

"Miss Hattie rode out the storm in an inner bathroom," Linc said. "We just freed her, and a neighbor down the road is taking her to the first aid station and then home with her."

"She was a lucky woman." Sarah stared at the house a little longer, then turned to Linc, running her gaze over him. "You're looking good."

"Yeah, well, thanks," he said. "You, ah, look good too."

"I've missed our talks," she said wistfully.

Linc swallowed hard. Sarah's brother had been his best friend since tenth grade at Natchez High School. They'd stayed friends through college and had joined the FBI together, Blake a field agent and Linc ending up being one of the FBI's best snipers until . . . until he wasn't.

"So do I," he said, hoping God would forgive him for not being perfectly honest. Sarah had been a couple of grades behind them, and while Linc had always liked Blake's kid sister, he'd never had any romantic feelings toward her. After her brother's suicide, they'd bonded for a while, but then Linc had backed off when he realized her interest in him went beyond being just a friend.

"You want to grab a cup of coffee when you finish up?"

Linc checked his watch. Past two a.m. Since today was his day off at Melrose, he planned to work until dawn. "I don't think you want to hang around that long," he said and cringed at the flicker of disappointment in her face.

"We'll see," she said, giving him a tiny smile.

A chain saw cranked up, and Linc nodded toward the sound. "I see my supervisor, and if anyone doesn't need to be operating a saw, it's Danny. I'll take his place and you can interview him," he said, forcing a chuckle in his voice. "Good to see you again."

"Don't be a stranger," she said. "Dad misses you too."

She didn't mean that last as a barb, but it pierced his heart anyway. Neither Sarah nor her dad blamed him for Blake's suicide, but that didn't stop Linc from feeling responsible.

6

It was four in the morning before Ainsley got her grandmother to go to bed. After a power nap in the room she'd slept in growing up, she showered and changed into her National Park Service uniform. Good thing she'd brought along several changes when she left East Tennessee for Jackson, Mississippi, and a week at the law enforcement academy. From there she'd dropped her things off in Natchez and drove to New Orleans for her cruise.

And now she was trying to get her head back in the game after Cora's accident last night. The girl who was murdered deserved no less.

At five forty-five, she grabbed her service pistol and left a note on the kitchen table. Once she stored the pistol in the hidden safe in her console, she drove to the hospital. The first visiting time for the ICU was from six until seven, and she should be right on time. Cora's nurse had said the doctor usually arrived early for his rounds, and she wanted to be there.

Pink clouds streaked the eastern sky as Ainsley pulled into Merit Health and parked the pickup. What was with the cloud that suddenly hung over her? Guilt? No, more like regret. Maybe passing her familiar haunts drove home how much she'd changed since leaving Natchez.

If someone had told her when she graduated from high school that she'd be working as an Investigative Services Branch special agent sixteen years later, she would've laughed. She'd had plans to make it big as a country singer, in spite of her dad's opposition.

Ainsley sighed. She'd ridden that train for eighteen months—dropped out of college after her first year and toured the country as a backup singer for a big-name artist long enough to prove her dad and Linc wrong. But when her big break came, her voice had failed her . . . so maybe they'd been right.

She loved what she was doing now. When she'd returned to college, she'd chosen a degree in criminal justice. Mostly because it was as far from music as she could get. Ainsley once again brushed away thoughts of failure as she climbed the stairs to the ICU.

Inside the waiting room, she pressed the button to enter the unit and was quickly allowed in.

Her aunt was dozing when Ainsley paused at the door, then her eyes fluttered open. "Ainsley? What are you doing here?"

She crossed the room to the bed and bent and kissed Cora's cheek. "Checking on you before I go to work."

Confusion crossed the older woman's eyes, and she glanced around the room. "Where . . . am I?"

Ainsley had been afraid something like this might happen. It was one reason she wanted to see her aunt first thing this morning. "You fell last night and hit your head." She filled her in on all the details, and tension eased in Ainsley's shoulders as understanding replaced her aunt's confusion.

"I remember now, at least some of it," Cora said.

The door opened, and Ainsley frowned when her father walked into the room.

"You're here early," he said.

He didn't have to sound so surprised. "I have a busy day, and I wanted to check on Cora before it got started."

"I didn't know you were planning to visit Natchez until last night, or rather this morning."

"It's not exactly a visit." Surely he wasn't upset that she hadn't let him know her plans—he hadn't expressed an interest in what she did since the day she defied him. "The park service rerouted me, and I got in late yesterday. I did plan to text you this morning."

"Too busy for a five-minute call, but not too busy to get a nice tan." He arched an eyebrow. "Mom said you just got back from a cruise."

Heat flooded her face. "I'm surprised to see you here this early."

"Had to come see how my girl was before I left town." He flashed his famous grin at Cora as he took her hand. "How are you feeling, sweetie?"

"I'd be better if you two would stop bickering with each other," Cora said sharply.

Ainsley swallowed the he-started-it reply on the tip of her tongue. One of them had to be the grown-up. "Sorry. I should have made a point to let you know I was here."

There. Now it was up to him to accept her apology, which he wouldn't.

"Thank you."

Ainsley clamped her jaw tight to keep it from hitting the floor.

Her dad turned to Cora. "You didn't say how you're feeling."

"Tired," Cora said, returning his smile.

"I heard you say you remember some of what happened?" he said.

"Only the part about coming to the hospital."

"How did you hear about her fall?" Ainsley asked. Gran hadn't indicated that she'd called him, and Ainsley certainly hadn't.

"I asked the nurse to call him for me after you and Rose left," Cora said.

That shouldn't have been a surprise. There was a knock at the door, and a man entered dressed in scrubs. "Ms. Cora Chamberlain?"

"Yes?"

He checked her bracelet. "I've come to take you for your CT scan." Then he turned to Ainsley and her dad. "Shouldn't take more than twenty minutes."

"Would you like me to go with you?" Ainsley asked.

"No, dear, you have work to do. I'll be fine." She turned to her nephew. "And Johnny, there's no need for you to hang around either. I'm sure you have campaign things to attend to."

Her aunt didn't see him flinch when she called him Johnny, a name he detested. Most people knew him by his initials—J.R., although the campaign flyers she'd seen at Gran's had John Ross Beaumont on them.

"I have a campaign appearance in Jackson this afternoon, but I'll be back tomorrow. I'll drop by to see you, hopefully at home."

"If I have any say-so, that's where I'll be."

Cora had grit, and it was gratifying to see how alert she was. Ainsley leaned over and gave her a peck on the cheek. "If I don't see you at the ten o'clock visiting time, I'll see you at one."

When Ainsley moved back, her father stepped beside the bed. "Don't give these nurses any trouble," he said, winking at his aunt.

They both stepped outside the room and waited until Cora was rolled out and down the hallway. "She'll be fine," her dad said.

"Yes, Cora's feisty." Ainsley managed to keep

her voice from breaking as a lump formed in her throat.

"Walk out with me?" he asked. He was actually asking instead of ordering.

"Sure."

Her dad held the ICU door open for her. "So, you're here on National Park Service business?"

"Yes."

They crossed the waiting room to the hallway. "Are you going to make me pry the information out of you?" Then his eyes widened. "Oh, wait. Are you here about that girl who was murdered?"

She nodded. "I'll be leaving for the crime scene as soon as I stop for some real coffee and then check on Gran."

He chuckled. "I had almost forgotten she only drinks decaf."

They walked outside into the sunshine, and Ainsley inhaled the humid air scented with the light fragrance from the row of crape myrtles in front of Merit Health. She'd hoped it would be cooler after last night's storm, but as the sun climbed above the trees, the rain had only made it more humid, if that was possible. Humidity and all, she'd missed this, not that she could tell anyone what "this" was, only that it was June in Natchez and no other place smelled or felt like it.

"I'm over here," her dad said, pointing in the same direction she'd parked the truck, and they walked toward the east side of the lot. "Oh, I saw your write-up."

She stopped and narrowed her eyes at him.

"I'm trying here, Ainsley." He faced her. "I know we haven't had the best relationship, but I'd like to bury the hatchet."

In her back, maybe? Ainsley didn't know what was going on, but she didn't trust her father any more than the gators in the swamps.

"I could use a little help from you."

When she stared blankly at him, he huffed. "I saw where you won an award for solving a murder up in the Smokies."

"You saw that?" Ainsley couldn't keep the surprise from her voice. The report of her award had only been on the National Park Service website.

"Of course. Google alerts me anytime your name appears on the web."

The toe of her shoe caught on a crack in the pavement, and she stumbled. Her dad caught her arm, steadying her.

"You're one of the few people who can fall up a set of stairs," he said.

He'd made fun of her clumsiness hundreds of times, but somehow it sounded different this time. More of a simple statement instead of ridicule.

"It's a talent. And thank you. That was a difficult case." It was the reason she'd booked a cruise—she needed to decompress.

"You seem to have done well with the park service."

"I like it."

An "I'm proud of you" or "Good job" or "I was wrong when I questioned your sanity when you chose the park service" would be nice right about now. But he hadn't changed *that* much. She relieved him of her arm and nodded toward her car. "I'm over here." She turned to face him and flinched under his intense gaze.

"Well, it was good to see you. Don't be such a stranger to Natchez." He looked away, then turned back to her. "I'm sure Mom's told you I'm having a fund-raiser tomorrow night at the house, and I'd appreciate it if you were there. She'll be in attendance . . . Cora had planned to come."

Actually Gran hadn't mentioned his fund-raiser. Ainsley calculated how long it would take to get the CT report back—an hour?

"Did you hear me?"

"I'm sorry, I was thinking about Cora." Ainsley swallowed. "Um, sure, I'll come."

"Don't get so excited."

She tempered her anger. "I'm sorry, but Cora is having a scan that will determine if she has to have surgery, and I'm about to start an investigation into the murder of a teenaged girl. Forgive me if your bid to be governor gets pushed back a little." So much for tempering her anger, but now she was on a roll. "And when did you ever show up for anything for me? Like my high school graduation."

His face turned splotchy red and then a mask clicked into place, smoothing his features. "Really, Ainsley?" His blue eyes so much like her own pinned her. "That was a low blow. I was out of the country when you graduated, and besides, your grandmother and great-aunt were there."

She crossed her arms and immediately uncrossed them, not wanting him to interpret the move as defensive. Why she ever argued with her father, she'd never know. She couldn't win. In his eyes, he simply never did anything wrong. "I'm sorry. I shouldn't have said that."

For a minute he said nothing, then his shoulders relaxed. "No, I probably had it coming, and you don't need to apologize."

"Then you shouldn't have left me to be raised by your mother," she said sharply. "Her first rule is to apologize for any hurt you've caused." Although that rule certainly hadn't taken with him.

He sighed. "Do we always have to argue?"

She let his question go unanswered as she stared at her feet.

Another sigh, this one louder. "Well, I have to be on my way. It was good to see you."

She raised her head in time to catch his smile. He'd already switched into the suave political candidate. "You too. See you tomorrow."

He turned to walk away, then stopped. "Oh, Cora mentioned something about diaries the last time I talked to her," he said. "Do you know where they are?"

Cora had talked about diaries last night before they brought her to the hospital. "Did you go to see Cora last night?"

"What? Of course not."

"Someone was there. The carpet around her desk was wet, like someone had stood there, looking for something."

"Wasn't me. I was with my campaign manager until the storm hit. Your job isn't making you see a crime around every corner, is it?"

"No. There were signs of a break-in and her carpet was wet, and since the library is on the first floor, it wasn't from a leaky roof."

He stared at her a minute. "Did you see the diaries?"

"No. When did you discuss the diaries with her?" Ainsley didn't like the thought that just crossed her mind.

He shrugged. "Probably every time I've talked with her lately. Forget I asked. I'll ask her when I return from Jackson." Her dad fobbed the door locks on his Lexus and without looking back, climbed in and drove away.

She'd thought for a minute he'd changed, but nothing ever really changed with him. He could be as charming as all get-out when he wanted to . . . or had something to gain, like her showing up tomorrow night. Her conscience poked her. That hadn't been exactly true today—he'd been different, softer, at least a little bit.

She checked her watch. Cora could be back from her CT scan. Pocketing her keys, she hurried back inside and was pleased when her aunt was in her room. "That didn't take long," she said.

A smile creased Cora's face. "I thought you'd left, but I'm glad you came back. Did you and your father have a good visit?"

"About the usual."

Cora twisted the sheet in her hand. "I do wish you two could get along better."

"It wasn't bad. Neither of us drew blood," she replied with a laugh. Then Ainsley sobered. "Last night you mentioned Charlotte's diaries."

"Diaries?"

"Yes. Like maybe you'd found new ones. You were quite insistent that we find them."

Her aunt searched Ainsley's face like she might find the answer in it. "My brain is just so foggy."

"Did anyone stop by the house last night?" Ainsley asked.

Her aunt's brows lowered. "I . . . I don't know." Tears glistened in her eyes. "What if my memory gets worse? I have to finish my book."

Before Ainsley could reassure her, they were interrupted by a light rap on the door and a doctor entering the room. "Dr. Morgan" was stitched on his lab coat. "Good morning, ladies," he said before turning to Cora. "How did you sleep, Ms. Chamberlain?"

"Fair-to-middling," she replied.

"Sorry about that, but this is a hospital," he said with a chuckle.

"How soon can I go home?" Cora demanded.

"Not today." Dr. Morgan glanced at the chart in his hand. "Your CT scan from two a.m. looks troubling, and the scan you just had doesn't show any improvement."

"Will you have to operate?" Ainsley asked and tensed when the doctor didn't answer right away.

He cleared his throat. "It won't be up to me. There's a small tear in the lining of the brain, and if the bleeding doesn't stop, the neurosurgeon will need to go in and relieve the pressure." Dr. Morgan patted Cora's shoulder. "He hasn't looked at the scan yet, and my thoughts are, he'll wait for a repeat scan later this morning before making a decision."

"Isn't all that radiation dangerous?" Cora asked.

"It's more dangerous to not stay on top of it."

"Does that mean you won't know if she'll need surgery until early afternoon?" Ainsley asked, glancing at the clock on the wall over the whiteboard with today's date and the day shift nurses' names.

He nodded. "And I can't speak for the surgeon."

Ainsley patted Cora's hand. "If I'm going to be back by then, I need to leave now. Don't give them any trouble," she said and realized she'd repeated her father's words.

"*Moi*?"

Her aunt couldn't be too bad off if she could joke. "Yes, you."

Cora's memory loss weighed on Ainsley as she hurried to her pickup. Given Cora's age, Ainsley didn't have a lot of time left with her aunt, but Cora had always been so sharp. The thought of what little time they did have being clouded with confusion and possibly dementia was more than she wanted to think about.

Her thoughts jumped to her father. Why was he concerned about the diaries? Things like that didn't normally interest him. A thought from earlier crept in. What if he'd been the person who'd tracked water into Cora's house? She tried to dismiss that thought. Besides, her father had a key and would have no need to break in through the basement.

Unless he'd forgotten his key . . .

7

Linc grabbed his chain saw from the back of his Tahoe and hustled to the SAR supervisor. "How about I do this?" he asked as the man pulled the cord on his saw yet again to no avail.

"Thanks, I never can get these things to crank. Need to check on some of the volunteers anyway."

Linc's saw roared to life on the first pull, and he went to work cutting away a tree on the now-dead power line. His thoughts drifted to earlier in the night. He hoped Cora was okay, but if she had a brain bleed . . . Linc shifted his thoughts, only to have an image of Ainsley crowd into his mind.

The chain saw blade kicked back, and he gripped the handle to keep from losing control. Better keep his mind on what he was doing.

Linc worked until dawn, thankful it was his day off. Not that he didn't enjoy his job conducting tours of Melrose Mansion—it was a nice quiet job. When he finished with his last tree, he trudged to his truck only to find Sarah's mint-green MINI Cooper parked beside his Tahoe with her dozing behind the wheel.

He rapped lightly on her window, and she jerked awake and lowered the window. "You should have gone home and slept," he said.

"I haven't been here long." When he questioned her with his eyes, she said, "I was helping some of Miss Hattie's neighbors. You ready to grab a cup of java?"

His stomach growled. Coffee sounded good, but he needed food as well. "As long as we add bacon and eggs to the menu."

Sarah grinned. "How about the Waffle House? They're open."

It was also on his route home. "See you there."

He'd planned to drive by Rose Beaumont's house. He didn't figure they'd stayed at the hospital because he was pretty sure Cora would have been put in the ICU, and he wanted to see if she or Ainsley was up. He could still swing by Rose's house after he left the restaurant.

As Linc drove to the diner, he worried that Sarah might make more of their breakfast than it was. The few times they'd eaten out together had never been a date, more of an impulse like now—*"I'm hungry, want to grab a bite to eat?"* sort of thing.

Somehow, he had to make Sarah understand that while he liked her, the spark just wasn't there. Ainsley was the only person he'd ever experienced that special feeling with, and a relationship with her was a lost cause.

Sarah pulled into a parking space on the other side of him and lowered her window. "They're busy," she said, nodding at the full parking lot. "Want to try McDonald's?"

He really didn't want to do fast food, and besides, with the diner so full, it might keep Sarah from getting personal. "Maybe it's not as busy as it looks."

Linc held the door open, and his stomach growled when the aroma of waffles and fried bacon wrapped around him. He spied an empty table near the cash register. Everyone who entered the establishment would pass by their table, but he didn't see another and guided her toward it.

"Be there in a minute," the waitress said as he pulled out Sarah's chair.

Linc sat across from her, not bothering with the menu. He knew what he wanted. Bacon and eggs and one of their plate-sized waffles.

"I love this place." Sarah scanned the menu. "I think I'll have their All-Star special."

True to her word, a few minutes later the waitress took their orders and quickly returned with coffee. "Be about fifteen minutes before your order is up," she said.

Linc took a sip of coffee, letting the hot liquid revive him. It wouldn't be enough to make it through fifteen minutes of small talk, something he'd never been good at, but ever since he'd gotten the feeling Sarah might harbor romantic feelings for him, he hadn't been sure of what to say.

"How are your parents?" she asked. "Aren't they in Ecuador?"

She'd kept tabs on his parents? "They're good. Should return next month."

"And your sister?"

"She's good too."

Sarah rolled her eyes. "Honestly, Linc, you can do better than that."

"Sorry. I'm tired and a little preoccupied. She loves living in Alaska," he said. "Did you get any good human-interest stories?"

"Yep. Got some footage of you using that chain saw too. When did you learn how to operate one of those?"

Her voice held a teasing note, but when he lifted his gaze, there was a note of sadness in her eyes. "Worked for a logging company one summer during college."

"There's a lot about you I don't know."

Before an answer formulated in his mind, the waitress plopped their plates on the table and then refilled their coffee.

"Thank you," he said. The cook had fried his eggs to perfection—crispy on the edges and runny in the middle. He said a brief prayer, and then they spent the next few minutes concentrating on their food.

"So, what has you preoccupied?" she asked, popping a bite of her raisin bread in her mouth.

He hesitated. "As friend to friend and not friend to reporter, Cora Chamberlain fell last night and hit her head. I haven't had a chance to check on her."

"You've been helping her with her book, right?"

Linc nodded, surprised she remembered.

"Was she alone?"

Again, he hesitated.

"I take it someone was with her. Rose?"

"Not when she fell."

Sarah frowned. "What happened?" When he hesitated, she said, "Never mind, I'll ask Cora or Rose."

He should have known better than to mention Cora's fall and wouldn't have if he hadn't been brain dead. Now he'd piqued her curiosity, and if he didn't give her a satisfactory answer, she would go straight to the older women. "It's nothing more than Rose couldn't raise her sister on the phone to warn her about the tornado, and she and Ainsley went across the street to Cora's house. They found her unconscious in the library."

"Ainsley's back?" She looked over his shoulder, and her eyes widened. "Indeed she is."

He turned just as the woman in question approached the cash register and gave the waitress her order. She was dressed in her National Park Service uniform minus the flat hat and had a gun strapped to her waist. As the waitress turned in the order, Ainsley did a double take.

"Linc?" she said, then her gaze slid to Sarah.

He nodded. "How's Cora?"

"I just left her. She's stable but doesn't remember any of the circumstances around the fall."

Ainsley's glance slid over to Sarah again, and he realized she didn't recognize the reporter. "You remember Sarah Tolliver, don't you? Blake's sister."

Ainsley smiled. "Sarah? Last time I saw you . . . goodness, you couldn't have been more than twelve."

Sarah's eyes narrowed. "No. I was fourteen, in my freshman year of high school. It was just before you and Linc broke up—that was, what? Fifteen, sixteen years ago? What brought you back to Natchez?"

"My job. And I'm really sorry about Blake."

Linc barely heard Ainsley's response as he wrestled with what Sarah had said. His instincts had been right. A person didn't remember those kinds of details unless there was a good reason— like having a crush on someone. Now he really did need a third party as a buffer. "You want to join us?" he asked, and couldn't help but notice the reporter stiffen.

Ainsley's eyes darkened as her gaze shifted from Linc to Sarah and then back. She thought they were a couple.

"You won't be intruding," he said. "We ran into each other while we helped with the tornado cleanup and decided to grab a bite."

"Was there much damage?"

"The storm got several houses," Sarah said. "My report aired on the six a.m. news—you can find it on the station's website."

"No one was hurt, though," Linc said. "Please, do join us."

Ainsley checked her watch and then shook her head. "Any other time I would, but I'm meeting Sam Ryker and the Claiborne County sheriff at nine to go over the Rocky Springs crime scene."

"What do you do?" Sarah asked.

Ainsley pointed to her badge. "I work for the National Park Service."

"As a . . . ?"

"Law enforcement ranger," she said. "I'm a special agent."

Sarah's face lit up. "Oh, you're here about the girl that was murdered." She took a card from her camera case and handed it to Ainsley. "I'd love to interview you on camera."

Ainsley glanced at the card. "I wasn't aware Natchez had a TV station."

"It doesn't, yet. I cover the Natchez area for WTMC in Jackson." Pride laced her voice. "I'm surprised you haven't seen one of my reports."

"She just got into town, Sarah," Linc said, and then hoping to put Ainsley on alert, added, "And when Sarah wants a story, she goes after it full speed."

The reporter shot him a look of gratitude. "I'm trying to get a local station started here. So how about it? Could you find time to let me interview you about the investigation?"

Ainsley pocketed the card as the waitress brought her order to the cash register. "Let me think about it. Right now, I have to get this food to my grandmother." She paid the waitress and grabbed the tall cup of coffee, then nodded good-bye before she hurried to the door.

"She's got it made," Sarah muttered when the bell jingled, signaling Ainsley's departure.

"What do you mean?"

The reporter gave him an I-can't-believe-you'd-ask-that look. "Got a great job, probably travels all over the country investigating crimes, and men drop everything to help her."

"Men do what?" He hadn't a clue what she was talking about.

"That's right, you didn't see that guy jump up and open the door for her. Or how all the men in here stopped eating when she walked in."

"Maybe they were looking at the uniform." Ainsley was beautiful, but he couldn't believe Sarah was jealous. Not with her looks. Not only was the willowy blonde very pretty, the camera loved her.

"Whatever." She narrowed her eyes at him. "You still have it bad for her, Lincoln Steele."

Heat started at the base of his neck, and he concentrated on his breathing to keep the blush from spreading to his face. "What makes you think that?" He wasn't about to admit to Sarah how he felt about Ainsley.

"I'm not blind. I saw how you looked at her." She leaned forward. "You might as well move on."

He didn't need Sarah to tell him something he already knew.

She placed her hand on top of his. "Linc, there are plenty of other women out there."

Like her. He didn't know what he was going to do with Sarah. He didn't want to hurt her, but neither did he want Blake's sister harboring ideas that they might get together. That would hurt her even more in the long run. She needed to be looking for someone who could give her what she wanted, and he wasn't that person. "Sarah," he said. "We—"

"You'll help me get an interview, right?" Her whole personality had shifted into the aggressive reporter he saw on TV.

"What?"

"An interview with Ainsley about the teenaged girl who was murdered. My news director has been pushing me to get a really big story, one that might go viral. I think this is it."

"I'll see what I can do," he said.

"Good. Something like that would really help take my mind off next week."

His mind blanked. What was happening next week?

"You haven't forgotten next Wednesday is the second anniversary of Blake's death, have you?"

Next Wednesday? His lips turned cold as blood drained from his face. How had the date snuck up on him?

"It's okay if you forgot," she said, her voice husky. Her eyes said otherwise.

"I didn't forget." More like pushed it out of his mind.

"I hope you don't still blame yourself for his death."

There would never be a day that Linc didn't blame himself.

Sarah squeezed his hand. "I don't blame you. Blake just couldn't take it any longer, and it was so hard to watch him suffer. He's in a better place now."

If she was trying to make him feel better, it wasn't working. Linc pushed the past away and concentrated on how they could honor him. "Blake loved the water. What do you say to a picnic lunch at Natchez Lake? Maybe take your dad?"

Her face lit up. "You'd do that? Take time to be with us Wednesday?"

"Of course. Blake was my best friend." Spending time with Blake's family on the anniversary of his death was the least he could do.

8

Ainsley set the to-go boxes on her grand-mother's table.

"What's that?" Gran asked as she entered the kitchen, cinching the belt on her robe. Even this early, every hair was in place. Did she still sleep in a silk hair bonnet?

"Breakfast."

While her hair looked great, last night's activities had taken their toll on Gran. Tired lines creased her normally smooth skin. Ainsley couldn't believe that at thirty-four she had more wrinkles than her eighty-five-year-old grandmother.

"I only meant to get coffee, but everything smelled so good." Ainsley frowned. "What are you doing?"

"Setting the table. I will not eat eggs from a foam box," she said, handing her a mug. "Here's something to put your coffee in."

"I like drinking from Styrofoam." It was what she was used to on the job, but when in Rome . . . She poured the coffee into the mug, popped it in the microwave, and heated it for half a minute. "I also went by the hospital and checked on Cora," Ainsley said as she sat down to eat bacon and eggs on the china plate.

"How is she?"

"About the same. The doctor came by, and if the next CT scan doesn't show improvement, they'll do surgery later today."

Gran laid her fork down. "S-surgery?"

"Yes." She explained what the doctor had told her. "If the bleeding doesn't stop, they'll have to go in to relieve the pressure."

Her grandmother leaned back in the kitchen chair. "Oh my," she whispered. "When can I see her?"

"Next visiting hours are at ten." Ainsley checked her watch. "And I have to leave in five minutes if I'm going to meet Sam Ryker and the Claiborne County sheriff at the Port Gibson ranger station. I won't be back in time to drive you to the hospital."

"Excuse me?" Her grandmother's blue eyes snapped. "Since when do I need a driver?"

"I just thought—"

"I know what you thought, and I'm not having it. Up 'til now, I've handled all kinds of emergencies without you. I can handle this."

Ainsley knew Gran didn't mean to make her feel guilty for not coming home more often, but the words stung. "I'll get back as soon as I can," she said.

"You just find whoever killed that poor girl and give her folks closure."

"I plan to." But what if she didn't? Doubt always swept through her at the beginning of a case. Didn't matter how many cases she'd solved or commendations she'd won.

Gran patted her hand. "I have total confidence you will."

Ainsley wished she was as confident as her grandmother. With breakfast finished, she rinsed her plate and put it in the dishwasher, mentally ticking off a to-do list.

Gran cleared her throat, getting her attention. "I made you an appointment with Harold Blackwell for Monday at nine o'clock."

Blackwell. The name rang a bell. "And this appointment is for . . . ?"

"Oh, Ainsley. Your trustee. You get the funds from the trust on your next birthday."

Ohhh. The inheritance from her mother that had been put in a trust fund. She'd forgotten the fund would end next year when she turned thirty-five.

She hadn't given it a thought in years, not since the last time her grandmother made an appointment for her with Blackwell that Ainsley'd had to cancel. Actually, she'd never thought of the money in the trust as "real" money. Sure, it would be nice to have, what was it, a hundred thousand dollars? She'd probably leave it where it was for retirement, but like the trust fund, retirement was the last thing on her mind.

"I'll try to make it this time," she said and hurried to the bathroom to brush her teeth.

When she returned, a man's voice in the kitchen sent her heart racing. Linc. Earlier she'd almost fled the Waffle House when she saw him. Maybe if she hung out in the hallway, he'd leave. Then she heard her grandmother say, "Here's your coffee. I'll go see what's keeping Ainsley."

"I'm here." She pushed the swinging door open. "And hello again."

He stopped with a cup of coffee halfway to his lips.

"I hope you know that's decaf," she said.

His eyes twinkled. "Actually, yes."

"And you're still drinking it?"

"A gentleman doesn't turn down his gracious host's offering."

He considered himself a gentleman now. Ha.

"Linc stopped by to ask how Cora was," her grandmother said.

Ainsley tilted her head. She'd just given him a report. Did he think Cora's condition had changed in the last thirty minutes?

"I actually stopped by to see if you wanted company on the drive out to Rocky Springs," Linc said.

"You what?" She wouldn't have been more surprised if he'd said he'd sprouted wings and planned to fly to the moon.

"I heard there were trees down on the Trace and

you might have trouble getting to your meeting." He seemed to have a problem meeting her eyes. "I have a chain saw in the back of my Tahoe."

Ainsley hadn't considered last night's tornado may have wreaked havoc on the Natchez Trace. But ride all the way to the crime scene with Linc? "You were up all night helping tornado victims," she said. "You probably need to go home and sleep."

"I'm good," he said with a grin.

"Honey, when a good-lookin' man offers to help you, let him," Gran said, winking at her.

"It's only a forty-five-minute drive, and I promise I won't bite or go to sleep on you."

"If you promise," she said. "But in my pickup."

"Let me grab my chain saw . . . just in case."

She kissed her grandmother on the cheek as Linc shut the door behind him. "I'll try to be back by early afternoon."

"Don't you worry. If I need you, I'll call," she said. "And go easy on Linc. He's had a bad few years."

"Do you know why he left the FBI?"

"I do, but it's not my story to tell."

Didn't matter. Ainsley didn't have time to listen right now anyway. She paused at the door. "If you need me and I don't answer my phone, call the ranger station at Port Gibson. Should be someone there who can get ahold of me."

"I won't need you. Cora is going to be just fine.

That's what God impressed on me this morning in my prayers."

Ainsley bit back what was on the tip of her tongue. Sometimes God's "just fine" was different from hers.

Linc had set his saw and gas can in the pickup bed and was waiting when she came around the side of the house. "I like your wheels," he said.

Ainsley did too, and was glad she'd chosen the Ford Ranger over an SUV. She would've hated to smell the fumes from the gas can for the next hour.

"I'm not surprised it's red—that was always your favorite color."

She pressed the button to unlock the doors. "And not yours."

"Evidently the color has grown on me," he said, nodding toward his SUV.

How had she missed his vehicle was maroon? He'd surprised her again. "You've changed," Ainsley said as she climbed into the truck.

"You haven't?"

She'd changed, all right, in a lot of ways. Ainsley wasn't that naïve young girl who thought she had the world on a string. She backed out of her grandmother's drive. "Everyone changes."

"Ainsley," he said softly, a tremor in his voice. "I, ah—"

"Why'd you leave the FBI? Gran said you loved it." If he was about to get personal, she did not want to hear it. She glanced at him as she turned right. His face was unreadable.

"It was time." The finality in his voice said *"Don't go there."*

She heeded the warning and fell silent as she drove to the Trace. Once she'd turned off Liberty Road onto the southern terminus, she tried again. "Since you're along, maybe you'll have some insight on the case."

He hesitated. "It's one reason I wanted to tag along."

His answer confused her. He didn't want to talk about why he left the FBI, but he was willing to help her out on the investigation? "I thought you were along to clear any trees out of the way . . . although I don't see any damage so far."

"When I talked to Sam Ryker, he said there was a tree across the road about a mile past Mount Locust."

"When did you talk to Sam?" Linc was on the interpretive side of the park service and normally had no reason to talk to the district law enforcement ranger. Sam investigated crime on the Trace, even murder, but he was shorthanded since his field ranger, Brooke Danvers, was on her honeymoon with Ainsley's fellow ISB agent, Luke Fereday. Luke had been the one who recommended bringing her in on the case.

"Before I left the Waffle House."

Sounded fishy to her, but she let it pass. "How about the campground? Any damage there?"

"The storm didn't hit that far north. The tree fell across the road at Mount Locust because of rain, not the tornado," he replied. "Sam said to meet him at the campground."

"Oh?" It made sense to meet at the crime scene, but why had he told Linc and not her? "You and Sam talk about anything else?"

When his reply wasn't forthcoming, she took her gaze off the road long enough to shoot a glance at him. "Did you call Sam . . . or did he call you?"

The pinched expression on Linc's face was answer enough. "Does he want you to take over the case since you're ex-FBI?"

"No." He swallowed hard. "He asked if I would help out on the investigation, though, and he sent me a copy of the report, which I've read."

She didn't breathe for five seconds. The district ranger didn't think she could do the job?

"It wasn't that he didn't think you could do a good job."

Linc was a mind reader now? *Think it through before you shoot off your mouth.* Her grandmother's voice echoed in her head.

"I do have eight years' experience as an investigator for the FBI."

As opposed to her almost eight years as a law enforcement ranger, four investigating as an ISB

73

ranger, but in some minds that might not compare to the FBI. "It's not my first murder case."

"I know."

She blinked. He'd checked up on her? This she wanted to hear. "And you know this how?"

"Your grandmother has kept me up to date on your life—especially how you walked away from a very promising singing career to become a park ranger. I never understood why."

Leave it to her grandmother to twist the story in Ainsley's favor. It'd been the story her agent-until-he-wasn't put out at the time, and maybe she'd let Linc believe it for a little while longer. "Like you, it was time."

9

Life does that to you," Linc said, thinking of Blake. For years, he'd wondered why Ainsley had left the career she'd fought so hard for, the career she'd ended their relationship over. "The news reports never explained why you walked away."

"No, they didn't," she said. "How are your parents, by the way?"

He wasn't getting his answer today either. "They're fine. In Ecuador for the summer, doing mission work." Maybe someday she'd trust him enough to share the reason.

Ainsley fell silent until they rounded a curve and orange lights flashed on the side of the road. "Looks like we may have found the fallen tree," she said.

A few yards down the road a maintenance worker held up a stop sign. When she brought the truck to a stop and lowered her window, Linc recognized the worker—Billy Norris.

"Tree down?" she asked.

"Yep." Voices came from the handheld radio. He replied and then turned back to the truck. "Be another few minutes."

"I have another chain saw if you need help," Linc said.

The worker bent down where he could see him. "Didn't recognize you, Linc. I think we have it under control, but thanks."

He shifted in his seat. "You were the one who found the teenaged girl who was murdered."

He grimaced. "Terrible thing, what happened to her. I don't think I'll ever forget seeing that poor girl's body."

Ainsley's breath hitched. "You're Billy Norris?"

"Yep." His radio crackled again, giving an all clear. "Okay, you folks can go now."

A car pulled up behind them.

"I'm Ainsley Beaumont with the Investigative Services Branch of the National Park Service. I planned to find you later today, but could we talk now?"

"Sure. It'll be a minute before they pick me up."

Ainsley pulled her pickup to the side of the road and grabbed a notebook. They both climbed out of the truck and waited until Billy crossed to their side.

She shook his hand. "I appreciate you recounting what happened. It can't be easy."

"It ain't, and I hope you can find the scumbag who did this."

Linc stood back as Ainsley took charge. It was her investigation, and he was pretty sure it'd stung that Sam had called and asked if Linc would assist. When he agreed, Sam had emailed him the case files that included Billy's statement, and Linc scanned over them on his phone before he left the Waffle House.

Ainsley fished her cell from her pocket. "Do you mind if I record our conversation?"

"Fine by me," he said.

She turned on the recorder app. After speaking their names, time, and date, she said, "Go ahead."

"Well, it was like this. We'd stopped at Rocky Springs to clean the bathrooms and generally police the area. It was about eight in the morning, and I, uh . . ."—he scuffed the dirt with his shoe—"took a break, walked up the road. It'd rained the night before, and it was kind of muddy on the side. I noticed these footprints. Barefoot, like a kid. Then there were shoe prints, but not like they were together."

Billy felt his shirt pocket, where the red top of a pack of Marlboros was visible, then seemed to think better of smoking and dropped his hand. "I followed the footprints and found her propped up under a bank with all these roots coming down. Like a cage, you know?"

She nodded and he continued. "It wasn't far from the old Methodist church. I don't know how long she'd been dead, but there wasn't a mark on her that I could see. Of course, I didn't look that close."

"Did you recognize her?" Linc asked.

Billy gave a sharp nod. "She was a cheerleader at Natchez High School with my Sherry. Been to our house, don't know how many times. My kid is taking this pretty hard."

"Did you notice any signs of a struggle?" Ainsley asked.

"No. Soon as I knew she was dead, I didn't want to disturb anything. Backed away from her and called Sam Ryker." He shook his head. "I hope I never see anything like that again."

"I hope not either, Mr. Norris." Ainsley shut off the recorder on her phone and wrote down Billy's contact information, then took a card from her pocket. "If you think of anything that might help with the investigation, give me a call."

He assured them he would, then before Linc could get the driver's-side door for her, Ainsley opened it and climbed behind the wheel. "Thanks for letting me know who he was," she said. "Saved me from having to track him down later."

"You're welcome." Maybe she was warming up to the idea of him helping with the investigation.

She started the truck and pulled out onto the Trace. "Don't take this wrong, but if you wanted to investigate, why didn't you become a law enforcement ranger?"

Or not. "I like what I do better." Linc stared out the passenger window, taking in the green vege-tation and the occasional Spanish moss hanging from the trees like ghosts. He wasn't ready to tell her why he didn't apply to the protection side of the park service and wasn't sure he ever would be.

His eyes grew heavy on the smooth road. Staying up all night was getting to him. Ainsley's cell phone rang, startling him awake.

She glanced at her phone. "It's my grandmother," she said and pressed the answer button on the steering wheel. "I have you on speaker. Has something happened to Cora?"

"The surgeon was just in." Rose's voice wavered. "The CT scan showed more bleeding and she's been confused this morning. He plans to take Cora to surgery at one. I called your father, but he was in Jackson. Something about a campaign appearance."

"Yeah, he told us about it this morning." Ainsley pressed her lips together and took a deep breath. "I'll be there," she said.

"Thank you. The doctor said I could stay with her in ICU until she went to surgery."

"Rose, I'll be praying for you and Cora," Linc said.

"I know you will be," her grandmother replied. "Thank you."

"Call me if there's any change." Ainsley disconnected the call. "I was afraid they would have to operate."

"Does Cora have a brain bleed?"

"Not sure exactly what it's called. When she hit her head, there was a tear in the membrane covering the brain. It's not as dangerous as bleeding inside her brain but still very serious because it causes pressure to build up inside her skull."

"Do you think you should turn around and go to the hospital?" He glanced at her as they passed a road sign that said "Rocky Springs—1 mile."

Responsibility and desire to be with her grandmother and Cora warred in Ainsley's face. She squared her shoulders, but not without a sigh. "We're here, and the surgery isn't for a few hours. May as well at least look at the crime scene."

10

With his tent packed, Troy Maddox dashed the remains of his coffee on the fire and forced his facial muscles to relax as the twentysomething kid from the next campsite approached. "Mornin'," he said and pulled his hat lower on his forehead.

"Morning," the young man replied and extended his hand. "I'm Ted Gilmore. My friends and I, we're from Nashville."

"Carter Stevens," Maddox said, ignoring the outstretched hand.

Ted dropped his arm. "Just wanted to be neighborly and offer to help you break down your campsite, but I see you're about done."

"Thanks anyway." The kid ought to help since he and his three friends were the reason for his move.

Ted cocked his head. "So, where're you from and where're you headed?"

Nosy kid. Maddox hesitated, hoping to send the message he didn't like questions. "From Kentucky," he said.

Ted glanced around. "You walking?"

Evidently, he hadn't gotten the message.

"Mostly hitchhiking. A couple dropped me off here at Rocky Springs two nights ago. They were going to Alexandria from here."

Ted rubbed the back of his neck. "I didn't know anyone did that anymore—hitchhiking, that is."

"It's a cheap way to travel."

An awkward silence fell between them. As much as Maddox wanted to rush Ted off, he didn't want to appear suspicious and fished for something to say. The bicycles. He'd seen Treks at their campsite earlier this morning. "Y'all bike all the way down on the Trace?"

"Yeah." Ted's face lit up. "We stopped at every site. Spent a day where Meriwether Lewis died. Then we stayed a couple of days up at Waterloo, Alabama, where the Trail of Tears crossed the Tennessee River."

"That so?" *Come on, kid. Go back to your campsite.*

"Yeah. We plan on hanging around here a couple of days. Looks like you're headed out."

"Yep." Maddox wondered what the kid would think if he told him he planned to stay at Rocky Springs, albeit at another campsite after the kids parked next to him, until he killed Ainsley Beaumont. He almost laughed.

On the other hand, maybe the kid had given him an opportunity to do a little misdirecting, because if he caught Beaumont here and killed

82

her like he planned, the police would be sure to question the boy. "I'm heading to New Orleans."

"Sounds good." Ted shifted from one foot to the other. "Well, I guess I better go see if the others are ready to explore the Old Trace. Have you hiked it yet?"

"Afraid not. Maybe some other time," he said. "Nice meeting you. Hope you enjoy Rocky Springs."

"I'm sure we will. Take care." With a half wave, he turned and jogged back to their campsite.

Maddox rubbed his back. He should have bought a good sleeping bag when he bought the tent. Maybe there was a Bass Pro Shop in Natchez. Or maybe not. His cash was going fast, but the tent had been a good investment. The cops wouldn't think about him hiding out in a national park.

He wished he could've seen the faces of the two bozos he'd broken out of prison with when they woke up and discovered he'd taken the car and left. Served 'em right for horning in on his deal. When they got caught—and they would since between the two of them, they didn't have enough brains to break out of a paper bag—they would point the cops toward Canada. That'd been the only destination he mentioned.

Maddox laid the tent poles in the middle of the folded tent and rolled it up and slid it into the case. Easy now, but it'd taken a video to show him how the first time. He couldn't get over what you could learn on the internet.

He slung the bag onto his shoulder and hiked to the restroom area where he'd left his car. After scanning the area to make sure his campsite neighbors weren't around, he popped the trunk and stowed the tent. As soon as he used the facility to clean up a little, he would find the guy in the camper with the marijuana again. First night here, he'd smelled weed and tracked down the source. The guy had been happy to sell him a baggie, but it was gone now.

Ten minutes later when he stepped outside the restroom, he did a double take as a pickup truck passed by the building. *Ainsley Beaumont?* Lady Luck was with him today. He'd known she would come to the crime scene. It'd been mentioned in one of the emails he'd found when he hacked the park service field office in the Smokies. He just didn't think he'd be lucky enough to see her when she arrived. Now to get to the perfect place he'd found to wait for her.

Last night he'd been curious and walked up to the old church near where the murder happened. Yellow-and-black tape marked the crime scene, and he'd wondered briefly why someone killed the girl. Not his concern.

Being the good detective Beaumont was, she would surely check out the church. And he'd be waiting for her . . .

Maddox shrank back when she and two other rangers walked up the road leading to the crime scene. Too late to beat her there, and with three of them, it would be tricky getting to the church. Since they were taking the campground road, he would use the Old Trace and wait until they were out of sight.

Visions of getting his revenge pushed Maddox as he trekked to the church. In the eighteen months he'd been in prison, his hatred for her had intensified. It'd been the motivating factor to break out. Night after night he'd dreamed of killing her, and while his dream was to wrap his fingers around her neck and squeeze the life out of her, he hadn't thought it would be possible. But maybe it was . . . if he could catch her alone in the church.

11

Ainsley slowed to make the turn. "Where did Sam say to meet him?"

"The maintenance building," Linc said, and she turned left once they entered the campground.

District Ranger Sam Ryker had parked and stood waiting in front of his vehicle when they pulled into the lot. He tipped his head at them as they climbed out of her pickup. "Good to see you, Linc. Appreciate your help." He turned to Ainsley. "I'm glad you could take the case."

It hadn't been her choice. Ainsley had hoped to catch up on paperwork before she took on another case. Instead, the minute the cruise ship pulled into port yesterday, her phone had blown up with texts and emails about the Natchez case. The rest of the day had been a flurry of calls and driving from New Orleans to Natchez. "Headquarters thought since I was familiar with the area, I'd be the best bet with Luke gone." She nodded to Linc. "And thanks for talking him into helping me out."

Linc wasn't certain whether she was being sarcastic or not.

A flush crept across the district ranger's tanned

cheeks. "It didn't make sense to have his experience available and not use it."

"I agree, just would have appreciated a heads-up. Where's Sheriff Randolph?"

The smile on her face went a long way toward taking the criticism out of her words, and Linc was glad that was out of the way. He admired how she handled herself in a professional way.

"About a mile out," Sam replied.

Suddenly, the skin on the back of Linc's neck prickled just like it had when he was an FBI agent and he sensed someone surveilling him. He scanned the area but nothing moved. Nothing human, anyway.

"You got the preliminary report I sent?" Sam asked.

Ainsley nodded. "And read it along with the report from Sheriff Randolph."

"Let me get what I wrote up yesterday. It has contact information for a kid that might be Hannah's boyfriend—it wasn't in the original report." Sam retrieved a folder from his SUV. "Clete may have a follow-up as well."

Sam handed them each a copy. Ainsley took her folder and flipped through it.

"They did the autopsy, but they're backlogged in Jackson so it'll be a couple of days until we get even the preliminary report," Sam added, "but I had a brief call with the medical examiner. There were small bruises around her throat, like someone had grabbed her. He'd found something he wanted to check out before he passed it along, but he did indicate the girl was about three months pregnant."

Linc winced. That had not been in the report he'd read.

"Did you see the body before they moved it?" Ainsley asked.

He nodded. "I saw the faint bruises, and there was no gunshot wound or any other obvious cause of death. She looked as though she was asleep."

The autopsy would pinpoint the cause of death. He flipped through the additional report as Ainsley scanned her copy. "I'll go over this in detail later today."

All three turned as a Dodge Charger with the Claiborne County Sheriff's Department logo on the side pulled into an empty space on the other side of Sam's SUV. Clete Randolph climbed out holding a large manila envelope. A gold badge stood out on a crisp white shirt with gold stars on the collar.

Linc liked the sheriff, and according to the reports he'd heard, the soft-spoken Randolph had been reelected four years ago by 80 percent of the voters. That spoke well of the man.

The sheriff adjusted the black tie he wore and strode toward them. Once he'd spoken to Sam and Linc, he turned to Ainsley and removed his flat hat. "Good to meet you, Ms. Beaumont.

Fereday said some good things about you."

"I'll have to thank him," she said and shook the hand he extended. "And I don't stand on formality, Sheriff. Call me Ainsley."

A smile of approval crossed his face. "If you'll do likewise. I answer to Clete." Then he turned to Linc. "I'm surprised but glad to see you here."

"Thanks," Linc replied. "It was Sam's idea."

The sheriff turned to Ainsley again and held out the manila envelope under his arm. "Unfortunately, I can't stay today. I have to testify in a murder case up in Jackson this morning."

Now Linc understood the white shirt and tie. Randolph usually wore a short-sleeved khaki uniform.

"Thank you," Ainsley replied, taking the envelope. "And thanks for coming in person to tell me you couldn't join us."

He nodded. "Call me anytime you have questions."

After the sheriff left, Sam asked, "You ready to see the crime scene? It isn't far and we can walk, or drive if you'd prefer."

"I need the walk," she replied.

Good. Walking to the Methodist church should revive him. But Linc couldn't shake the sense of someone watching as he trailed behind Ainsley and Sam. He heard a snap and whirled around, spying a skinny teenaged boy not ten yards from him. "You startled me," he said.

The boy, dressed in cutoff jeans and a torn T-shirt, shrugged. "Just wanted to see what was going on," he said. "Pays to know those kinds of things after that girl got murdered."

Linc identified himself and then said, "What's your name?"

"Colton."

"You have a last name?"

"Mason."

"Thank you, Colton. Were you here Tuesday night?"

He nodded. "We—I'm here with my folks—talked about pulling out after the rangers got through questioning us, but then my dad figured her killing was a one-off kind of thing. And they like the campsite."

"Did you hear anything?"

"I don't think so."

That was an odd answer. Either he had or he hadn't, and Linc was betting he had. He waited Colton out, keeping his gaze pinned to the boy.

Colton scratched his arm, picking at what looked like a mosquito bite. His Adam's apple bobbed and he cleared his throat. "Maybe a motorbike around one."

"A motorcycle?" No one had mentioned that.

"No, not a cycle. It didn't sound that big. More like the whine of a motocross bike."

Linc instantly recognized the difference between the Harley in his mind and a smaller cross-country bike. Something a teenager might ride. What if this was a simple case of teenage love gone bad rather than the human trafficking suspicions he'd been having?

"Anything else?" Linc asked.

Colton stared at the ground a few seconds, then looked up. "I heard she was a pretty girl."

"Where'd you hear that?"

He shrugged again in the universal teen language. "Around school."

"You two went to school together?" When Colton nodded, Linc said, "Then you knew she was pretty. What school?"

His face turned red. "Yeah, I'd seen her around Natchez High, but we didn't run in the same groups. I hope you catch whoever did it."

"We will." He pulled a card from his pocket and handed it to the boy. "Thanks for your help. If you think of anything else, call me. And if you don't mind, hang around. I'm sure the ranger I'm with will want to talk to you." Linc turned to walk away and then stopped. "Have you seen anyone else in the woods in the last hour?"

Colton shook his head. "Not on this side. Haven't been over by the Trace, though."

Linc nodded, then quick-timed it to catch up with Ainsley and Sam. It'd probably been Colton who had raised his body alarm.

So why did Linc still have this sense he was being watched?

12

Muggy air wrapped around Ainsley as they walked to the crime scene. Air so thick you could stir it with a spoon. She couldn't wait to get back to the mountains in Tennessee where she'd lived for the past four years. Before that, it'd been a new park almost every year.

She barely kept pace with the district ranger as they hiked to the old Methodist church. Right now Sam was a good thirty feet ahead of her and had barely broken a sweat, whereas perspiration rolled down Ainsley's face.

He stopped and waited for her. "Forgot you're not used to the heat."

It wasn't the heat that slowed her down. "I'll have to get acclimated to breathing water again," she said, catching her breath.

He chuckled. "Yeah, it's not the heat that kills you—it's the humidity."

Standard joke in the South. "Absolutely. Has a time of death been established?"

"Unofficially, the ME estimates Hannah died sometime between eleven and three. When I get the report, I'll send it to you."

She was glad he used the girl's name. Let her

know he viewed her death on a personal level.

They left the road for a narrow gravel path. Sam pointed to the dirt beside the path. "Before the storm last night, you could see footprints in the mud. It'd rained Monday and she was barefoot. You could tell she was running, and in a few places closer to the church, you could see a bigger shoe print. The man was running as well," he said. "Photos are in that folder, and you can see the casts at the Port Gibson office."

They stopped under a huge live oak at the base of a hill, and she flipped through the pictures. Whoever took the photos had done a good job, zeroing in on the deep prints of the front of Hannah's bare foot and the even deeper ones of her pursuer. They both were definitely running. "Looks like he was wearing boots."

"Yeah, but we haven't identified the shoe tread."

Ainsley looked up from the photos as Linc joined them. "Get lost?"

"Nope. Ran into a kid who was here that night. Said he heard a motorbike either late Tuesday night or maybe in the early hours of Wednesday morning." She listened as he recounted his talk with the boy. "I told him to hang around, that you'd want to speak to him."

"Thanks. I'd like to speak with his parents too." Ainsley turned to Sam. "How much farther to the crime scene?"

"Just up the hill," Sam replied. "If you look close, you can see the church through the trees. Her body was found right over here."

Before she looked at the actual crime scene, Ainsley peered through the leaves, making out glimpses of a brick building. Looked like Hannah may have been running toward the church. Did she think she could hide there? Steeling herself, Ainsley flipped to the photos of Hannah and compared them to the area where tape fluttered from a huge oak growing at the edge of an over-hang, its exposed roots grasping the eroded ground below like a three-foot claw. Almost cave-like.

Hannah had been running from someone. Did the girl crawl inside the roots to hide and the killer found her? Or had the footprints been innocent? The girl was pregnant . . . the area was isolated. Was she meeting the baby's father and they argued?

It was also a perfect place to do drugs. "Were any needles or drug paraphernalia found at the scene?" she asked.

"No."

"When do you expect to get the toxicology report back?" One look at the district ranger's face gave her the answer. "Backlogged again?"

"Yep."

Ainsley used her phone to snap photos and hoped the last thing Hannah saw wasn't the grotesque tree roots. She pocketed her phone, and they walked closer to the site. All three of them removed their flat hats and stood silently for a minute. Ainsley never visited a murder scene without thinking about the life lost and the family left behind. Hannah Dyson had her whole life ahead of her until someone took it away. *Lord, help me find whoever did this.*

The prayer caught her by surprise. It'd been more than ten years since she'd last uttered any kind of prayer. Not since . . . She shook her thoughts off. Solving this crime was up to her.

She turned to Sam. "Were there any shoe prints leaving the area?"

"Not that we could find. Either he—and judging by the size and the type of shoe, it was a he—returned by way of the gravel path or walked to the Old Trace and left that way."

"How about on the other side of the church?" Linc asked.

"That's a possibility, as well. Could've cut through the cemetery to a hiking trail," Sam said. "There are several of those around here."

So many ways he could have left after he killed Hannah. "Is the church open?"

"I've never found it locked," Sam replied.

Ainsley tilted her head. "What do you say we split up. I'll take the church and cemetery."

Sam nodded. "I'll take the Old Trace and meet up with you back at our vehicles."

Ainsley glanced at Linc, and the expression on his face indicated he didn't like her idea. "Problem?"

He didn't answer right away but instead turned and scanned the area.

"Linc," she said impatiently.

"It's nothing, I guess. Just a gut feeling someone's watching us."

"Have you seen anyone?"

"Just the boy." He shook his head. "Probably my overactive imagination. I'll check out the cemetery with you and then hike the trail on the other side that leads back to where we're parked."

"Good idea."

Sam walked toward the Old Trace while Ainsley and Linc walked the short distance to the opening in the chain-link fence around the cemetery.

"To save time, why don't you go ahead and check out the church while I look around here," Linc said. "Then we can walk back to the truck together."

She agreed and checked the names on the tombstones as she walked to the brick building. Proof people had lived here once. Barrett, Harrison, Lum, Powers, Winters . . . it was so hard to imagine a town in this overgrown wilderness. She paused a minute under the towering trees, their limbs draping Spanish moss like gray streamers.

It was peaceful here, but she wasn't here to relax. She kept her attention on the ground, looking for signs the murderer had passed this way. When she reached the edge of the cemetery, she strode to the front of the building, stopping to read the sign between the two entrances. The church had been built in 1837. Ainsley climbed the steps on the right and tried the front door. Like Sam said, it was unlocked. A shiver ran down her back, and she looked over her shoulder to see where Linc was. Maybe he would like to search the building with her.

Where did that thought come from? Ainsley shrugged it off and entered the church, the coolness surprising her. The musty odor did not. She paused to take stock of her surroundings. Three sections of wooden pews. Two aisles. At the front, a white altar and pulpit. Exits on either side matched the entrance doors. It was much like the old country church where she'd gone to homecomings with her grandmother and aunt every spring.

Ainsley didn't detect any movement signi-fying anyone was here, and she wandered farther inside. Had Hannah ever been here before? If so, maybe the familiarity was what drew her to the church? Otherwise why hadn't she run to the families who were camped at Rocky Springs?

Ainsley paused in front of the altar. The peace she'd felt in the cemetery wasn't here. Instead, a heavy atmosphere weighted her down. A sense she wasn't alone stood the hair on her arms on end.

Someone was here.

Ainsley unsnapped her holster and pulled her gun, holding it with two hands as she turned and scanned the room. "I know you're here. Show yourself."

Her voice echoed in the empty room. Had she imagined someone was here? If so, why did she still feel as though her heart would jump out of her body? Keeping her gun raised, she slowly walked toward the entrance she'd come in.

A blow struck her from behind. She stumbled and caught herself.

Linc! She had to get his attention.

Ainsley squeezed the trigger, the report echoing in her head. Another blow to her arm, and her Sig skittered across the floor. A sweaty arm snaked around her throat and held her fast, blocking her airway.

She kicked at her assailant's legs, and he lifted her off the floor. Ainsley elbowed his ribs.

He swore and squeezed tighter. She kicked the back of a pew, but the more she moved, the less air she had. Black dots filled her line of vision.

Ainsley fought the blackness encroaching her brain. *No!* She would not die this way. She let her body go limp. His grunt was one of surprise as she slipped out of his grip. Before he could clamp back down, she jerked back and headbutted him.

Her assailant bellowed and yanked her in the crook of his arm again. "You'll pay for that." The guttural voice didn't even sound human.

Ainsley struggled to get loose. Lack of oxygen to her muscles drained her strength, but she kept fighting him. Once, she thought Linc called her name. Then again.

It was the last thing she heard before pain shot through her head and she blacked out.

13

Blood dripped from Maddox's nose as he bolted out the door behind the altar. He grabbed a handkerchief from his back pocket and pressed it against his nose. He'd barely gotten out before the other ranger busted through the front door.

The bleeding staunched, he peeked around the corner of the church building and ducked back. The third ranger ran toward the front door. When he disappeared, Maddox slipped into the woods beside the building, a plan already forming in his mind.

14

After hearing the gunshot, Linc raced across the cemetery. He bounded up the church steps and shoved the door open. It took precious seconds for his eyes to adjust to the change in lighting, and then he saw Ainsley's crushed hat on the floor. Just beyond, she lay in a heap. He reached for his Glock that wasn't there, and for the first time in three years, he regretted not carrying one. But could he even use a gun if he had it?

He pushed the thought away and rushed to Ainsley, kneeling beside her. His heart ratcheted down a notch when he felt a strong pulse beating in her wrist. *Thank God.* Linc cradled her in his arms, dismayed at the intensity of his feelings for this woman who had rejected him. He thought he'd buried them for good.

She groaned, and then her eyes fluttered open. They were unfocused. Concussion maybe? Suddenly she swung at him, her fist just missing his jaw as she fought to get out of his embrace.

He pinned her arms to her body. "Ainsley, it's me, Linc," he said softly. "You're all right. No one is going to hurt you."

She stilled in his arms, her body tense. "Linc?" she whispered.

"It's me. You're safe."

She tried to move and groaned. "My head. It's killing me."

Gently he ran his fingers over her head, and she yelped when he found a goose egg at the back. "You've been hit. I heard the gunshot and came as fast as I could. What happened?"

Ainsley leaned against his chest and sucked in a deep breath. "I couldn't breathe. He . . . Something hit me from behind, then knocked my gun out of my hand." She swallowed. "Then he used some kind of choke hold."

He tightened his arms around her. "Did he say anything?"

Ainsley shuddered and took another breath. "That I would pay for headbutting him."

"Did you recognize his voice?"

She smoothed her fingers across her forehead, massaging it. "No. The voice wasn't normal, more like a growl."

They both turned toward the sound of the front door opening. "Find my gun," Ainsley whispered.

Before Linc could move, Sam entered the church. "What's going on?"

"She was attacked," Linc said as Ainsley pushed away from him and tried to get her feet under her. "You sure you want to stand?"

"Yes."

Before he could help her, she struggled to her feet. Ainsley hadn't changed one iota. Independent as all get-out. "I would've helped you," he said.

"I'm good."

She didn't look good. Her face was pale, and her hand shook as she holstered her gun. "You need to rest. You could have a concussion," he said.

Ainsley ignored him and picked up her hat, examining it. "I hope I can reshape it." Then she dusted off her pants. "Do you think he could've left shoe prints?"

She had shifted into full investigator mode, and that meant she was okay. Relief had him almost light-headed. But it shouldn't surprise him, thinking of her grandmother and great-aunt. All three of them were like the sturdy oaks outside the church. Strong. Resilient. But a tad too independent.

Linc glanced down at the pine floors. They didn't look like they'd seen a broom in ages. "Maybe, since there's plenty of dust," he said.

"I have a few gelatin lifters in my SUV," Sam said. "And a flashlight."

The flashlight would help illuminate the prints. While Sam went for the lifters, Linc studied the room. "You didn't see your assailant at all?"

"No. I sensed his presence, though." She shuddered. "I should've listened to my gut earlier."

"I get it. Ever since we got here, I've felt like someone was watching us."

She glanced toward the pulpit. "That was the same feeling I got standing at the altar."

"I shouldn't have dismissed it, but after I talked to that kid, I thought it was him." If anything bad had happened to her . . .

Ainsley turned back to him. "Don't beat yourself up. I'm just glad you were here. If you hadn't yelled my name . . . you did yell my name? I wasn't dreaming that, was I?"

"No. I called for you several times," he said.

"That saved my life."

Their gazes locked, skyrocketing his heart rate. Her blue eyes, framed by thick lashes, held him spellbound. It was like the years fell away, and thoughts of their last kiss before everything went south made him want to take her in his arms again.

Linc brushed a smudge of dirt from her forehead, the touch burning his fingertips. A tremor ran down her delicate throat, and he trailed his fingers along her face, stroking it. A bolt of electricity arced in the inches that separated them, and he leaned closer.

Sam's tires crunching the gravel jerked Linc's head back. Air whooshed from his lungs as he released the breath he'd been holding. "I, uh, guess we better see if we can find any prints."

Ainsley was the first to move as color flooded her face. "Yeah."

Her breathy voice didn't help his heart rate to slow.

"Find anything?" Sam asked as he entered the room.

"Not yet," Linc replied. Heat burned his neck as he looked anywhere but at the district ranger.

"Where have you searched?"

"We hadn't exactly started."

"I'll check the podium—he could have been hiding behind the pulpit," Ainsley said, her voice almost back to normal.

Linc took the smaller of the two flashlights that Sam offered, ignoring the question in his eyes. "I'll see if I can find anything on the aisles."

"I'll take the front entrance," the district ranger said. "But first, let me get our shoe prints for comparison."

Sam wore Redwings while Linc and Ainsley had on lightweight hiking boots. Getting the impressions gave Linc time to pull himself together. With his attention refocused, he studied the layout of the room, taking in the two sets of doors at the front and back of the church as Ainsley knelt behind the pulpit. The assailant could have entered any of them, especially if he got to the church before they arrived at the crime scene.

If it was later, he probably came in through one

of the front doors, given he and Ainsley had been in the cemetery with a direct line of sight to the back entrances. And since Linc came in from the front of the church, the assailant must have fled out the back.

He turned to the pews that were unlike any he'd ever seen. A wooden divider was built in the middle of the row that went all the way to the floor. Perfect hiding place. The man could have hidden on any row.

Linc started with the aisle to the left and turned on the flashlight before he knelt on all fours, angling the light so that any prints would show up. Inching forward, he examined the floor all the way to the front of the room. The dust was undisturbed. To keep from contaminating the other areas, he backtracked to where he'd started and then moved to the other aisle.

"Nothing up here," Ainsley said. "I'm going to check in front of the altar on the off chance I didn't walk over his tracks when I came in."

Linc gave her a thumbs-up and continued his search. Halfway up the aisle on the right, he found shoe prints in the dust, and he tracked them to the back door. It looked as though the assailant had entered through the back, probably before they got to the church, and walked straight to the pew where he hunkered down.

"Over here, Sam," he called. "I need your larger flashlight and gel sheets."

Once he had Sam's flashlight, he laid it on the floor and pointed out the prints to the other two. "It looks like he hid here," he said and shined the light on a space up under the pew beside him. "See, the dust is all smudged."

"I never looked under the pews when I entered the church, and he must've gotten behind me while I was at the front," Ainsley said.

Sam opened the box he'd brought in and took out a rectangular sheet and peeled the back off. Linc shined the light on the floor again.

"Hold it lower." Linc obliged, and Sam laid the sheet on the floor and used a roller from the box to press the gel lifter onto the floor. After a minute, he lifted the sheet and showed them the print.

"It doesn't look like the same shoe that you cast," Ainsley said.

The district ranger agreed. "But the shoe size looks about the same so it doesn't mean it's not the same person."

"Why would anyone be hiding in the church? And why attack you?" Linc's jaw clenched as he stared at the shoe print.

Sam tilted his head. "What if he followed you two to Rocky Springs and overheard that Ainsley was searching the church?"

Her eyes widened. "But why? Unless . . ." Color drained from her face.

"He meant to kill you," Linc said, finishing her sentence.

15

Ainsley's head swam. Fainting was not an option. She already chafed at not apprehending her assailant. With a deep breath, she squared her shoulders and immediately gritted her teeth to keep from groaning when pain shot through her head. Linc was probably right about a concussion.

Linc. Ainsley refused to think about how he'd almost kissed her before Sam returned. A kiss she would have welcomed. *Don't go there.* She sucked in air to clear the thought away. Linc had let her down once, nothing said he wouldn't do it again. She made the mistake of looking up into his hazel eyes that had a green cast today.

"You okay?" His voice was tender, reminding her of what they'd had together once.

Ainsley nodded, the movement making her head throb even more. Until now, adrenaline had kept her going, but the rush was wearing off, leaving exhaustion and pain in its wake. That's all it was. Exhaustion made her vulnerable to him.

"None of this makes sense," she said. "Do you think we were followed?"

"It'd be hard to tell. There were a few cars behind us. A couple of them passed us, but you were only driving the posted fifty-miles-an-hour speed limit. When we stopped for the tree that was down, there were two or three cars behind us." He frowned. "Nothing suspicious, though."

"And no one else turned into Rocky Springs," she said.

"He could have gone past the campground and then turned around, or he could have antici- pated where you were going and was already here," Sam pointed out. "We need to check out the campers. See if anyone has abruptly left or seemed suspicious."

She massaged her temples. "How did he even know I'd be here this morning?"

"Who knew you were meeting me at Rocky Springs?" Sam asked.

"Hardly anyone knows why I'm here other than my boss in East Tennessee. My grandmother and Cora, but who would they have told?" She looked at Linc. "There was that reporter with you . . . and my dad."

Sam shook his head. "None of them are likely candidates."

"He may not have followed us at all," Linc said. "Let me throw this out there—what if he followed you from East Tennessee? If he knows you're investigating this crime, he could have assumed you'd come to the crime scene. Came here, saw the tape, and then noticed how close the church is, and could have hidden in the church, waiting for you."

"Or . . ." Sam said, "like I said earlier, if he overheard us before we split up, he would've known you were the one checking out the church. He had time to get into place."

Cold chills ran over her body. She knew no one in Natchez who would want her dead, and trouble *could* have followed her from East Tennessee. Over the years, she'd made a few enemies of the people she'd arrested. When she finished here, she would call Brent Murphy, the special agent in charge of the East Tennessee district and ask him to pull the records of all the criminals who had threatened her.

"I'll notify Randolph of your attack," Sam said. "You two want to interview the people at the campground while I dust for fingerprints and get a few more of these shoe prints?"

Linc looked at her. "You up to it?"

She warmed under his intense scrutiny. "I am."

Her phone rang and she glanced at the number. Her grandmother. Her heart clenched, and she quickly punched the green answer button. "Hello?"

"Oh good. I got you." Gran's voice sounded shaky. "Cora's surgery has been moved up to noon."

That meant the bleeding in her skull had gotten

worse. Ainsley checked her watch. Eleven forty-five. She should have stayed at the hospital instead of coming to Rocky Springs.

"I'll get there as soon as I can," she said.

"You stay and do your job. Cora and I will be just fine—like always."

Guilt rubbed like a too-tight shoe. Ainsley had never been there for any of their other emergencies. Hadn't even known when they had one until it was over.

"Okay, but keep me updated." When she disconnected, she looked up into Linc's concerned eyes.

"Everything okay?"

"They're taking her to surgery right away."

"Do you want to go to the hospital? Sam and I can do the interviews, and then I can catch a ride with him back to Natchez."

She was torn, wanting to be there for her grandmother and Cora but knowing this might be the only chance to interview some of the campers before they scattered. Not that Sam and Linc wouldn't do a good job, but secondhand testimony wasn't the same thing as hearing it firsthand.

"Gran told me to stay here and do my job. Besides, I can't get to the hospital in time for the surgery anyway." She turned to Sam. "Send me the report on the prints when you get it."

"Will do."

Ten minutes later they approached the campground loop where RVs and trailers were parked. Ainsley counted ten campers. "I'll take these five," she said, pointing to the first campsites.

"Good deal. I'll get the rest, and if I finish first, I'll check out the tent campers."

She walked to the first site, a nice fifth wheel with a diesel pickup parked to the side, and knocked on the screen door. "Hello! Anyone home?"

A teenaged boy appeared in the doorway. "I am, but my parents are hiking."

Was this the boy Linc had run into? She told him her name. "Can I ask you a few questions?" she asked.

He regarded her suspiciously. "About?"

"Just checking to see if you've seen anyone suspicious or an unoccupied car parked around here."

He opened the screen door and stepped outside. "What kind of car?"

"I'm not sure." She glanced at the picnic table in the shade. "Mind if we sit over there?"

He shrugged, and taking it as a yes, she walked to the table and sat down. At first, she thought he wasn't going to follow, but after a minute's hesitation, he did and sat across from her. "Did you talk to another ranger earlier?"

He nodded silently.

Joy. She might as well be asking the trees

questions. She searched her memory for the name Linc had called him. Oh yeah . . . Ainsley smiled. "He indicated you heard something Tuesday night, Colton."

He flinched when she said his name. "How . . . ?" Then he frowned. "Oh yeah. I told that other ranger, and then I made the mistake of telling my dad. He said I probably imagined it."

Sounded like the dad wasn't very supportive of the kid. Then again, maybe he had reason not to be. "Mind telling me what you saw and heard?"

Another shrug that she took for a yes.

"If you don't mind, I'm going to record our conversation. My memory isn't what it used to be."

It'd been a risk asking, and she breathed easier when he didn't object. Ainsley took out her cell phone and laid it on the table, wishing she hadn't left her electronic tablet in the truck—she'd gotten in the habit of using one instead of the small notebook she was stuck with today.

Colton repeated basically what Linc had told her, which made her think he was telling the truth. Liars often weren't able to repeat a story accurately. "So, you knew her from school?" When he nodded, she asked, "Did you talk to her?"

The boy's mouth twitched before he shook his head. A twitch she wouldn't have seen if she hadn't been watching him closely. "Look, you won't be in trouble if you two talked."

"But we didn't!"

Yet he wouldn't look at her. Was he lying or was he afraid of something? "What happened here Tuesday night? You want to tell me, I can see that," she said, softening her voice.

Colton rubbed his face. "You won't tell my dad?"

What was it with the boy's father? "Why wouldn't he want you to tell the truth?"

"You'd have to know my dad, and you don't want to do that." His hands curled into fists. "If I tell you, will you leave before he gets back?"

Did she want to promise that? "I'll leave, but I'm not telling you I won't return."

"I don't care if you come back. I won't be here."

"Your parents are leaving?"

"No. I'm leaving. I can't take living with my dad anymore."

"Where will you go?"

"Not sure, but I saw this flyer, and it said I could make twenty dollars an hour, no experience necessary."

Ainsley didn't like the sound of that. "Doing what?"

"I called and the man who answered said I'd be doing landscaping. He said I could make 160 to 200 bucks a day. He's going to pick me up at Port Gibson later today."

She thought of the cases of human trafficking

that had come across her desk. Traffickers promising not just teenagers but older people good jobs and then paying them practically nothing. Ainsley wanted to warn him, but first she needed his information. "Tell me about Hannah."

He clasped his hands together. "You're right. I saw her Monday night with a boy about my age. They were on a motorbike and then they had a fight, and he left. She didn't have a way home."

The words rushed from him almost in one sentence. "So, you did talk to her."

He barely nodded.

"Was he her boyfriend?"

"It looked like it."

"Does this boyfriend have a name?"

"Kingston. Drew Kingston. He's a big jock around school."

And Colton wasn't. "Why do you think they came *here?* Rocky Springs is fifty miles from Natchez."

He shrugged. "Probably to smoke weed. Hannah had some Monday night. Offered to share it." He stared at his thumbs pressed together. "Told her I didn't touch that stuff. My dad, if he smelled it on me, he would've killed me."

"Is that when you talked to her—Monday night, not Tuesday?"

He nodded.

"Start at the beginning and tell me what happened."

His response was slow in coming. "I . . . couldn't sleep and was out walking when I saw them. They were arguing and didn't see me. She was at one of the picnic tables up near the church . . ." He crossed his arms over his chest.

"And?" she prompted him.

"After he left, I said something to her and about scared her to death. When she saw I wasn't going to hurt her, she calmed down. Told me her name, but I already knew it was Hannah. She said she'd called someone to come get her. We talked until her friend showed up, and then I went back to our camper."

"Who picked her up?"

"It was a girl she hung out with sometimes at school."

Ainsley wasn't sure whether to believe him or not. He clearly had issues, and she'd had to push him to get answers. Still, his story had the ring of truth in it. "And she came back Tuesday night?"

Colton nodded. "*He* was with her again. Guess they made up."

And maybe they fought again and he killed her. "Did anyone else come around?"

"I didn't see nobody."

"Can you think of anything else that might help find her killer?"

He chewed his bottom lip as he looked up toward the sky. After a long minute, he shook his head.

"Well, if you remember anything, give me a call." She gave him one of her business cards, and then closed the recorder app and pocketed her phone. "Thanks, Colton. And do me a favor."

He looked up from the table.

"Don't take that job."

"I have to. I can't stand living with my dad."

"How old are you?"

"Just turned seventeen."

"Then you're not out of school yet."

He shook his head.

"No one is going to pay you twenty dollars an hour without experience in landscaping or any other job. You've heard of human trafficking?"

"This ain't nothing like that—it's just working! The man said I'd be driving a mower."

"Legally you can't operate a mower or weed trimmer or any other motorized equipment. Legitimate companies don't do that. And there are more people caught up on the labor side of human trafficking than the other," Ainsley said. "And if that company has no problem breaking the law by letting you operate a machine, they won't have a problem lying to you about the job. Or the pay."

Hope faded from his face.

"I'm sorry. Can I give you some advice? My dad and I fought like crazy when I was your age," she said without waiting for his answer. "Until I finally learned to agree with him and—"

"I can't do that. He puts me and Mom down like we're trash."

"You didn't let me finish. Just because I agreed with my dad doesn't mean I let him win. You only have a year until you're eighteen. Do whatever it takes to get through the year. Stay away from home as much as possible. Go to the library or hang around school in the afternoon. Study hard and find a scholarship, or do whatever it takes to get a good education. That's your best revenge."

He shot her a skeptical look.

"My dad didn't think I'd make it as a law enforcement ranger, and here I am now, working in an elite group with the National Park Service. One of thirty-three. If I can do it, so can you."

Ainsley put Colton's phone number and Natchez address in her phone. "I'll be in Natchez until the investigation is over. If you need to talk or remember other details about the murder, give me a call. My number is on that card I gave you."

He seemed about to say something, then his face closed down. "Thanks."

She left him sitting at the picnic table and walked to the next campsite. Colton Mason was holding something back. She just didn't know what it was . . . yet.

16

L inc had no luck with his five campsites. Two of them, fancy RVs traveling together, had arrived an hour earlier and hadn't seen anyone. The other three campers had not arrived at Rocky Springs until Wednesday and, like the first two, had not seen anything out of the ordinary.

When he finished with the last campsite, he looked for Ainsley. She hadn't made it past the first camper and was talking with the boy he'd run into in the woods. He considered joining them, but something drew him to the trailhead. There'd been a couple of tent campers on the main road, and he could walk the Old Trace for a piece, and then veer off to talk with them.

Dappled sunlight shaded the colors of the trees on the historical path as he walked a carpet of pine needles, his thoughts drifting to Ainsley. Being around her was more painful than he'd expected when he agreed to help Sam. His sigh blended with the birds singing above him.

She hadn't forgiven him for siding with her father. Linc hadn't opposed her trying to make it in the music industry because she didn't have a good singing voice. Ainsley had a beautiful alto—at least that's the label that music critics gave her voice. To him it was pure and unaffected and touched his soul.

Linc had discouraged her because he feared the cutthroat music business would chew her up and spit her out, and he hadn't wanted to see her hurt. At least that's what he'd told himself at the time, but if he'd been honest with himself, he would have realized he feared losing her.

When she was asked to sing backup to one of the top names in gospel music, he and her dad staged a mini-intervention, trying to make her see the dangers that lay ahead. She had not taken it well and broke it off with him. He'd lost her anyway.

Linc thought she was on her way to stardom, and then after a year and a half, she disappeared. The next time he heard anything about her, it was through her grandmother, who relayed that Ainsley had returned to college and was a year from graduation. By then, Linc had been recruited by the FBI and was caught up in that world. Truth be told, he'd been more than a little upset that Ainsley had given up her dream so easily.

He'd like to know what happened to her music career. Linc had asked Rose, and she'd told him he'd have to ask Ainsley. So far there hadn't been a good opportunity.

Why was he doing this? Torturing himself

with thoughts of Ainsley? He shifted his focus to his surroundings as a light breeze rustled the leaves. The Old Trace he was hiking was the original road that had begun with bison traveling to salt licks and then morphed into a highway for Native Americans, then French trappers, then Kaintucks . . . even Andrew Jackson's army.

Something within him stirred at the thought of adding his footsteps to the same path that over ten thousand travelers a year had walked in the early 1800s. He eyed the towering oaks shading the trail. It was even possible some of these huge trees had been saplings at the time.

Movement ahead caught his eye. Two people hiked toward him. If they'd been out long, maybe they'd seen something or someone.

"Morning," he said when they reached him.

"Good morning to you as well," the man answered.

Linc catalogued the man's dragon tattoo that started on one side of his neck, then wrapped around to the other side and disappeared into his long-sleeved pullover. It was a habit left over from his FBI days.

He met Linc's gaze while the woman barely nodded before she looked down at the ground. From her gaunt frame, she could possibly be ill. Still, she reminded him of someone . . . Colton. The woman had to be his mother.

Linc identified himself to the couple. "Have you met many hikers on the trail this morning?" he asked.

"Nope."

The man's reply had been a little too quick. "You didn't see anyone at all?"

The woman lifted her head slightly and cast a sideways glance at her husband.

"No one at all," he replied. "Right, Alma?"

She tucked her head down. "Right."

Linc barely heard her reply. "And you would be . . . ?" He took a notepad from his shirt pocket.

"Jesse and Alma Mason. We're camped at site 1. Been there since Monday."

That's where he'd last seen Ainsley talking to Colton. Linc jotted down their names. "Address and phone number? Just in case I need to get in touch with you."

Once he had their information, he asked if they'd heard anything Tuesday night and almost missed seeing Alma's shoulders flinch.

"Terrible thing, what happened to that girl," Jesse said. "But we didn't see or hear anything until the sirens and lights woke us up."

Linc tapped his pen on the notebook. Whatever Jesse knew, he wasn't telling. Linc gave them two of his cards from his wallet. "If you remember anything, give me a call," he said, tipping his hat. "Appreciate you talking with me."

"Anytime, Ranger."

Yeah, right. But if Linc could get the woman away from her husband, he might actually learn something. He'd have to work on that.

17

As Ainsley walked to the next camper, she listened to the recording of the conversation with Colton on her phone, pausing it when the Kingston name was mentioned. There'd been an Austin Kingston a couple of grades ahead of her in high school. His father, Jack, had relocated the family to Natchez after he married a Natchez socialite in a second marriage. Even though he'd been new to the area, it didn't take him long to become a power player in city politics. But Natchez had not been big enough for him, and about the time Ainsley left for college, the prominent attorney moved to Jackson and later became mayor.

She hoped Drew didn't belong to *that* set of Kingstons.

Alpha males. It was the only description she could think of for the Kingston men, especially Jack. Like a wolf pack leader, he raised his hackles at any perceived slight to his son, whether it was on the football field or in the classroom.

Jack was also running against her father for governor.

She approached the trailer at the next campsite, calling out, and when no one answered, moved on to the third one. The older couple in the Airstream hadn't seen anything unusual. Same story at the camper beside them. When Ainsley finished with the fifth campsite, she walked toward her Ford Ranger. She didn't see Linc and figured when he finished his five campsites, he'd probably taken the other side of the circle to check for more campers.

Before she reached the trailhead, Ainsley heard voices, and then a man and woman emerged from a side trail. Scruffy. That was her first impression of the couple, especially the man, who made no effort to hide his blatant once-over of her. Ainsley could only imagine how the thin woman beside him felt.

"Good morning," she said, focusing on the woman, who looked a lot like Colton. Besides their features, they had the same beaten-down expression about them. If these were Colton's parents . . . She barely kept herself from shuddering.

She tapped her badge. "I'm ISB Ranger Ainsley Beaumont. Got a minute for me to ask a couple of questions?"

"We just talked with another ranger," the man replied. "We know nothing about the poor girl who was murdered, and my wife and I have seen no one acting suspicious this morning."

She took a card from her pocket, which the man waved off.

"The other ranger provided us with his contact information in case we remembered anything, even though I explained there was nothing to remember," the man said. "If you'll excuse us . . ."

"Take it anyway," she said.

The man took the card and examined it before he handed it off to his wife. "Just what does the Investigative Services Branch of the National Park Service do?"

Ainsley ignored his question for the moment and opened her notebook. "I need your contact information for my report."

"We already—"

"I still need it."

His eyes narrowed. "Jesse and Alma Mason."

She ignored his snappish tone. "Phone number and address."

"We gave that information to the other ranger."

"Then it should be fresh in your mind." Ainsley didn't look up as he recited phone numbers and an address. "Is that in Natchez?"

"It is. And if that's all . . ."

She tipped her head. "Sorry to have hindered you, but thank you for your cooperation. If you remember anything, no matter how insignificant, give me or the other ranger a call," she said with a smile and pocketed her notebook. "Oh, and as for what the Investigative Services Branch of the National Park Service does, think FBI—we're a small but effective branch of law enforcement rangers."

Ainsley had only gone a few yards when she heard her name called and did an about-face. She almost asked if he'd remembered something already. "Yes?" she asked instead.

"Should you happen to talk to my son," he said, "I would advise you to take anything he tells you with a grain of salt."

Colton hadn't exaggerated the issues with his father. "I'll keep that in mind."

18

Linc cut across to the main road, where he'd seen tents set up. He found four young men in their late teens or early twenties and learned they'd been traveling together and had arrived Wednesday afternoon.

They reported there'd been another camper at the next site, but he'd broken down his tent maybe two hours ago. They hadn't seen which way he went but described him as an old guy who was there when they arrived, and he wasn't very talkative. *Old guy.* Given their age, that could mean the man had been anywhere from forty on up. One of the boys volunteered the man was hitchhiking and going on to New Orleans from Rocky Springs.

He took their contact information and then walked to the parking lot where Ainsley's pickup was parked. She was sitting on the tailgate, typing into her tablet, the retaining strap on her Sig Sauer unhooked. His shoes crunched on the gravel, and her hand went to her gun as she looked up, her eyes wary.

"Oh good. It's you." She relaxed and removed buds from her ears.

"Where's Sam?"

"He got a call. Something about an alligator down the road," she said. "When I was growing up around here, I don't remember that happening hardly at all."

"According to Sam, it happens a couple times a week," he replied with a chuckle. "Did you get Colton to talk to you?"

She held up her phone. "Better than that, he let me record our conversation. I was just transcribing my notes into my tablet. You want to listen to it?"

"I'll listen on the way to the hospital," he said. "Would you like me to drive back to Natchez? That way you can finish up your notes."

Linc thought Ainsley was going to decline his invitation, but then she nodded and hopped off the tailgate. "Good idea. Once I get to the hospital, I won't get a chance to get my thoughts down on paper or rather in the tablet."

She tossed him the keys, and once he was in the driver's seat, he familiarized himself with the pickup. Not too different from his Tahoe. He shifted into reverse and backed out of the parking space. The pickup handled well as he pointed it toward Natchez. "Any luck with the other campers?"

"Not really. Either they'd just arrived at the campground or they didn't hear anything. I understand you met Colton's parents," she said.

"Yeah. They indicated they hadn't seen anything suspicious around the campground this morning either. Seemed nice enough, but I thought the woman might be more willing to talk if her husband wasn't around."

"I got that impression too and asked Sam to run a background check on them." She glanced down at her tablet. "I have an appointment to meet with Drew Kingston at four. And I called Hannah's mother, but she didn't answer, so I left word on her voicemail to call me back," she said.

"Kingston, as in Austin Kingston?"

"Yep. Would've been a lot easier if it'd been anyone but one of the Kingstons."

As far back as Linc could remember, the Kingstons had been acting like the rules didn't apply to them. If Austin or his father, Jackson mayor Jack Kingston, decided Drew didn't need to talk to Ainsley, it would practically take a court order to override either of them. "Will you have to go through his dad to talk to him?"

"Not really. Sam's report states he's seventeen, but I thought it might be a smart move to ask Austin's permission to talk to Drew. I'm interviewing him at Austin's law office. And I can always play the old school-spirit card as a last resort."

"Get ready to play it," he said and added, "Mind if I tag along?"

"Not at all, and if you think of something to ask

that I've overlooked, feel free to speak up." She looked over her notes. "Do you still write your notes in longhand?"

She remembered? Warmth radiated through his chest, then he realized she was waiting for an answer. "I'm afraid I switched over to the computer for my notes in college and now a tablet. Quicker and easier to read. Although sometimes when we're stumped, your aunt gets after me to grab a notepad and start freewriting."

"How long have you been helping her?"

"About six months now. Wish I'd started earlier though. I could have seen that first diary she found."

In the passenger seat, Ainsley clicked on the recording, and Colton's voice filled the cab. When it ended, he said, "That's pretty well what he said when he was talking to me."

"I didn't think he'd contradicted what you told me." She slipped her phone in her pocket. "I'm going to finish these notes."

Ten minutes down the road, the sedate fifty-mile-an-hour speed limit made it hard for Linc to keep his eyes open. "I think I'll come off at Port Gibson and switch over to Highway 61. It'll be the quickest way to get to the hospital."

She rolled her shoulders. "Good idea."

An approaching pickup sped past them and Linc flinched when a rock came flying toward them. The impact sounded like a bullet when it hit the windshield. Ainsley ducked and grabbed for her gun.

"It's okay! It's only a rock."

"Looks like a bullet hole to me!"

If he hadn't seen the rock coming, Linc would agree with her. The round hole with cracks spiderwebbing in every direction on the windshield did look like it was caused by a bullet. "Trust me, it's not."

He slowed and pulled over on the side of the road and put the flashers on. "You okay?"

She sat with her head braced against the back of the seat, her eyes closed. "Yeah. Or I will be after I get past thinking someone was trying to kill me again." She sat up. "Sorry. Overreacted a little bit. Let's see what the damage is."

They got out and examined the hole and jagged cracks, which looked like they might run anytime. She narrowed her eyes. "You sure this isn't a bullet hole?"

"I saw the pickup tire fling the rock. Happens sometimes, especially with those plus-sized tires on the truck. It's safe enough to drive back to Natchez, but you're going to need a new windshield."

She groaned. "Another thing on my to-do list."

"You ready to get on to the hospital?"

Ainsley nodded and climbed back in the passenger side. Once they were back on the road, he suggested she get some rest.

"I'm too wired," she replied.

He was glad. Having someone to talk to would keep him alert. Linc's thoughts kept returning to the attack in the church. "Did you call your supervisor in East Tennessee?"

"I thought I'd wait until I got closer to Natchez so service wouldn't be interrupted."

"Good idea. Have you come up with anyone?"

"There's only one person who comes to mind—Troy Maddox, a guy who almost killed his ex-wife and did kill her new husband. They were spending their honeymoon near Cades Cove in the Smokies. I was the special agent in charge of the case, and somehow he blames me for ruining his life."

"Sounds like he might be a little unbalanced," Linc said.

"And you would be right." She shook her head. "Maddox got twenty-five years without the possibility of parole so I'm pretty sure he's incarcerated. After the threats he made against me, surely I would be notified if he wasn't."

"We need to make sure," Linc said. "Do you have body armor with you?"

She jerked her thumb toward the back. "There's one in the storage box in the bed of the truck."

"When we get to the hospital, I'll get it so you can put it on."

Ainsley nodded. "I didn't wear one this morning because I only expected to walk over the crime scene, maybe interview any campers who were at Rocky Springs Tuesday night. Never expected what happened at the church. I still wonder if I could've disturbed a druggie."

"Nothing's impossible. Maybe Sam found fingerprints. If it was a drug user or dealer, he might have a record."

Still, Linc couldn't shake the sense of foreboding that hung over him. He was afraid they hadn't seen the last of her attacker.

19

When they neared Mount Locust, a text dinged on Ainsley's phone, and her heart stuttered. Cora's surgery was over, but it would be a while before anyone could see her.

"From Rose?" Linc asked.

She nodded. "I hate that I'm not there."

"It can't be helped, and I'm sure your grandmother understands."

"She always does." Pattern of her life. Her grandmother needed her, and something always kept Ainsley from helping her.

After promising to text if a problem came up, Gran told her not to worry. Easier said than done. Ainsley concentrated on her breathing. If she didn't, she'd be wringing her hands, not something she wanted Linc to see.

Was it a drug addict who'd attacked her? Her gut said no. It also said the attack had nothing to do with the investigation, but where did that leave her?

"There's cell coverage at Mount Locust," Linc said. "We can pull in and you can call your supervisor."

His voice startled her, setting off a flurry of

heartbeats. She wasn't sure if it was because the truck cab was so quiet or if it was the deep timbre of his voice. If it was the latter, she was in trouble.

"I'll try, but I don't want to spend a lot of time here." She took a breath and dialed Brent Murphy's number. She groaned when she got his voicemail but left a message asking for Troy Maddox's status. "I can't believe he's been released."

"Maybe he escaped."

"I think someone would have notified me if that had happened. Maddox has been pretty vocal about what he'd do if he got out. I was counting on those twenty-five years to change his mind and decide harming me wasn't worth going back to prison for."

"Still, I'll feel better once you get in touch with your supervisor," he said.

So would Ainsley, if nothing more than to verify Maddox was where he was supposed to be. She leaned her head back on the seat, the sound of the tires calming her. She liked the man Linc had become, not that she'd admit it to him. Her heart sped up at the memory of his fingers stroking her cheek. Was he dating anyone?

Immediately Sarah came to mind and the way she'd put her hand on his arm. Maybe they were a couple. The thought pained her. Why? Ainsley had no claim to Linc. Her time would be better spent trying to figure out who wanted to kill her.

Half an hour later, they rolled into the hospital parking lot. There'd been no more texts from her grandmother and nothing from her supervisor. "I'll take you to get your SUV as soon as I've talked to Gran," she said and slipped into the vest he retrieved from the toolbox. She hated wearing the vest inside the hospital.

"No hurry. I want to see how Cora is." He tilted his head. "What's the matter?"

"Just trying to figure out how to keep Gran from worrying when she sees me in this vest."

"I think you'll be safe in the hospital, so why don't you see if you can stash it at the front desk until you get ready to leave?"

"Good thinking."

When they walked into the hospital, she slipped out of the vest and asked the volunteers manning the reception desk if she could leave it there. They agreed but eyed the Sig Sauer in her holster. "I'll keep this," she said.

As they walked to the ICU waiting room, she asked, "How did you get roped into helping Cora with her book?"

"I wasn't 'roped' into it," he replied. "She told me she was writing a book about her great-grandparents and she needed my assistance. It seemed like such an interesting story that I offered to help."

"Really?" Ainsley supposed someone hearing

the story for the first time would find it interesting. She'd heard the story a hundred times. How Gran and Cora's great-grandfather was arrested for murdering his brother-in-law and then killed by an angry mob made up of friends of the murdered man before he could stand trial.

"Cora has her own theory formulated by the first diary she found almost a year ago. She believes there are more diaries, if she just knew where to look. Evidently the diary that went missing was written well after the murder, and according to Cora, it's rich with history about the Reconstruction era."

"Cora mentioned diaries last night. Do you think she may have found more?"

"She was certainly looking for them," he said. "Had been since before I started helping her."

Talking about the diaries reminded Ainsley of the wet carpet. "Once we leave here, do you have time to go by her house?"

"I was hoping you would ask," he said with a grin.

It surprised her that she looked forward to his help searching for evidence that someone else was in the library.

20

Maddox pulled into the hospital parking lot and parked several rows over from the pickup he'd followed from the Trace. His information about Beaumont hadn't included her location in Natchez, so following her to wherever she was staying was a must.

Time ticked by slowly as Maddox slouched down in the seat and waited for them to exit the hospital. A slight breeze through the open windows barely kept him awake. He tipped his hat down on his forehead and watched the front entrance.

21

When they entered the ICU waiting room, Linc narrowed his eyes. Sarah was sitting with Rose. The videographer he'd seen with her last night was leaning against the wall. What were they doing here?

That was a dumb question. The news reporter was looking for Ainsley to interview her. Beside him, Ainsley caught her breath.

"I'm sorry," he said. "I'll see if I can get rid of them."

"No. Let's get this over with unless I can visit Cora right away."

"Don't breathe a word to her about the attempt on your life at the church."

"I've dealt with reporters like Sarah before, so you don't have to worry about that."

Ainsley didn't know Sarah. The girl could smell a story a mile away.

The reporter's broad grin faded when her gaze slid over Linc's shoulder to Ainsley. "I thought I might catch Ainsley here," she said. "But I didn't expect you to be with her."

"He's helping with the investigation," Ainsley replied, then she turned to Rose. "How is Cora?"

"She's back in her ICU room, and the doctor said we could go in, probably in about thirty minutes," Rose said. "Not that I expect her to be awake."

"I'm sorry it took me so long."

"I told you not to worry about that. This young lady has been kind enough to sit with me." She turned to Linc. "Sarah said she was your very good friend. And she's been entertaining me with some of her stories. Did you know she broke the recent gambling scandal?"

Linc masked his irritation. Sarah had traded on their friendship to worm her way into Rose's good graces, probably to get personal information about Ainsley.

"So," Sarah said, "do you think we could do that interview now? That way it'll run on the five o'clock news."

"On one condition," Ainsley replied. "That I can ask people to contact me if they have any information on the murder."

The reporter waved her hand. "No prob. How about we step outside in the hallway?"

Linc followed them out the door and leaned against the wall as Sarah set up for the interview. When her videographer was ready, she spoke into her microphone, framing the interview with the murder details, and then turned to Ainsley. "ISB Ranger Ainsley Beaumont is heading up the investigation in the death of Hannah Dyson, the teenager found murdered at Rocky Springs. Do you have any suspects in her murder?" she asked. "Or persons of interest?"

"This is an active investigation, and those are details I can't reveal," Ainsley replied. "Besides, it's early in the investigation."

"So that means you'll talk to me later, when you have more evidence?"

"I didn't say that, but perhaps."

Sarah's smug expression indicated she'd get the second interview. "Are you looking at her boyfriend as the possible murderer? I understand that—"

"We're not even certain she had a boyfriend," Ainsley said, cutting her off. "We're looking at everyone who has a connection to Hannah."

Good answer, and he released the breath he held. But how did Sarah learn about the Kingston boy? Or was she just fishing?

Sarah didn't try to hide her irritation. "Can you reveal how she was murdered?"

"I'm sorry, but no."

"Well, then could you explain to our audience exactly what an ISB ranger is?"

Ainsley switched directions seamlessly. "ISB stands for the Investigative Services Branch of the National Park Service. We're sort of the FBI for the park service."

"I understand there are only thirty-three ISB investigators. Is that correct?"

"Yes."

Ainsley's short answer didn't deter the reporter. "So why did your field office send you?"

"Partly because I'm familiar with the area since I grew up here, and why not me?"

Sarah ignored Ainsley's question. "I understand your great-aunt, Cora Chamberlain, fell last night and you suspect foul play."

"I have no idea where you got that information, but it is not correct," Ainsley said, her voice icy enough to chill even Sarah.

She gave Ainsley a quick smile and then looked into the camera. "Thank you for taking the time to talk to our viewers, Ranger Beaumont."

Before Sarah could turn away, Ainsley said, "I would like to ask your viewers to contact me if they have any information on Hannah Dyson's murder. They can call the Port Gibson ranger station and leave their number and I'll return the call. Thank you for giving me a platform to ask for the public's help in bringing Hannah's murderer to justice."

The camera cut away from Ainsley to the reporter. "You can also contact me at the news station. This is Sarah Tolliver in Natchez for WTMC, reporting the latest news on the murder investigation of Hannah Dyson."

As soon as the camera shut down, Linc strode to Sarah. "Why in the world did you ask Ainsley about her aunt?" He should've nixed the interview.

Sarah palmed her hands. "It wasn't anything personal. Just following up on information her grandmother gave me."

"And you had to ask me about it on-air?" Ainsley demanded.

"It's my job." She handed the videographer the microphone. "Now if you will excuse me—"

"If you get a tip, I expect you to pass it on," Ainsley said.

"Of course." The reporter grinned.

Linc fumed. Probably not until she investigated it.

"I'm going to check on Cora," Ainsley said over her shoulder.

Once the door closed behind her, Sarah said, "Are we still on for next Wednesday? I've already told Dad about the picnic."

If he said no, it would hurt Ed Tolliver's feelings, and Linc didn't want more guilt. "Yeah. I'll be in touch about the time."

Linc entered the waiting room and joined Ainsley and her grandmother at the front desk. "How is she?" he asked.

"The nurse said we could see her for five minutes," Rose replied. "Would you like to come with us? I know how fond you are of Cora."

"I don't want to intrude." He glanced at Ainsley.

"You won't," the older woman said, patting his arm.

"She'll be glad to know you're here," Ainsley said.

Her approval was what he'd been waiting for. "Okay, then."

A nurse met them at the door and led them back to her room. Rose faltered at the door and Linc saw why. A line of staples closed the incision on the left side of Cora's head, and above the staples was a drain tube.

"The nurse said she might wake up," Ainsley said. "But she probably wouldn't make much sense."

Rose stood by the side of the bed, her hand covering her sister's. Cora's eyes fluttered open, and her gaze focused on her sister, then Ainsley, and she smiled before she closed them. A minute later she opened her eyes again and scanned the room as if trying to place where she was before her gaze came back to rest on him. "Linc?"

He was surprised she recognized him. "You're going to be fine," he said.

"The diaries," she whispered. "Don't let him have . . . keep them safe."

The diaries again. "Where are they?" he asked.

"They're . . ." Confusion filled her eyes. "I . . . don't know."

"Who wants them?"

Her brows pinched together, then she grimaced. "I . . . don't know."

The nurse appeared at the door. "I'm afraid

your time is up, and she needs to rest. You can see her again at six this evening."

Rose bent and kissed her sister on the cheek and whispered something in her ear. Then Ainsley did the same. When they stepped away from the bed, Linc walked close enough to take her hand. "Hurry up and get well so we can finish that book," he said.

"You work on it," she said softly.

"I'll wait on you."

Back in the waiting room, he suggested that they pick up something to eat and meet Rose at her house. Hamburgers from the Magnolia Grill were decided on.

Ainsley turned to her grandmother. "Did you say anything to that news reporter about the journals?"

Rose pressed her fingers against her lips. "Maybe. While she was telling me her funny stories, sometimes she'd ask me a question about Cora."

Linc shook his head. That was Sarah at her best. "I don't think we should discuss anything with Sarah Tolliver," Linc said. "When she asks a question, just say 'No comment.'"

"But she seemed so nice," Rose said.

"Oh, she is," he replied, "but never forget, she is first and foremost a reporter."

After they left the waiting room, Linc said, "I'll get the pickup and meet you at the door while you're getting your vest."

"Good idea."

"Have you heard anything from your supervisor?" he asked a few minutes later as they drove to pick up the hamburgers.

"No, and I tried to call him again. I don't understand why it's going straight to voicemail unless he's in a remote area of the mountains."

"Is there anyone else you can call?"

"We're the only two ISB rangers in the Smokies." Ainsley scrolled through her phone. "But I can try one of the law enforcement rangers in the area."

He pulled into the drive-through and ordered the burgers.

"Goes to voicemail, just like Brent's," Ainsley said. "Something big must be going down."

Linc drove to Rose's and pulled the pickup into the drive behind the older woman's Prius and parked beside his Tahoe he'd left earlier. He followed Ainsley inside, remembering the countless times he'd trailed her through the old-fashioned kitchen that was spotless as usual.

"I was about to send out a search party for you two," Rose said. "And why are you wearing that thing?"

Ainsley looked down at the vest Rose pointed to. "SOP." She pulled the Velcro tabs loose and slipped the vest off.

"And standard operating procedures don't

apply to Linc?" she asked, sniffing. "You didn't have it on in the hospital either."

Rose didn't miss anything.

"I'm hungry," Ainsley said, pulling out one of the ladder-back chairs and plopping down. She reached for the bag. Linc had a feeling the subject wouldn't be ignored long.

"Not until I get plates." Rose's lips twitched.

He laughed at the way the older woman looked over her glasses at Ainsley when she said they didn't need plates. He wondered if Rose had ever eaten on a paper plate other than at a picnic. Once they'd eaten, he helped clear the table and put everything in the trash while the plates and utensils went into the dishwasher. Then he looked at his watch. "It's almost three thirty. Do we have time to check out Cora's house?"

Indecision played on Ainsley's face. "Let's at least look at the library, but I need to run to my room first."

She returned wearing a better-fitting vest under her park service shirt and tossed him the one she'd been wearing. "Now you have one—you can adjust it to fit you." Then she kissed her grandmother on the cheek. "Try to get some rest before you go back to the hospital."

Rose eyed Ainsley over her glasses again. "I could say the same thing to you." Then she turned to Linc. "See if you can get her to at least take a nap."

"Yes, ma'am." He swallowed the chuckle that almost escaped his lips. From the look on Ainsley's face, she didn't find the order amusing.

"Put the vest on," Ainsley said when they were outside. "If I'm in danger, then you are too."

She was right, and he donned the body armor as she grabbed two pairs of latex gloves from her pickup's console.

The awkwardness that had been between them this morning was gone. They'd settled into comfortable, and maybe that was all he'd ever get from Ainsley. But he hoped not.

"Do you have a key?" he asked as they approached the antebellum house.

Her blue eyes widened. "I should've gotten one from Gran."

"No worry. There's one inside the frog in the backyard."

"You're kidding."

"I tried to tell Cora she didn't need to leave a key where someone could find it, but she was afraid of getting locked out."

"I wonder how many other people know it's there."

"She has assured me only Rose and her house-keeper know the key is there . . . and I hope that's true."

"It probably is. Cora is very discriminating about what she shares with others."

They walked around the side of the house to

the back, and he found the key inside the frog. "Would you like me to get a piece of glass cut and replace the broken one for the basement door?"

"You'd do that?"

"Of course. I'm very fond of your aunt."

"And she seems fond of you as well. And she trusts you, not something she does with many people."

"I guess when you've lived as long as she has, you've seen enough to be skeptical."

He followed her down the hall to the library, remembering Cora's admonition to him. *"Don't let him have them."* Who could she have been referring to? She'd been very upset about the diary she thought she'd misplaced. Now he wondered if she'd misplaced it or if someone had stolen it.

"Did you ever see the first diary Cora found?" he asked as Ainsley knelt beside the desk.

"No. Yesterday we were discussing how she'd found it in an old desk in the attic, and as far as I know, it was the only one she'd found." Ainsley sat back on her feet. "I wish we'd had time last night to look closer." Then she stood and pulled out a desk drawer. "Today made at least twice she's mentioned the diaries, as in plural. Do you think she may have found more?"

"That's what I'm wondering. Could they be in her bedroom?"

"Only one way to find out."

He followed Ainsley as she led the way to Cora's bedroom, where the scents of lavender and menthol met them at the door. Two things he associated with the older woman. The bedcovers were thrown back, like she'd gotten out of bed quickly.

He glanced around, noting papers on the floor around her nightstand.

Ainsley knelt and used a pencil to move the papers. "Cora would not have left these papers like this," she said.

"Maybe she knocked them off when she climbed out of bed?"

"I know my aunt, and the only way she would have left them lying on the floor would be if she were hurrying to investigate a noise."

"You think someone else was in the house?" he asked.

"It's the only explanation I can come up with," she replied grimly.

22

Maddox drove the streets in the residential area, searching for Beaumont's red pickup. He was still kicking himself for losing the pickup when it turned into the neighborhood with its maze of streets. A kid on a skateboard zoomed toward him, and Maddox pulled over.

The boy hopped off the skateboard and held it in front of him. "Looking for something, mister?" he asked, stepping to the back edge of the sidewalk.

The kid needn't worry. He wasn't going to grab him. "Yeah," he said, putting warmth in his voice. "A friend of mine. I lost his address, but he has a ruby-red truck. You seen one in the neighborhood?"

The boy started shaking his head, then his eyes widened. "Wait . . . yeah. I saw one this morning. Early."

"Where?" He kept himself from snapping the word.

"On this street. It was going that way." The boy pointed in the direction Maddox had just come from.

"Don't happen to know who owns it, do you? Might be my friend."

He cocked his head to the side. "I don't think so, unless your friend is a woman."

Maddox tamped down his irritation. "Could've been his girlfriend."

He thought about offering the boy money, but that might send him running to his parents.

"If you made it worth it for me, I could show you where I last saw it."

The little punk. "What do you think it would take to be worthwhile to you?"

"Ten bucks?"

Maddox swallowed a chuckle. He'd thought about offering him twenty. "You got a deal."

The boy didn't move.

"Oh, you want the money first."

He nodded, and Maddox pulled a ten from his pocket and held it out the window.

Faster than he could blink, the boy snatched the bill from his hand. "It's parked on the next street over. House is on the corner," he called over his shoulder and took off on his skateboard.

If that was the case, Maddox had quit too soon. He turned around in the next drive and drove to the end of the street and hung a right. Old, ritzy houses. At the next corner, he turned again, and at the next crossroad he saw the pickup in the drive of a two-story antebellum house. A darker red Tahoe SUV sat parked beside it.

Just like he figured. The woman who'd ruined his life had it made.

23

Ainsley knelt beside the bed and used her pen to check the scattered papers again. A sheet of yellowed paper peeked out from between two sheets. "What's this?" She carefully separated the yellowed paper from the others and picked it up with her gloved hand before laying it on the bed.

They both leaned over to read it, their shoulders touching, the contact like a magnet pulling her closer. It didn't help that the clean linen scent of his aftershave brought back memories of him holding her in his arms.

"Look," Linc said. "It has a date. October 16, 1870, so it's not from the journal that went missing. If this is what I think it is . . ."

She jerked her mind back to the task at hand. The cursive letters covered only one side of the paper with flowing strokes. "Maybe a page from one of the diaries she's been looking for. Can you read it?" she asked, hating that her voice sounded breathy.

He was quiet a minute. "I'm pretty sure it's written by a woman, and she's recording a visit from someone named Elizabeth." Linc looked up at her. "According to some of the papers I've helped Cora with, Elizabeth was married to Robert Chamberlain."

"Their great-grandmother and great-grandfather! Cora said the diary she found earlier was written by Charlotte Elliott, her great-grandfather's sister and Zachary Elliott's wife."

He scanned the room. "Did Cora say there were two?"

"Yes. Maybe he stole the other one."

"Who is 'he'?"

"Whoever left the wet carpet in the library," she said impatiently. "And maybe he was responsible for Cora's fall."

"We keep saying 'he,' but we could be talking about a woman," Linc said.

"True. Whoever it was could have been looking for the diaries Cora mentioned. Which means maybe she's found more?"

"They're definitely on her mind. Where does she keep her valuables?"

Ainsley closed her eyes and pinched the bridge of her nose. "Yes," she said, opening her eyes and turning to Linc. Wrong move. She could easily get lost in those hazel eyes. She gave herself a mental headshake.

"Once, when I was a little girl, Cora opened a wall safe and showed me this beautiful ruby and diamond necklace. Said it'd be mine one day . . . I haven't thought of that in years," she said. "If

Cora found more diaries, I'm pretty sure that's where she'd keep any she wasn't reading."

Ainsley checked behind the floral painting over the bed. Of course it wouldn't be there. It'd be too difficult for her aunt to reach. A bold abstract painting across the room caught her attention. She checked behind it and found a small black safe embedded in the wall. "Here it is, but I don't know the combination. And I don't feel right about opening the safe without her permission. Let me call my grandmother and see what she thinks."

Gran answered on the first ring. "Find anything?"

Ainsley described the yellowed paper.

"That sounds like the first diary she found."

"If Cora found more of Charlotte's journals, do you think she would keep them in her wall safe?"

"Definitely."

"Two questions, then. Would she mind if we opened the safe in her bedroom to look for them? And do you know the combination?"

"It's your dad's birthday, 11-16-60, but . . ." Gran sighed. "My sister is funny. I know if you asked, she'd tell you it would be fine, but I'm not sure how she'd feel if you opened the safe without asking."

That's what had hovered in the back of Ainsley's mind. "That's what I thought you'd say. I'll drop by tonight and talk to her. Thanks,

Gran." She hung up and turned to Linc. "I guess you could tell by the conversation, I'm not unlocking the safe until I talk to Cora."

"I think that's wise," he said.

She checked her watch and then took in his tired eyes. "I have to leave for Austin Kingston's office right now. I know you said you wanted to go with me, but don't you want to get some rest? You were up all night."

"So were you. Neither of us are hitting on all cylinders, so it might take both of us to conduct the interview."

She laughed. "It'll be good to have your back."

Their relationship had started out rocky this morning but seemed to have smoothed out, and now they were clicking. Her stomach fluttered. They weren't just clicking. Whatever had attracted her to Linc years ago was alive and well. Not a good thought, and Ainsley pushed it to the back of her mind to think about later, when she wasn't so sleep deprived. That was probably the problem anyway.

"Where did you say we're meeting them?" Linc asked as they walked out the door.

"Austin's law office," she said as she walked to her vehicle and opened the driver's side.

"I think we better go in my Tahoe."

"Why?"

He pointed to her windshield. "We might get

stopped. Or, those jagged cracks might decide to run."

"I guess you're right. Know of a good place I can take it for repairs?"

"Yep. I'll get his number for you," he said as she hopped in on the passenger side of his Tahoe. "Did you talk to Austin when you made the appointment?"

"Yes. He didn't sound too happy that I wanted to interview his son."

Linc made a turn. "I hope this doesn't get sticky."

She'd already thought of that. "You mean because of the governor's race?"

He nodded.

She turned and stared out the window at the passing houses. There would be very little room for error in dealing with the Kingstons. If the boy was involved with the murder, Jack Kingston could very well accuse her of trying to affect the election. "I haven't kept up with the campaign. Gran mentioned it when I first arrived, but then Cora fell, and we simply haven't discussed it. How many candidates are running? And when is it, anyway?"

"Primaries are in August, and there are six candidates running against your dad, including Jack Kingston. Your dad and Kingston lead in the polls." He made another turn. "Did you know Kingston's wife is related to the Elliotts?"

"You're kidding."

"No. Cora told me not long ago when we were working on her book that Adele Kingston is Zachary and Charlotte's great-great-granddaughter."

Adele Kingston. Why did the name send a shiver of dread through Ainsley's stomach?

"Somehow Ms. Kingston found out Cora was writing a book about the murder. She phoned your aunt and threatened a lawsuit if she published anything defamatory about her relatives."

"I'm sure that went over well with Cora."

"Like a ton of feathers. She asked Ms. Kingston how something that happened 150 years ago could possibly upset her."

Ainsley's breath hitched and she gasped.

Linc glanced at her. "What?"

"When you mentioned her name, I had a sinking feeling, and now I know why. I remember Adele Kingston when she was Adele Platte, and back then if there was a society event going on, she was in the middle of it. She was the crème de la crème of Natchez society and had definite views on dress and what was proper and what wasn't." Ainsley hadn't thought about Adele Kingston since the woman left Natchez with her husband for a bigger pond to swim in.

"And?"

She leaned her head back on the headrest. "I was maybe eight and at the top of the old oak in the front yard when she came to visit Gran once. Something about the garden club—I don't remember now. This was before she married Jack Kingston. Anyway, she made me climb down from the tree and marched me to the front door. Told Gran she'd saved me from getting my arm or leg broken."

He chuckled. "How did she know you were in the tree?"

"Could've been the water balloon that just missed her."

Linc laughed out loud this time.

"It's not really funny since I'm sure she remembers the incident. I hope it didn't play a part in why she's so upset about Cora's book."

"I doubt it did. Cora thinks it's because Zachary wasn't a very nice person and plays a prominent role in Cora's book about her great-grandfather Chamberlain. According to Cora, and she got her information from the diary that went missing, Charlotte talked about Zachary in the past tense, how he'd been an alcoholic and a womanizer. After the war he fought bitterly against Reconstruction because it cost him his workforce. Without workers, he couldn't farm his plantation, and he lost everything except his house."

"I've never heard that part of the story, but it explains why Adele wouldn't want the book published," Ainsley said.

"Yep," Linc said. "Pedigrees and family trees matter more than they should to some people."

"And that especially includes Adele Kingston."

They pulled into the parking lot at Austin Kingston's office building, and Ainsley unbuckled her seatbelt. "Nice clientele," she said, eyeing the Mercedes and two Cadillacs parked in visitors' slots.

"People want to be associated with winners," Linc said. "And Austin has his daddy's touch—he wins most of his cases."

She gathered her thoughts and climbed out of Linc's SUV. "This should be fun, then," Ainsley said dryly. *It's not about you.* The thought gave her the kick she needed, and she lifted her chin. *Bring it on, Kingston.*

Inside, the office reflected the clientele—thick carpet, leather seating, and not one piece of furniture that looked like it might've come from IKEA. On the wall, an Ansel Adams black and white of a mesa was paired with another mesa print by Georgia O'Keefe. At least she figured it was a print. Given the Kingstons' money, it could be an original.

She gave her name to the receptionist, and they were quickly ushered down a carpeted hallway to an empty conference room. Evidently Austin didn't want them lingering in the reception area.

"Nice." Linc pulled out a leather chair for her and then took the chair adjacent to hers.

"Yeah," she replied in the same hushed tone as she laid her iPad on the table and sat down. She glanced around the room. Bookcases lined the walls with huge tomes. Heavy curtains closed the room to the outside world and absorbed sound. How many secrets had been shared here?

The quiet was broken when a side door opened, and the attorney marched in, his cell phone ringing. The teenaged son lagged behind. "Sorry. I need to take this," Austin said, but before he swiped his phone, he eyed his son. "Don't say anything until I get back."

"Gotcha." Drew saluted as his dad closed the door behind him. He sauntered to the table and slouched in a chair. "Good afternoon. I guess that's allowed," he said.

"I don't see any harm," Ainsley said. "Afternoon to you."

Linc echoed her greeting, and Drew took out his phone and quickly became absorbed in it.

Mr. Cool Teen. Except he gripped his phone a little too tightly, and the muscle in his jaw worked a little too fast, spoiling the effect. The boy was probably the football captain—he just had that look. Had Hannah been his only girlfriend? Since the girl had been three months pregnant, she hoped so. Had Drew even known? The side door opened again, and Austin stepped into the room followed by his father, Jack. She swallowed her surprise.

Drew sat to attention as Ainsley and Linc stood and shook hands with both lawyers.

"I didn't expect you," Ainsley said to the older man.

"Drew is my grandson, and I'm very involved in his life," Jack said.

Meaning he was here to make sure no one railroaded the boy. She sat in her chair and turned to Austin. "Good to see you again."

"Been a while," Austin said. His father pulled out the captain's chair at the end of the table and sat down while Austin sat to his left. "Didn't I hear you were backup for one of the top gospel groups?"

"Briefly," she said. Heat rose in her cheeks in the silence that followed.

"Nice office," Linc said, filling the void.

She pretended to take in the furnishings and then curved her lips in what she hoped didn't look like a grimace. "Whoever decorated has great taste."

"Thank you," Jack said, "but I'm sure you're not here to admire my son's office. What can we do for you?"

Ainsley had made it plain over the phone what she wanted. "I'd like to ask Drew a few questions."

At the mention of his name, the teenager's Adam's apple bobbed up and down. "W-what about?"

"Hannah Dyson." She took out her phone. "Do you mind if I record this?" she asked Austin.

"Feel free. I plan to record it as well." Austin set his phone on the table.

Once Ainsley had the recorder app turned on, she shifted her gaze to Drew. A light sheen of perspiration dotted his unblemished forehead. Somehow he'd missed the teen acne curse. "What was your relationship with Hannah?"

He darted a glance toward his dad, then shrugged. "We, uh, hung out sometimes."

"Does that mean you dated?"

Drew looked at her like she'd grown a second nose. "No."

She'd heard that teen dating wasn't like it'd been when she was that age. "What did you do when you hung out?"

"We'd grab something to eat, maybe meet for a movie, that kind of thing."

Sounded like dating to her. At the end of the table, Austin stiffened, and Ainsley turned to him. "Were you aware they were hanging out together?"

"Actually, no. Drew wasn't supposed to be going out, period. He was grounded until summer school was over."

"Hannah was helping me with math," Drew said defensively.

Austin made no pretense of believing his son. "Just how was she helping you?"

"Uh, we were studying together. At the library."

"Were you studying together at Rocky Springs Monday night? And Tuesday night?" Ainsley asked.

The boy's eyes widened. "How did—"

Jack cleared his throat. "Are you accusing my grandson of murdering the girl?"

She held the senior attorney's gaze. "No. Just trying to get a picture of what happened those two nights."

"Continue, then, because I'd like to know the answer to that question as well."

Linc leaned forward. "Do you own a motor-bike, Drew?"

The teen's shoulders drooped as he barely nodded.

"You want to tell us what you were doing at Rocky Springs?" Ainsley asked.

The room was quiet for a minute. "I snuck out at night and picked Hannah up on my bike. We rode up to the campground. Hannah said she knew this dude we could score some weed off of."

Ainsley had to lean forward to catch his words.

"Did she?" Linc asked. "Score some weed?"

"I don't know. We got into this argument, and I left her there." He dropped his gaze to the table.

"What night was this?"

"Monday."

"How about Tuesday night?"

"She asked me to take her back to Rocky Springs that night. Said she'd left her phone at that church the night before and wanted to get it."

"Did you two argue Tuesday night?"

He looked up. "She lied to me, said she just wanted to grab her phone and leave. But when we got there, she didn't want to leave." He gave a side glance at his dad. "Mom and Dad went to this thing in Jackson, and I was afraid they'd get back early and find out I wasn't there."

She believed he was telling the truth to this point. "Look at me, Drew." He turned. "Did you kill Hannah Dyson?"

Drew held her gaze. "No ma'am. I-I liked her, and I hope you find whoever killed her, but it wasn't me."

"Did you know she was pregnant?"

The boy's face paled.

24

Austin Kingston leaned forward. "Did you get that girl pregnant?" he demanded.

Linc almost felt sorry for the boy as his mouth worked but no words came out.

Then Drew palmed his hands. "No way that baby could be mine," he said, finding his voice. "I never slept with her. I mean, I'd heard around school she was . . . but . . ." He shook his head. "Not me."

"Then you won't mind giving a DNA sample?"

"Tell me where and when."

"We'll have to think about that."

Drew's dad and his grandfather spoke at the same time.

"Did you see anyone else at Rocky Springs on Monday night? Or Tuesday night?" Ainsley asked.

He flinched at her blunt tone. His thumb went to his mouth, and he chewed his fingernail until his father shifted forward in his chair.

"Did you?" Austin's voice was impatient.

Drew dropped his arms to the table and clasped his hands together. He was digging in, and this was getting them nowhere.

"I don't think you killed Hannah," Linc said softly, shifting into the "good cop" role.

Drew jerked his head toward him, suspicion in his eyes.

"I think you've gotten caught up in a bad situation. Now's the time to tell your side of the story."

The boy should never play poker. Suspicion and the desire to set the record straight played out in his face. "I . . ." He licked his lips. "I saw this kid we go to school with when I peeled out of there. He was standing on the road that goes to the church."

"What's his name?" Ainsley asked.

Drew scrunched his forehead. "Colby?" He shook his head. "No . . . he's a nerd, hangs out with the weirdos." He snapped his fingers. "Colton. That's who it was, but I don't know his last name. Maybe that's who killed her."

Linc hoped not. While he'd only met Colton today, he'd felt sorry for the kid.

"Do you think he was going to meet Hannah?" Linc asked, still keeping his voice soft.

"I don't know. Maybe." Then he shook his head. "Even Hannah wouldn't mess around with Colton."

"Do you know anyone else Hannah was dating?" When he gave her a blank stare, Ainsley added, "How about hanging out with?"

Red crept up Drew's neck and into his face.

169

"She, uh, might've been hanging with some of the other guys on the football team."

Great. The suspect pool just grew substantially.

"Could you make us a list of guys she might've been friends with?" Linc asked.

Drew flinched. "I'd rather not."

"And the reason would be . . ." Austin's stare bore into his son.

"I'm not snitching on my friends."

"I admire your loyalty," Linc said. "But it wouldn't be snitching."

"Maybe not to you," Drew shot back, folding his arms across his chest. "Ask around. Someone else will tell you. Or look at her TikTok page."

"I'll get you that list," Austin said, his voice tight. The jut of the teenager's jaw promised a battle.

"Can you tell me if Hannah had any enemies?" Ainsley asked.

He shifted his gaze to her, his chin relaxing. "Some of the girls at school didn't like her, but they wouldn't have killed her."

Linc looked over the list of questions he had in his notebook. Drew was shutting down, and they wouldn't get much more from him. "Do you know if she was involved in anything illegal other than marijuana?"

Drew's hesitation was followed by a quick shrug, but no information was forthcoming.

His grandfather cleared his throat, and the boy jumped. "Answer the question."

"Just the weed, but—" He looked up at Linc, his eyes pleading. "I just knew her from school, that's all, I promise." Drew sagged against the back of the chair. "Hannah was really smart and was just helping me with my math class."

Linc waited to see if the boy would add any other information. When he didn't, Linc glanced at Ainsley, and her expression mirrored his feelings. They were done here. She stopped the recording.

"Can I go now?" Drew asked.

"As far as I'm concerned, we're through for today." Ainsley plucked a card from her backpack and wrote on the back before she handed it to the boy. "I'll probably be back with more questions as the investigation progresses. If you remember anything, no matter how insignificant you think it is, give me or Linc a call. I wrote his number on the card."

Drew hadn't told them all he knew, and the threat of them returning should keep the teen's anxiety level up. Might even loosen his tongue a little when they did. The boy shot out of the chair and out the door without giving a backward glance. At least he hadn't thrown the card on the table but tucked it in his back pocket.

Ainsley stood and Linc followed suit. "Thanks for talking to us," she said.

Austin nodded tersely without replying.

"I hope this is the end of it," Jack said, leaning back in his chair with his arms folded across his chest.

"It's like I said—"

"I heard what you said, but don't make a big deal out of his relationship with that girl just to help your father get elected governor."

"Excuse me?" Ainsley's voice held ice in it.

"Look, I know what you're doing," Jack said. "You better hope a reporter doesn't get hold of this and blast all over TV that Jack Kingston's grandson is being investigated for the murder of Hannah Dyson."

For a second when Ainsley's face lit up like a flaming match, Linc feared she might not hold her temper. Then she took a breath and shook her head like she was shaking off an annoying mosquito.

"Mr. Kingston, I would've hoped you knew me better than that," she said, her voice even. "But you will not intimidate me. I have a murder to solve and I plan to do it. If your grandson has information I need, I will get it. Thank you for your time."

Mentally, Linc applauded her spunk as he followed her out of the office.

Austin's voice stopped them at the door. "I heard about Miss Cora's fall. I hope she recovers quickly."

Ainsley gave him a nod. As they walked across the parking lot to his SUV, Linc said, "Good job back there."

"I cannot believe he thinks I would do what he accused me of."

"He probably doesn't, just wants to get his point across and keep you off-balance."

Ainsley checked her watch. "It's too late to check with the school today, but first thing Monday morning, I plan to be there. Hopefully the principal will be willing to give me the names and addresses of the boys Hannah hung around with."

"You might get more than that," Linc said. "I read in the paper that the high school coach was holding a football camp next week."

"You're kidding! That's great."

The broad smile she gave him kicked his heart up but at the same time triggered the ache that was always with him. Then he remembered their shoulders touching at Cora's and how her voice shook afterwards. Maybe it wasn't such a lost cause after all.

Linc opened the passenger door for Ainsley, and she shot him a questioning glance before stepping onto the running board and sliding across the seat. "What? I can't be gentlemanly?"

As he slid in on the driver's side, her phone rang, and she glanced at the caller ID. "Brent Murphy. Finally."

Her supervisor in East Tennessee. Linc drummed his fingers on the steering wheel as she answered.

"Did you get my message?" Ainsley asked.

His mouth dried when she fell silent, listening.

"I didn't see any messages. When were they sent?" Ainsley closed her eyes. "I see." She sat up straight. "No. You can't take me off this case. We don't have absolute proof it was Maddox who attacked me." Her jaw clenched as she listened to her supervisor. "You didn't take Harold Jones off his case last year when someone was stalking him."

Linc wished he could hear Murphy's side of the conversation.

"Today's attack could've been from someone hyped up on meth or worse," she said. "Look, Sam Ryker and his field rangers are here and Sam's asked Lincoln Steele, a former FBI sniper, to help out with the investigation. He and Sam Ryker will have my back."

A minute later she disconnected and released a long breath.

"You okay?"

Ainsley straightened her shoulders and stared straight ahead. "Yeah."

"Are you still on the case?"

"Yes. Don't know for how long, though."

"So Maddox is on the loose?"

"For a week now. Him and two others. They're

armed with both a pistol and rifle. His ex-wife's family was notified and put in protective custody at a safe house. I was notified as well, but I was on the cruise."

He frowned. "You didn't check your email or your messages?"

She shook her head. "I turned my phone off and didn't turn it on again until we docked. The emails and texts alerting me about Maddox were buried in the hundreds of emails and I have no idea how many texts."

He couldn't believe she'd turned her phone off. "What if there'd been an emergency with Rose or Cora like what happened last night?"

"I left Gran detailed instructions on how to get in touch with the ship if that happened."

"But—"

"Linc, I'd just wrapped up an exhausting week at the law enforcement academy in Jackson, this after being involved in a search and rescue mission for a ten-year-old boy that did not end well." She breathed in and crossed her arms. "I was stressed. Wanted, no, *needed* to get away from everything. After the training, I drove to Natchez and left my computer, my files, service revolver—everything—at Gran's. Then I drove to the Port of New Orleans and boarded the ship."

Linc got it that law officers needed to decompress sometimes, had needed to himself. He just wished she'd checked her phone occasionally on the ship.

"Is there any possibility he's made it to this area?" he asked.

"Brent didn't know." She turned to him. "That's not all. I didn't mention it to Brent, but Maddox knows computers. What if he hacked into our system and found out where I was?"

The tent campers at Rocky Springs. Linc wished he'd gotten a better description from the other campers of the man who'd left. "Would he be considered old?"

She tilted her head. "It would depend on who was doing the considering."

He told her what the campers had said.

"Yeah, they'd probably think so. Did you get their contact information?"

He nodded and flipped his notebook open. "Even got their email addresses. Can we get a photo of Maddox to send them?"

"Should be able to. What's your email address and I'll have Brent send it to you too." Ainsley called her supervisor and requested the photo. "I'll be careful," she said before disconnecting.

"Want to just wait here until it comes?" he asked.

"Let's go to Gran's. At least in her house I won't feel like he has me lined up in his cross-hairs." Suddenly, she sucked in a breath. "I can't go there. It would put Gran in danger."

Linc thought of his small apartment and winced. He'd been meaning to get a bigger place but hadn't gotten around to it. "I'd offer for you to stay at my apartment, but it's only one bedroom."

"Thanks, but if that was Maddox at the church, it'd be too dangerous for the other people living in the building," she said.

Both fell silent, then Linc said, "How about Cora's house? Could you stay there?"

Ainsley pulled her bottom lip through her teeth. "Until she gets home. Then I'll have to find another place."

"We'll catch him by then," he replied.

25

All Ainsley wanted to do was lean back against the seat. The price for getting little sleep last night was making itself known, especially after talking to Brent.

"I'm beat, but I'm probably not as tired as you are. I don't have someone trying to kill me," he said. "Why don't I take you to Cora's and let you get a little shut-eye in her recliner? I'll let your grandmother know what we're doing, and if the photo comes in, I'll send it to the campers."

A nap sounded like heaven. "Just for an hour."

It took all of her energy to climb out of the seat when they got to Cora's. She removed her vest, then set her alarm on her phone. As a backup, she made Linc promise to wake her.

When the alarm went off, Ainsley jerked awake, unsure of where she was. Linc was leaning back on her aunt's sofa, asleep as well. The alarm became louder and she silenced it.

Linc's eyes popped open. "Sorry," he said. "The photo came in, and I sent it on. Then I must have dozed off."

"No problem. Is there an answer yet?"

"Not yet, but they should respond to both of us."

She opened Brent's message, tensing at a booking photo of Troy Maddox taken as he looked defiantly at the camera. There was something off about the photo. She closed the message as both their phones alerted to a text. "Was one of the men a Ryan Peterson?" she asked.

"Yes. I have it too."

She opened it and quickly scanned the message.

I'm not sure if the men are the same. We all looked at the photo in your email and it's possible it was the same man at the campsite next to us. But the man in your photo didn't have a beard and our man did, so it's hard to tell. Sorry we can't be more specific.

The beard. That's why the photo looked off. At the trial Maddox had started growing a beard. Ainsley checked her other messages. "Did you get any other replies?"

"No. It looks like he's speaking for them all." Linc looked up. "Do you have a photo of him with a beard?"

"No, but we might find one on the internet," she replied. "He had a short beard at the trial and several news organizations covered the proceedings."

Ainsley's phone rang, startling her. "It's Gran," she said and answered. "How's Cora?"

"Her nurse called just now. Cora is agitated. Wants to see us, and the nurse thought it might help if we came."

"Why don't you go ahead. I'll be there shortly."

"You don't want to ride together?"

There wasn't enough time to explain about the danger involved if they rode together. "Hold on a minute." She glanced toward Linc. "I know you need to go home, and I hate to ask, but could you ride to the hospital with my grandmother and explain what's going on?" she asked.

"Sure."

"Gran, Linc is going to ride with you. Okay?"

"Ainsley, I don't need a chaperone. The only reason I suggested riding together is that I didn't see the need to take two vehicles."

"Normally we wouldn't, but I'm waiting on an important call. If it comes in, I'll have to leave and don't want you stranded." Hannah's mother had yet to return her call, and if she didn't soon, Ainsley planned to call her again and try to set up a meeting for later this evening.

"So, I'll take my car. Problem solved."

After saying goodbye to Gran, she disconnected and started to slip her phone into her pocket.

"Does she want me to ride with her?"

"No," she said. "She's probably backing out of her drive now, so we better get a move on.

I'll explain to her what's going on at the hospital."

When they were on the road again, she dialed Hannah's mother. The call didn't go through the first time, and she tried again. A woman answered on the fourth ring.

"If this is one of them insurance calls, you can hang up now." The raspy voice sounded as though it'd been cured with tobacco.

"This isn't an insurance call," Ainsley replied and identified herself. Silence answered her. "Are you still there?"

"Yeah. I got your message. Don't know what I can tell you that I didn't tell the other cops when they brought the news about Hannah."

"I'm really sorry about your daughter," Ainsley said. "But I do need to speak with you. I think we both want to catch whoever committed this crime."

"Good luck with that."

"Is there a good time today for me to talk to you in person about your daughter? It would give me insight into people she might have come in contact with." Ainsley caught herself holding her breath as she waited for an answer.

A deep sigh came through the phone. "My husband leaves for work at six thirty. Can you be here at the house around seven?"

"I'll be there. Thank you, Mrs. Dyson," Ainsley said.

"It's Hanover," she said. "Caleb Dyson was my first husband and Hannah's father."

After ending the call, she turned to Linc and repeated what Connie Hanover said, including that Hannah and her mother's last names were not the same. "Not sure why, but she doesn't want me to come until after her husband leaves. I'm going to call Sam to meet me there at seven, but you're welcome to tag along."

While Ainsley didn't want to be taken off the case, she didn't have a death wish—she wasn't too proud to ask for help and protection.

"Of course." Then he laughed. "If you hadn't asked me, how did you plan to get there?"

She had to get her windshield fixed.

Gran texted that she was already in Cora's ICU room, and this time Linc left his vest in the lobby before they took the elevator to the waiting room.

Linc squeezed her hand, sending a tingle up her arm. "Do you think it'd be okay for me to step in and say hi to Cora after you've had some time with her? Say in about fifteen minutes?"

"She'd love that." Ainsley should've thought of that and invited him to see her aunt. "You want to come now?"

"No. You visit first." He made a shooing sign with his hands. "Go on and see her. I'll find a corner and take a quick nap."

Ainsley didn't remember this Lincoln Steele. Kind, caring, considerate . . . Had he changed that much or had she been so focused on her dream that she really hadn't known him at all? "Thank you," she said softly, then turned to leave.

With a lighter heart, she walked to the double doors and pressed the button. Almost immediately, the doors opened and she hurried back to Cora's room.

Gran looked up as she entered the room. "She dropped off to sleep, but she's been asking for you," she said, worry furrowing her brow.

"Do you know why?"

"No. She keeps mumbling something about diaries, but I can't unscramble her words."

Ainsley took Cora's hand gently in her own. Her aunt stirred, and suddenly her eyes flew open. She clutched Ainsley's hand, her bony fingers squeezing tight. "What are you doing in my house? No!"

"Aunt Cora, it's me, Ainsley."

At first she didn't respond, then turned her head. "Ainsley? Oh good. You're here." The fear in her voice was gone.

"Yes ma'am. Who was in your house?"

Confusion clouded Cora's eyes. "What do you mean?"

"You said someone was there." Ainsley leaned closer as her aunt searched her face.

Tears formed in her eyes. "I . . . don't remember." She sighed. "It's like fog has rolled into my brain."

"It'll get better." At least Ainsley hoped it would. "Linc's going to pop in for a few minutes."

Cora loosened her death grip on Ainsley's hand. "That boy," she said affectionately. "Don't know why you let him get away."

She supposed to her aunt, Linc was still a boy, but he was thirty-four, just like Ainsley. "He thinks a lot of you," she said. "And he told me about the book he's helping you with."

"Book . . . ?" Her aunt squeezed her eyes shut.

"The one about your great-grandfather."

Recognition lit her eyes. "Oh. Yes. How did I forget that?" She frowned, her face a picture of concentration. "There's something I wanted to remember . . ."

"Could it be about diaries?"

"Charlotte's diaries. Yes. That's it."

"Do you know where you put them?" Ainsley held her breath, waiting for Cora to answer.

"Somewhere safe . . ." She closed her eyes. "I'm so tired."

She hated to push Cora. It wasn't like a crime had been committed, or at least Ainsley had no proof of a crime.

"Would it be okay if I stayed at your place? Maybe keep an eye on it for you?" she asked, ignoring Gran's wide-eyed stare. "I can check the safe and see if the diaries are there."

"You know you can," Cora said. "I can't seem to stay awake."

Gran walked to Cora's bed and smoothed her sister's short hair back. "Go to sleep if you can. We'll be here as long as they let us."

When Cora's breathing slowed, Gran pulled Ainsley away from the bed. "I want some answers, missy."

"Can it wait? I don't want Cora to overhear us."

Just then, Linc stuck his head in the door. "How is she?"

"Better, and you're just the person I want to see," Gran said. "Would you sit with her for a minute? Ainsley and I need to talk."

Linc questioned Ainsley with his eyes, and she nodded. "Do you mind?"

He stepped into the room. "Not at all."

Gran pulled her outside into the hallway and away from the nurses' station. "Now, what's going on?"

Ainsley gave her an abbreviated version of the attack at the church and the information about Maddox. "It's not certain Maddox is in the area, but just in case, staying at Cora's until she comes home should keep you out of danger."

"I'm not worried about me." Gran's gaze narrowed. "That's why you were wearing that vest! Why don't you have it on now?"

Ainsley patted her chest. "I changed into one I could wear under my uniform."

Her grandmother crossed her arms. "You need to drop this case. Let someone else handle it."

185

"Gran, I can't do that. You didn't raise me to quit the first time I ran into a problem."

"You didn't have someone trying to kill you then."

"We don't know that for sure." Somehow she had to make her grandmother understand. "I'm in danger in every investigation I conduct. It's the nature of my career. Besides, I have Linc and Sam backing me up."

"You're going to do it whether I like it or not, aren't you?" Ainsley didn't answer, but finally, her grandmother squeezed her hands. "Just be careful."

"Always." She relaxed. "Thanks."

"Not sure 'You're welcome' is the right response, but you are." She looped her arm in Ainsley's as they walked back to Cora's room. "I know you love that job of yours, but times like this I wish you'd get a different career."

26

In the bedroom that had been hers since she was five, Ainsley quickly packed her clothes, except for her hanging garments. Linc would help her with those. He'd dropped her off and would return in twenty minutes, he'd said. Something about going by his apartment.

Her heart fluttered as she remembered the look on his face in the church. *Stop it.* Out of everything that had happened today, their near kiss was what she remembered? Sheesh, what was wrong with her? They'd had their time together and it hadn't worked out.

She gathered her toiletries from the bathroom. Linc had definitely changed. While he was still confident, he wasn't . . . what had she called him when they'd broken up? High-handed. Acting like he knew what was best for her. Even undermining her confidence in her voice. Just like her dad.

But that was the old Linc. Had he changed enough for them to have a second chance? Did she even want a second chance with him? She had her life planned out—keep her focus on solving crimes and one day head up the Investigative

Services Branch of the National Park Service. She didn't want any distractions. And Lincoln Steele would definitely be a distraction.

A text dinged on her phone, and her face flushed. Linc. It was like she'd conjured him up.

"Just letting you know I'm here and coming in the back door—don't shoot."

She sent him a thumbs-up and rolled her suitcase to the kitchen as he entered. "Thanks for helping me move these things. I'll be right back with my hanging clothes."

A Natchez patrol car was idling in front of the house when they walked her things over to Cora's. "I called Pete," Linc said. "There'll be extra patrols in this neighborhood until Maddox is caught."

While the extra protection was necessary, Ainsley didn't like being the recipient. "I'll have to call and thank him."

Linc waited by the SUV while she stored her things in Cora's spare downstairs bedroom, then she called Sam to meet them at the Hanovers'.

He opened the passenger door. "Is he coming?"

"Might be a little late, but he'll be there." She programmed Connie Hanover's address into her phone and buckled up as the GPS spit out the directions.

Linc was quiet as he worked his way to Highway 61, occasionally glancing in the side mirror. Ainsley did likewise. "You think someone might tail us?"

"It doesn't hurt to be careful even though I haven't seen anyone."

Neither had she. The GPS took them down deserted country roads. At least it was easy to spot anyone following them. The Hanover house turned out to be a single-wide mobile home set back off the road in a wooded area. One car sat jacked off the ground with the wheels removed and weeds growing around it. Another had the hood missing and the motor hoisted overhead. *Don't make snap judgments.* Connie's husband could be some sort of mechanic.

A dog barked to her left and Ainsley turned, catching her breath. The dog, a boxer, strained against the chain tethered to his collar. He'd worn a perfect circle in the grass. She hated seeing a dog chained. At least the Hanovers had staked him in the shade and provided what looked like a bucket of water.

"Did Sam say how late he'd be?" Linc asked.

"No." Ainsley scanned the area. Nothing unusual caught her eye, and she checked her watch. Seven on the dot. Her cell rang. "It's him. I'll put the call on speaker."

"Where are you?" she asked.

"Tied up with an accident near Mount Locust. A deer jumped into the path of a motorist. Probably be here forty-five minutes to an hour. I'm sorry."

Ainsley drummed her fingers on the armrest. "I'm going ahead with Mrs. Hanover's interview. We didn't have a tail and I don't see how anyone could know we're here."

"You sure no one followed you?"

"Didn't see anyone behind us at any time."

Once Sam reluctantly agreed, she disconnected and turned to Linc. "Ready?"

They climbed the block steps to the porch, and Ainsley knocked on the door, hoping Connie Hanover would hear it over the rattling air conditioner in the window. She was about to knock again when the door jerked opened. Ainsley stepped back as the woman she assumed was Mrs. Hanover stepped onto the porch. A baby screamed in the background.

"Mrs. Hanover? I'm ISB Ranger Ainsley Beaumont. I talked with you earlier," she said, showing her badge before nodding toward Linc. "And this is Lincoln Steele."

"Mrs. Hanover is my mother-in-law. Just call me Connie," the large-boned woman replied. A cigarette dangled from her fingers. Probably the reason for the raspy voice. "Mind if we talk out here? The baby is having a fit right now."

"Do you need to see about—"

"My older daughter is seeing to her. Don't know what she meant getting pregnant so soon after marrying that no-good . . . bum. He hit the road already." She grabbed a pack of cigarettes and closed the door. "Tried to tell her she needed to get an education first, but no, she had to do things her way."

"I'm sorry," Ainsley said.

She sighed. "Got a beautiful grandbaby out of it, though, so I oughtn't to complain too much." She pointed to lawn chairs under a huge live oak. "Let's sit under the tree over there."

The dog barked as they followed Connie to the tree where chairs sat around a small firepit. "Hush up, Buster!" Connie shook her head. "Dog barks all the time."

Ainsley took in the low rock fence and a raised bed of forget-me-nots. "Your flowers are pretty, and someone has put in a lot of hard work on the wall."

"Thanks. Hannah helped me build it." She looked away from them, her chin quivering. "We hauled those rocks in from the river. She was a good girl."

Ainsley had interviewed parents of murdered children only twice before, and it was the hardest assignment she'd ever had.

When they reached the metal chairs, she sat in the middle chair while Connie took the one to her left. Linc sat across from them both, so that they made a semicircle around the firepit.

"I'm very sorry about your daughter," he said and Ainsley echoed his sentiments.

Hannah's mother took one last draw off the

cigarette, dropped it beside her shoe, and ground it into the dirt. She pulled a handkerchief from the pocket of her shorts and dabbed her eyes. "Thank you. I don't think I'll ever get done crying. A mother shouldn't have to bury her child."

"Do you know anyone who might have wanted to harm her?" Ainsley asked.

"No! Everyone loved her." Connie swallowed hard. "Just last year, they voted her most beautiful in her sophomore class. That wouldn't have happened if everybody didn't like her, right?"

"Could that have made someone jealous?" Ainsley asked softly.

Connie turned and stared into the ashes of the firepit. "Surely not enough to kill her just because she was pretty." She looked up. "Have you . . ." Her chin quivered again. "Nobody's told me exactly how she died. Those officers just said it was murder."

"We haven't gotten the autopsy report yet."

"You can't tell me anything?"

"Whatever I told you might be wrong and subject to change." Ainsley didn't want to be the one to tell her about the bruises around her daughter's throat.

Linc leaned forward. "Do you know what she was doing at Rocky Springs that night?"

"No. She told me she was going to the library to help that Kingston boy." Connie dabbed her eyes again. "She was like that, always wanting to help somebody."

"Did you know she smoked marijuana?"

"Don't all kids? I mean, I never asked, but once or twice I thought I smelt it on her," Connie said. "But what can a parent do? Lock 'em up until they're twenty-one?"

"Do you know where she might have gotten it?" Linc asked.

She turned to him. "Are you a cop ranger too? I mean, I don't see no gun on you."

"No," he replied. "I'm the ranger at Melrose. Do you know her dealer?"

The thin shoulders raised in a half-hearted shrug. "No. Figured she got it from some of her friends. Are you saying she didn't?"

"A witness indicated she went to Rocky Springs to meet up with a dealer."

"You think the dealer killed her?"

"We're considering that as a possibility. Tell me about your husband. Did he and Hannah get along?"

"Not always."

"What was their problem?" Ainsley asked.

"She was a teenager, and Wally works long hours. Her music drove him crazy, but he tried." Connie nodded toward the car with the motor hoisted above it. "He was fixin' that Camaro up for her graduation next year."

"How about boyfriends?" Ainsley asked.

"She never brought any of her friends around here . . . always met them somewhere else, not that I blame her." Connie flipped the top on the cigarette box and lit another cigarette, her fingers shaking as she lit it.

The smoke drifted toward Ainsley, and she stood and walked out of the line of the fumes. "Did you know Hannah was pregnant?" It was a question she'd dreaded asking.

The girl's mother sat stock-still, then she ground the cigarette into the dirt. "No," she said. "I thought she was smarter than that, especially after her sister . . ."

The dog started barking again. Ainsley walked to the back of her chair and then thought better of sitting again. They were almost finished and the chair was too low to be comfortable. "Do you know who the father might have been?"

"Could've been the Kingston boy. They been thick as thieves since school let out."

"He says not."

Connie's snort indicated what she thought of that. "And you believed him." It wasn't a question. "Oh, that's right. He's a Kingston, so of course, he wouldn't lie." She jumped up, her hands fisted.

Her body jerked just as a rifle report split the night air. Connie fell face forward to the ground, a red stain spreading on her white tank top.

Ainsley whipped her gun from the holster, scanning the area.

"Get down!" Linc yanked her arm.

Ainsley dropped to the ground and dialed 911 as another bullet whizzed over her head. When the operator answered, she reported what had happened and gave their location. As soon as she ended the call, she crawled to where Connie lay.

Linc had already reached her and had his finger on her wrist. "She has a pulse, but it's weak and fast," he said.

Connie didn't seem to be bleeding out. Maybe a main artery hadn't been hit. "An ambulance should be here soon."

She scanned the wooded area behind the mobile home. Except for the barking dog straining against his chain, nothing moved, not even a leaf. "Do you think he's gone?"

The door to the mobile home opened. "Mom? What's going on?"

Ainsley had forgotten the other daughter. "Stay there—don't come out!" she yelled. "There's a shooter!"

The girl slammed the door, leaving a deadly quiet. Then, the high-pitched whine of a motor-bike broke the silence. Ainsley turned her head toward the woods again. "You think there's a road behind the woods?"

"Could be. I'll crawl to the trailer and ask the girl."

"I'll do it," she said.

"You have the gun—you need to stay here and protect Connie."

He was right and she nodded. Ainsley wanted to know why he didn't carry a gun—another one would have been handy just now. She kept a watch on the woods, but nothing stirred.

When he reached the mobile home, Linc eased up the steps and banged on the door before he opened it and disappeared inside. Seconds later, he reappeared. "There is a road," he called out. "Pretty sure our shooter is gone."

The faint sound of sirens reached her ears, and relief swept through her. She felt Connie's wrist again. Her pulse raced. *Lord, help her.* It was the second prayer that had crossed her lips today.

"Hang on," Ainsley said. "Help is coming."

An hour and a half later, she was sitting in Nate Rawlings's SUV relating the details of the shooting. Now she understood why her grandmother had sung the Adams County sheriff's praises yesterday when Ainsley made her list of people in Natchez to contact. Nate, as he'd said to call him, was easy to talk to, and she could take a page or two from his low-key questioning that helped her to recall details she'd missed when his deputy took her statement.

He looked up from his notepad. "Your statement dovetails with Linc's. One more time, did you see anything out of the ordinary before Connie Hanover was shot?"

"Not one thing," she said. "Like I said, the shots came from the wooded area, and the shooter could have been on a motorbike—we heard one leave on the road behind the woods." She glanced out the side window to where Linc and Sam were searching for one of the spent bullets.

"Do you think this shooting had anything to do with Hannah's death?"

"Since a motorbike was heard the night Hannah died, it's possible. But . . ." Ainsley had given Nate the details on the case as well as the case that followed her from East Tennessee. "I can't rule out this had nothing to do with Hannah and everything to do with Troy Maddox."

Nate made a few more notes. "How would he have known you were going to be here?"

"That's the big question. And brings it back to it possibly being linked to Hannah." She cocked her head. "Are either of the Hanovers involved in anything illegal?"

"As far as I know, not in years." He palmed his hand. "I've only been sheriff six months, but I've lived in Adams County most of my life except for a stint in the army. While Connie's never had any problems with the law, Wally was a different story. As a teenager, he was in and out of trouble, but as far as I know, that was in his past."

So it was possible someone was out to get the Hanovers. Wally Hanover could have crossed someone in a deal and this shooting could've been revenge. She had another thought. "Does Wally Hanover's alibi check out?"

"Yeah. A deputy checked the factory where he works. Wally clocked in at seven, and several people saw him loading out trucks."

Scratch the husband as the shooter.

Nate put his notepad away. "Sam is sending me the report on the church incident, and I may have more questions after I read it."

"You know how to find me," Ainsley said and stifled a yawn.

"I know Linc is sticking close to you, but I'm also going to assign deputies to cover you. One will be following you home."

It's what she would do in his place, but she hated that it was needed. "Thanks. I think I'll pack it in. Any news on Connie Hanover's condition?"

"Last report, her condition had been upgraded from critical to serious."

"Good." Now if Ainsley could find out who the bullet was meant for.

27

L inc scanned the dark, wooded area. The investigation was winding down for the night, but before darkness set in, Adams County deputies had found where the shooter was standing when the shots were fired. No casings, though, which told something about the shooter. The person was familiar with guns.

Sam shined his flashlight where Linc was digging in the trunk of an oak tree. "Sorry I didn't make it here sooner, but—"

"No need to apologize. You were doing your job," Linc said. "Shine the light a little more to the left."

Sam obliged, and Linc turned back to digging out the chunk of wood with the embedded bullet. Even if the slug was badly damaged, the weight should tell the type of rifle they were dealing with.

Linc clenched his jaw as he stabbed his knife into the tree again, and it yielded his target. If he'd had a gun . . . Face it. His gun was on the top shelf of his closet. He jerked a paper bag from his shirt pocket and dropped in the evidence. He handed the bag to Sam.

"It's all my fault," Ainsley said.

He hadn't heard her come up.

"It's the fault of the madman who pulled the trigger," Sam said.

She pressed her lips in a thin line. "I should've interviewed her inside the trailer."

"Would've, could've, should'ves do nothing but make you doubt yourself." Linc ought to know. He squeezed his hands into fists. Maybe he should see the therapist again. He looked over Ainsley's shoulder, and his stomach sank.

"What?"

"Sarah Tolliver is what, and she's fast approaching. If you're done here, let's leave."

Ainsley followed his gaze. "It's too late." Lifting her chin, she turned to face Sarah.

"Do you have time to answer a few questions on camera?" the reporter asked, pinning her gaze on Ainsley.

"Sorry. You have questions, you'll have to ask Sheriff Rawlings. This is his investigation."

A frown crossed Sarah's face, but she quickly erased it. "Can you just tell me what happened?"

"No comment."

"Hannah Dyson is Connie Hanover's daughter. Is this shooting related to that murder?"

Linc's patience was stretched as thin as a rubber band about to break, and he shot Sarah a warning glance.

"No comment." Ainsley crossed her arms.

Linc put a protective hand at Ainsley's back. "Are you ready to leave?" When she nodded, he turned to Sam. "We'll touch base in the morning."

His heart skipped a beat when Ainsley raised her gaze to his. Pain filled her blue eyes. The reporter needed to know when to ease up. When they reached his Tahoe parked under an overhead light, the dark circles under Ainsley's eyes concerned him. He opened the passenger door.

She glanced toward the firepit. "I feel like I'm abandoning my post."

"Don't. It's like you said—this is Nate Rawlings's investigation. Let him do his job."

"He's assigning a deputy to follow us home," Ainsley said.

"Good." The news would have made him happy if it hadn't underscored his inability to protect her.

The cab of his SUV was quiet as they drove down the sand road from the Hanover place. True to Rawlings's word, a deputy was close behind them. Linc had just turned onto another county road when Ainsley's phone rang. She glanced at the screen. The phone rang twice more before she answered. "Hello." She listened for a few seconds. "How did you—"

Quiet ensued.

"No. I'm fine. No need to worry about me. Thank you for calling." She hung up and blew out a breath. "My dad. It appears I was the lead story on WTMC tonight. How did Sarah get the story turned in so quickly?"

"Modern technology."

She shook her head. "I should have turned this assignment down."

"Why? You're a good investigator."

"I don't know about that right now. I do know Natchez is the last place I want to be."

"I for one am glad you're here." He focused on the road. "But is it time to let someone else investigate Hannah's death?"

"No. We don't know who the target was tonight." She was quiet a moment. "I knew when I took this job it would be dangerous. You knew the same thing when you became an FBI agent. Did you quit every time you ran into a threatening situation?"

Danger had not been the reason he'd walked away from the FBI. "This feels different. Some-one is targeting you—"

"We don't know that for sure. We don't even know how the attack at the church figures into this. It could've been an isolated incident."

"And it could very well be Troy Maddox," he said grimly.

"You never had someone come after you on a case?"

There'd been a couple of times before he joined the FBI SWAT team that drug dealers he'd arrested had put out a contract on him. "Yeah."

"What'd you do about it?"

"Wore my body armor and took whatever precautions I needed to and caught the bad guys."

"That's exactly what I'm doing."

He didn't have a response to that.

She rested her head against the back of the seat. "Thanks for being here for me today."

"I didn't do anything."

"Yes you did." She was quiet a minute, then turned toward him. "Why don't you wear a gun?"

His chest tightened, and for a few seconds, he didn't breathe. "It's a long story." He felt her gaze on him and glanced toward her. "It's not one I want to get into while I'm driving."

Ainsley dipped her head slightly. "I understand."

She wouldn't once he told her.

When they arrived at Cora's, he pulled around to the back. At the hospital Rose had given Ainsley her key to Cora's house so they didn't have to fish one out of the frog. "Wait until I come around before you get out."

For once she didn't argue with him. Linc hopped out and took a minute to scan the backyard that backed up to a wooded area. Night vision goggles would be nice, but nothing moved that he could see. He turned to the back of the house. A floodlight left no shadows where anyone could hide.

Linc jogged around to her side of the Tahoe

and hurried Ainsley inside, using his body as a shield.

"I need to call Gran. I'm sure she saw the news too," she said once they were in the kitchen but made no move to make the call.

"Want me to do it?"

Ainsley shook her head as if to clear it. "No. She would really think something was wrong if you did that."

"Put it on speaker. Maybe I can reassure her."

She made the call, but before she could say a word, Rose said, "Why didn't you call me! I've been worried to death ever since I saw the ten o'clock news! Why didn't you let me know you were all right?"

"I'm sorry, Gran. I had no idea the shooting would make tonight's news. We just got to Cora's."

"We?"

"I'm with her, Rose," Linc said.

"Oh good." Relief sounded in Rose's voice. "Ainsley, are you sure you're okay?"

"Yes, ma'am. Just a little wound up."

"You don't have to stay at Cora's, you know."

Ainsley sighed. "I won't worry as much about you if I stay across the street."

"Who's going to keep me from worrying about you?"

Linc spoke up. "I'm staying the night in one of the guest rooms upstairs."

Ainsley jerked her head toward him, her eyes wide.

"That's a wonderful idea," Rose said. "You both sound exhausted. Get some rest."

A minute later, Ainsley pocketed her phone and turned to him. "What did you mean about staying overnight here?"

He hadn't meant to spring that on her. "You don't need to be alone."

"Cora has a perfectly good alarm system, and you don't have any . . ." Her face blazed.

"I packed a bag when I went by my apartment."

"Oh. But—"

"How about we talk about it over a cup of Cora's decaf?" he said before she could protest further. "She usually has cookies in the cabinet. Might help you unwind."

"I was thinking of some of her medicinal Jack Daniels." She laughed when his eyes widened. "Decaf and cookies sound good."

Ainsley sat at the round wooden table, and he popped a K-cup into Cora's new Keurig. While the coffee brewed, he looked in the cabinet where she usually kept her snacks. "How about lemon snaps?"

"Sounds good."

A few minutes later he set their coffee and the cookies on the table and sat across from her.

"This kitchen is like Gran's. Homey," Ainsley said.

"That's the right word for it. Cora and I usually enjoy a cup of coffee or hot tea the days I help her with the book."

Ainsley laughed. "I wondered how you knew where she kept her cookies."

A comfortable silence surrounded them. Ainsley took a sip of coffee, her shoulders relaxing a bit. "I'm glad you talked me into this."

"I'm glad I did too."

How different their relationship was from last night, when he could've cut the tension with a knife. Did he dare hope . . .

His past washed over him like a tsunami. Linc couldn't allow himself to even contemplate a relationship with her until she knew the whole story of why he wasn't an FBI agent. He wasn't sure this was the right time, though, and reached for her cup. "You need to get some rest."

She stayed his hand, her fingers lingering on his. "I'd rather hear that story you said you'd tell me."

Her touch was like an electric current burning its way to his heart. He raised his head. Ainsley waited expectantly, her blue eyes soft, trusting. If he told her what happened, she would never trust him again. His head said don't do it, but the words that came out of his mouth were different. "Are you sure?"

"It can't be that bad. You're not in prison, so you didn't kill anyone."

"But I did."

"I don't believe you. Tell me what happened."

He leaned against the back of the chair, sorting out his thoughts. Linc had played the scenario out so many times in his head. "It started one day in October," he said slowly. "The team was sent to a housing project in Chicago. This gang leader was threatening to blow up the block. Had two hostages. Never did know who they were. Adrenaline was pumping. The target was pacing in front of a window . . ."

This wasn't a story Linc shared with many people. He didn't know why he was telling Ainsley, but he found the words spilling out of him.

"I had him in my crosshairs, and then he disappeared. Through my earpiece, I heard my supervisor say the target was coming down the steps."

Beside him, Ainsley tensed and leaned closer.

Linc couldn't pull himself out of the movie playing in his head.

Two hundred yards away, he scanned the area through the rifle scope, lining the crosshairs on a spot in the alley between the two apartment buildings. Intel indicated the alley was where the target would emerge.

A figure darted into his line of sight from the alley, a kid with his arm pulled back and a round object in his hand. Grenade? It wouldn't be the first time the gang leader used a boy to kill. Linc's finger tightened on the trigger.

His breathing stilled. Sound faded to nothing.

He'd never killed a boy before.

Motion to the right. Another boy appeared and the first kid tossed the object to him.

Linc backed his finger off the trigger. Sweat poured down the side of his face. A baseball. Nothing but a baseball. He swallowed down the bile racing into his throat.

Now he looked at Ainsley's ashen face. "So, I almost killed an innocent boy." He swiped his forehead with the back of his hand. "Even now, thinking how close I came to killing this ten-year-old kid, it breaks me out in sweat."

"You never would have gotten over it," she said softly. "And that's why you quit the FBI?"

"No, but it was the beginning of the end," he said. "The end came a couple of months later in a similar situation. Terrorists were holed up in a farmhouse in Iowa. They were planning to bomb the state capitol, and I was supposed to provide cover while the other agents stormed in . . ."

"What happened?"

He licked his bottom lip. "Our supervisor held us back. An hour or two passed without any action, and I was getting bored. That's when Blake and three other FBI agents moved into place. They had to be ready when the command was given. Suddenly there was movement in the window. I had the terrorist in my crosshairs . . ."

Linc stared straight ahead.

Ainsley placed her hand on his. "You don't have to tell me."

But he did. He wanted her to know what happened so she would understand why he couldn't carry a gun. He gripped the coffee mug, and she released her hand from his.

"Like I said, I had him in my crosshairs. The command was given for Blake to move in. I was ready. Then, in the blink of an eye, I was seeing the kid instead of the target. I . . ." He licked his lips. "I couldn't pull the trigger. I just stood there. The terrorist saw Blake. I snapped out of it when I heard the gun fire. Then I took the terrorist out. I was only a millisecond late . . ."

"But Blake was shot," she said softly.

"Yes. In the leg." Linc swallowed. "He lost his leg. Two years later, he killed himself."

"Oh, Linc, I had no idea you blamed yourself for Blake's death. I'm so sorry," Ainsley said. "Blake didn't know you hesitated, though."

"Yeah, he did. I told him. He never blamed me, but sometimes I think if he'd gotten angry at me, I would've felt better."

"That's a hard load to carry around," she said. "Have you seen a therapist?"

He barked a laugh. "Several." Linc shifted his gaze to Ainsley, not sure what he'd see in her eyes. Hopefully not disappointment . . . or pity.

"Ever since that night, I haven't been able to pick up a gun, let alone fire one."

Tears glistened in her eyes. "We all make mistakes," she said.

"Most of them don't cause someone to take their life."

"You don't know what was in his mind before he took those pills."

"Sarah told me he was suicidal. I should have done something, but I didn't believe her. Blake seemed to be getting better. He was making plans . . ."

"Did she say it was because of losing a leg?"

Had she ever come out and said that point-blank? "She didn't have to. He'd been depressed ever since it happened."

Ainsley's hand covered his, squeezing it.

"I'm okay most days . . . it's just that Wednesday it'll be two years since Blake died, and I've promised Sarah to spend part of the day with her and her dad. Blake loved the water, so I thought we could have a picnic at Natchez Lake."

"I'm sure they'll appreciate it . . ."

He looked up. "There's a 'but' in your voice."

Her shoulders lifted. "Don't take this wrong, but from the tone of your voice—it sounds like you're doing it more out of guilt than because you want to."

Ainsley could still read him, even after sixteen years. Linc raked his fingers through his hair.

"To tell the truth, the anniversary had slipped my mind until Sarah reminded me."

"She guilted you into it?"

"It's hard to tell Sarah no."

She laughed. "So I've noticed. I've also noticed she still has a crush on you."

"I keep hoping she'll get past it." Sarah'd had a crush on him when he and Blake hung out together as teenagers, but Linc had never had eyes for anyone except Ainsley. "She's a beautiful woman, and there are a couple of nice guys at church I want to introduce her to, but she never comes."

Ainsley tilted her head, staring at him, and he warmed under her scrutiny. "You had such a strong faith when we were dating. Do you still?" she asked.

He dropped his hands from the mug. "It's the only thing that gets me through the days."

28

Troy Maddox drove slowly by the two-story house, searching for the SUV he'd followed earlier, but there was only the pickup and a Prius parked in the drive.

He knew it! He should've kept following the SUV earlier, but the ranger and Beaumont turned off the main highway onto a deserted county road. He feared they would catch him tailing them and backed off, driving back to the highway to wait. Except he'd somehow missed them. Maddox turned around in a drive and retraced his path, halting at the four-way stop. He glanced to his right and a sign caught his eye. "No Thru Traffic."

But that wasn't the only thing that caught his eye. A maroon SUV was parked behind the house. Looked like the same one he'd been tailing. If he could get the license plate, he could hack into the DMV and learn who it belonged to.

Maddox craned his neck to see if anyone was out and about. The area was deserted, but he did see a dark house with a for sale sign. He could park there and sneak across the street to get the license plate number.

He pulled in front of the empty house, opting not to use the drive. A few minutes later Maddox crept through the adjoining backyard and stood across from where the SUV was parked.

The floodlight shining against the back of the house posed a problem. If he tried to approach the vehicle, he'd stand out like a lighthouse. Just as Maddox turned to retrace his steps, the back door to the house opened and the man he'd seen driving the SUV walked to it. Now he didn't need the license plate.

Maddox narrowed his eyes. The ranger was a complication. Might as well plan on killing him when he took care of Beaumont. He scanned the neighborhood, looking for a place where he could easily surveil the house in the daylight hours. First he'd have to do a little research, and he knew just the place to do it.

29

He had problems. Sonny stood at his window, fingering the key to the Chamberlain house that he'd copied from the one hanging in the kitchen.

Cora had said she'd found diaries, and he'd only found one last night. Earlier in the day he'd searched her house to no avail. If there were more, and he believed there were, they had to be in the safe he'd found in her bedroom. Problem was, he had no idea how to get it open. He could bring in someone to crack the safe, but that meant involving another person. Instead he'd spent the afternoon researching how to break into a safe like the one in the Chamberlain house.

Sonny took a list he'd compiled from his wallet. He'd read most people used a date they could easily remember for a safe combination. He figured Miss Cora had used a relative's birthdate. At least he hoped she had. Otherwise he'd spent the afternoon looking through public records for nothing.

But now he had four birthdates—hers, her sister's, the nephew's, and Ainsley Beaumont's. He doubted she'd used her great-niece's—the safe had been installed way before she'd been born—but he'd tracked it down all the same.

He pinched the bridge of his nose. What if he didn't get the third diary? He had to have it. If Beaumont got her hands on it first, Sonny could kiss the fifty grand goodbye.

30

It was almost midnight when Linc went out to the Tahoe and grabbed the overnight bag and uniform that he'd picked up from his apartment. Back inside, he checked the locks before he climbed the stairs and stowed his things in a guest room. Linc would've preferred being on the same floor, but there were only two downstairs bedrooms, Cora's and the one Ainsley was in.

He was too restless for sleep and remembered seeing a copy of *Moby-Dick* in the library. It had put him to sleep in school, maybe it'd do the same thing tonight—if he could remember where Cora shelved the book.

While he searched, he admired the craftsmanship of the ten-foot ceilings and the beautiful hand-carved crown molding—mostly to keep him from questioning his presence in this case.

Without a gun, his options for protecting Ainsley were limited. He'd hoped talking to her about what happened with Blake would release him from the paralysis that kept him from using a gun, but it hadn't. Fear still held him in its power. Linc knew without a doubt that if he drove to his apartment right now, he wouldn't be able to get his gun off the shelf in the closet and strap it to his waist. He doubted he'd even be able to take the gun out of the closet.

He scraped his hand against his jaw. Today had proven his presence couldn't deter an attack. If anything, he was a liability to this case. All he had to offer was his expertise. And what good had that been?

Linc turned as Ainsley entered the room. "I thought you would be asleep by now," he said.

"I could say the same to you." She cinched the long robe she wore over striped pajamas. "I heard you come down and thought something might be wrong."

"No, just couldn't face trying to sleep just yet. I remembered Cora had some of the classics and came down to find something boring. Then I couldn't help admiring the room."

She ran a hand over the smooth finish. "Gran says the lumber came from cherry trees on the property."

"Too bad all that land wasn't kept with the house," Linc said.

"I think the family fell on hard times and barely kept the house after Robert Chamberlain was killed." She sank into one of the wingback chairs in front of the fireplace and stared at the blackened hearth. "Gran left me here with Cora when she had errands to run and didn't want me tagging along. I remember sitting in the library on cold winter days watching the flames and Cora sitting at her desk telling me stories about our family."

Linc sat in the other wingback chair. When they'd dated years ago, Ainsley had told him how Rose had taken her in when her mother died and her dad opted to live in Jackson most of the time.

She turned to him. "Cora was in her seventies when she decided to learn how to use a computer. We used them at school, so I was her 'expert.'" She laughed softly. "I couldn't understand why she wanted to learn it so badly since I thought she'd die any day. Twenty-some odd years later, she's still going strong. Or was until she fell."

"When we were kids, someone Cora's age seemed ancient," he said, laughing with Ainsley.

"Not so much anymore."

"Not when the person is as active as Cora or your grandmother."

Ainsley leaned back in the chair and closed her eyes. "I have to get some sleep, but first, tell me about Cora's book. She'd talked about writing one for years, and I didn't realize she'd started it until I came home this time."

Linc hesitated. He didn't think Cora would mind if he shared the story she was writing and leaned forward. "Cora has completed the Chamberlain family history through the Civil War. Her great-grandfather couldn't bear the thought of fighting against his country and joined the Union forces. We found old newspaper articles that show Robert Chamberlain was instrumental in uniting the town after the war and was a huge proponent of Reconstruction. He'd only just begun implementing his plans when he was killed by the mob."

"Were there articles about his murder?"

"Haven't found any yet. That's one reason Cora wanted to find more of the diaries, hoping Charlotte's writings would verify the stories that had been handed down through the family."

Her eyes widened. "I remember one of them. Charlotte's husband forbade her from helping former slaves to learn to read and write."

He nodded. "That's what Cora wants to verify. The story she'd always heard was that Zachary went into a rage when he discovered his wife helping with the freedman's school here in Natchez.

"The night Zachary died, for some reason, Charlotte sent for her brother, Robert. From that point on, it gets muddled since there was little record of what happened. Evidently, after the sheriff arrived and found Zachary dead of a gunshot wound to the chest with Robert holding the gun, he took him into custody to stand trial. It was later that night that Zachary Elliott's drunken friends broke into the jail and killed Robert."

Ainsley tilted her head. "Is there any record that

Robert Chamberlain denied shooting Elliott?"

"I haven't found any."

"Then why does Cora believe he didn't kill him?"

"The first diary that Cora found alluded to Robert being innocent. It's the one that she found before I started helping her."

"The first one that went missing." Then she yawned. "What I'm trying to figure out is why anyone would break in here and steal the journals.

"*If* someone did."

She nodded. "I'm too foggy to think it through. I have to get some sleep."

"You and me both." He stood, offering Ainsley his hand. Without hesitation, she took it, sending a current of electricity through his arm. Her blue eyes widened. She'd felt it too.

"Up you go," he said, tugging her to her feet. Inches separated them. His desire to take her in his arms and kiss her sent blood thrumming through his body. Her lips softened and she leaned into him. He caught his breath. He'd never wanted anything as much as he wanted to feel her in his arms, his lips on hers.

Linc tucked a strand of her black hair behind her ear and forced himself to step away from the woman he'd never stopped loving. Kissing Ainsley right now would be taking advantage of her lack of sleep and stress. When he did kiss her, it would be the right time and place.

31

Ainsley slept so soundly, it took a few minutes to figure out where she was when she woke. It wasn't the first time she'd slept in a place that wasn't her own and wouldn't be the last. And yesterday wasn't the first time she'd gone twenty-four hours without sleep.

She took a couple of deep breaths to shake the fogginess from her brain. To her chagrin, the image of Linc pulling her to her feet, his intentions clear, replaced the fog. But then he hadn't kissed her. Even now, disappointment surprised her.

This wouldn't do. Linc was her past, not her future. *Go forward, not backward.* That had always been her mantra. She'd left Natchez behind without a backward glance. Same thing when she'd walked away from her singing career.

But Linc wasn't the same person he'd been fifteen years ago.

Could she get past the fact that he'd sided with her father, and eventually gave her an ultimatum—choose him or her singing career? She'd chosen the career. And he'd been right. It was a cutthroat business, one she was ill-prepared for.

That hadn't been the point. Like her father, Linc had demanded that she turn down the opportunity to join a group that opened for one of the top country/gospel singers in the country.

He's changed. And for the better.

Ainsley ignored the voice in her head and sat on the side of the bed. She called the hospital to check on Cora, and after learning she was a little confused, she asked about Connie Hanover. Her condition was still rated as serious. Ainsley stood, and the faint aroma of coffee beckoned her to the kitchen. Clothes first.

She padded across to the bathroom and wet a cloth with warm water and pressed it to her eyes as details of the shooting bombarded her. It wasn't like her to miss someone tailing her, twice possibly. So why yesterday? Or, in both instances had the person figured out where they were going and hadn't needed to tail them at all? That would rule out Maddox as the shooter at the Hanovers' since he wouldn't know them or where they lived.

It was something to discuss with Linc. But first she needed that coffee. Ainsley pulled her hair back and wrapped a band around it. She slipped the gray pants from the hanger that she'd hung on the back of Cora's door and pulled them on. She quickly donned her body armor before grabbing her shirt.

A tap at the door startled her.

"Are you decent?" Linc's voice came through the door.

She finished buttoning her shirt and tucked in the tail. "Yep. Come on in."

He pushed the door open and entered with two mugs in his hand. "Thought you might need this," he said, handing her one of the steaming cups of coffee.

"I need something stronger than decaf," she said.

"You didn't see the text?"

"What text?" She pulled her phone out. She'd completely missed Gran's message telling them she'd left a bag of assorted coffee pods on the front doorknob. All caffeinated. Grinning, she looked up. "Real coffee."

Ainsley nodded toward a sitting area in the bedroom with two chairs and a small table between them. She almost asked him what he'd done with the *real* Lincoln Steele. It never would have occurred to the old Linc to bring her coffee, further proof he'd changed. "Join me. I'm not quite ready to face the sunshine pouring into Cora's kitchen."

Once they were both seated, she sipped the strong brew. "You make a mean cup of joe."

"I picked out one that read full-bodied since I thought that fit you."

"Really?" She hadn't meant to tease with her

voice and swallowed a grin when his face turned crimson.

"You know what I mean," he said. "What's the plan for today?"

"First thing is to call Sam to see what he's learned."

"Sounds good. And don't forget your vest."

"I already have it on. Do you have yours?"

"Grabbed it when I got my change of clothes. It's in the Tahoe."

She hoped it wouldn't be hot and humid today. As if. This was Natchez in June. "I want to check Cora's safe first."

"You asked her about opening it?"

"Same time I asked if I could stay here. Then everything that happened at the Hanover place blew it right out of my mind."

"What are we waiting for?" he asked, setting his mug down.

They both stood, and she led the way to the safe. After taking the picture down, Ainsley twirled the knob four times to clear it.

"I hope this works like a combination lock," she said. "Dad's birthday is November 16, 1960, so the combination should be 11-16-60."

She turned the dial and lastly landed on the 60 and turned the handle to the right. It silently swung open. "We did it!"

Linc used his phone light to shine in the dark safe, illuminating several packets and a couple of boxes. And a small leather-bound book. Ainsley gently removed the book held together with a thin leather cord.

A shiver went down her spine. She held in her hands the diary of someone who had lived over 150 years ago. Ainsley took the diary to the chair she'd been sitting in. "I wonder where Cora found this," she said.

"Good question—it's not in the best of shape," Linc said, pointing to the cracked leather binding.

Ainsley carefully untied the cord and opened the diary. The first entry was dated August 1870. She looked up at Linc. "Do you know the date of the first diary Cora found?"

He rubbed his chin. "I think she said it was 1871, the year after Zachary Elliott died."

"This is fascinating," Ainsley said, carefully turning the weathered pages. "Look," she said, reading an entry. "Charlotte was holding a graduation ceremony for her students."

"This needs to be in a museum," Linc said softly.

"I agree." Holding the words of her ancestor sparked something inside Ainsley. She'd never understood Linc's deep interest in history, but reading Charlotte's words birthed a desire to know more about her. With a sigh, she carefully closed the diary. "I have a murder to solve. This will have to wait."

He grinned. "I'd love to read through this . . . maybe later?"

"Definitely." Her cell phone rang, and she picked it up from the table, glancing at the caller ID. Her dad. Ainsley silenced the phone and slipped it into her pocket.

"You're not going to answer his call?"

"You saw who it was?"

"Kind of hard not to. Your screen was in plain sight."

She fished it out of her pocket. He'd hung up. "Oops, just missed him." Then it rang again, and she sighed.

"I'll get you a refill," he said and grabbed her coffee cup.

After Linc shut the door behind him, she punched the answer button. "Hello, Dad."

"How are you this morning?"

"I'm fine."

"You didn't mention last night you were attacked at Rocky Springs. You want to tell me about it?"

"Nothing to tell. It was probably someone high on drugs, and I stumbled on him. How did you know about that?"

"Clete Randolph and I go way back. You think the murdered girl's mother was the target last night, not you?"

"It's early in the investigation." She smoothed her hand over the diary.

"You do have help on this case, right?"

Nothing ever changed. "Why? Do you think I can't handle it?" Without giving him a chance to answer, she said, "If that's all you called about . . ."

There was a sigh on the other end. "No. I wanted to remind you about the fund-raiser tonight and ask if you'd come maybe a little early so we can talk."

"I'll try."

"Good. Oh, and wear something dressy instead of your uniform. The park service might not be happy to see one of their employees support a political candidate."

She clenched her jaw. Did he think she was a complete idiot? Although the uniform would have made it easier to hide the Kevlar vest. "Do you think it's wise for me to be there? I mean, in case I was the target last night? It might endanger your donors."

"I'll have plenty of security in place," he said. "But at least you're admitting you were the target."

She couldn't win. "I told you it was too early to tell. Have you talked to Cora?"

"I talked to her ICU nurse. Cora's somewhat confused this morning. But, according to the nurse, that's to be expected."

That's what the nurse had told her. "I'll check on her later today. How about Gran? Have you spoken to her?"

"Not yet, but since you asked that, it sounds like you're not staying with her, and that begs the question of why."

She was slipping. How could she forget that he never missed anything? Ainsley started to say she'd already left the house. But she wasn't a fourteen-year-old who'd broken some rule he'd made up. "With the hours I'm keeping, it's easier to stay at Cora's. And I'm not certain someone didn't break into her house Thursday night."

"I'd think you had enough on your plate without creating a new crime."

Ainsley caught the retort on her tongue.

"Playing devil's advocate," he said, "why would someone suddenly decide to break in? Everyone in town knows she has an excellent alarm system."

Ainsley frowned. The alarm hadn't gone off Thursday night when they came to check on Cora. "Evidently she doesn't always set it," she said. "Or maybe the person who broke in knew the code." Like him. Why was he trying so hard to make her think no one had broken in?

"Who would know that, and besides, no one's ever broken in on her before. Why would they now?"

"Maybe someone with a vested interest in those journals she found."

He was quiet a minute. "So, she really did find more journals?"

Ainsley was very good at detecting evasion in voices. So good that she taught classes on it at the police academy every summer. She'd bet her career on it that her father already knew Cora had found the journals.

Before she could form an answer, he said, "I want to see them."

"There was only one in the safe." He was quiet and she could almost hear his brain whirling. "Why do you want to see it?"

"It's nothing I want to discuss over the phone," he said. "How soon can we meet?"

This was something she could control. "Not this morning. I'll try to get to the house early tonight."

"Ainsley—"

"Why is this journal so important?" she asked.

"It just is."

32

Holding a cup in each hand, Linc waited outside the door until he was certain Ainsley was off the phone before he entered the room. "Here you go," he said, handing her the fresh coffee.

"Thanks," she said.

"Doesn't look like the conversation went too well."

"Does it ever with him? He wants me to attend his fund-raiser tonight."

Linc had gathered that much. "Are you going?"

"If I don't, I'll never hear the end of it. He said there'd be plenty of security."

"I could be your plus-one."

Her eyes warmed. "You'd do that?"

That and a whole lot more, if she'd let him. "Sure."

"Maybe it won't be so bad after all."

He'd try to make sure it wasn't. "Would you like breakfast? We could do a drive-through."

"Cereal will do." Her cell phone rang, and she glanced at the ID and then at him. "Do you know a Hugh Cortland?"

"FBI," he replied. A call Linc had been

expecting after last night's shooting on top of the attempt at Rocky Springs. "Sam Ryker probably called him."

Hurt flashed in her eyes.

"It's protocol and has nothing to do with your ability," he said softly.

"I know." She pressed the answer button. "Beaumont."

Cortland's voice boomed from her phone as he identified himself. Somehow, she must have hit the speaker button.

"How can I help you?" Ainsley thumbed buttons on her phone.

"I'd like to"—Cortland's voice dropped as she found the right button, but he had a voice that carried, allowing Linc to hear the conversation—"meet with you later today. I'll be at Rocky Springs by one to take a look at the crime scene. Would that be a good time and place for you?"

"I'll make it work," she said.

"Good. See you then."

Ainsley pocketed her phone and turned to him. "I hate to ask, but could I get you to follow me to that body shop you mentioned, then take me to a car rental?"

"No problem. I'm off today and at your disposal. But the body shop owner may not work on Saturdays. Let me call and see while you grab a bite to eat."

"Thanks. How about you?"

231

"I had cereal before I drank coffee." He followed her to the kitchen while he made the call. As he suspected, the body shop wasn't open but the owner said he'd meet them and put her truck inside the fence.

"Good," she said when he relayed the message. "Did he say how long it'd take to repair it?"

"I explained why you needed your truck, and he'll order your windshield Monday and install it Tuesday." She nodded her approval, and he added, "I noticed Cora's station wagon in the garage last night. Maybe you could use it."

"Good thinking. I'll ask when we go by and check on her." She looked at her watch and groaned. "How did it get to be nine thirty? Let me call Gran and then I'll grab the diary and we can go."

Linc cleaned up the kitchen while she made her call and looked up as she reentered the kitchen.

"Gran said Cora wouldn't mind if I use her car. She has the keys and will give them to me at the hospital. That way I won't have to rent wheels when you go to work tomorrow at Melrose."

While Sam had cleared working the investigation with Linc's supervisor, the ranger subbing for him had a family emergency. "If I could take off, I would, but short of shutting the tours down, I can't."

Her eyes narrowed. "Look, I appreciate your

help, but this isn't my first murder investigation and it won't be my last."

"I bet it's the first murder investigation where you've become the target," he said, matching her argumentative tone. His pride stung when she glanced to his side.

"Linc, no offense, but—"

"I don't need a gun to help protect you." But he did. They both knew that. "There are other ways I can help."

He held her unwavering gaze until she dipped her head slightly. "Suit yourself. And when this is over, I want a private tour of Melrose."

"You got it," he said. "Are you ready to leave?"

"I haven't closed the safe, and I need to check my backpack to make sure I have everything I need."

"I can close the safe," he said and followed her down the hall. Once he had it shut, he twirled the lock.

"What number is it on?" Ainsley asked.

"Twenty-six," he said. "Why?"

"Just in case someone breaks in, I want to know if they try to open it."

Linc frowned. There was something he should remember, but what was it? "You really think someone will try to break in while you're staying here?"

"I won't be here all the time. Like now. I don't believe that carpet got wet by itself."

He snapped his fingers. "So much has hap-pened, I forgot the water in the basement."

"What are you talking about?"

"I needed a board when I fixed the broken window and looked around the basement. There was water behind the stairs."

"You're kidding. And you're just now telling me? Show me."

"Do we have time?"

"We'll make time. Someone was here Thursday night, I feel it in my bones."

He flipped the light on at the top of the stairs, then led the way down the steps to the basement. "It was right here," he said, rounding the corner.

"How much water?"

"A puddle. Like someone had been outside in the rain and stood there a minute. Hiding, maybe?"

Ainsley scanned the room. "But why? There's nothing here. No door, no anything."

"Do you think there might be another safe here?" Linc tapped on the wall just as Ainsley's phone rang again and she answered.

"We're on our way," she said and then dis-connected. "We'll check this out later. Right now Cora is asking for us."

33

Sonny waited until Steele and the Beaumont woman drove away. He'd come by Cora's house at midnight, and two vehicles had sat in the drive. One probably belonged to Ainsley Beaumont, but who had the other one belonged to?

What if they'd opened the safe and found another journal? He had two and needed all three to get what he was asking in order to pay the people he owed money to. What if he didn't pay them, instead took the took the money and ran? Fifty grand would be enough to start over in a little Mexican village. Then he'd never have to deal marijuana again. No more selling on the sly to *upstanding* businessmen or the dealers who sold to high school kids.

Sonny had about croaked when he'd discovered the Dyson girl's supplier was one of his dealers. Sonny needed to talk to him. Make sure he kept his mouth shut.

He entered the house through the kitchen. Once in Cora's bedroom, he removed the painting before he took out the slip of paper with the entire family's birthdates. If she hadn't chosen one of their birthdays for the combination he'd have to bring in a professional.

The first one, Rose Beaumont's, didn't work, and he tried the niece. No dice. He doubted it was Cora's birthdate, but he tried it anyway. Why was the last option always the correct one?

He froze as the back door scraped open. There was no way to get to the library and in the hidden stairs without being seen. He took a step toward the bathroom and stopped. Might be the first place whoever it was stopped. That left either under the bed or in the closet to hide.

He opted for the closet and stepped inside the narrow space between hangers of Miss Cora's flowery dresses. The scent of lavender tickled his nose. What was it with old women and lavender? If he sneezed . . . He'd have to somehow not do that.

With the door barely cracked, Sonny peered through the narrow opening, his breath catching as J.R. Beaumont stalked into the room and stopped in front of the safe. Sonny took pride in knowing about the men he dealt with. J.R. Beaumont worked out to stay in shape, and from what he'd read, he had a left hook that had found its mark more times than not in his amateur boxing days. Something Sonny did not want to experience.

"Can't believe Ainsley didn't rehang the painting." J.R.'s voice carried to the closet.

"Definitely not like her." He opened the safe and swore.

Sonny shrunk back as J.R. swung around and scanned the room. "Where is it?"

That was what Sonny wanted to know. Sweat ran down the side of his face in the claustrophobic space. He was going to pass out if he didn't get out of the closet.

J.R. banged the safe door shut and stormed out of the room.

Sonny took his first good breath when the back door slammed hard enough to rattle the windows.

He slipped out of the hiding place on legs like rubber. That was close. And evidently for nothing. Ainsley Beaumont must have the diary with her. Which would make getting it more difficult. Or, she'd hidden it somewhere.

He had all day. He might as well use it searching the Chamberlain house.

34

L inc had let Ainsley out at the hospital entrance, and she waited in the lobby for him to park. Since she was wearing her body armor under her shirt, she didn't have to stash the vest at the reception area.

Cora was sleeping when they walked into her ICU room. "She's been asking for you and mumbling something about the diaries," her grandmother said.

As Gran talked, Cora's eyes opened and she tried to sit up. "You're here. Did you find them?"

As Ainsley raised the head of her bed, the nurse stepped inside. "She's only allowed two visitors at a time, so one of you will have to leave."

Gran stood. "She was so excited when I told her Linc was coming. I'll step out since the doctor said I could stay and help with her lunch." She hugged Ainsley and handed her the keys to Cora's car. "The garage opener is in the kitchen. Third drawer from the sink."

"Thanks." Ainsley turned to Cora. The six-inch line of staples on her head reminded Ainsley how close they'd come to losing her great-aunt. At least the black eye she'd suffered when she fell was healing, although it was turning greenish. "You look better today."

"Don't ever play poker," Cora said. "At least my head isn't hurting like it was. Did you find the diaries?"

Her aunt was much clearer today, and her grit amazed Ainsley. "The diary in your safe? Yes, we found it."

"Only one?"

"How many should we have found?"

Cora's brow furrowed. "Two . . . maybe . . . I think I was reading one in bed . . . but my memory is still fuzzy."

There was no diary on the bed, further confirming someone had been in the house. "Where did you find them?" Ainsley asked.

Cora's expression went blank. She pinched the bridge of her nose like she had all of Ainsley's life when she was thinking. "I can't remember . . ." She looked past Ainsley. "Is that Linc with you?"

He stepped around her. "Yes, ma'am. How are you today?"

A smile was slow in coming. "The doctor said I was better, but it's so frustrating to be unable to recall anything." Tears formed in her eyes. "He said I might never get all my memory back."

"Don't believe everything someone tells you," Ainsley said. "Do you remember the events of Thursday night at all?"

Cora's brow furrowed again in concentration.

"No," she said, closing her eyes. "I remember reading one of the diaries . . . and putting one in the safe . . . It's like something is hovering in the back of my mind, but I can't pull it out."

"You remember that much. Did you set your alarm Thursday night?"

"No." Cora opened her eyes. "I knew storms were predicted and Rose would be checking on me. I didn't want to fool with turning the alarm off and on." She looked toward Ainsley. "I'm sure you two have other things to do, so don't hang around here."

Ainsley patted her aunt's hand. "I hate to leave, but I do have to meet someone at Rocky Springs."

She turned to go and recalled the water in the basement Linc had mentioned. "Is there another safe in the basement?"

"A safe?" Her voice reflected the puzzlement on her face. "No . . . but . . . there's something I should remember about the basement . . ." Her fingers gripped her sheet, bunching the corner. Then she huffed a sigh. "Maybe it will come to me later."

"Don't worry about it. The diary is in a safe place, and I'll keep looking for a second one. You rest now."

When Ainsley reached the door, she turned, and her heart caught at how frail Cora seemed. Ainsley should have been home more often.

240

She had no excuse other than not wanting to be around her father. And Linc. That was a poor excuse. It wasn't like her to avoid difficult situations—she usually met them head-on. But both men had hurt her deeply. *If you hold anything against anyone, forgive them.* The Bible verse that she had learned in her youth blasted from her past.

No. Maybe Linc. He'd changed, but her father . . . that would be harder. He'd always made her feel like she was such a bother. *Forgive as the Lord forgave you.*

Linc's hand on her arm made her jump, and she refocused.

"You okay? Cora's tough," he said when they were in the hall. "She'll make it."

"I know." But there was no telling how many years this injury had shaved off her life. In the waiting room, she held her grandmother extra close.

"She's going to be fine," Gran said.

"I know," Ainsley repeated.

"I'll call you if there's any change or she says something I think you should know."

Ainsley hugged Gran again before her grandmother hurried to Cora's room. She wasn't getting any younger either. Blinking back tears she didn't quite understand, she walked with Linc to the elevator and waited. When the door slid open, her heart sank as her father stepped out.

"Ainsley. Linc. Just the two people I wanted to see."

She didn't miss that the smile was the same for-the-camera smile she saw in every political ad. "I thought I told you this morning I don't have time to talk—we have to get to Rocky Springs," she said, tapping her watch.

Her father stiffened. "Yes, of course. You're very busy. All I want is the diary that you found."

Ainsley folded her arms across her chest. "You checked Cora's safe."

He at least had the decency to look sheepish. She really needed to see what was in the diary that was so important. "She entrusted it to me, and until she tells me otherwise, I'm keeping it."

"She would not mind if you gave it to me."

"Why do you want it?" Ainsley asked.

"I'm your father. I shouldn't have to explain myself to you."

"Try again."

His mouth twitched. "I'm running on a plat-form of true equality for minorities, and not just because over 40 percent of Mississippi's voters are classified as minority. It's the right thing to do."

Ainsley would have to give him that. "What does that have to do with the diaries?" she asked.

"I'm afraid they'll paint a different picture. I need to know what's in the diaries to be prepared if Kingston gets his hands on them."

"Who's going to care what happened 150 years ago?" Linc asked.

"I know most voters won't care, but the race is projected to be so close that I can't afford to lose even one vote." He held up his hand. "Elections are about perception. If there is damaging information in the diaries and that information went viral, it would have a negative impact on my campaign."

"But how would the diary get into Kingston's hands?" Ainsley cocked her head. "And how do you know what was in the first diary?"

"Cora told me." His face flushed under her scrutiny.

He'd chosen not to answer how Kingston would get the diaries. If that first diary had been stolen, and it was beginning to sound like it was, maybe the thief was offering it to the highest bidder. And Kingston and her father were the bidders.

Ainsley shuddered. It amounted to political blackmail, but if her father wouldn't admit someone was blackmailing him, there was little she could do. "I have to go," she said.

"Wait. If the diary isn't in the safe, and you don't have it with you, where is it? Surely not in your pickup."

"Nope," Ainsley said. "Linc is chauffeuring me around."

"Good. Relieves my mind to know you're not handling this by yourself," he said, changing like

243

a chameleon as he slapped Linc on the shoulder.

She ground her teeth. Why couldn't he have confidence in her? The thought almost made Ainsley snort. She could count on one hand how many times he'd said "Good job" on anything she'd ever done.

But why was that so important to her? She pushed the question away. It wasn't important. Her medals and citations proved her worth. She didn't need his approval.

35

Linc studied Ainsley. The conversation with her father had drained her—it showed in her tense jaw and the tired lines around her eyes.

A text chimed on his phone. Linc groaned. His request for tomorrow off had been denied since no other ranger could take his place.

"Ready?" he asked as she joined him at the door.

"Yes. What did you make of my dad's conversation?"

"He knows a lot about the journals to claim not to."

"He's hiding something, for sure, but I need to switch gears and focus on the reason I'm in Natchez," she said. "I checked on Connie Hanover just now and her condition has been upgraded to good."

"That's great news. I still hate that I can't take off tomorrow."

"Don't worry about it. I rarely ever have someone working with me anyway."

They walked toward the automatic doors. "Wait here until I get the Tahoe."

Once he picked her up, he pointed the Tahoe

out of the parking lot. "Any word from your supervisor on Maddox?"

"No. I'll text Brent for an update." She sent the message on her phone, then scrolled through it. "Last night before I went to sleep, I requested a drawing showing a beard." She held her phone up. "This is what they just sent. Do you think we can go by Cora's and print this?"

When Linc stopped for a light, he glanced at the drawing. "That should help. I'll turn back at the next intersection."

A horn beeped behind him as he let the traffic clear out so he could get into the left lane. Impatient drivers. Then the car switched lanes with him. Were they being followed?

He noted the color and model as he turned left and it shot past them. A mint-green MINI Cooper. Sarah? He hadn't been able to see the driver in the tinted windows, but he didn't have a good feeling about it.

Could she have followed them to the hospital? He hadn't seen her, but she might not have made her presence known . . . especially if she'd overheard their conversation with J.R. But surely he would have seen her. Or not. Their conversation with J.R. had been pretty intense. "You think someone is blackmailing your dad?"

"You felt that too?"

"Yes, and I think you should advise the chief of police about your suspicions that someone broke into Cora's house." He turned at the next intersection. "Do you know the chief of police, Pete Nelson?"

"Vague memory of him from school. He was a couple of years ahead of us."

"He's a good guy." Linc pulled into Cora's drive and parked near the back door.

"This won't take a minute," she said as they piled out of his Tahoe.

"Toss me the keys to the station wagon, and I'll crank it up and let it run in case you need it."

"Thanks, but you'll need the garage opener too."

He followed Ainsley to the kitchen and waited while she found the remote. Outside, he walked to the large stand-alone building that had at one time held a carriage on one side and stabled horses on the other. The door creaked up and he smiled at the 1991 Mercury Colony Park station wagon sitting inside. Someone washed and waxed it regularly because it looked practically brand-new.

After unlocking it, he slid across the leather seat. While it didn't smell brand-new, it had that luxurious leather smell. When he turned the key, the motor instantly turned over. It only had fifty thousand miles on it, and someone kept the car in good running shape. J.R., maybe? If it was J.R., then he had a better relationship with Cora than he had with his daughter. They were almost like strangers to each other.

Had Linc been so blind all those years ago when he aligned himself with J.R. that he couldn't see they both had their own interests at heart and not Ainsley's? Linc, because he feared losing her, and J.R. because he arrogantly thought he knew what was best for his daughter?

36

While the sketch was printing, Ainsley walked to her aunt's bedroom and checked the safe. The dial was no longer set at twenty-six, the number Linc had left it on. As she suspected, her dad had been here and opened the safe.

Why couldn't he trust her enough to be honest with her? And why did she care? Because every child wanted their father's approval, even as adults. Maybe that was why she had so much trouble trusting God.

Her lips tugged upward in a wry grin. Gran would have an answer to that.

"Honey, never compare God to your dad. He has frailties and weaknesses. I should know—I raised him. God will always be there for you, and he'll never give up on you."

Ainsley wished she could grab ahold of that. A scent tickled her nose and she lifted her head, sniffing the air. If there was one talent she had, it was picking up scents. Lavender. She turned to the closet. Why was the door ajar? It hadn't been when she left this morning.

She crossed to the closet and checked Cora's clothes. The lavender scent filled the enclosure.

It was a scent she would always associate with her aunt. Her grandmother on the other hand preferred the clean fragrance of lily of the valley and bergamot.

Ainsley picked up another scent, heavier, like musk. A man's scent. She tried to remember how her father had smelled at the hospital. She didn't think it was the scent she smelled now. Too heavy for her dad. She rocked back on her feet. Had someone been here other than her dad, or was she, like he said, seeing a crime everywhere she looked? If only she could get him out of her head.

Realizing she no longer heard the printer, Ainsley closed the closet door and hurried back to the library. Four sheets were in the tray. That should be enough for Rocky Springs. She frowned and sniffed the air again. The heavier scent from the closet had followed her to the library. Not as strong, but definitely there. She still didn't think it was her dad's cologne, but neither could she rule it out. Shaking her head, she walked to the kitchen. She would ask him point-blank about it later today.

Ainsley paused at the kitchen door. She couldn't shake the feeling of someone's presence in the house . . . it just didn't feel empty. She pulled her gun and backtracked, checking the first floor. Nothing unusual. At the foot of the steps going up to the bedrooms, her phone chimed an incoming text. Linc asking if she was ready to leave.

"Be there in a sec," she texted back. Did she want to tell him what she was doing? She wasn't sure she trusted him not to make fun of her . . . but if her instincts were right, she might need his help. *"Clearing the house."*

He texted back. *"Why?"*

"Vibes." If he didn't understand that, there was no need to say anything else.

The back door opened and footsteps came toward her.

"Ainsley?" Linc called.

"At the stairs going to the second floor," she called back, surprised at how pleased she was that he'd showed up. He might not be able to use a gun, but he wasn't afraid to cover her back. She hoped one day he could get past what happened with Blake.

"What's going on?" he asked.

She paused at the landing and turned to him. "I don't know. Nothing I can explain, but either someone is in the house or they were here right before we arrived."

"I'll go with you," he said and climbed to the landing.

Ainsley nodded, and they cleared each bedroom one by one. By the last room, she questioned why she'd felt the need to check out the house. "Guess you think I'm crazy, like my dad does."

He cocked his head. "Investigators have to go by their gut instincts."

251

"Thanks, but as you can see, no one is here."

"Tell me why you thought there might be."

She explained smelling the musky scent in the bedroom and library. "And you know how a house feels when it's empty? When I was in the library, it's like there was a presence . . ."

"Like someone was nearby?"

"Yes! I hadn't thought of it that way, but that's exactly how I felt." Warmth filled her heart. Linc got it.

"We'll check the house again when we return—if you don't mind me staying another night."

"Actually, I'd be glad if you did."

He handed her the keys and the remote for the garage as they walked out the back door, and she stuffed the items into her backpack. Linc had turned and was surveying the house. "This house was built before the war, right?"

"Yes. Around 1850."

"A lot of these homes had secret passages in them. I wonder if this one does."

"Never heard any talk of one, but Cora could tell you."

"Maybe your dad knows."

"You could ask him tonight."

He nodded and opened the passenger door. It seemed so odd for someone to do that. None of the men she worked with had ever opened a door for her . . . probably thought she'd take their head off if they did.

Within minutes they were weaving in and out of traffic as they drove to the Trace. Summer in Natchez had always meant a lot of vehicles because of all the tourists visiting the old homes and historical sites.

"Are you going to church tomorrow with Rose?" he asked.

"I imagine." Short of dying, there would be no other option. "I'll miss you tomorrow."

"Really?"

Ainsley was surprised that she would and even more surprised that she'd told him. "You're getting to be like an old shoe—comfortable."

"Gee, thanks," he said with a laugh.

"Be glad—that's much better than some of the other thoughts I've had about you."

His smile disappeared. "About that . . . I was an idiot fifteen years ago."

"That was one of the thoughts."

He turned onto the Trace. "Thanks for making me feel better."

Before he could bring up their past, she steered him away from the subject by asking how he liked his job at Melrose. They talked about their respective jobs, and the hour passed quickly. Soon he made a left turn into Rocky Springs.

"Looks like we're the first to arrive," Linc said.

"Good. We can see if the tent campers are still here."

Just as he parked in front of the maintenance

shed, her cell phone rang. Her supervisor. "Beaumont," she answered and glanced at Linc. "I'm putting you on speaker."

"Sure," Brent said, his voice echoing in the SUV. "The Tennessee Bureau of Investigation just notified me the three escapees are holed up in a cabin near Chattanooga. They've had them under observation since midnight."

"Midnight? Are you certain Maddox is one of the men at the cabin?"

"He was ID'd along with the other two escapees," Brent said. "TBI thinks the three have been together the whole time, so I don't think he could have been your shooter."

Ainsley gripped her phone. If Maddox wasn't her attacker, who was?

37

Linc's stomach clenched. In a way, it'd been easier to think Maddox was the attacker. If he wasn't, and it looked like he wasn't . . . maybe Ainsley's assaults were connected to Hannah Dyson's case. Could the Hanovers be involved in something that got Connie's daughter killed?

She'd wanted them to wait until the husband left for work to even talk to her. If they were involved in illegal activities, that opened the possibility that Connie Hanover really had been the target last night.

They needed to interview Mr. Hanover as soon as possible. Maybe he was at the hospital with his wife . . . Linc tuned back in on the conversation.

"Thanks," she was saying. "Sam Ryker called in the FBI, and I'm meeting Hugh Cortland."

"Good call. Keep me informed."

Ainsley hung up and released a long breath. "Well, back to square one."

"We need to make a list of people who might want you out of the way, starting with this murder investigation," Linc said.

"I agree. Once we get back to Cora's, I plan to set up a whiteboard and walk through the case."

A visual of the investigation would be helpful. "I'll help you—that is, if you'd like my assistance."

"Absolutely," she said. "I have a problem with these attacks being related to this case. Taking me out will only bring more heat—and has. We wouldn't be meeting with Hugh Cortland right now if someone hadn't attacked me at the church and shot Connie Hanover."

"Ignoring this case, can you think of anyone in Natchez who holds a grudge against you?"

"Besides my dad?"

"Be serious," he said. But he was glad she could still joke.

She bit her lip and then shook her head. "I haven't lived in Natchez since high school, and I never had an enemy that I know of. Who would hold a grudge that long anyway?"

Ainsley was right. There had to be another angle. "How about the Kingstons?"

"That would bring it back to the investigation, but you don't seriously think they would try to kill me over this, do you?"

If he hadn't seen so much of the wrong side of the law, he wouldn't. "Power corrupts sometimes," he said. "Your dad and Kingston are leading the pack of candidates—neck and neck in the polls. If it became public knowledge Kingston's grandson is a suspect in Hannah's murder, it could sway the election against him."

"I can see them being upset after we interviewed Drew, but I don't see them trying to kill me over it," Ainsley said.

She had a point, but that brought them back to no viable suspect. He grabbed the enhanced photos of Maddox. "I still think we should ask our tent campers if the sketch resembles the man camped near them yesterday."

"You don't think Maddox is with the other escapees?"

He shrugged. "Doesn't hurt to have a backup plan."

They turned around and slowly drove down the road where he'd last seen the young people, but there was no sign of them at the campsite. "Let's see if Colton and his parents are still here," he said.

They circled back around to where the RVs and trailers were parked. Colton's dad, Jesse Mason, was sitting at the picnic table, a small pipe lying near his hands. When Linc pulled parallel and climbed out of the Tahoe, Mason scooped the pipe up and slipped it in his pocket. He eyed them calmly as they approached.

"What can I do for you?" he asked.

A faint odor lingered in the air. "Have a skunk come through?" Linc asked.

"Early this morning," Mason replied, tugging at the sleeves of his pullover. "Mating season, you know."

Linc handed him one of the drawings. "Have you seen this man around here?"

Mason looked over the sketch. "No. What'd he do?"

"Is your wife around?" Ainsley asked. "Or Colton? Maybe one of them saw him."

He shifted his gaze to Ainsley. "I doubt it."

"We'd like to ask," Linc said.

Mason spit on the ground. "Alma!" he called without looking around. "These nice folks want a word with you."

Alma appeared at the camper door almost instantly.

"Don't keep 'em waiting," Mason snapped. "Get yourself out here."

She eased out the door and walked to the picnic table, her steps hesitant. Linc repeated his question as Mason handed her the sketch. She cast a sideways glance at her husband and shook her head. "Sorry, I can't help you."

"Is Colton around?" Ainsley asked.

"Naw. He took off early this morning, walking the Old Trace. But he didn't see him either," Mason said.

Ainsley rested her hand on her gun. "How can you be so sure?"

"If I didn't see him, neither did Colton. I check out everybody around here as soon as they set up."

"You hanging around Rocky Springs much longer?" Linc asked.

"Plan to."

"You don't have a job?" Ainsley asked.

"Not that it's any of your business, but I'm on medical leave. I get antsy in town. It's why we hit the road as soon as I was able."

A text chimed on Linc's phone, and he opened it. "Mind if I step into the shade? Sun's too bright for me to see my screen."

"Suit yourself."

Linc stepped into the shade, noting a message from the FBI agent. Then he silenced his phone and snapped a photo of Mason. "Cortland is here," he said to Ainsley.

They both turned to leave and Linc stopped, handing Mason a card. "In case you lost the one I gave you. If you happen to remember seeing the man in the sketch, contact me."

"Will do." Mason took the card and handed it to his wife. She bobbed an acknowledgment and then scurried back inside the trailer.

Ainsley was already in the Tahoe when Linc climbed in on the driver's side and pulled away. "That was interesting."

"Yeah. Did you smell the marijuana?"

"The skunk, you mean?" he asked with a chuckle.

"Do you think he could have been Hannah's supplier?"

"That occurred to me, but I get the feeling he's messing with us."

"Yeah. I get the distinct impression he believes he's smarter than we are. Sam should have the background check on him by now."

"Whether he does or not, I'll get Cortland to run a facial recognition scan of the photo I snapped when I stepped into the shade."

They turned out of the loop and drove toward the meeting point. Seconds later, Colton came into view. "Pull over," Ainsley said. "I want to talk to him."

Linc parked and both climbed out and waited for Colton to reach them. The boy was having a bad hair day with his hair sticking out in every direction under his cap. He wore the same cutoff shorts and tank top from yesterday. "You okay?" Linc asked when Colton drew near.

"Not sleeping too good," he said, scanning the woods behind them.

"Do you recognize this man?" She held up the sketch of Maddox.

The boy pressed his lips together as he stared at the photo, then he shrugged one shoulder.

"Does that mean yes or no?" Ainsley asked.

"Means I can't swear I've seen him. I saw a guy that could've been him, but a lot of the old guys who come in here look the same."

He was lying. Linc took out a notepad. "Can you give me the names of some of the guys Hannah hung out with?"

Colton took off his ball cap and ran his hand through his hair. "The jocks."

"Do they have names?" Ainsley asked.

The boy rattled off four names, and Linc wrote them down.

Ainsley crossed her arms. "You indicated your dad would be angry if he smelled marijuana on you. He uses it, so why would he care?"

Colton's eyes widened. "How did you know?"

Linc touched his nose. "It has a distinctive odor . . . as you well know."

The boy half shrugged again. "Case of do as I say, not as I do, I guess."

"Where does he get it?"

His gaze dropped. "I dunno."

Ainsley stepped into the boy's space. "Did he give Hannah marijuana?"

He jerked his head up. "No!"

"Are you sure?" Ainsley asked.

"I . . ." Colton closed his eyes, then he took a deep breath and opened them. "I, uh, asked him, and he said he didn't."

"But now you're not so sure?"

"No. He would have bragged about it if he had."

"Maybe he got scared after she died."

"I gotta go," Colton said and pushed past them.

"Don't protect him," Ainsley said.

"I don't know anything," he replied and kept walking.

"Colton," she said.

He stopped and turned around. "Do you know what he'd do if I snitched on him?" The boy was near tears. "You just don't get it. All I ever wanted was for him to be proud of me."

"I do get it, Colton." Ainsley's voice broke, and something shifted in Linc, making him want to take her in his arms and hold her. "I know how it feels to do everything you can to get someone's love." She walked over and touched the boy's arm. "But you can't get something a person doesn't have the ability to give."

The teen blinked and started to say something, then swallowed hard and stared at Ainsley. A minute passed. "Thanks. If I remember anything, I'll call you," he said and walked away.

"That was a bust," she said as they pulled away.

"You never know, he might call."

"Don't hold your breath."

"He's hiding something, and his conscience might get the better of him," Linc said as he pulled in beside a black Camry as the lanky FBI agent climbed out. He hadn't seen Cortland since leaving the Bureau. "I see Hugh got a new car."

"How's life treating you?" Cortland asked after Linc introduced him to Ainsley.

"Good," Linc replied as Sam Ryker's Ford Interceptor pulled in behind them. "Love my job at Melrose, and I can sleep at night."

"So why are you working the investigation?"

"That'd be my fault," Sam said as he joined them. "I wanted his input."

"And he's been a good sounding board for me," Ainsley added.

"But now that you're here, I'll back off." Disappointment was swift, surprising him that he didn't want to back off.

"No need for that," Cortland said. "I was just hoping you were rethinking your retirement."

Was he? No. He might, except Linc had never heard of an FBI agent without a gun.

38

Ainsley liked the serious FBI agent. She briefed Sam and Hugh on the escaped criminals and gave them the updated sketch of Maddox. "Until there's positive identification of him in Chattanooga, I'm not ruling him out as my assailant."

"Do you have a photo without the beard in case he's shaved it?" Hugh asked. "I'd like to run them on the Jackson TV station. If he's in the area, maybe someone will recognize him."

Linc pulled Maddox's mug shot from a folder and handed it to Hugh. "Maybe we'll get lucky."

"We can always hope," Sam replied.

Her phone rang, and Ainsley glanced at the ID. Brent. "Excuse me." She walked away from the men as she answered.

"Got some news for you," Brent said.

She held her breath, waiting for the worst.

"TBI breached the cabin, killed one of the men. Two of them got away."

"Was Maddox the one killed?"

"I don't know yet. TBI is running his prints through AFIS."

The Automated Fingerprint Identification Sys-

264

tem should identify them pretty quickly. "How long since this happened?"

"Fifteen minutes ago."

She tapped her fingers against her leg. AFIS should have already identified them. "And you haven't heard anything?"

"No, but informing me may not be high on their priority list. I believe they'll capture the other two pretty quickly."

"Keep me updated."

"I will, but stay on guard. Even if Maddox wasn't your shooter, you still have someone out there hunting for you."

Ainsley thanked him and pocketed the phone, then adjusted her Kevlar vest. Until Maddox was positively identified by the Hamilton County Sheriff's Department, it would be hard to relax her guard. Not that she should anyway—if the attacks *were* connected to the case, right now she was probably in the most dangerous place she could be.

While it didn't feel like she was being watched, it wasn't hard to imagine danger lurking in the dark woods. Rain from Thursday's storm had stirred the spores in the soil, releasing a damp, earthy aroma, reminding her of the cemetery not far from them. Spanish moss draped from the trees like in a Southern gothic horror film. She suppressed a shiver and hurried to where the three men stood.

Linc queried her with his eyebrows.

"TBI killed one of the escapees but two of them got away. Don't know if Maddox was the one killed yet," she said.

Hugh held up his hand. "But if it wasn't Maddox who attacked you here, it's someone else—someone who might still be after you."

"Spoken like a true FBI agent," Linc said with a dry laugh.

She rubbed the back of her neck. "But why?"

"If we can figure that out," Sam said, "it'll lead to the who."

"Did you get any hits on Jesse Mason?" Linc asked Sam.

"Nothing. Of course, that might not even be his name," Sam replied. "We need his prints."

"How about a photo? I snapped one of him just now." Linc held up his phone and turned to Hugh. "Can you run it through your FACE program in case he's using an alias?"

FACE was the Facial Analysis, Comparison, and Evaluation Services that the FBI used to identify unknown subjects, and Ainsley had requested the service in the past for cases in East Tennessee.

"Shoot it over to me," the FBI agent said. "And if everyone is ready, I'd like to see the crime scene."

"You two can walk if you'd like, but I'm driving Ainsley to the site."

"I have no desire to tramp around these woods in this heat," Hugh said. "Sam can ride with me, and we'll meet you there."

The other two men pulled out first, and they fell in behind them in the Tahoe. Ainsley's phone rang.

"It's Brent," she said and punched the answer button. "What do you have for me?"

"Bad news, I'm afraid," he said.

Dread coiled in her stomach. "Hold on and let me put you on speaker so Linc can hear you." A second later, she laid the phone on the console. "Go ahead."

"Turns out Maddox wasn't with the other two escapees." Brent's voice sounded tiny inside the Tahoe. "They'd stayed together as far as the cabin around Chattanooga," Brent said. "Some-time Friday night Maddox stole the weapons and the car they'd made their getaway in, leaving the other two stranded."

"But I thought there were three men at the cabin in the mountains," Linc said.

"There were, but one was a friend they'd called to help them out. He was supposed to find them another car, but he got killed for his trouble," Brent said grimly. "Thing is, they confirmed that Maddox really had it in for you. It was all he talked about—getting even for what you did to him."

Ainsley clenched her hands. "What I did to

him? What about what he did to his wife and her new husband?"

"I know, but this morning my IT specialist informed me we've been hacked. He's not sure when yet, but if it was Maddox, he definitely knows where you are, so take every precaution."

"Don't worry, I will," she said. "Keep me posted."

"Oh, and he's changed vehicles. The one they made their escape in was found in a bad area of Chattanooga, stripped. Witnesses indicated the car had been there for at least twenty-four hours."

"Any lead on what he'd be driving?" Linc asked.

"Three cars and a motorcycle were reported stolen earlier yesterday, but there's no way to know if Maddox took one of them."

She and Linc exchanged glances. "We heard a motorcycle leave Connie Hanover's area last night."

"Just be careful," Brent said.

Ainsley wanted to punch the dashboard but instead punched the red button, disconnecting the call. "How did he know we would be at Connie Hanover's place?"

"There was no motorcycle following us," Linc said. "We both would have noticed that. And it sounded like a motorbike last night, not a big cycle."

If she was the reason Connie was lying in a hospital bed, fighting for her life . . .

Ainsley didn't want to think about it and focused on the road.

"Is that one of the tent campers?" she asked when a young man with a backpack walked toward them.

"Looks like it," Linc said. "Text Sam that we'll be a few minutes."

He pulled beside the hiker and lowered his window. "How's the hiking?"

"It got too hot for me. I left the others about thirty minutes ago. Figure they'll be along soon," he said. "You still looking for that guy?"

"Yes." Linc handed him the sketch. "Does this man look familiar?"

The hiker examined the sketch and then raised his head. "Could be . . . except the beard was shorter. And darker." He studied the paper again and then shrugged. "It's hard to tell. I never saw him up close. That was Ted."

"Keep the sketch and call me when your friends return."

"Will do."

"Do you remember if he had a car or a motor-cycle?" Ainsley asked.

The kid shook his head. "Ted said he was hitchhiking."

She did not believe Troy Maddox was on foot. He could have parked a car at the restroom area and no one probably would have thought anything about it. And he could've hidden a motorcycle in the woods. As they pulled away, Ainsley drummed her fingers on the armrest. "I want to talk to Ted before we leave."

Ainsley's phone rang. She didn't recognize the number. "This is ISB Ranger Ainsley Beaumont. How can I help you?"

"Uh. This is . . . uh . . ."

Sounded like a teenaged boy. "Drew? Is this Drew Kingston?"

"Yes, ma'am."

"Lincoln Steele is with me. I'm putting you on speaker."

"Did you remember something?" Linc asked.

"No. It's . . . I was there last night. At Hannah's house."

Ainsley gripped the phone. "What? Where are you?"

"Home. Dad's got me washing all the cars because I broke curfew."

"What'd you see last night, Drew?" Linc asked.

His voice rose and fell like he was pacing. "I uh, wanted to talk to Hannah's mom, tell her I was sorry about what happened. But I saw you guys there and—"

"Where were you? We didn't see you," Ainsley said.

"I motorbiked to the road behind their house. I was going to wait until you left, but then I saw a hunter with a rifle dressed in camouflage, but then the hunter shot Mrs. Hanover."

"Can you identify the shooter?" Linc asked.

"I . . ." Suddenly he gasped. "No!"

39

Ainsley brought the phone closer to her ear, hearing a faint *thwack,* followed by a groan and the sound of the phone hitting the ground. Then she heard nothing.

"Something's wrong!" She started hitting numbers. "I'm calling 911! And let Hugh and Sam know."

When the operator answered, she alerted him there was a possible shooter at Austin Kingston's residence. "I don't know the address."

Minutes later Ainsley grabbed the armrest as Linc peeled out of Rocky Springs behind Hugh. Sam's flashing blue lights led the way.

They lost the phone signal just outside Rocky Springs, but when they neared Port Gibson, Ainsley called Drew's dad. "Are you home?"

"No." Voices murmured in the background. "I'm having coffee with friends at the Donut Shop."

She sucked in a breath. "Drew called me and I think someone shot him while we were talk—"

"What! No—I just left him half an hour ago washing cars. He was fine."

"Listen to me, Austin. Get home as fast as you can and check on him."

She looked at her phone to see if the call had dropped. It was that or Austin hung up. Then, surprising herself, she lifted up prayers for the boy. She'd prayed more in the few days she'd been home than she had the entire time she'd been away.

When they arrived at the Kingston mansion, police cars filled the driveway and more patrol cars sat on the tree-lined street. Linc parked behind Hugh, and Ainsley bolted from the Tahoe. She raced to the back of the house. Police were combing the backyard. Her gaze went to a bucket of soapy water and a water hose that sat next to a silver Lexus.

"Is Drew all right?" she asked the Natchez chief of police, Pete Nelson.

"He's on his way to the hospital, hanging on by a thread," Nelson said. "Austin Kingston said you were talking to his son when this happened. Did he give any indication of who shot him?"

"No."

"Why did Drew call you?"

She rubbed her arms. "He was at Connie Hanover's place last night and saw the person who shot her. The shooter must've ID'd him as well. Were there any witnesses to what happened here?"

Nelson rested his hand on the butt of his gun. "Apparently not."

Ainsley scanned the area. "How about security cameras?"

The chief pointed to the back of the house. "One there, but where Drew was washing the car is out of its range." He turned and pointed to the far side of a detached garage. "One there too, but the same problem."

She turned to Linc. "Do you think this could've been Maddox?"

He chewed his bottom lip. "I figure it's the same shooter who was at the Hanover place last night. Evidently, whoever it was missed their chance to silence Drew last night. Probably followed him home and waited for an opportunity to do this."

She pinched the bridge of her nose. Too many people were getting shot. "If Drew dies . . ." She couldn't finish the sentence.

"He's not dead yet," Linc said. "The person who shot him is the bad guy, not you."

If only she could believe that.

Once it was evident there was nothing they could do at the crime scene, she said, "Now would be a good time to set up that whiteboard I was talking about."

"I have a conference room at my office. There's a board already set up," Pete said. "My officers can take care of the crime scene."

Doing something constructive would ward off

the helplessness engulfing Ainsley. They followed the chief to the jail.

"Coffee?" Pete asked.

"No thanks. I've had your coffee," Linc said, laughing.

Ainsley and Sam and Hugh declined as well and followed the chief to the conference room, where a large whiteboard was center stage.

"It's all yours," Pete said.

Ainsley hesitated. She had done this dozens of times, but never with so much riding on her ability to put together all the pieces floating around this case. Now was not the time to doubt her ability. She marched to the board and picked up a dry erase pen and with a firm hand wrote Hannah Dyson's name at the top. Then she made three columns. In the right column, she wrote Connie Hanover's and Drew Kingston's names.

"Autopsy report?" she asked, writing "Autopsy" in the left column before looking at Sam.

"Got an email from the medical examiner in Jackson this morning." He opened his phone. "Here's his summary—Hannah Dyson died from hypertrophic cardiomyopathy. It's an inherited condition where the walls of the heart muscle thicken, disrupting the heart's electrical system, causing irregular heartbeats."

Stunned silence followed his announcement.

"She died a natural death?" Ainsley said.

"No." Sam was still looking at his phone. "The

doc says there were no ligature marks around her neck, but she had those bruises that show up in the photos. Further examination revealed skin tissue under her fingernails, and that's been sent for DNA analysis. The ME figures she fought for her life. And once he started looking closer, he discovered slight bruising inside her nose and mouth."

He looked up from his phone. "The ME speculated the assailant caught her by the throat, and she got away. He caught her again and blocked her breathing by covering her nose and mouth with his hand. That could have thrown her heart out of rhythm, resulting in her death. He thinks when we find the killer, he'll have scratch marks on his hands or arms."

"Forward that to me," Ainsley said as she wrote the medical term on the board. She pictured the scene. Hannah was a beautiful girl and, from what Colton and Drew said, liked attention from the boys. But she might not have welcomed attention she hadn't sought. The footprints showed she ran from her attacker—that alone could have caused the abnormal heart rhythm. He could have caught her and restrained her in a choke hold like Ainsley had been in at the church or covered her nose and mouth with his hand. Either way, she struggled, scratching him.

Linc held up a photo. "How did she get under the tree roots?"

Sam leaned forward. "I asked the ME about that. She had dirt on her knees. With an abnormal rhythm it's very possible Hannah fainted and her assailant thought she'd died and left her there. She could have come to and crawled up under the tree, where she died from the irregular heartbeat."

"That sounds a whole lot better than thinking this might be a serial killing," Hugh said. "I ran a query in the regional database for cases that have similarities, and there were no hits for this area. I'll check the national database when I get to a computer, just to be sure." He cleared his throat. "I have a court case next week, so I won't be available to help you until probably the end of the week. It'll depend on how the trial goes."

"I understand and appreciate your help today. I know you could be preparing for the trial," she replied.

He nodded, and Ainsley turned back to the board. She listed Drew, Colton, and Maddox in the middle column under possible suspects. She stepped back and stared at the board. What if Hannah's murder was an accident? She quickly dismissed that thought—her assailant had run her down. She added one more name to the middle column. Jesse Mason. She tried to remember if he had any scratch marks on his hands or arms . . . pretty sure his hands had been clear. She shuddered. Every time she was around the man, her internal alarm went crazy.

40

Maddox stood at the scarred sink and trimmed his beard with scissors he'd bought at the Dollar General just before closing time last night. The clerk was so busy trying to get out of the store, she didn't even look at him closely.

A roach scurried across the lavatory, and he squished it with the empty bottle of platinum hair coloring. He'd paid cash from his dwindling supply for one night at the motel that was probably as old as he was. At least he had gotten a decent shower and changed into a pair of jeans and a plaid short-sleeve shirt he'd found at the Salvation Army discount store. He'd found a washer and dryer near the front office and used the facility to launder the two sets of clothes he'd worn for the past week.

Maddox eyed himself in the mirror, pleased the hair dye had changed his brown hair and beard to silver, adding years, even distinction, to his face. The man staring back at him bore little resemblance to the prison escapee. He turned and used the small mirror he'd bought to check out his profile. Good.

No one would mistake him for a thirtysomething. More like a fiftysomething. And if he needed to, he could add a stoop and a limp that would give the impression he was even older—like the old men he never looked at once much less twice.

Now to offer his services to Grace Johnson, the old woman who lived on the southeast side of the street, across from Cora Chamberlain. He'd used the library computers to look up the owners of the houses on the corners of Walnut and Elm streets.

The Chamberlain house was where he'd seen the SUV parked. According to the librarian he'd chatted up, Cora Chamberlain's sister was Ainsley's grandmother and lived across the street. And the house on the other corner was the empty one with a for sale sign in the yard.

Maddox grabbed his clothes and the trash with the hair dye bottles in it. No need to take a chance. After ditching the trash, he pulled out of the motel parking lot and drove straight to Walnut Street and slowed as he passed by the house.

Good. No one had picked up the branches in the Johnson yard. Now he wanted to make sure Beaumont wasn't home. Even with his changed appearance, she was no fool and might see through it if she saw him.

There was no sign of the ranger, and he parked in front of Grace Johnson's house and walked up to the front door and rang the bell. It wasn't long before a white-haired woman peeked through the window in the door.

"Mrs. Johnson," he said loudly, "I'm from one of the churches in town, and I noticed you have a lot of limbs in your yard. Do you mind if I pick them up for you?"

Her eyes rounded, and she cracked the door. "You say you want to clean up my yard?"

Maddox risked taking off the ball cap. "Yes, ma'am."

Her blue eyes twinkled. "Why, how thoughtful of you. My grandson was supposed to come do that today, but he hasn't shown up yet."

"I doubt he'll mind if I get it cleaned up before he arrives."

"I'm sure you are right," she said. "I think I missed your name . . . and of course, I'd want to pay you something."

As much as he needed the money, he shook his head. "No, ma'am. I consider it my Christian duty to help you."

"Oh my. I can't say no to that." Then with a slight frown, she tilted her head. "What church did you say?"

He ground his teeth. What was the name of that church he passed? "Uh, Faith Gospel," he said.

Her frown deepened. "That's not that snake-handling church, is it?"

"Oh no, ma'am. Full gospel." That's what had

been on the sign. "If you don't mind, I'll get to work."

He found a wheelbarrow behind the house and started at the back and slowly hauled leaves and debris to a spot near the street. It gave him time to familiarize himself with the two houses and find a place where he could watch from later.

He was glad the ranger wasn't staying with her grandmother. Of the two, the grandmother's would be the harder to breach. While it had a privacy fence, it backed up to another two-story house, and if someone happened to be on the second floor looking out, they might see him enter through the back door. No, the Chamberlain house would be much easier to break into.

After he'd been working an hour, Mrs. Johnson brought out a glass of lemonade. "Thank you," he said and quickly drained it.

"I just appreciate what you're doing. Did you tell me your name? I'm so forgetful I can't remember."

"Sorry, I don't think I did. Doug Banks," he said, tipping his head.

"That's a nice solid name," she said. "Have you been going to that church long?"

He hoped she wouldn't ask a barrage of questions. "Just got in town a couple of weeks ago. Only been once."

"So, you're not from here?"

"No, International Paper transferred me to the Natchez plant." It had paid to research the area. "I'm looking forward to living here."

"Natchez is a lovely town," she said. "Have you found a house yet?"

"Not yet. I'd love to find something around here," he said, "but I don't see any houses for sale other than the one next door to you."

"I think that's the only place for sale in the neighborhood right now, but of course, several of us are getting on in years." She pointed to the house diagonally across from them. "Rose Beaumont has lived there ever since she married, but I expect her sister will move in with her one day. Her granddaughter, Ainsley, was staying with her."

He'd hit the mother lode on information. "And she's not now?"

"No."

Now was not the time for her to clam up. But how to ask without seeming to ask? "That house there," he said, pointing to the one straight across from them. "Who does it belong to?"

"Cora Chamberlain, Rose's sister I mentioned. She's in the hospital, but Ainsley is looking after the place." Mrs. Johnson frowned. "Who is that?" she murmured.

He looked to see what she was talking about. A Lexus had pulled into the Chamberlain drive.

When the driver got out, she chuckled. "Oh, that's J.R., Cora's nephew and Ainsley's dad. Cora told me they fight like hummingbirds. And that's Ainsley now with her friend," Mrs. Johnson said, pointing toward an SUV that pulled into the drive behind the Lexus.

Maddox quickly turned his back to the street and checked his watch. "Well, if I want to get finished here before dark, I better get back to work."

After thanking him again, Mrs. Johnson started toward her house, and halfway there, she turned around. He bit back a sigh.

"Seeing J.R. reminded me—be sure to register to vote. J.R. is running for governor, and he'll make a good one too," she said. "Tonight he's having a big barbecue shindig at his mansion downtown."

Maddox's stomach growled. He hadn't had a decent meal this week. Besides, he'd bet Ainsley Beaumont would be there, and it might be his golden opportunity. "Don't suppose you have the address? I might like to hear him speak."

"Oh, this one's for his biggest contributors and invitation only, but I'm sure he'll have one soon that'll be for everyone."

"Say he lives downtown?" When she frowned, he palmed his hand. "Just want to make sure I avoid the area he lives in—bound to be lots of traffic."

"Oh, there will be! His house is near the River-walk and overlooks the river."

"Good to know." With that information, getting to Ainsley Beaumont was easier than shelling peas.

41

It was nearly four when Linc pulled into Cora's drive behind a late model Lexus. A low groan escaped Ainsley's lips. "Dad's here," she said. "I wonder what he wants."

"I was going home to change and come back to pick you up for the fund-raiser, but if you'd like, I'll come in with you," Linc said.

Ainsley almost said yes but then shook her head. "No need to drag you into whatever it is."

If she didn't dread talking with her dad so much, she would've teased him at his relief. But Linc always liked her dad, and she was pretty sure he'd want to keep it that way.

"What time do you want me to pick you up?" he asked.

"The fund-raiser starts at six . . . I think I'll be fashionably late, so six or a little after is fine."

He grinned. "You do like to push his buttons."

"Not really. What I'd like is to stay home tonight with a book and get a good night's sleep. That way I'll be in better shape to face the church crowd tomorrow."

"So, you decided to go with Rose?"

She bit back a smile. "I don't want to disappoint Gran. Besides, there's not much I can do investigation-wise. My main witnesses are in the hospital, and it won't take long to check on them tomorrow afternoon. It'll be Monday before I can talk to anyone at the high school about the boys Colton told us about. And the park service isn't big on overtime pay unless I can justify it."

"I think I'd go straight to the coach," Linc said. "I've heard the principal is somewhat of a stickler—you know, goes strictly by the book."

"I won't be interrogating the boys, just having a conversation with them, which is perfectly legal." That said, some principals were easier to deal with than others. It wasn't like she wanted to browbeat the boys.

"I know." He cocked his head. "You know, if you showed the list to Drew's dad, Austin might know the boys and who their parents are and where they live."

"I must really be tired to not figure that out." She rubbed the back of her neck, wishing she had time for a massage.

"The curtain in the window looking out on the drive just moved," Linc said. "I assume your dad has seen us."

She steeled herself to face him. "Might as well get this over with. See you about six," she said and climbed out of the Tahoe.

"You sure—"

"I can handle this." She hoped. She opened the

back door and strode inside the house, giving her dad a curt nod when he came into the kitchen.

"You and Lincoln getting back together?"

"What Linc and I do is between us." She needed to nip this in the bud. "But no, we are not getting back together."

Even as she said the words, her heart sank at the thought. Had she actually begun to think she and Linc might have a second chance? "Why are you here?"

"I thought maybe you'd give me the diary you found in the safe."

The diary Linc just drove off with. "Why do you need it so badly?"

"We went over this at the hospital. I really need to know what's in it."

"It's not here right now." A horrible thought flashed in her mind. "Do you have the other diary Aunt Cora found?"

"What? No." Then he sighed. "We're fighting again. I wish I knew how to fix our relationship—I don't like butting heads with you all the time."

"It's a simple fix," she said. "Stop ordering me around." Then remembering how he'd campaigned against her singing career, she added, "And stop telling me what to do."

"I'm a parent. What else am I supposed to do?"

It would be funny if it weren't so sad that he didn't have a clue. "I'm not a child anymore that you can demand I do something and expect me to do it."

"You're not giving me the diary?"

"It's not mine to give. Ask Cora for it," she said. "I still don't understand why these diaries are so important to you."

"How many times do I have to tell you? It's all about the election and Kingston dragging our long-ago history into the campaign."

"Why not answer with the truth—that was a terrible time in our history, and yes, your great-great-grandfather Robert Chamberlain inherited slaves, but he freed them all?"

He laughed, but there was no mirth in his voice. "I can just hear my campaign manager's response."

"Dad, you have a reputation for fighting for minorities. Trust the voters to do the right thing."

"You're being naïve." But his voice had softened. He dipped his head toward her. "How do you know about my reputation?"

"I, uh . . ." What had made her say that? Ainsley wasn't even sure where it came from. "You have great cheerleaders in Gran and Cora."

"They are that." He checked his watch. "I'm running late. Look, in case you're worried, there will be enough security to keep you safe—the firm I've hired is even providing a helicopter to sweep the area. But do get Linc to drop you off at the front entrance." Just before closing the door, he looked over his shoulder. "And wear something dressy, but not too dressy."

"I planned on it." It wasn't an order, more like a suggestion. Was it possible there was a thaw in their cold war?

Ainsley had been trying to envision what to wear tonight that would accommodate the Kevlar vest and so far had come up with zilch. Maybe she could leave the vest off since security would be tight with not only his rent-a-cops but probably state police as well. Nope. Not happening.

The sketch! She grabbed her backpack and hurried after him, catching her dad before he got into his car.

"Wait!"

He turned around, and Ainsley fished one of Maddox's sketches from the backpack. "Would you make copies of this and distribute them to your security detail?"

He took the sketch. "Is this the man you think is after you?"

"I'm not sure, but it won't hurt for them to be on the lookout."

"I'll make sure they get this."

Ainsley watched as he backed out of the drive. Her dad seemed to be mellowing a bit. Was it possible they had turned the page on a new relationship?

42

The Tahoe had left with only the man in it, and before long the Lexus drove away. Could he risk breaking in now and taking care of Beaumont? The desire to get it over with and leave Natchez was tempting. All he had to do was slip in the back door, and after he made sure she knew who was killing her, do the job.

"Yoo-hoo, Mr. Banks!"

Maddox ground his teeth and then turned to see Mrs. Johnson making a beeline for him.

"I hate to impose, but could you change a lightbulb or two for me?"

He forced his jaw to relax. "Of course, Mrs. Johnson."

She pressed bills into his hand. "I know you don't want me to pay you, but I just have to give you something."

He glanced down at the two twenties and slipped them in his pocket. He'd spend five of it for something to eat. The rest would go into his gas tank. "Thank you, ma'am. I'll donate it to the church tomorrow."

Just as he laid his rake against the porch, a woman crossed the street carrying two bags, and he watched her walk up to the Chamberlain front door. Had to be Beaumont's grandmother.

Mrs. Johnson may have just saved him from a close call.

43

As soon as her dad left, Ainsley went through her clothes. The outfits she'd worn for dinner on the ship were too dressy for a barbecue, and the rest of her cruise wardrobe consisted of shorts and tank tops. Her phone rang. Gran. "Has something happened to Cora?"

"No, dear. She's much improved and the doctors are talking about moving her into a room on the surgery floor Monday," Gran said. "Have you dressed yet?"

Ainsley groaned into the phone. "No. I was just trying to pull something together."

"Good. I have something for you. I'll be there in a jiffy."

Gran was there by the time Ainsley unlocked the back door, and she was carrying a hanging bag from Soiree Boutique. Another bag dangled from her arm. "I saw this in the window and thought of you." She handed the garment bag to her.

Ainsley slipped the plastic off and caught her breath. A sleeveless black dress. Perfect.

"I figure you didn't bring any sandals either." Gran pulled out a pair of rose-gold sandals that went perfectly with the outfit. "You do still wear an 8?"

"Yes. I love these. Thank you." She kissed her grandmother on the cheek. "You are the best."

"Put them on so I can see how you look. I'll wait in the library."

Ainsley showered and quickly blew her hair dry. It would be too hot to wear it down so she pinned it up in a messy bun just off her neck. She took the time to put on a little mascara and lipstick and then took out the formfitting vest she'd bought specially to wear under clothes like the dress. Made like a tank top, it fit snugly against her body.

There would be all kinds of security at the house. Was it absolutely imperative that she wear it tonight? Especially since it would be hot and humid. What would she advise anyone else? With a sigh she slipped it on and zipped it. It would also be the first thing Linc asked about.

Ainsley slipped into the dress and stood in front of the floor-length mirror in the bedroom, checking the fit. The hem struck her just above the knees. She smoothed the fabric with her hands. Even with the vest, she actually had curves, and unless someone bumped into her, no one would know she had the vest on.

Earrings . . . She needed something besides the gold studs she usually wore to complete the outfit. Her spirits sank as she thought of the dangly gold earrings in her apartment in East Tennessee. They would have been perfect. The studs would have to do.

"Ta-da!" she said to her grandmother when she walked into the library.

"You look beautiful!" Gran pressed her hands together at her lips. "I have the perfect necklace and earrings. Follow me to the house."

Ainsley dutifully followed her across the street. The jewelry was a perfect complement to the outfit. Dangly rose-gold chains for her ears and a matching necklace. Gran checked her watch, then handed her a bottle of nude nail polish. "Those sandals cry out for polish on your toes, and maybe even your fingernails."

"Text Linc, and tell him where I am," she said, looking at her hands. They did need a dab of *something.* "I didn't tell you earlier, but you look snazzy." And Gran did in a geometric silver and black top with black slacks.

The curtsey Gran did was nearly perfect. "Thank you. I want to do my son proud."

"Would you like to ride with us?"

"No, ma'am. I'm sure I'll leave way before you do—probably before dark."

"Don't be too sure about that," Ainsley said with a grin. "But I understand you wanting your own wheels."

Gran handed her a towel to cover her clothes as Ainsley uncapped the polish. "Don't forget

Monday at nine you have an appointment with Mr. Blackwell."

Ainsley must have looked puzzled.

"Your trustee."

"Would you mind rescheduling it until I solve this case? There's no hurry anyway. The trust doesn't end for another year."

"Actually, he reminded me it ends six months prior to your birthday."

"What? Since when?"

"Since always, dear. Which you would know if you'd ever kept one of the appointments I made for you with him."

"You're right, but actually receiving the funds always seemed so far away. It's what, a hundred thousand?" she said. "That's a lot of money, but it's never been something I dwell on."

"I think it's more than that, although I'm not privy to the amount. Your father is, though, and you could ask him." Gran patted her arm. "But it'd be better if you kept the appointment with Mr. Blackwell. He'll give you all the details."

"I'll try." She had a crime to solve, and visiting the school was first on her list for Monday.

The polish was barely dry on her nails when Linc rang the doorbell. Her heart fluttered as he entered the den where she waited. Linc's biceps and pecs filled out the fitted short-sleeve shirt he wore over a pair of khakis. Then he stunned her with a low whistle. "I could do the same thing," she said, finding her voice. "You look good."

"And you look better." His husky voice raked her senses. "If you're ready."

He crooked his elbow, and she slid her arm through his, electricity sparking through her as they walked to the Tahoe. This wouldn't do. She could not let her defenses down—but her heart definitely had a mind of its own.

"I hope you have your vest on," he said, opening the passenger door.

"Of course I do." She held up the small clutch. "But I don't have my Sig."

"Want to get it?"

"No. Dad said there'd be a lot of rent-a-cops present, so I shouldn't need it." Ainsley looked up, and his hazel eyes captured hers. She never wanted to look away. Every ounce of resistance to Linc melted away as he brushed his knuckles along her jaw before gently cupping her chin.

She leaned into his touch, the gentleness in his fingers overwhelming her. Linc lowered his head, pausing briefly as if to make sure she wanted him to kiss her. She slipped her arms around his neck and brought his lips to hers, ignoring the voice in her head that whispered to stop.

His lips commanded hers, igniting a fire within her. When he released her, he kissed the tip of her nose.

"Wow," she whispered.

"Yeah." His arms wrapped around her as he drew her close and kissed her again.

She'd never felt this way before when he'd kissed her. Fireworks exploded in her head, and she returned his kiss with passion that had been locked away for fifteen years.

Slowly he released her. "Ainsley," he said, breaking the silence.

"Shh," she said, putting her fingers to his lips. "Don't think. Don't say anything."

He caught her fingers and kissed them, then released the clasp that held her messy bun in place. Her hair fell to her shoulders.

"I've been wanting to do that for two days," he murmured.

She laid her head on his chest, feeling the rapid rhythm of his heart. Hers matched his beat for beat. She refused to think about their past and that she shouldn't be standing here in his arms. It was time to just be in the moment. She'd worry about the consequences later.

44

It's getting late," Linc said, breaking the spell. He searched her face for regret, and his heart lifted when he saw none. "We better go."

"As much as I hate to agree, you're right," she murmured. "Why don't we skip out early?"

"Sounds like a winner to me." His heart was still beating ninety-to-nothing. Linc wasn't sure what the kiss meant, but it gave him hope that Ainsley was willing to rekindle their relationship.

A few minutes later, he turned into a roped-off cul-de-sac. J.R. had bought the house after Ainsley and Linc broke up, so this would be his first visit. He lowered the window as an attendant stopped the car.

"Oh, it's you, Ms. Beaumont." He waved them on.

"Know him?" Linc put the car in the drive.

She shook her head. "Dad probably circulated my photo—he's good with details most people don't think of."

Linc turned into the long drive that circled in front of a two-story white brick on the river bluffs. He could imagine the view as the sun sank over the Mississippi River each day, especially from the second-floor veranda. Not that there was anything wrong with the wraparound porch on the first floor.

Linc surveyed the cars lining the drive. "I didn't expect this many people," he said, unease crawling down his back. "You did give the security detail a photo of Maddox?"

"I gave it to Dad and he said he'd make sure they got it," she said. "And I didn't expect this many people either. After you drop me off, park where we can get out if we leave early."

When he stopped in front of the entrance, another attendant opened the passenger door for Ainsley and whisked her inside the house. Evidently J.R. had meant it when he said she'd be safe. Bluegrass music played from speakers at the edge of the house as he walked up the drive.

Ainsley met him on the porch. "Let's go around this way to the back."

He linked hands with her, and she didn't pull away. Something had changed, and if he got a second chance with her, he didn't plan to blow it this time.

"Uh-oh," he said softly.

Instantly her body tensed. "What?"

"Sarah. With her videographer, and she's coming this way."

"You didn't expect her?"

"I didn't think about it one way or the other, but I should have known she'd be reporting for her station." He released Ainsley's hand as Sarah flashed him a big smile.

"I didn't know you were coming," she said.

"I'm Ainsley's plus-one."

Her smile faltered and she turned to Ainsley. "I almost didn't recognize you out of uniform."

"I've heard that before," Ainsley replied.

He glanced sharply at Sarah as she swung her backpack off her shoulder and set it down. It wasn't like her to be snarky, but Ainsley hadn't seemed to notice.

Sarah glanced toward the house. "It's a beautiful place. Your dad said I could tour inside later, and I thought I would before the fireworks start."

"Good. He doesn't make that offer to everyone," Ainsley said.

"Any chance of getting you on camera?"

"As long as you keep your questions to his campaign." Ainsley smiled, but her voice was firm.

"No problem . . . that's what I'm here for. The station is giving equal time to your dad's opponents. I would like an interview later on another topic, like tomorrow? I understand you have an escaped prisoner after you."

Linc stiffened. "Where did you hear that?"

"Hugh Cortland, the FBI guy. He came by the station and left a couple of sketches. Asked us to run them on our six and ten p.m. news."

He'd briefly forgotten Hugh's plan to post

the sketch and Maddox's mug shot on the TV station.

"Yours will be my first clip. Oh, and by the way, this is Russ." Sarah nodded toward her videographer as she took a mic from the backpack and held it toward Ainsley. "Can you give me three reasons to vote for your dad? You can take a minute to think about what you want to say."

Even though Ainsley wore a game-on smile, Linc sensed the panic beneath it. "Why not let me go first," he said.

Sarah shot him a quizzical glance. "Oh. Well, sure," she said. "Same question."

Linc took a few seconds to compose his thoughts, then began. "J.R. Beaumont is one of the smartest men I've ever met," he said. "If he gives you his word, you can bank on it. He has great plans for Mississippi as the next governor. I'm certainly voting for him."

"Cut," Sarah said as Russ lowered his camera. "Very good."

"Yes, very good," Ainsley echoed.

"You ready now?" Sarah asked.

"I suppose." After a deep breath, she spoke into the mic Sarah had now turned toward her. "My father is J.R. Beaumont, and one thing I've learned over the years is that he cares for Mississippi. Not just the movers and shakers but those who don't have a voice as witnessed by his many pro bono cases. A vote for him will be a vote for all the people in our state."

"Cut," Sarah said. "Wow. Great plug."

"Very good!" Linc squeezed her hand. Ainsley had surprised even him. At least she did have some good thoughts toward her father.

Color flooded Ainsley's cheeks. "I only told the truth."

"I'm sure your dad will appreciate your words." Sarah slung her backpack onto her shoulder and nodded to Russ. "I'm off to interview more people."

"I hope she incorporates the music," Ainsley said as the duo disappeared around the house. She tapped her fingers on the side of her leg in time with the bluegrass song. "She has a crush on you, you know. I'm guessing you haven't talked to her yet."

"No, I haven't." His heart sank. He'd hoped it hadn't been that obvious. "I think it's a hold-over from way back. That, and I'm a link to her brother. She was really devastated by his death. I'm not quite sure how to discourage her. I mean, she was my best friend's sister, and that's the only way I've ever thought of her."

"She definitely doesn't think of you in terms of a brother."

He sighed. "I'll try to set her straight Wednesday."

"The picnic. Seems to me taking her on a

picnic is sending a mixed message," Ainsley said.

"Her father will be with us," he said. "I feel I should be there for them."

"Of course," she said softly. "I wish you didn't feel his death was your fault."

Linc wished he didn't either, but facts were facts, and if he hadn't hesitated on the mission, Blake wouldn't have lost his leg.

For the next hour they mingled with the crowd, and Ainsley thanked people for coming and asked them to vote for her dad.

"You're getting good at this," he said as they relaxed under a live oak near the bluff.

"My dad owes me big-time," she said, "and I'm only half joking."

He laughed with her, and she slipped her hand into his, her touch electrifying. Ainsley looked westward and stilled. Linc followed her gaze and stared mesmerized. Everything faded except for the sight of the yellow ball reflecting off the waters of the Mississippi before it dropped below the horizon amid a brilliant array of orange and golden streaks in the sky.

"That was about perfect," she said softly.

"It was," he agreed.

They sat in comfortable silence until she stood. "I guess I better mingle a little more, and then you want to leave?"

"You're not staying for the fireworks?

Shouldn't be much longer now that the sun has gone down."

"We'll see."

"Can I get you something from the buffet line?"

"Not right now. I think I just want to enjoy the music for a bit before I mingle," she said as a musician drew his bow across his fiddle.

He understood. Even his two left feet wanted to dance to the lively music as the band played "Uncle Pen."

"Look," Ainsley said, nodding toward the stage where two small girls clogged.

"They're good," he said. One of J.R.'s security people stood at the edge of the bandstand, scanning the crowd that seemed to have grown since Linc last checked. He'd identified several of J.R.'s security detail, all good men, which should have reassured him. "Big crowd."

"I didn't realize he'd invited this many of his donors," she said.

Linc wasn't sure that was a good thing, not with Maddox on the loose. Across the way, her dad worked the crowd, shaking hands and slapping a few men on the back. "Your dad seems to be having a good time."

"He's in his element," she said. "Although I haven't seen him kiss any babies yet, but the night's young."

J.R. looked their way and waved.

"I think he wants you to join him," Linc said.

"So I see. I saw Sarah talking to him, and he probably wants me to redo the clip. Be back in a minute."

A helicopter made a pass overhead, then swung toward the river as Ainsley struck out across the lawn. Halfway there, she turned and motioned for him to come too.

"Me?" he mouthed and touched his chest. She didn't have to nod twice, and he jogged toward her. Just before reaching her, he sensed someone watching him and glanced over his shoulder and up toward the back veranda.

A dark figure stood hunched over something. Linc's breath caught in his chest as he made out a rifle. Muscle memory had him reaching for a gun that wasn't there.

Time slowed to a standstill. Sound ceased except for the pounding of his heart in his ears. "Get down!"

His own voice sounded like a record slowed to half speed as the crack of a rifle echoed. Ainsley turned in slow motion, her gaze raising to the veranda, eyes widening just as Linc tackled her.

He covered her with his body as another report broke the silence, returning everything to normal time. Screams came from different directions.

"On the veranda!" he shouted to the security guard who raced to them.

Then he noticed Ainsley wasn't moving.

45

Ainsley's chest throbbed. A weight held her pinned to the ground.

"Are you all right?" Linc's anxious voice in her ear penetrated the fog in her head.

"Can't move," she whispered.

Suddenly the weight lifted as Linc shifted his body, and her memory flooded back. Gunfire, Linc tackling her, screams—everything muddled together in her head.

"Sorry," he said, helping her sit up. "Someone just took a shot at you. Are you okay?"

Her ribs ached. Her head felt as though it would explode. "Good question."

Ainsley felt her chest, her fingers finding a tear in her dress where the bullet sliced across her body. The vest had saved her life.

His jaw clenched. "I saw them, but—"

"Are you all right?" J.R. Beaumont's voice cut off Linc, and Linc moved out of the way as her father knelt beside her and rubbed her hand.

"I think so." She'd never heard him this concerned before. Multiple sirens drew near. "Was anyone else hurt?"

"I'm not sure, but no one around us was hit," he replied.

"Did they get the shooter?"

"No." Her father looked grim. "The security people are looking for him now, but they did find the rifle he used."

Ainsley looked past her dad as one of the security detail rushed up.

"Mr. Beaumont, we have another casualty."

"What? How bad?"

"Possible concussion. That reporter was inside the house when the shooter ran past her. He shoved her, and she hit her head on the door-jamb."

"Can she describe him?"

"Said she didn't get a good look at him."

Linc stepped forward. "I'll check on her."

"Thanks."

The side of Ainsley's head was sticky when she touched it. She must have hit the walkway when Linc tackled her. Her dad turned back to her and pressed his handkerchief against her forehead. "Somebody get me some ice," he called over his shoulder.

She struggled to stand, and her dad turned back to her. "Don't try to get up. An ambulance is on the way." One of the security guards handed him ice wrapped in a towel. "Let's see if this stops the bleeding," he said.

The ice felt good on her head, but it was hard to

fathom this was her dad taking care of her. He'd always been a Beaumonts-don't-show-pain type of guy.

"Do you have the diary?" he asked, keeping his voice low.

She gaped at him. Surely he hadn't just asked that question. One look at his face, and Ainsley knew he had. So much for the concern. "Someone's just shot at me, and you're worried about a diary?"

"No. You totally misunderstood . . . I just wondered if that's what the shooter was after. That's all."

"I don't believe you," she said through clenched jaws. "Did you hire someone to shoot at me? Is that diary that important to you?"

He jerked his head back like she'd slapped him. "Are you accusing me of . . ." He stared at her, his mouth trying to form words that didn't come out.

"Cora found two diaries and one is missing. Did you go to her house the night she fell? Maybe pushed her out of the way so you could take it?"

"Ainsley Beaumont! What in the world do you mean?" Gran said, kneeling beside her.

She had not heard her grandmother come up.

"She's not herself." Gran placed her hand on Ainsley's forehead. "She doesn't know what she's saying."

Ainsley rose up. "Gran, I don't have a fever, and I know exactly what I said."

Her father stood, towering over her. "I can't believe what you've just accused me of doing."

The hurt in his face took her aback. He turned and marched away. Ainsley used her hands to push herself to her feet. A wave of dizziness hit her. Maybe she shouldn't have stood. She stumbled to a nearby chair and collapsed in it.

"That probably wasn't your best move," Gran said, sitting beside her as she held the ice to Ainsley's head again.

"Me getting up or the thing with Dad?"

Her grandmother was slow with her answer. "Both."

"I just call it as I see it."

"Maybe you're not seeing clearly."

Wasn't she? The thought that her dad might have hired someone to shoot her turned her stomach. But why else had he been so insistent that she come? Were the diaries that important?

What if it wasn't the diaries but was something else altogether? Like the trust fund she would receive when she turned thirty-five? Her mouth dried.

She caught her grandmother's hand. "Who's the beneficiary of the trust if I die before I'm thirty-five?" she asked.

Color drained from her grandmother's face.

"Your father. But I can't believe you think . . . he would never harm you."

Maybe not, but Ainsley couldn't stop the tiny seed of doubt from exploding. "Did he know I was going to question Connie Hanover?"

"Of course not." Gran frowned. "I might have told him when he called yesterday afternoon. He asked how your investigation was coming . . . but that doesn't mean a thing."

Unfortunately, Ainsley had seen the worst in people, the greed that sometimes caused family members to . . .

She blocked the thought before Gran could see it in her face.

"I know what you're thinking, and you're wrong." Gran's broken voice cut Ainsley to the quick, and she raised her gaze. Her grandmother's pale-blue eyes were shiny with tears, and she looked every one of her eighty-five years.

"You're right," she said. "Dad would never do anything like that."

Gran sagged against the chair and squeezed her hand. "That's my Ainsley."

She wished she believed her own words, but there was the trust to consider, and his suggestion that someone shot her to get the diaries didn't make sense. How would getting her out of the way aid the person? Unless . . . it *was* her dad—Ainsley was the only person who stood in the way of him getting his hands on them.

No. Reason worked its way into her brain. She'd seen too many evil, sick people in her job. Her dad wasn't one of them. Genuine hurt had been in his face. She and her dad might not get along, but he wouldn't physically harm her. There had to be another explanation—it made much more sense that Troy Maddox was the one who shot at her.

In her peripheral vision, Linc carried Sarah across the lawn to the ambulance that had just arrived. She palmed her hand in their direction. "Do you know if Sarah Tolliver is okay?"

Gran looked toward the ambulance. "I think I heard someone say she might have a concussion."

She hoped Sarah would be all right. Ainsley would hate to be responsible for another person going to the hospital. Her heart quickened when Linc walked her way, bringing a paramedic with him. Kanesha again.

Linc knelt beside the chair. "How are you?"

"I feel like I've been hit by a Mack truck." She removed the towel with ice in it. "And that's just my head."

"Can't you and Cora stay out of trouble?" Kanesha asked, kneeling on her other side.

"Doesn't look like it," she said.

"Well, you know the drill. I need to examine you."

Linc stood. "I'll move out of the way."

311

"Wait," Ainsley said. "Is Sarah okay?"

"She has a headache," Linc said. "She's refused to be transported, says she's fine."

"You think she needs to go to the hospital?"

He shrugged. "Hard to tell, but I don't think she's badly hurt."

That relieved her. "Did she see the attacker?"

"Briefly before he shoved her into the wall. She said he could be the person in the sketch, but she couldn't be sure."

As Kanesha wrapped a blood pressure cuff around Ainsley's arm, she muttered, "I'm not going to the hospital."

The medic chuckled. "Why does that not surprise me. Looks like that vest saved your life, but it could've bruised a rib or two."

"My ribs aren't sore except where Linc tackled me." She traced her finger along the rip in the vest where the bullet had traveled across her chest. "If I hadn't turned, it'd be a different story. Not sure this vest would've taken a frontal attack." But it had changed the trajectory of the bullet enough that she hadn't been wounded.

She turned back to Linc. "Did you see the shooter?"

"Barely. Just long enough to know someone presented a danger to you."

Before she could respond, Kanesha held up her hand. "I need you to hush so I can get your blood pressure."

Ainsley forced herself to relax. If it was high, she might push harder for her to go to the hospital, and like Sarah, Ainsley didn't intend to.

"A little high, but not bad," she said and removed the cuff. "Pulse is a little high too. Let me look at the gash in your scalp."

She managed to yelp only once when she felt around on her skull.

"Looks like you hit your head on a patio stone. I think Steri-Strips will take care of the wound, but I need to trim a little of your hair," she said.

When she agreed, Kanesha sprayed something on her skin that numbed the gash. She heard the scissors snipping rather than felt them. Probably have a permanent part there now. The feeling started coming back after she cleaned the wound, and the strips stung as she applied them.

"That should do it, unless you'll let me transport you to Merit."

She very carefully shook her head. "I'm good."

Kanesha laughed and elbowed Linc. "We raise some tough women in Natchez."

Ainsley didn't know how tough she was, just that she had better things to do than spend half the night in the ER.

"I'd like to talk to Sarah before she leaves," she said, then turned to Kanesha. "But would you first check out Gran, make sure all this excitement hasn't raised her blood pressure?"

"You sure you're ready to walk to the ambulance?"

"We'll see." She stood and steadied herself until her head stopped swimming, then took tentative steps. So far, so good. Her strength returned by the time she reached Sarah. An angry-looking bruise covered half the reporter's forehead.

"I'm so sorry," Sarah said, staring at Ainsley. "If I had just seen him earlier, I—"

"I'm sorry you got caught up in this," she said. "Linc said the man might fit the sketch you saw earlier."

"It was hard to tell. He had on some kind of goggles and a floppy black hat and a black plastic poncho."

"Could you tell how tall he was?"

"No. It happened so fast . . . the last thing I expected was a man to barrel into me."

"What were you doing up there?" Linc asked.

"I was touring the house, and when I got to the second floor, I, uh, needed to use the restroom. When I came out of the bathroom, he was just there. I think I surprised him as much as he surprised me."

Ainsley squeezed Sarah's hand. "If I can help you in any way, let me know."

"How about that interview?" she asked with a wicked gleam in her eyes.

The reporter never gave up. "I'm sorry, but the only thing I'd have to say is 'No comment.' "

Sarah huffed, then lifted her gaze to Linc. "My equipment is still on the second floor. Would you mind getting my backpack for me?"

While they waited for Linc to retrieve Sarah's belongings, the reporter tried again to lock Ainsley into an interview. And again, she refused. Ainsley froze as her dad approached the ambulance. He must not have seen her, because when their gazes met, he faltered, then recovered.

"I hope you're better," he said, his voice flat.

She nodded and he turned to Sarah, taking her hand. "I'm so sorry this happened. Please get checked out at the hospital. I'll cover the cost."

Ainsley backed away from the ambulance. The seed of doubt sprouted in her mind again. What if he had tried to get rid of her? The question was, did she want to mention her suspicions to Pete Nelson, who was walking toward her?

"You okay?" Pete asked when they met. The resignation in his face and slumped shoulders indicated he was taking today's crimes personally.

"Headache, but it could have been worse." Much worse. Like Drew Kingston. "How is Drew?"

His lips pressed together briefly in a thin line before he answered. "The doctors are keeping him sedated to allow his body time to heal."

"Prognosis?"

He rested his hand on his gun. "Barring complications, he should recover, but it'll be a few days before I can interview him," he said. "Think back over your phone conversation with him this morning. Is there anything new surfacing from your memory?"

If only she'd had the presence of mind to record the call, but she remembered it almost word for word. "No. Wish there was something new."

"He was there last night to see Hannah's mother. Do you know why?"

"Drew didn't get that far. He'd just told us he saw who shot Connie Hanover when his assailant shot him."

Ainsley twisted the wet cloth she still held. Hannah, Connie Hanover, Drew Kingston, now Sarah. How many more people were going to be hurt because she hadn't caught the person responsible? Maybe her supervisor needed to call in someone who was more capable.

46

Linc grabbed Sarah's backpack from the floor near the bedroom door on the second floor of the house. He looked around for a purse but didn't see one. Maybe like Ainsley, the reporter used the backpack for one. He walked out on the veranda, where a deputy was snapping photos of a black AR-15 type rifle. When he looked up, Linc nodded.

"Don't suppose there were any prints," he said.

"Afraid not." The crime scene tech snapped from another angle. "I googled this model. It's only been around a couple of years. Folds up enough to fit in something as small as that backpack you're holding."

Linc glanced down. "You're kidding."

"Afraid not. These foldable models are going to make police work a whole lot harder, especially for those trying to stop terrorists."

"Think you'll be able to trace it?"

"If it could be traced to the shooter, he wouldn't have left it behind. Probably got it off the dark web."

Linc agreed. But to leave a gun like this behind meant the assailant didn't care what it cost to take Ainsley out. "You said you googled it—what does a gun like this cost?"

"Stripped down like this one? Twelve, fifteen hundred."

That was a lot to leave behind. He and Ainsley needed to explore other people who might have it in for her, people who had access to the dark web and had that kind of money. Linc slung Sarah's backpack onto his shoulder and left the deputy to his picture-taking.

He crossed the lawn to the ambulance, where J.R. was talking to Sarah. "If you need anything at all," J.R. was saying, "just let me know."

"I'm fine, really, Mr. Beaumont."

"Call me J.R.," he said, and then turned to Linc. "I don't think I've properly thanked you for what you did."

"I didn't do anything," Linc said.

"You saved Ainsley's life. If you hadn't assessed the situation and acted so quickly, the outcome might have been a lot different."

Linc started to shake his head, and Sarah put her hand on his arm, stopping him. "Just accept the man's thanks," she said. "You're a hero."

He definitely was no hero, but for the sake of ending this conversation, he dipped his head. "I'm glad Ainsley wasn't hurt any worse than she was."

J.R. nodded to Sarah, then turned and shook Linc's hand. "I have a few other guests I need to reassure, but thanks again." He turned and walked away, avoiding the stage, where Ainsley and Pete were in a deep conversation.

"You want me to take that off your hands?"

Sarah's voice startled him, and he realized he still had her backpack on his shoulder. "Not necessary. You want me to take it to your car?" he asked.

"Would you mind? And thanks for getting it. I don't think I could've climbed those stairs."

"Maybe we should drop you off at your house on our way home," he said.

"No. I'm good to drive," she said. "Wouldn't want to horn in on your date." Her voice held a tremor.

"If you're sure . . ."

She glanced toward Ainsley. "I'm sure. Are we still on for Wednesday?"

"Of course," he said. "I'll bring the food."

"No. I'll take care of the food," she said. "It'll be a chance for me to show you how well I can cook."

He grinned at her. "You don't cook for a picnic—just throw sandwiches together."

"Spoken like a man. Now I know I'll take care of the food," she said, returning his grin with a megawatt smile that reached her eyes.

His chest tightened as vulnerability and something he couldn't put his finger on replaced the haunted look in her face. He'd meant to be careful with his words around her so she wouldn't get the wrong idea. Linc wasn't sure how to fix it. "I'm looking forward to spending the time with you and your dad."

"We're looking forward to it too. If you'll help me down, I'm ready to leave."

"You sure you feel up to driving?" Linc asked.

"I'm good. Dad always said I had a hard head."

He laughed. "You're not driving to Jackson tonight, are you?"

"No. I'm still staying with him here in Natchez." Sarah took the arm Linc offered and climbed off the back of the ambulance. "My car is parked out front," she said.

He guided her around the house to the circle drive and spotted the green MINI Cooper.

"Thanks again." She took the backpack and stashed it in the back seat.

"It was nothing. See you Wednesday." He tried to make his tone light, and from the disappointment in her face, he had.

"Yeah, see you Wednesday. About eleven?"

He gave her a thumbs-up. A few minutes later he rounded the corner of the house. Someone had turned on floodlights, and Linc shaded his eyes as he searched for Ainsley. She was still talking to Pete near the stage, and both looked up when he approached.

"Did Rose check out okay?" he asked when he didn't see her grandmother.

"Yes, but she was tired, and Kanesha suggested that she go home."

"And she actually complied?"

"Tried to get me to go with her, but I wasn't finished here." Ainsley looked totally exhausted.

"How about you?" he asked. "Are you ready to leave now?"

"I might as well since I've gotten about all the information out of Pete I'm going to get."

"I'll email you a full report in the morning," the chief replied and turned to Linc. "Before you go—the security officers gave me their version of what happened. I'd like to hear yours."

Linc wanted to do anything other than relive the moments seared into his brain. If he'd just . . . He focused on collecting his thoughts. "We were listening to the music, and J.R. waved Ainsley over. About halfway across the lawn, she motioned for me to come too. I was jogging to meet her when I got a feeling I get sometimes— you know, like when your neck tingles. I don't know where it came from, just that something seemed off. I looked up toward the veranda. That's when I saw the shooter."

He clenched his hands as the thoughts he'd held at bay flooded his mind. If he'd had a gun, he could've taken the shooter out. This had to end. Tonight. No more being held a prisoner to his fear. No more being vulnerable to attack.

Ainsley could have died tonight, and if he'd

been the man he should be, he could have prevented the attack. Even as he vowed to change, the thought of holding a gun soured his stomach.

"Can you describe the shooter?" Pete asked.

The image of someone draped in black surfaced. "The sun had gone down, but it wasn't dark yet. Couldn't tell his size because of what he wore. Looked like some kind of poncho with a hood."

He glanced up at the second floor. "He was hunched over the rifle, right next to a big grill in the middle of the veranda, kind of blending with it. If I hadn't been looking for something out of place, I doubt I would've noticed him."

Pete looked up from his pad. "Sarah indicated he wore goggles."

"I couldn't see his face for the hood."

"How about the rifle?"

When had he seen the rifle? "Everything was happening split-second and came together at one time. I don't remember much about the gun, just the flash from the muzzle. I must have already thrown myself at Ainsley."

She squeezed his hand. "You know, you ought to try out for the Saints."

He stared at her. "Don't joke about this."

"It's that or cry," she said, rubbing her arms.

"If I'd had a gun—"

"Don't do that to yourself," she said softly.

He managed a tiny smile, then looked at Pete.

"If that's all, I'd like to get Ainsley home, where she can rest. And I'd appreciate it if you'd have one of your officers follow us home. One of the deputies followed us here, but once we arrived, he returned to his county duties."

"Sure." He spoke into his mic, requesting an escort. "He'll meet you out front. Wish I could provide round-the-clock surveillance, but we're always shorthanded. I'll have my patrol officers drive by at least once an hour though."

They both nodded their appreciation, then Linc helped Ainsley to stand. "Want to say good night to your dad?"

"No."

"You sure?"

"Yes."

Something was going on. He just didn't know what. "Anything happen I don't know about?"

"It's nothing I want to talk about right now." Her tone brooked no argument.

"Yes, ma'am."

Pete's officer fell in behind them as soon as they pulled away from the drive. Ainsley was quiet as they drove the short distance to Cora's house, but it wasn't a peaceful quiet. Linc glanced down, and her hands were fisted in her lap, her body rigid. He turned into her aunt's drive and gave a thumbs-up to the officer before pulling to the back of the house. Neither of them made a move to get out of the Tahoe. "It's evident something's wrong. Sure you don't want to talk about it?"

She leaned her head against the headrest and closed her eyes. He waited. Minutes slipped by before she opened them and looked at him.

"What if my father is trying to kill me?"

"What?" He couldn't have heard her right.

"What if it was my dad who knocked Cora down when he came looking for the diaries? You know how badly he wants them. What if he hired someone to take me out?"

He stared at her, the unthinkable taking root. As an FBI agent, he'd seen how depraved people could be. But J.R. Beaumont? The man was running for governor. "It's hard to believe—"

"I knew you'd take his side."

"I'm not taking his side, but you have to give me more than the diaries as a reason."

She crossed her arms. "I just found out today that I have a trust worth quite a bit of money. If something happens to me before I turn thirty-five, it all goes to him." She turned to him. "I turn thirty-five my next birthday."

He tried to remember the articles he'd read about J.R. If there was a hint that he had financial troubles, his opponent would have splashed it all over the news. "Why would your dad need your money?"

"Who knows—maybe he's lost it all. He's the only person who stands to gain from the trust if I die."

"Listen to yourself, Ainsley. This is your dad you're talking about."

"Don't you think this is tearing me apart?"

"I'm sure it is," he said softly. He needed to be careful with his words. "Let's go in and look at this rationally."

"I think we better end this right here. That way we can keep it *rational,*" she said, making air quotes.

He'd used the wrong words.

47

Rational. Ainsley hopped out of the Tahoe and hurried to the back door before Linc could get out. He didn't believe her.

She'd thought voicing the words running through her mind would dispel her anxiety, that maybe Linc would help her understand, but all he wanted to do was convince her she was wrong. Nothing had changed in fifteen years.

And now she might just throw up.

Ainsley fumbled in her pocket for her key, remembering too late that it was in her purse. In his SUV.

"Looking for this?" He held out her clutch.

His deep baritone sent a tremor through her heart. No matter how hard she fought it, she was drawn to him. Ainsley took the purse and fished her key out while Linc waited.

"May I come in?" he asked when she pushed the door open.

"Linc . . ." she started.

"I'm not leaving you alone. Have you forgotten Maddox is still on the loose? Either I come in, or I'll spend the night in the Tahoe."

She leaned against the door. "Probably a good idea for you to come in."

Ainsley pushed the door open, and Linc followed her inside. Had she totally lost it? Why had she gotten so caught up in trying to prove to herself her dad's guilt when Maddox had more reason to kill her than anyone? She reset the alarm, then joined him in the library.

"I want to apologize."

Ainsley turned around and stared. She'd been ready for anything but an apology. And she should be apologizing to him . . . and her father. "For?"

He propped himself against Cora's desk. "I didn't mean to make it sound like I was dismissing your suspicions. I just want you to keep an open mind."

"No, you're right. I'm not thinking clearly."

Surprise showed on his face. "Then how about we examine the situation?"

"Okay."

"I've been thinking . . . you believe your father stole the diaries, and I'm not so sure."

She really didn't think her father was trying to kill her, but she wasn't so sure about the diaries. "I—"

"Hear me out. First, if your dad had asked Cora for the diaries, would she have given them to him?"

"I don't think my aunt would have given them to anyone."

"I agree. Suppose he came over and asked her for them Thursday night, and she refused. Can you really see him shoving her down and then leaving her on the floor to maybe die?"

Would he? It was really hard to believe her dad would ever leave Cora unconscious and injured.

Why did she think he was the type who would hire someone to kill her? She pressed her fingers tightly against her temples as though the pressure would clear her muddy thoughts. She paced in front of the fireplace.

"Maybe his ambition to be governor changed his core personality." When he started to object, she stopped pacing and held up her hand. "I need to follow this thought to a logical conclusion. Let's look at this a different way."

"What do you mean?" he asked.

"It's easier to see the motivation behind a crime when you don't know the people involved, like we do in this instance. Can you pretend you have no connection to anyone in this case?"

"I think I can do that. Can you?" A tiny grin quirked his lips.

"Of course I can." Heat crept into her cheeks as she remembered those lips on hers. Ainsley forced her thoughts back to the topic. "Let me lay out the motive, means, and opportunity of my case. My father has two motives—the diary and my trust. He definitely has the means to hire someone since he is, after all, a criminal defense lawyer. The political rally created an opportunity."

When he didn't object, she said, "Let's start with the trust—"

"Totally circumstantial. If he wanted your trust money, he wouldn't wait until the year before you receive the trust to kill you. He especially wouldn't want to draw that kind of attention when he's running for office." He tilted his head to one side. "What about Maddox?"

Ainsley sank onto the sofa and pressed her hand to her mouth as she tried to still her whirling thoughts. It made much more sense that her assailant was the escaped convict.

So why couldn't she get rid of this niggling thought about her dad? "Okay, let's say Maddox shot at me tonight. That still leaves whoever broke in here Thursday night."

"And you think it's your dad," he said. "Tell you what. There's one way to ease your mind about that."

She stared at him. "Go on."

"You think he wants that diary, so what if we set up a situation for him to get it?"

"What do you mean? How?"

"Why don't you call him tomorrow, and while you're talking to him, casually mention you're moving the diary to a lockbox Monday morning."

Ainsley's muscles tensed. She saw through what Linc was trying to do. He didn't think her father would show up to steal the diary. Could she pull it off? Of course she could. She'd worked more than one undercover operation that required her to snow the suspect. "Where is the diary?"

"In the Tahoe," he said. "Locked in the console. I meant to put it in the safe when I came to pick you up, but you were at Rose's . . . and once I saw you, everything else left my mind. Be back in a sec."

As hot as her face was, she was glad he'd left the room. What she wasn't glad about was the way her attitude toward Linc was softening. But his plan made sense.

If her father was guilty, he would be here tomorrow night to get the diary, and if he was innocent . . . she could apologize for real, but she didn't think she'd be doing that.

48

Ainsley closed the safe and twirled the knob. Since her father knew the combination, she would remove the diary in the morning and take it with her.

Linc took her hand. "Are we good now?"

This was where she should tell him they didn't have a future. That as soon as this case was over, she would be heading back to East Tennessee. But when she looked into his eyes, she couldn't bring herself to say the words. "We're good."

Linc brushed a strand of hair out of her eyes that had escaped the band she'd used to put her hair in a ponytail while the medics dressed the wound. He pulled the band off, allowing her hair to fall around her shoulders.

"You never wear your hair down," he said, winding a strand around his finger.

If she didn't shut this down, she'd be in his arms again. "It's usually too hot in Natchez," she said, taking a step back.

Disappointment glinted in his eyes. "The style becomes you," he said softly. Then he sighed. "You're tired and need to get some rest. I'll bunk down in the extra bedroom again."

Tension eased from her shoulders, and she smiled. What was that Scripture verse? Something about two being better than one . . .

"What are you smiling about?"

"A verse Gran always said . . . two are better than one so if one fell down the other could help him up . . . I can't remember it exactly."

"Two are better than one, because they have a good return for their labor," he recited. "If either of them falls down, one can help the other up. But pity anyone who falls and has no one to help them up."

"That's it," she said. "You read your Bible much?"

"Most days . . . lately on my phone, though." He stroked her cheek with his thumb as desire lit his eyes. He took a step back. "With that, I'm saying good night."

She listened as his footsteps echoed on the stairs leading to the second floor. Linc had a peace she didn't. Was it God? And reading the Bible?

Ainsley picked up Cora's Bible on her desk and took it to the recliner. She wouldn't even know where to begin. She thumbed through it, stopping where the ribbon bookmarked a page. It was probably the last passage Cora had read.

Her aunt had underlined verses in the fourteenth chapter of John, and she read it. Could she really have the peace it promised? She read it again, the words soothing her mind. When had she stopped believing God would help her? With a sigh, she closed the Bible and returned it to the desk. Linc said he read his on his phone. Maybe tomorrow she would download an app.

After sleeping fitfully, Ainsley dragged herself out of bed at eight o'clock. She'd heard Linc's footsteps on the stairs and had purposely not gotten up. But now, the tantalizing aroma of coffee beckoned her. Cinching a robe at her waist, Ainsley trod the ancient oak floors to the kitchen that was miraculously empty except for bright sunlight.

A mug sat beside the pot of coffee along with her favorite hazelnut creamer. Seconds later, she lifted a cup of the strong brew to her lips. "Thank you, Lincoln Steele," she murmured.

"You're welcome."

Ainsley jumped, almost spilling the hot liquid. "I thought you'd left," she sputtered.

"I'm sorry. I didn't mean to startle you. Are you sore?"

"From the top of my head down."

"I was afraid of that." He filled his cup. "How does your day look?"

"Church with Gran, then lunch at her house—probably should be called Sunday dinner since she has pot roast and all the fixings—then visit Cora."

"You have a perfect excuse for missing church. Someone just tried to shoot you."

Ainsley had thought about it, but except for the singing part of the service she looked forward to going. "I'm not going to be held prisoner." She gave him a wry smile. "And I doubt he thinks I'll go out in public so soon." If he knew much about her, he wouldn't expect her to go to church. She hadn't been since she walked away from her singing career.

Her phone chimed with a text. "It's Pete Nelson, letting me know there's a police officer parked outside on the street, and he would take me to and from church if I want to go."

"Good. I texted him I had to go to Melrose today."

She wasn't used to someone looking out for her. "Thanks." Ainsley responded to Pete with a thank-you as well, then refilled her cup and held it up as she walked toward the door. "And thanks for the coffee too."

"You're welcome. See you at five, and we'll call your dad unless you want to call him before then," he said. "And don't forget to eat something!"

She grabbed a breakfast bar and hurried to her room. Maybe eating would help her with the tinge of anxiety she had about attending the only church she'd ever gone to. She'd even sung in the choir. How many would remember she'd wanted to make singing her career?

She wouldn't let what others thought of her

keep her captive either. Ainsley flipped on the shower while she finished her coffee. Even though she'd showered last night, she needed the hot water on her muscles. When she stepped into the glass enclosure, she adjusted the shower-head to massage and let the jets pound her sore body, glad Cora hadn't stuck with keeping her renovations to the antebellum time period.

A jumble of thoughts ran through her mind before settling on one. Maddox. Had he somehow slipped through the safeguards? The man was wily, and even though the chief had assured her the security people her dad hired were top-notch, he could have breached the property. The man had escaped prison after all.

49

The music was just starting when Linc slipped inside the small church and searched for Ainsley. He'd unexpectedly gotten the day off when a water main ruptured at Melrose and tours were canceled. His gaze landed on her long raven ponytail where she stood four rows from the front. No surprise there since that was the same pew where her grandmother and aunt sat every Sunday.

He didn't like being late but was glad to be here, even dressed in his NPS uniform. Going home to change after unexpectedly getting the day off would have taken too much time, and he couldn't wait to surprise her. At least everyone was standing so it wasn't so hard to slip in unnoticed.

Ainsley's eyes rounded when he stepped beside her. "I thought—"

"I'll explain later." He looked past her and nodded to Rose before joining in on the last stanza, expecting to hear Ainsley's velvety smooth voice rise above those singing around them. He leaned in closer, then glanced at her lips, which were moving though no sound was coming from her. She was only mouthing the words?

The song ended, and the congregation sat down as the pianist launched into one of Ainsley's favorites, "In the Garden," but once again, she didn't sing. The song ended and the worship leader who had been at the church since Linc was in high school took center spot. But instead of starting another song, he said, "I see one of our former soloists is back with us today. I'm hoping I can persuade Ms. Ainsley Beaumont to grace us with a song."

The congregation clapped, but beside him, Ainsley froze, the color draining from her face. Linc leaned over to encourage her and caught Rose's plea in her eyes for him to do something. Ainsley looked as though she might pass out any second.

Once again, the worship leader prompted her, and she shook her head. Unable to bear seeing her in such distress, Linc stood. "It's been a tough week for Ainsley. You all know Miss Cora is in the hospital," he said. "Maybe next time."

The man finally got it and motioned to the pianist, who broke into "His Eye Is on the Sparrow." Linc sat down, and she slipped her hand into his as the solo began.

"Thank you," she whispered.

The song had been Ainsley's favorite, and the longing in her face as she listened broke his heart. By the time the song ended, Ainsley's lips were moving silently in sync with the music.

He barely heard the pastor's sermon, thinking instead about the fear on Ainsley's face. Something terrible had happened to her the year she was on the road, something she'd never told him.

And it was no wonder. Their last time together, they'd argued, and he'd yelled at her, told her she was making a terrible mistake, that she had to make a choice. She did, and it hadn't been him. She probably thought he was just waiting to say *"I told you so."* Three years ago, he might have. But not now.

When they stood to sing the benediction, Ainsley slipped past him and hurried toward the door. Rose motioned for Linc to go after her.

He nodded and quickly walked to the back of the church. The officer he'd seen when he first arrived was already out the door, escorting her to his patrol car. "Ainsley," he said just loud enough for them to hear. They both turned, and he said, "Okay if I take you home?"

She hesitated, then said something to the officer before she turned to him and nodded.

"My SUV is right over here," he said when he reached her. "You have your vest on, right?"

"Yep." She tapped her chest. "Brand-new one. Bought it before I left East Tennessee."

Even so, he put his body between her and the road and guided her to his Tahoe. "Rose's house?"

"I guess, although I don't think I can eat. I'd rather go to the hospital and check on Cora and Drew and then stop by Connie Hanover's room and talk to her."

"I think your grandmother is expecting you at her house," he said as she climbed in the passenger seat.

"I know."

The defeat in her voice pierced him. He shut her door and walked to the driver's side and slid across the seat. "You want to talk about what happened in there?"

"No."

O-kay. Without another word, he started the SUV and drove to Rose's with the patrol car following them. "Good service," he said.

"I suppose. Are you going to eat with us?"

"Hadn't planned on it, but if that's an invitation, I accept."

That got a tiny smile from her. "Gran will expect you to stay. Along with Shawn."

"Shawn?"

"The police officer."

He hadn't known his name, and Ainsley was right—Rose would want the officer to come in and eat. The faint aroma of cinnamon and baked apples greeted them when they entered through the back door to the kitchen. "Something smells good," he said.

"Gran made an apple pie." Her phone dinged, and she fished it out of her purse. "She will be fifteen minutes late," Ainsley said, looking up.

Linc suspected she was giving them time to talk. "Feel like talking about what happened back at church now?"

"No." She turned and stared out the window. After a minute, she released a breath. "If I'd had any idea anyone would ask me to sing, I would've stayed home."

"Is there something wrong with your voice?" he asked.

"Other than I can't sing? No."

He tried again. "You've always had a beautiful voice. What happened?"

"I don't know," she said. "The doctors don't know." She grabbed a napkin from the table and blotted her eyes. "You really want to hear this?"

"I do."

Ainsley got a glass of water from the tap and took a sip. "It was supposed to be my big break," she said, her back to him. "I'd worked my way up to singing duets with the lead singer, and they were going to let me do a solo near the end of the show. Halfway through the song, my voice cracked and then no sound came out of my mouth."

He'd expected anything but this. "I'm sorry."

She hugged her arms to her waist and continued like she hadn't heard him. "I rested my voice for a month and then another month, but it didn't help. That's when my agent cut me loose." She turned to him with tears in her eyes again. "And now you know the whole truth. You and Dad were right. I didn't have what it takes to be a singer."

Ainsley looked so miserable he wanted to take her in his arms. Instead, he said, "How do you know after all this time your voice will fail you?"

"Don't you think I've tried? Not as much as I did early on, but it doesn't make any difference—my voice still cracks. I can't hold a note."

He didn't know what to say. "I'm so sorry."

"It's not that I want to sing professionally again. I'd just like to sing, like today at church."

He never expected to see Ainsley broken like this. And some of it was his fault. "I had no right to tell you what to do," he said softly. "I was being selfish."

Ainsley raised her gaze, a question in her eyes. "I don't understand."

"I knew what a good voice you had, and that you had the potential to be a big star. And that scared me." *Tell her you still love her.* His heart hammered his ribs. The words stuck in his throat. Intuitively he knew she wasn't ready to hear them.

50

Ainsley stared at Linc, not sure she'd understood him. "You believed in me? But I thought you discouraged me because you didn't think I was good enough."

"That absolutely was not the reason I discouraged you. When you quit singing, the world lost a beautiful voice. I had no idea there was anything wrong with it."

He thought her voice was beautiful? The words washed over her like a balm. But even though his voice had the ring of truth in it, she still had questions. "Why didn't you call me when you learned I wasn't on the road any longer?"

Regret filled his eyes. "You'd been around famous people. All that glitz and glamor. I thought once you had that taste of fame, you'd never be happy with someone like me." He took her hand. "I think you should see a specialist. Maybe there's something that can be done, something that wasn't available eleven or twelve years ago."

See another doctor? The round of specialists she'd seen when she lost her voice had resulted in one disappointment after another. And even if she regained her voice, she wouldn't want to resume her career. Being on the road had been harder than anything she'd ever faced. She was older now and didn't have the fire in the belly to pursue such a demanding dream. Especially since it wasn't her dream any longer.

"If you could do anything in the world," he asked, "what would it be?"

"What I'm doing," she said without hesitation.

"Why?"

Ainsley had never thought about why she enjoyed her work so much. "When I returned to college after leaving the group, I took a criminal justice course. That one course hooked me," she said.

Linc tilted his head toward her. "I've been meaning to ask how you ended up as a ranger."

"That's an easy question—I had a roommate whose brother was a seasonal ranger, and he kind of opened the door for me." A car pulled into the drive. "I think I hear Gran."

When her grandmother entered the kitchen, she took one look at them and said, "Am I interrupting something? Like maybe a proposal?"

"Gran!" Ainsley's face felt as red as Linc's had turned.

"You both looked so serious," she said, setting her Bible on the counter beside her purse.

"It wasn't like that," Linc said, "but if anything

of that nature ever happens, you'll be the first person we tell."

"Good." Gran surveyed the kitchen. "I'm hungry. Let's get dinner on the table. Somebody tell that officer to join us."

An hour later, Ainsley put her fork down and stretched. "I don't want to get used to eating like this," she said. Shawn had said much the same thing before he returned to his patrol car.

"You could use a few pounds," Gran replied.

She grinned for an answer. "You want to take a nap before we go to the hospital?"

"Nope. Visiting time is in twenty minutes. Let's load the dishwasher and go." She turned to Linc. "You coming?"

"Can you wait until I change clothes? I have jeans and a shirt at Cora's."

After he hustled out the back door, Gran turned to her. "I'm sorry about church. I didn't think about Brother Reece asking you to sing."

"No problem," she said lightly.

"But I think it is a problem. One you need to resolve." Gran tilted her head. "Do you wish you were back on the road again, singing backup and occasionally a solo?"

"Not that it's a possibility, but no. I like what I'm doing."

Gran patted her arm. "I always prayed for God to put his desires in your heart. And if it was that singing career that you worked so hard for, then doors would open. And if that wasn't what he wanted for you, that your desires would change." Gran squeezed her hand. "I think I have my answer."

Could it be possible that God really did care for her? Care about what she wanted? Ainsley wished she could believe God wasn't out there just waiting for her to mess up so he could squish her with his thumb. Like her dad.

Can't you do anything right? That is so stupid. What were you thinking? All her growing-up years, he'd pronounced those words over her. "It's kind of hard to see God when the only example I have of a father is Dad. We've butted heads ever since I can remember. Nothing I've ever done has been good enough or the right decision."

"I'm afraid he got that from his daddy— James said the same words to J.R. I told my son when you were first born to break that generational curse. But I guess it was too ingrained." Gran's eyes had a sheen to them. "Honey, I wish . . . James was my husband and J.R. is my son, but sometimes I just wanted to shake them both."

A picture of Gran shaking Dad like a rag doll made Ainsley smile. "Why doesn't he love me?"

The older woman snatched up a napkin and blotted her eyes. "He does, but he's afraid of losing you. It started after he lost your mom."

She stared at her grandmother. Ainsley had so few memories of her mother.

"You're the spittin' image of her. I think that's what makes it so hard for your dad. He loved her something fierce. She was thirty when you were born and had waited a long time for you. Thirty-four when that drunk driver killed her."

Thirty-four. Same age Ainsley was now.

"Your dad has made a lot of mistakes where you're concerned, but not loving you isn't one of them. He would never knowingly hurt you."

If only she could believe that.

"You two ready?" Linc asked from the doorway.

"That was fast," Gran said.

"I didn't want to keep you waiting," he said. "And with Maddox still on the loose, when we go to the hospital, I think it's a good idea for Rose to go in her own car. Shawn will follow us."

Ainsley agreed, but her thoughts were still on Gran's words. Down deep she really didn't think her dad was trying to kill her. And even if he came after the diary tonight, it wouldn't prove anything other than he wanted it. She gave her brain a mental shake and focused on what they were saying.

"I'll probably want to stay longer anyway," Gran said. "That is, if the nurses will allow me to, and sometimes they do if Cora requests it."

They followed Gran until she turned off at the

drugstore to pick up a box of candy for Cora.

Linc let Ainsley out at the door, and she waited inside while he parked. It did feel good to have someone watching out for her.

The waiting room was empty when they entered. "I'll wait here until you see if she's up for company other than family," Linc said.

She tilted her head. "Who are you and what did you do with the real Lincoln Steele?" Years ago he wouldn't have been that considerate.

"Was I that bad?"

"Let's just say, you may have felt entitled," she said with a laugh. "If you want to come with me, I think she'd be glad to see you, family or not."

"Well, if you insist." Then as they crossed to the open ICU doors, he muttered, "I wasn't that bad."

"Yes. You were." As they walked the circle around to Cora's room, she noticed that most of the curtains were open and she could see into the rooms. She searched for Austin, Drew's dad. Her stomach churned when she didn't see him. What if Drew had died? Then Austin stepped out of a room and turned and stared straight at her.

"How is he?" she asked.

His eyes narrowed briefly, then shuttered. "Still sedated. Have you found the person who shot him?"

"Not yet. It's not my case." She wasn't sure he

wanted her sympathy, but she had to try. "I'm so sorry—"

Austin palmed a hand. "Don't even go there."

Linc stiffened beside her. "She was only doing her job," he said.

"Yeah, well, maybe if she hadn't made him feel so guilty, he wouldn't have been at that Dyson girl's house."

"Did he tell you he was going to see Connie Hanover?"

"No. If he had, I would've stopped him, and if I'd known he was there yesterday, he wouldn't have been out in the open washing cars." He pinned a hard glare on Linc. "I hope you're both satisfied. At least maybe this will make you admit he had nothing to do with that girl's death."

"Hannah," Ainsley said, forcing herself not to snap at the man. "That girl's name was Hannah."

Austin's face hardened. "Don't lecture me, Beaumont. *That girl* almost got my son killed."

She bit back the retort on her tongue that would only make matters worse. "I hope he pulls through."

"I bet you do." He brushed past them, and Ainsley stopped him.

"Would you let me know when he's able to talk?"

"Yeah, right." He stalked away from them.

Her jaw ached from clenching her teeth. She'd

wanted to ask if Drew had given him the names of the boys Hannah had hung out with, but even if she'd asked, it was doubtful Austin would have told her.

A nurse was in Cora's room, hanging a new IV bag. "How is she?" Ainsley asked, glancing at her dozing aunt. Seemed like she was sleeping a lot lately.

"Her vitals are good. A little confused still, but that's to be expected in an ICU."

"Are you Drew Kingston's nurse?" she asked.

"Yes." Her tone was guarded.

"Can you tell me how he is? Generally," she added quickly when the nurse frowned. Maybe her badge would help, and Ainsley fished it from her purse. "I'm with the Investigative Services Branch of the park service, and Drew's shooting is involved in a case I'm working on."

"That little girl who was murdered? Hannah Dyson?" Her face softened. "She was my daughter's friend. I didn't know Drew's shooting was connected to that."

"We think it is." She took a card from her purse. "Could you call me when he wakes up? I believe he has vital information on Hannah's murder."

She hesitated only a few seconds before taking the card. "If I'm here. I'm off tomorrow, but I work Tuesday."

"Thank you," Ainsley said as Cora coughed and her eyes blinked open.

Linc took her hand. "You been playing possum, Miss Cora?"

"A person learns a lot that way," she replied.

Ainsley was happy to see that her eyes were clear. "So, you're feeling better?" she asked.

"If you're about to ask me what happened that night, I'm afraid you're wasting your breath. Everything is a murky haze in my mind."

"Then I won't ask," Ainsley said. "How about the diaries? Did you tell Dad about them?" Cora stared at her like she'd spoken a foreign language. "You don't remember any diaries, do you?"

"Diaries." Her eyes narrowed. She shook her head. "They seem very important to you. What's in them?"

Maybe if she put the diaries into context for her aunt. "I'm not sure exactly . . ."

"Miss Cora," Linc said. "I was helping you work on the book about Robert Chamberlain—"

"My great-grandfather," she said, looking pleased with herself.

"Yes," Ainsley said. "And what started it all was a diary you found and then misplaced."

"I did not misplace it," she said, stubbornness in her voice. "I believe someone stole it." She gripped Ainsley's hand. "Sonny. I told him about it, and he wanted to read it, and then it went missing."

"Who is Sonny?" she asked.

"You know," Cora insisted. "That little raga-muffin is always getting into trouble!" She squinched her eyes and shook her head. "No, no, that's not right."

Cora stared at the wall, and Ainsley waited, hoping she would continue.

With a sigh, her aunt turned to her. "I'm sorry. What were we talking about?"

"Don't worry about it," she said as her grand-mother bustled into the room. Ainsley needed to be careful about putting pressure on Cora.

"Sorry I'm late, but I couldn't find a parking spot near the door." She laid a box on the bed. "And here are your chocolates."

"I'll step out," Linc said.

Ainsley gave him a thumbs-up. "Be out in a minute."

Gran plumped her sister's pillow. "I was talking to the nurse, and she said for us to encourage you to sit up."

Cora's lips pinched together. "I don't want to sit up."

"Too bad." Gran grinned. "If I were lying there, you'd make me get up, so come on, let's at least raise you to a sitting position in the bed."

Ainsley should have already done that. What was wrong with her, pushing her aunt to remember something she obviously couldn't instead of trying to help her.

Suddenly Cora gripped Ainsley's hand. "I

remember now. Johnny did ask me for that diary, but I told him he'd have to wait until I was finished with it. And now it's lost."

Her heart caught. Her aunt had always called her dad Johnny.

51

Linc stopped at the nurses' station to ask if Connie Hanover was still in the unit and was told she'd been moved onto another floor. He tapped the room number the clerk gave him into the Notes app on his phone.

While he waited for Ainsley, he checked Drew's room for his dad. Austin hadn't returned, and Linc stepped inside. The rhythmic click and whoosh of the ventilator reminded him of how close the boy had come to dying. *Who shot you, Drew?*

Two good possibilities. Maddox or Hannah's killer. Maddox could have followed them to Connie Hanover's place. *If* he was the shooter who fired at Ainsley and instead hit Connie, did he see Drew before he took off?

He cocked his head as Ainsley's voice caught his attention. She must be ready to leave. Linc covered Drew's hand with his own. "We're going to find who did this," he promised softly.

His heart caught when Drew frowned and his shoulder stiffened. For a second, Linc thought he would open his eyes, then the lines of his face smoothed out as he became still again.

Linc squeezed his hand. "Just get better, okay?"

Ainsley was standing at the nurses' station when he stepped out of the small room. "I thought that's where you might be," she said.

"He tried to wake up, so maybe it won't be long before we can talk to him." He nodded toward the nurses' station. "They gave me Connie Hanover's room number. Let's go see her."

Ainsley nodded in agreement.

When they reached Connie's room, Ainsley knocked on the closed door.

"Come in," a faint voice called.

Linc pushed open the door to a strong smell of room deodorizer that barely disguised the odor of cigarette smoke. Connie was sitting in a chair by the bed, an IV pole beside her with the clear plastic line attached to a vein on the top of her hand.

The expectant look on her face morphed into a frown. "What do you two want?"

"A few words," Ainsley said. "How are you?"

"Alive, no thanks to you."

Ainsley stiffened. "I'm sorry for what happened to you—"

"You ought to be. That bullet had your name on it, not mine. If I hadn't jumped up when I did, it'd be you in that bed."

Ainsley took a step back, her face ashen.

Linc wanted to steady her but knew she wouldn't appreciate it. He turned his attention to Connie Hanover. The woman was on the offensive, and that usually meant a person had something to hide. "We're not sure that's what happened," he said. "Are you involved in anything that might cause someone to come after you?"

"Excuse me?" Color flooded Connie's face. "Are you implying—"

"No, ma'am." Linc held up his hand. "Just trying to look at all the options."

"Well, that's not one of them."

Her voice shook, and Linc didn't know if it was from anger or fear.

"Can you think of *any* reason someone might take a shot at you?" Ainsley asked, recovering her composure.

"Like I said, I don't think they were shooting at me." She stopped and took a deep breath. "Wish they hadn't taken the oxygen away already."

"Do we need to call the nurse?" Linc asked.

"No. Probably wouldn't come anyway. Waited an hour for pain meds last night before anyone showed up." She shifted in the chair and winced. "I'm tired. I think it's time for you to leave."

"One more question and we'll go," Ainsley said. "Have you thought of anyone who might have wanted to harm your daughter?"

"We went over this Friday night. Drew Kingston was with her that night. Have you talked to him?"

Connie hadn't heard about Drew? "No. Some-one tried to kill him yesterday morning," Ainsley said.

Her hand flew to her mouth, and then she fumbled for a red-and-white box that had been hiding under her leg. "Wh-what do you mean?"

"Someone shot him."

"Oh, wow. I'm sorry." She took a cigarette from the pack and rolled it between her thumb and finger. "Why?"

"The case is still under investigation," Linc replied.

Connie turned and stared out the window. "I always thought he was using Hannah, but I never wanted him to get hurt."

"Can you give us the names of some of her friends?" Ainsley asked. "It would help a lot."

She turned to face Ainsley. "Like I told you Friday night, Hannah never brought her friends around." She put the cigarette to her lips and seemed to remember where she was and care-fully returned it to the box. "There was this other boy she helped with math. Hannah was real good with numbers." She lifted her gaze toward the ceiling. "Peyton, that was his name."

"Does he have a last name?" Linc asked.

"I don't remember."

"Phone number?"

Connie shook her head.

"Do you know who his parents are?" he asked.

Another headshake. Linc took out one of his business cards and wrote Ainsley's number on the back, then handed it to her. "If you remember his last name, give one of us a call."

"I doubt I'll remember anything."

Linc stood. "Would you like help getting back into bed?"

She lifted her chin. "I can manage."

"We don't mind helping you." Ainsley's voice was soft.

"I don't need your help. I got to get out of here and plan a funeral."

52

Ainsley followed Linc out into the hallway, closing Connie Hanover's door behind her. "That went over worse than I expected."

He nodded. "At least she's stronger than I thought she'd be. The bullet must not have hit anything major."

Ainsley was thankful for that. The woman was right. If Ainsley hadn't gone to her house and questioned her, Connie Hanover would not have been shot.

"If you're ready, I'll take you to Cora's," Linc said. "And then we can call your dad, that is if you still want to."

Did she? She thought about it as they took the elevator to the lobby. Just as they passed the reception area, she heard Linc groan and looked up. Sarah Tolliver was hurrying toward them, followed by her videographer.

The reporter stuck her microphone out. "Ranger Beaumont, could you answer a few questions for me?"

"Sorry, no comment."

"Hannah Dyson's murder—was her mother's shooting related to it?"

"No more questions," Linc said. He took Ainsley's arm and tried to brush past the reporter and cameraman.

"Hold up a minute," Ainsley said to him. "Not commenting doesn't seem to be working. Why don't you go get the Tahoe while I answer a couple of her questions—that way maybe she won't pop back up."

"You sure?"

"Yes." She turned to Sarah as Linc hurried out the front doors. "I'm not involved in Connie Hanover's investigation so you need to direct your questions to Sheriff Rawlings."

"How about Drew Kingston's shooting? Is it related?"

"I'm going to sound like a broken record," Ainsley said, "but I'm not involved in that investigation either."

Small frown lines appeared between Sarah's brows. "Let's turn to the attempts on your life. Do you think the person trying to harm you is Troy Maddox, the man we've been circulating photos of at the station?"

"I have no way of knowing." She might as well use this interview to ask the public for help. Ainsley turned and looked into the camera. "If anyone recognizes the man in the photo, please do not try to apprehend him. If you see him, call the sheriff's office immediately. Thank you."

"I understand Maddox threatened you. How are you handling his threat?"

"The way I handle all threats—by staying watchful and taking the necessary precautions." She'd borrowed Linc's answer to her.

"Thank you for your input. The station will certainly do all it can to help spread the word about him." Sarah turned toward the camera and repeated the warning to call the sheriff's office before she signed off.

While the videographer put his equipment away, Sarah turned back to Ainsley. "I understand your aunt unearthed a couple of diaries from the mid-1800s that shed light on a murder that occurred during Reconstruction."

"I only have one and haven't had time to read it," Ainsley said. "Probably won't since I'm putting it in a lockbox tomorrow where it will be safe until my aunt recovers from her recent brain surgery."

"I hope she recovers soon. I understand Linc is helping her with a book about that murder."

"You'd have to ask him about that."

A knowing smile spread across Sarah's face. "I hope to be able to ask your aunt once she gets out of the hospital—your grandmother indicated Miss Cora might let me interview her. It'd make a great human interest piece and be good publicity for her book." Sarah's cell phone buzzed, and she glanced at it. "I need to catch another story. This will air at ten tonight."

Linc's SUV pulled up and Ainsley hurried to get in. Once she was buckled up, he exited the parking lot with the patrol car behind them. "How'd it go?"

"Mostly no comment on my part. I did get a chance to warn the public not to approach Maddox if they thought they recognized him, so it wasn't a total waste of time. Your friend is very persistent."

"I'm sorry. She wants to move up the ladder at the news station, and a story like Hannah's murder is giving her an opportunity to show her stuff. Mostly she covers things like your dad's shindig."

"I definitely want to see the newscast tonight and make sure she included what I said about Maddox."

He turned into Cora's drive. "Speaking of your dad, are you going to call him? Or would you rather just drop the whole thing?"

Call or drop it? The options warred in her mind. If he didn't show up, maybe the niggling suspicion would go away. Ainsley squared her shoulders and put the call on speaker as she dialed his number.

"I hope you're calling to apologize," her father said in a flat voice.

She lifted an I-told-you-so brow at Linc. "I, uh . . . I am. I was upset last night." At least that wasn't a lie.

"What changed your mind?" His tone hadn't softened much.

She glanced at Linc. "A very wise friend pointed out a few things." Again, not a lie, although she didn't understand why it was so important for her not to lie to him. "And I wanted to give you an update on Cora."

"How is she?" Cora at least warranted a warm response.

"She's still confused but does seem to be improving."

"Good. How about the diary you have? Are you going to give it to me?"

She took a deep breath. He was making this easy. "Not right now. I'm putting it in a lockbox at the bank tomorrow until Cora can make the decision of what to do with it."

His obvious dislike of her decision came through in a loud huff. "She would give it to me, is what she would do."

"She didn't before when you asked for the first one."

"She wasn't finished with it."

"And she hasn't even read this one."

"Have you even asked her about letting me have it?"

Cora was in no condition to make a decision

on anything. "I've been waiting for her mind to clear."

He was silent for a minute, then he asked, "Have you read it?"

"I haven't had time." Ainsley had meant to scan through the diary last night, but she'd been too shaken. "But I plan to read it when I get back to the house tonight."

"Where are you?"

"Oh, I'm on my way to Cora's right now, but Linc and I are going out to dinner at the Duck's Nest. I'm hoping to be home by around nine so I'll have time to read it before bed."

"Well, I'm glad to hear you and Linc are spending time together," he said, and it sounded as though he meant it. "I . . . kind of blame myself for what happened to you two. Someday I want to talk to you about it, but face-to-face."

"Sure," she said. "See you maybe this week?"

"I have rallies up around Oxford and the Northern District the first part, but I'll be free later in the week."

"Okay then . . ."

"Ainsley, I hope you know I'd never do anything to hurt you. I've only ever wanted what's best for you."

His version of what was best without any consideration of what she wanted. But was it possible she was wrong about him? He sounded sincere, humbled, even. "See you later this week, maybe." If not before.

After they disconnected, she turned to Linc. "How'd I do?"

"Very good. I know you two have always had differing opinions of what's best for you, but maybe he's changing."

"*That* would take a miracle," she said.

53

At eleven p.m., Sonny stood in the copse of trees outside Cora's house, his hand resting on the semiautomatic in his belt. At least this time it wasn't raining. The house looked empty, but if it wasn't . . . he was prepared to do whatever it took to get the diary.

Shouldn't have spent more than your take of the drug money. "Shut up!" The words came hissing out. He scrubbed his face like that would make the voice go away. *Just get in the house, get the diary, and leave.*

It'd been pure luck that he even heard the news broadcast about Ainsley Beaumont. She had found the diary he missed the night of the tornado. He'd read the one he snatched, and it hadn't been worth his time to steal. But it did reference a diary written in 1870, a year earlier. And if J.R. Beaumont got his hands on that one, Sonny could kiss his money goodbye. Maybe his life as well.

The ranger probably had it all this time, and according to the interview, she planned to stash it in a lockbox. If she did that, he'd never get it.

He eased out of the woods, crossed to the

cellar door, and opened it, using the key he'd had made. Once inside, he listened for sounds of someone being in the house, but it was still and quiet.

54

A little after seven, Linc had parked his Tahoe down the street so J.R. would think they were still out, and they'd been waiting in the library ever since, reading the leather-bound book. Now he counted the chimes coming from the grandfather clock in the hallway. Eleven.

"Not yet," Ainsley said quietly to the question he hadn't asked.

"If your dad was coming, I think he would have come before nine." He shifted in his chair. Light from the streetlamp filtered through the blinds, breaking the darkness just enough to see the outline of the fireplace and the furniture. His familiarity with the room filled in the rest.

Ainsley stood and peeked through the blinds. "I cannot believe Sarah mentioned the diaries on-air. We weren't even on-camera when she asked about them." She returned to her chair. "You want to read more of the diary?"

"Yeah. I want to know what happened after we stopped to watch the newscast." He didn't know about Ainsley, but he hadn't been able to get the words of the diary from his mind.

They'd taken turns holding a penlight to read the chilling account written in Charlotte Elliott's precise penmanship. The details of the night Elliott was killed were laid out in a rational and dispassionate manner. How he'd discovered his wife was teaching former slaves to read and write. His anger and how he'd threatened to horsewhip her if she didn't agree to stop. This, after he'd beaten her almost unconscious.

Linc picked up reading where Ainsley had left off. When he reached the passage where one of the former slaves saddled a horse and rode to get Charlotte's brother, Robert Chamberlain, a slight noise arrested his attention, and he stopped, cocking his head to listen.

"It's him!" she whispered.

Linc held his finger to his mouth as muffled footsteps came up the stairs . . . but which ones? Definitely not the basement steps.

Linc held his breath, and seconds later a door slid open near the fireplace. A man too thin to be J.R. stepped into the library and crept toward the hallway.

Linc flipped on the light, and the man whirled around, a ski mask covering his face and a gun in his hand.

No! Not a repeat of last night.

"ISB! Drop your gun!" Ainsley aimed her Sig at the intruder.

The man fired, and she dropped to the carpet

and returned fire, hitting him in the chest. The gun fell from his hand, and he crumpled to the floor.

Linc kicked it across the room and then rushed to Ainsley's side and helped her to her feet. "Are you all right?"

"I think so."

She didn't look all right. Her hands shook and she had her lips pressed together like she might be sick. Linc knew the aftermath of shooting a suspect, and none of it was good.

"You had no choice but to fire."

She barely nodded, feeling the hole in her T-shirt. "The vest took the bullet again."

Linc's heart dropped to his knees. He hadn't noticed she'd been shot. "Are you sure?"

"Yeah. The intruder . . . Is he . . ."

Linc needed to see if the man was alive. He squeezed her hand, then crossed the room to where the man lay. What was he doing here? Had he come after the diary or was he the person trying to kill Ainsley? He knelt beside him. "He's breathing."

His words seemed to give her a second wind. She straightened her shoulders and knelt with him beside the fallen man. Her bullet had hit him a little to the right, missing his heart. Otherwise, he would be dead.

Linc pulled out his phone and dialed 911. "Do you know him?" he asked as the call went through. Even with a mask on, the man didn't look like the sketch of Maddox.

"I don't think it's Troy Maddox, but it's hard to tell with the ski mask on."

"Check his pulse," he said as the operator answered, and he gave their address and the condition of the man.

"Pulse is weak."

Before he disconnected, he relayed the message and assured the operator there was no danger to the paramedics.

The man's lips moved, and Linc leaned closer. "Don't want to die . . ."

"An ambulance is on the way. You'll make it," he added, hoping it was true.

"What were you doing here?" Ainsley asked.

The intruder shifted a dazed look at her. He reached for the mask, but his hand never made it to his face before he let it fall. "Beaumont . . . got to . . ."

"What about Beaumont?" Linc leaned closer. Maybe this was Ainsley's attacker.

He mumbled something and coughed, then he closed his eyes.

It sounded like he said kill . . . or tell. Linc couldn't make it out. "Did you understand what he said?"

When she shook her head, he turned back to the man.

"What were you doing here?" Linc demanded.

The shrill wail of an approaching ambulance was the only answer he got.

Ainsley jumped up. "I'll get the door," she said.

The siren died with a yelp, and within minutes, paramedics knelt beside the man, loosening his pants and removing the mask and his shirt.

Blue lights flashed outside the window, creating garish shadows on the wall as Linc joined Ainsley by the desk, waiting for the onslaught of officers. From where he stood, the man appeared unconscious. Could this be the man who'd been trying to kill her?

Once the paramedic removed the mask, Linc took a good look at him. "Do you recognize him?"

She shook her head. "I don't think I've ever seen him before."

The man looked familiar in the way people did when Linc thought he knew someone but couldn't pinpoint where or how. "I heard someone say Pete was on his way. Maybe he can tell us who he is."

"I called Sam—he's issuing me another Sig tomorrow until I get mine back."

That was right. Ainsley would have to turn in her service pistol for ballistics. "You have a backup, right?"

"A small Glock, but I like my Sig better."

Linc used his phone to photograph the crime scene, something he would have done before everyone arrived if he'd had time. Ainsley took her phone out and fumbled it.

"I'll share my photos with you," he said. Her adrenaline was crashing and would soon be followed by the guilt of shooting the man. It came with the territory, even though it'd been self-defense. He'd been there, done that, and if he'd had his gun, he could have taken this one for her.

"Thanks," Ainsley said in a shaky voice. She turned to the fireplace. "I never knew there was a hidden stairway. I'm going to see where it leads."

"Wait." Linc motioned to Jonathan Rogers, a sergeant with the Natchez PD. "Okay if we check out the stairway?" he asked.

"I better come with you."

The two men followed Ainsley down the steps to the basement. "You didn't know this was here?" Jonathan asked.

"Not a clue," Ainsley said over her shoulder. "I'll ask Gran and Cora if they knew about it."

The secret stairway exited through a panel right behind the regular stairway. "This is where the water puddled last Thursday night," Linc said, pointing to the floor.

"It's likely the guy upstairs *was* responsible for Cora's fall," Ainsley said.

"Are you talking about Miss Cora?" Jonathan asked. "I sure hated to hear she'd fallen, but I thought it was an accident."

"We can't prove it wasn't," Linc replied, "unless the intruder admits he was here Thursday night. Do you know who he is?"

"Ronald McClain, the manager down at the Blue Lantern Coffee Shop. I've heard a few people call him Sonny—seems like that might have been a childhood nickname."

That's where he'd seen the man. Not that Linc went there often, and in fact he didn't go enough to even know the man's name.

"But that's not where I know him from." Jonathan crossed his arms over his ample chest. "I've had him on my radar for a few years now. Pretty sure he supplies the dealers around here who sell marijuana and cocaine to the high school students."

"Why hasn't he been arrested?" Ainsley asked.

"Because he's slick. And very careful who he sells to. Plus, his runners are loyal, won't roll over on him."

"If Ronald McClain was dealing drugs, is there any chance he sold Hannah Dyson the marijuana the night she died?"

Jonathan shook his head. "Only decent thing I can say about him—he didn't deal to teenagers. But that's not to say one of his dealers didn't."

Ainsley's phone rang as they climbed the stairs back to the library. "It's Gran."

She silenced the call and then her fingers flew as she texted her grandmother. She tapped send and then looked up. "I told her everything was under control and that I'd see her in the morning."

Her phone rang again, and she groaned.

"You might as well answer," Linc said.

Ainsley shoved the phone into his hand. "You can do more with her than I can. I need to talk to Pete."

Linc took the phone while she joined the chief. "Rose, this is Linc," he said.

"What's going on over there? Where's Ainsley? Is she all right?"

"She's talking to Pete Nelson." He glanced toward where the paramedics were loading Sonny McClain onto a gurney. "We had an intruder. She'll tell you all about it in the morning."

"I hope you don't think I can sleep until I know what's going on," she said, her voice snappish.

"I'll pass the word along to her, but it may be a couple of hours before she's free."

She sighed. "Okay. I suppose I can nap until then," she said, her tone softer. "And Linc, I'm sorry I was so short, but I'm worried about my granddaughter. I want to see for myself that she's okay."

He assured her it was no problem, and after a few more words, he disconnected and walked to the fireplace, where Ainsley was showing Pete the hidden staircase. "She's waiting for a report," he said and handed her phone back.

"I figured that."

Even though she sounded stronger, she hadn't regained her color. They both turned as Nate walked into the library.

The sheriff nodded to Pete Nelson. "Thanks for giving me a call on this. I've never been able to get enough on McClain to take to the district attorney, but maybe this will put him behind bars."

Pete nodded his agreement. "The coffee shop was the perfect place to make connections."

"Your sergeant mentioned the Blue Lantern, and it rang a bell," Ainsley said. "I think Cora and Gran go there, but I'm sure they had no clue he was involved in drugs. That may have been where McClain learned about the diaries."

"Then we'll need to talk with Ms. Rose," Pete said. "Maybe tomorrow. Wouldn't want to disturb her tonight."

"I doubt you'll disturb her," Ainsley said with a wry grin. "I'm sure she's watching out the window."

"What's this diary you're talking about?" Nate asked.

"And Sergeant Rogers mentioned something about you not thinking Miss Cora's fall was an accident," the chief said.

Linc exchanged a glance with Ainsley, and she nodded for him to take the lead. "We don't actually know why he was here. Ainsley never believed Cora simply fell but that someone assaulted her. There were damp spots on the carpet around her desk the night it happened."

"Why didn't you report it?" Pete asked.

"We had no proof she'd been attacked," Ainsley said. "Cora didn't remember the details of why she fell, and by the time I got back to the house, the carpet was dry, and nothing seemed to be missing. But Cora kept rambling about two diaries she'd found dating back to the 1870s and asking me to keep them safe. I started looking for them. Found one in her wall safe, but I never found the other one."

"Add to that a diary she'd found previously that had definitely gone missing," Linc said. He explained how Miss Cora had found her ancestor's diary that was the basis for a book she was writing to clear her great-grandfather's name.

"I still don't understand," Nate said. "Why would something over 150 years ago be important enough to risk getting shot and jail time?"

"To the right person, a diary from this era could be extremely valuable," Linc said.

Nate shook his head. "I thought about it all the way here—I think McClain was after you tonight, Ainsley. And I don't think it was his first attempt."

"I don't even know the man. What could his motive be?"

"That's what we'll have to find out."

55

A dog barked a street over as Maddox surveyed the Chamberlain house from the spot he'd picked out yesterday in Mrs. Johnson's yard. Cop cars lined the driveway.

Ainsley Beaumont had at least nine lives, and she'd about used up all of them.

Three hours ago, he'd seen the man who'd been sticking to Beaumont like a tick drive away and then return to the house on foot. Then there'd been nothing until he'd watched a man sneak from the wooded area behind the property and enter the house through the basement.

Maddox had thought maybe he wouldn't have to risk his neck after all. His money was running out—he'd already pawned his tent. It no longer mattered how Ainsley Beaumont died, just that she did. His heart had about stopped when he heard the gunfire, and then sirens. Unfortunately, it'd been Beaumont who came to the door and let the paramedics in.

Looked like the intruder had drawn the short straw, and once again, she'd cheated death. But not for much longer. With this break-in, it made sense that everyone, including Beaumont, would think the intruder was the one who had been trying to kill her. She would drop her guard. Maybe get rid of the sidekick. Maddox didn't relish tangling with someone who had biceps like the guy hanging around her.

Without thinking, he lit the last joint he'd bought from the guy back at Rocky Springs. It hadn't been hard to score a couple of dime bags—he'd smelled marijuana at the campsite and at first thought it was the kids in the tents next to him. And it had been, but he quickly realized they weren't selling but were getting it from the guy in the camper.

He should've been more careful with his money, but he hadn't thought it would take this long to get rid of Beaumont. Maddox pulled in a slow, deep draw, and held it in his chest. Tension eased away. Halfway into the second draw, he stopped. While he was too far away for anyone to smell the scent, in the dark the red glow could give him away if anyone looked toward the Johnson property. Maddox took one last puff, licked his finger and thumb, and squeezed the tip. He'd finish it later.

He needed to get out of here anyway. With all the cops milling around inside the house, he couldn't get to Beaumont. Maybe he ought to just pack it in and find a place to spend the night. Except he didn't have the money even for a cheap motel room. Maybe he'd go back to Rocky

Springs. No one would notice if he slept in his car.

Suddenly the Chamberlain front door opened, and Ainsley Beaumont hurried down the porch steps. A perfect opportunity.

With the suppressor on his rifle, no one would hear the shot, giving him plenty of time to get away. He raised the rifle, his finger on the trigger, and lined her up in the crosshairs of his scope.

Raised voices drew his attention away from Beaumont, and he lowered the rifle. He hadn't seen the cop. Or the woman getting out of her car. That nosy reporter. He folded the rifle and slipped it in his backpack. There would be a better time.

56

Gran and Cora would be appalled when they learned the manager of the coffee shop they frequented dealt in drugs. "Did McClain ever sell direct to anyone?" Ainsley asked. Her phone buzzed with another text. Gran.

"I never could catch him," Pete said.

"Is there any way we can find out who's selling to the high school kids?" Linc asked.

Both the sheriff and chief gave a negative response. "And don't think we haven't been trying," the chief said. "But the kids won't give up their source."

"Maybe that will change with what's happened to Hannah and Drew. And maybe when Drew wakes up, he'll be willing to give us some names," she said and checked her watch. "It's almost one. Why don't I walk across the street and calm my grandmother down? She's blowing my phone up. I'll let you know if she's up to talking to you tonight."

"I'll get an officer to meet you and walk you across," Pete said.

Ainsley hurried out the front door. Sarah Tolliver had her back to Ainsley and appeared to be arguing with the officer getting out of his patrol car. Probably the one who was supposed to walk her to Gran's. With so many police cars on the street and officers milling around inside, she should be safe enough to cross the street. Ainsley ducked her head and made it across without being noticed.

A lamp glowed in Gran's living room, but that didn't mean she was still awake. A headache started at the base of Ainsley's neck. She hadn't realized how tense she was and inhaled a deep breath. Honeysuckle mingled with . . . marijuana? She sniffed the air again and turned in a circle, scanning the neighborhood. Nothing here but older homeowners who wouldn't be smoking pot.

Someone was out there. A shiver raced down her spine as her heart rate jacked up. Her gaze swept the area again. Anyone could be hiding in the shadows.

Cora's front door opened again and Linc bounded down the porch.

"Linc!" Sarah jogged toward him.

"What are you doing here?"

"My job. What happened here?"

Their words carried on the night air, and Ainsley stepped back into the shadow of her grandmother's front porch. She was in no shape emotionally to talk to the reporter. The shooting was too fresh.

"Sorry, Sarah, not tonight," Linc said, his voice

firm. "Pete Nelson will probably hold a press conference in the morning."

"I want to talk to you. And her."

"Then call tomorrow and set up an appointment," he said. "Now please, just leave."

The reporter hesitated, then nodded. "You owe me one."

"Whatever," Linc said and waited until she walked to her car and drove away.

"Thanks," Ainsley said when he reached her. She took a deep breath and released it to quell her shaky insides. Although faint, the marijuana scent lingered in the night air. "Do you smell marijuana?"

He sniffed the air. "Maybe. Can't tell where it's coming from though."

"I know. Probably somebody's grandkid." She cocked her head. "What are you doing out here? I was only going across the street."

"I'm not sure I agree with Nate that the guy you shot is your assailant. I think he was coming after the diary."

"How would he have known I had it?"

"He could have heard the information on the ten o'clock news."

The mention of the reporter reminded Ainsley she'd have to deal with her tomorrow. She shoved the thought aside. Tomorrow was soon enough to think about that.

He slipped his hand into hers, his touch like

an electrical current. She never remembered her feelings for him being so intense. Which meant if he betrayed her again, it would be worse than before.

"Linc . . ." she said, pulling her hand away.

"I wish you'd give us a chance," he said. His voice didn't reflect disappointment, but when she turned to him, it flickered in his face under the light from overhead.

"I don't know—"

Gran's front door jerked open, and Ainsley jumped. "Are you two going to stand out there all night, or are you coming in and telling me what's going on?"

"We're coming in, but first let me text Nate and Pete."

While they waited for the two law officers to walk across the street, Ainsley filled her grandmother in on what had happened. "They want to talk to you about the guy."

"Who is he?"

"Ronald McClain."

Gran gaped at her. "Sonny? He shot at you?"

"I'm afraid so," Linc said.

"Did you . . ."—Gran bit her bottom lip—"shoot him?"

"Yes." Her voice cracked. "I don't know if he'll make it."

Her grandmother sank onto the floral sofa. "I can't believe Sonny? . . . You're sure it's him?"

"Both Pete and Nate ID'd him. How well do you and Cora know him?" she asked as the sheriff and chief came through the door.

"We've known him all his life. His mother worked for both of us as a domestic. She often brought him along with her in the summers." Her shoulders slumped. "He was such a polite boy, always saying 'yes, ma'am' and 'no, ma'am.' We were so tickled when he took over management of the Blue Lantern. We went by to see him every week."

She shifted her attention to Ainsley. "You remember his mother—she looked after you sometimes when I had errands to run and Cora was busy."

Ainsley searched her memory, and a hazy figure emerged. A large woman with red hair and freckles. And with her a tall, skinny boy older than Ainsley . . . Her insides cringed. He'd been creepy, skulking around the house, hiding and then jumping out at her, yelling, *"Gotcha!"*

"That was Ronald McClain?"

"We called him Sonny," Gran said.

"Why didn't you ever tell me about the secret staircase?"

"We were afraid you'd fall down it. The entry in the basement was supposed to be boarded up—come to think of it, Sonny's father did the work."

That was how he knew about the stairs.

"Did you ever talk to him about the book Cora's writing?" Linc asked.

"Oh yes, and sometimes she went on and on about that book . . ." Gran's brow furrowed. "Oh, wait . . . I remember now. He came over to Cora's, and she let him read that first diary she found. It was about a week later that it went missing. I always suspected he took it somehow—as a kid he had sticky fingers, if you know what I mean."

"Did he steal from you?" Nate asked.

"I remember him now," Ainsley said, "He took my Matchbox cars!"

Gran nodded. "We never could prove it, though, and it wasn't just your little cars. He took food, candy, and the like that we had lying around. Not that we begrudged him the food."

Linc inclined his head toward Rose. "Did you ask him about the diary?"

"Cora wouldn't, but I did. He swore on his mama's grave that he didn't take it."

"You should've made a report," Pete said.

"I told Cora that, but she would never do anything to get Sonny in trouble. She's always had a soft spot for him." Gran's face fell, and she cupped her hand to the side of her face. "Oh my, I hate to be the one to tell her what he's done."

"Don't worry about it," Ainsley said. "I'll tell her."

"Would she have told Sonny about the new diaries she found?" Linc asked.

Gran stared at the floor a minute, then lifted her gaze. "She might have called him since he seemed really interested in her book, more than almost anyone else. Have you checked the log on her caller ID?"

Ainsley wanted to slap her head. "No. But until tonight, we weren't certain a crime had been committed." She stood and hugged her grandmother. "I'm going back to Cora's to check that out. I hope you're going to bed."

"You're going to stay over there again tonight?"

"Yep." Ainsley wasn't convinced McClain was her shooter either, and if someone came after her again, she didn't want her grandmother caught in the crossfire.

The chief and sheriff left directly from Gran's, and only Jonathan Rogers from Natchez PD remained at Cora's when Ainsley and Linc returned.

"If you need me, I'll be in the basement dusting for prints," Jonathan said. "And then I'm leaving."

She gave him a thumbs-up and walked to the desk, where Cora kept her landline, her gaze drawn to the blood on the carpet where McClain had fallen. She added cleaning the carpet on her mental to-do list. Ainsley did not want Cora coming home and having to deal with the man's blood.

She picked up Cora's landline phone. It was

cordless, unlike the wall phone in the kitchen. Linc looked over her shoulder as she checked the caller ID and wrote down the last few numbers on the received calls list. Next she checked the redial list and listed them, leaving off Gran's number, which occurred more than any other.

On a hunch, she redialed the last number Cora called and put it on speakerphone. After four rings it went to voice mail.

"Hello. You've reached Ronald McClain. Hours for the Blue Lantern are ten 'til ten. For anything else leave me a message."

Ainsley disconnected. "It looks like Cora called him, probably Thursday night, but we'd have to contact her service provider or check McClain's phone to see what time."

"If McClain had his phone with him, it should have been bagged." Linc asked, "I wonder if Pete took the evidence to the police department?"

"Check with Jonathan. He should know," she said. While Linc went downstairs, Ainsley transferred her mental to-do list for tomorrow to the Notes app on her phone, starting with an interview with the principal at the high school.

She massaged her neck, wincing as her fingers probed the tight knots. It was already tomorrow. Hopefully she could get to bed in the next hour. Ainsley looked up as Linc returned.

"Crime scene tech took it to the police department evidence room. I asked him to check

McClain's call log for Thursday night and ring us back."

"Thanks. Did Jonathan say how much longer he'd be here?"

"He was finishing up when I left."

"Good." She started for the kitchen.

"Where're you going?"

"To get cold water and something to get the blood up."

"I'll help you."

"You don't have to," she said, giving him a tired smile. If he kept being this nice, she would have to change her opinion of him. Like she hadn't already.

57

Linc dipped a brush in the bucket of water, baking soda, and vinegar that Ainsley had mixed up. He was amazed at how well the concoction worked to remove the blood. "Where'd you come up with this recipe?"

"Gran, of course." Ainsley used a dry towel to blot moisture from the carpet.

"Of course. Would you write down the formula?" In the past, Linc had gotten blood on his clothes during a takedown, and it would be handy to have something that dissolved it so quickly. He scrubbed that thought. He wasn't with the FBI any longer and doubted his duties at Melrose would call for something to remove blood.

At least this time he hadn't frozen. He had to be getting better, right? Linc clenched his jaw and scrubbed at the carpet, even though no sign of blood lingered. No. He wasn't getting better.

What if Ainsley had been shot, maybe killed, because he hadn't had a gun? Linc would never forget the helplessness that slammed him when he reached for a gun that wasn't there. He scrubbed the carpet harder.

"Hey! We got it," Ainsley said, placing her hand on top of his.

He sat back on his heels.

"You okay?" she asked.

No, he wasn't okay. He didn't believe they'd caught her shooter, not with Maddox still at large. Ainsley's life could depend on him, and without a gun, he was as useless as a tire jack without a handle.

Linc had never had a weakness he couldn't overcome. Somehow, someway, he had to beat this. "Have you checked with your supervisor about Maddox?"

"I texted him earlier tonight. He hasn't been apprehended."

"I won't be with you, so you'll be careful tomorrow, won't you?"

"Of course. I'm always careful."

He couldn't keep kidding himself that he was adding anything to this case. "I wouldn't be any help if I was with you and Maddox showed up."

"It worked out fine tonight," she said.

"No thanks to me. What if you'd missed? I might as well have grabbed at a shadow when I reached for my gun."

"I said it worked out fine. Don't beat yourself up." She tilted her head to the side. "But if it bothers you this much, you might think about talking with the psychologist again."

"Six months of counseling didn't work, what good would it do to go back?"

"How about a different counselor?"

Linc had thought about a different therapist and dismissed it, but maybe it was time . . . "I'll look into it. Why don't you go on to bed? I'll lock up."

"I think I'll let you. Thanks for the help." Her smile erased the tired lines around her eyes, but more than that, it lit his world until his failure taunted him again.

Failure. He tried to block the word from his mind as Ainsley walked out of the library. All his old fears settled in his heart. She deserved better than him.

When he'd stopped seeing the counselor, Linc had vowed to overcome his fear on his own. He had God—what more did he need? Except God had been silent. Maybe he didn't deserve his help.

Linc shook the thought off. He would not buy into that garbage. *Lord, give me more faith.* He wasn't sure what he expected—maybe a magic bullet or a sudden infusion of strength, but it wasn't forthcoming.

When you don't know what to do, do the next thing. That had always been Linc's mantra.

He emptied the bucket in the sink and rinsed it out, then descended the stairs to make sure Jonathan had locked the basement door, which he had. After he checked the other two doors, he climbed the stairs to the guest bedroom.

Pain radiated from his neck when he rotated his head. He was tight as an overwound spring, and he rolled his aching shoulders and neck. The joints popped and cracked, but they released. Now if he could just release . . .

"God, I need your help." His gaze fell to the Bible on the nightstand beside the bed. While he read the Bible every day, lately he hadn't really studied it . . . it'd been more like checking off a box. Maybe that was why God had been silent.

He thumbed through the Bible, and a bookmark fell out. Linc picked it up. It listed ten problems with accompanying Scripture verses and one that was handwritten, probably by Cora. Deuteronomy 8:2. *"Remember how the LORD your God led you all the way in the wilderness these forty years, to humble and test you in order to know what was in your heart, whether or not you would keep his commands."*

Humbling. Testing. If that's what God had been doing, once again Linc had failed the test. He'd never liked asking for help. Evidently that was part of his problem. He was too proud to acknowledge he couldn't overcome this on his own.

But he had acknowledged it. To the psychologist, to Ainsley, even to God . . . But had he really? Or had he just been giving it lip service?

He'd certainly not searched the Scriptures for answers.

Truth seared his soul. He was like the alcoholic who admitted he had a problem but went right on drinking. Deep down, Linc believed if the reason was compelling enough, he could pick up his Glock again. If protecting Ainsley wasn't compelling, what was?

Cora had written one more Scripture reference on the bookmark. Joshua 1:9. *"Have I not commanded you? Be strong and courageous. Do not be afraid; do not be discouraged, for the LORD your God will be with you wherever you go."*

"Okay, God, I'm claiming this." And starting tomorrow, he would be looking for other verses.

Linc set his phone alarm for six and crawled into bed. When the alarm went off three and a half hours later, Linc was tempted to ignore it. But he had to be at Melrose at eight, and he had a stop to make beforehand. Groggy, he staggered to the shower and turned it on. Minutes later, the stinging water pounded him awake. After he dressed, he eased downstairs to keep from waking Ainsley.

The new pod coffee maker sat on the counter, but hadn't Cora made coffee in a percolator when he first started helping her? He searched the cabinets, hitting gold when he discovered the stainless-steel coffee maker along with filters and coffee. Decaf. He eyed the pods beside the new coffee maker and quickly emptied several into the percolator basket. Once he had it going, the aroma of freshly brewed coffee filled the kitchen.

Footsteps down the hall alerted him that Ainsley was up, and he poured her a steaming cup and added a dash of creamer. "Hazelnut, right?" he said, handing it to her.

Even in an oversized bathrobe and with messy hair, she was beautiful. What would it be like to spend every morning with her?

Might as well get that thought out of his head. While he loved Ainsley, the problems in their past needed to be worked out, and they hadn't even discussed what happened. Today wasn't the day to discuss it either. Too little sleep and a long agenda for them both would not bode well for that kind of talk.

"Where'd you find the percolator?" Ainsley took a sip and, judging by the way she half closed her eyes, savored it.

"It was under the counter. I knew Cora had one somewhere, and I didn't think she would mind if we used it. What's first on your docket today?"

"Call the hospital. Talk to the principal at the high school, and after that, hopefully talk to a few of the boys Hannah hung out with. Maybe we can get a lead from one or more of them."

"How about your dad?" he asked.

Ainsley tensed. He could tell she didn't want to add him to the list.

"He's probably on the road. Maybe I'll talk to him tomorrow."

He nodded. "I'll be at Melrose until four thirty, but let's touch base later."

"How about you?" she asked. "Anything special going on?"

"No, the same old same old—check everything out, tours of the house, that sort of thing." He took a sip of coffee. "What would you like for breakfast?"

"Cereal." When he started to protest that she needed something more substantial, she palmed her hand. "That's all my stomach will take right now. I'll pick up something more later." She fished her phone out of the robe.

He listened to her end of the conversation with the nurse at the hospital as he set the cereal box on the counter and put out the milk. Evidently there'd been no change in Cora.

"Thank you," she said into the phone. "Can you tell me Drew Kingston's condition?" Her jaw set as she listened. "I see. Well, thank you anyway." Ainsley disconnected and looked up. "She wouldn't discuss Drew with me. Confidentiality."

"Definitely not the nurse we talked to yesterday," he said.

"No." She poured cereal into the bowl and added milk. "I'll check on him when I visit Cora later today."

Linc checked his watch. "I talked to Pete, and

one of his officers should be here by now. You could ride with him instead of taking the station wagon."

"I like the idea of having my own wheels. Besides, I don't think Maddox would expect me to be in a thirty-year-old car."

"Just be sure to watch the gauges. No telling how long since Cora has driven it."

She nodded and walked to the hall with her cereal in one hand and a fresh cup of coffee in the other. "Hope you have a good day," she said over her shoulder.

"You too."

Linc quickly washed out the percolator and his cup and left them to drain. He'd put them away tonight. Wouldn't do for Cora to return home to a messy kitchen.

Half an hour later, he parked in front of his apartment and hustled inside, hoping what he planned to do wouldn't take long. In his bedroom, he took a deep breath and repeated the verse in Joshua he'd read last night. He could do this.

Linc's hand shook as he reached for the box holding his service Glock and set it on the bed. At least he got that far, but it wasn't the box he needed. He turned back to the closet and fished out the smaller container that held a Glock 19, a smaller semiautomatic.

He stared at the two boxes, and the familiar

roiling of his stomach kicked in. It was as though something had sucked the air out of the room. Sweat broke out on his forehead.

Someone was trying to kill Ainsley. Her life could depend on him. Linc swallowed hard and straightened his spine. *Lord, help me.*

In one motion, he flipped the lid off the box and took out the smaller Glock 19 that was comfortable yet foreign in his shaky hand. He tamped down the nausea that threatened to come up his throat. Maybe if he just strapped the gun to his ankle and didn't load the magazine. That seemed doable.

Once he had the holster around his leg, he was tempted to just wear it and not the gun. He almost laughed at himself. Why was he having so much trouble? He'd worn an ankle gun hundreds of times in the past.

Fear not, for I am with you. Gritting his teeth, he shoved the magazine into the Glock, holstered the gun, and concealed it under his pants leg. *There.* He straightened up and took a deep breath.

"Thank you," he said softly, looking up. At least he hadn't had a full-blown panic attack.

58

Ainsley returned to the kitchen, noting Linc had put away the cereal and milk and had poured out what was left of the coffee. She meant to tell him to leave it, and turned on the pod coffee maker. Sometimes the man was too efficient. Ainsley washed out her bowl while the water heated. She needed one more jolt of caffeine before getting dressed.

At eight, she called the high school and was told the principal would not be in until ten. When she asked about the coach, the secretary indicated he could be found at the school anytime today. Then she called and canceled her appointment with the trust lawyer. She simply didn't have time for it today.

An hour later, Ainsley waved at the police officer in the black and white cruiser before she backed her aunt's station wagon out of the garage. She and Cora were about the same height so the seat was already adjusted for her long legs, but her pickup sat up much higher. She didn't like being this close to the ground.

The school wasn't far from Cora's house, making the drive short. Ainsley pulled into the almost empty parking area and found a spot she could pull through. Driving the station wagon was like driving a boat. Then she took a minute to admire the new high school. About time the county built a new building, and what a contrast it was to the old one she'd attended— sleek, modern lines, a new gym, Astroturf on the football field . . .

Staring at the new building wasn't getting her job done. She grabbed her backpack and remembered to take the keys before she climbed out of the station wagon. "I'll be inside," she said to the officer who had parked behind her. "No need for you to come in."

She checked in at the principal's office and was told he wasn't in yet. "Do you mind if I find Coach Andrews and talk to him?"

"That should be fine since he's the assistant principal anyway. Today is the first day of football camp, and Coach Andrews said something about showing films. You'll find them in the gym."

The secretary gave her directions, and after getting lost in the cross corridors only once, she found them. When she stepped inside the huge gymnasium, it struck her that this one hadn't been used enough to pick up the smells common to gyms in South Mississippi, where the kids in the bleachers were as sweaty as the players.

As she crossed the gym floor, Ainsley rested her hand on the Sig that Sam had dropped off right after Linc left. She didn't count the boys, but figured there were at least twenty-five football players laughing and cutting up in the lower section of the bleachers. A big-screen TV had been rolled out and a formation had been paused on the screen. A couple of heads turned in her direction as she approached.

"Coach Andrews?" she asked, holding out her hand to the dark-skinned man with a remote in his hand. "Ainsley Beaumont, Investigative Services Branch of the National Park Service."

His hand swallowed hers, the handshake gentle but firm. "What can I do for you?"

"Could we talk in private? It's about Hannah Dyson." She said it loud enough for the group to hear, and a hush settled over them. A couple of the boys exchanged looks while one bounced his knees, and another boy rubbed his pants leg as he eyed the exit to her left.

Andrews handed the remote to his assistant. "Carry on. I'll be right back."

Talking resumed, albeit quieter as he led her to his office just off the gym floor. He pulled cut the chair behind his desk and motioned for her to take one across from him. "I'm not sure how I can help."

"I'm the investigating officer for the NPS in this matter, and I understand Hannah was friends with several of the football players. Do you know if this is true?"

He rocked back in his chair. "She was a sweet girl, and from what I gather, quite a whiz in math. She liked to help some of the boys who were behind in those studies. Drew Kingston was one of them, but I understand you've already talked to him."

"Yes. You do know he was shot Saturday morning?"

"I do. I've visited him, or at least his dad, at the hospital. I'm really praying he pulls through."

She wasn't sure how to broach the subject of marijuana and decided on a frontal attack. "How many of your boys use marijuana?"

"Hopefully none of them," he said, rocking forward in his chair and clasping his hands together on the desk. "At least starting this week. I've told them there would be mandatory drug testing, and anyone who failed the test was off the team."

"Do you know who's selling marijuana to the kids around here? It's my understanding Hannah had gone to Rocky Springs to buy marijuana."

He stared at his hands, pressing his thumbs together, then he lifted his gaze. "Pretty sure. It's a couple of the boys in the senior class. It's not like I have any proof, but I hear stuff."

"Do you know who they buy from?"

"Probably, but I don't have proof of that either, so I'd hate to say."

"Could it be Sonny McClain?"

His eyes widened, then he chuckled. "For someone who hasn't been in Natchez long, you've learned a lot about our town."

She smiled. "I grew up here. And I don't think he'll be selling any drugs for a while. Could I speak to the boys who were friends with Hannah? Or those she tutored?"

He considered her request, then nodded. "As long as I can sit in."

"Of course. I just want to have a conversation with them."

"Wait right here. I'll be right back."

Five minutes later he returned with a lanky, wide-shouldered boy who walked in like he owned the room. He'd been the one who kept looking at the door.

"This is Peyton Cordell," the coach said. He pointed to a chair for Peyton to sit in.

"I'd rather stand," the boy said.

Peyton . . . that was the name Connie Hanover had mentioned. After she introduced herself, she said, "I understand you were friends with Hannah. That she tutored you."

"She was friends with a lot of guys." He flipped his dark brown bangs out of his eyes with his hand and they fell right back.

She didn't know how in the world the kid saw

to catch a football with his hair in his eyes. "Did she buy her weed from you?"

"No! Where did you hear that?" The boy jammed his hands into his pockets. The question had knocked some of Peyton's composure off.

"She bought it from someone. If not you, who?"

He shrugged. "I dunno."

She paused for a long moment. "Where were you Tuesday night?"

He jerked his head up, his eyes wide. "H-home. My parents will vouch for me."

She bet they would. "I need their phone numbers." She wrote down the numbers he sputtered out, then looked up. "I'm going to ask you once more. Where did Hannah get her weed?"

He side-glanced at the door and licked his lips. "Look, I ain't no snitch."

"We think whoever she bought the weed from could be her killer. If you know and withhold that information, it could be interpreted as impeding an investigation."

Peyton flinched as Coach Andrews placed his hand on the boy's shoulder. "Son, if you know anything, now's the time to tell it."

The bravado drained out of him. "Colton Mason."

Colton? That was the last name she'd expected to hear. "Are you sure?"

He nodded emphatically.

"Do you know who he gets it from?" she asked.

"He steals his dad's stash."

"And he's selling it?"

"Nah." He gave a contemptuous laugh. "The loser thinks people will like him if he gives it away."

She didn't know which made her sicker—Colton fooling her like he had or thinking he could buy friends with marijuana. "Where does his dad get it?"

"From the guy at the Blue Lantern. Everybody knows he deals. Just won't deal to kids directly."

Ainsley didn't think it was because Sonny was altruistic. More likely because if he were caught, the jail time would be more. "Thank you for helping," she said and some of his bravado returned.

"Sure."

He'd almost reached the door when Ainsley said, "Hannah was pregnant. Was the baby yours?"

He turned. All color had drained from his face. "She was supposed to get rid of it."

He'd just lost any points he might have gained by giving them Colton's name. Ainsley nodded to the coach, dismissing the boy.

"You can go now," Andrews said. "Send in Jacobs."

Peyton stopped at the door. "You won't tell him I snitched, will you?"

"No," she said. Tiredness or disappointment, she didn't know which, enveloped her. The boy was more worried people would think he was a snitch than that a pregnant girl had died.

Forty-five minutes later three of the boys had confirmed Peyton's story about Colton and the marijuana. She couldn't believe he'd lied to her or that she'd bought it. "I think this wraps it up," she said when the last boy left the office.

"I'm surprised that Colton is supplying the kids here with marijuana," Coach Andrews said. "I always liked the kid, felt sorry for him. His dad is a piece of work."

"Yeah, I've met him." She stood and grabbed her backpack. "Thanks for your help."

Ainsley approached the officer who had patiently waited for her outside the school. "I'm going to Melrose, if you want to follow me there. After that, I'll be heading to Rocky Springs, and I know that's out of your jurisdiction. The sheriff's too," she added. "I'll get Sam Ryker to meet me there."

"I'll check with the chief and see what he wants me to do," the officer said.

She stowed her backpack in the passenger seat and then walked around to the driver's side, her mind still on what the boys had told her. She had not expected them to accuse Colton of selling. No, not selling, but giving Hannah marijuana. Were Ainsley's skills slipping, or was she getting sloppy in her investigations? Or could the boys have gotten together and concocted their stories? Nothing was impossible, but it hadn't sounded like the boys had rehearsed what they'd told.

She dialed Sam's number, but he didn't answer and she left a voicemail asking him if the Masons were still at Rocky Springs. Ainsley disconnected. Right now she wanted to tell Linc what she'd learned. If she was slipping, so was he since he'd bought Colton's story too.

59

Linc fought the impulse to remove the gun strapped above his ankle all morning. It hadn't helped that in the first tour group a ten-year-old boy had reminded him of the kid he'd almost shot. He hung up his out-to-lunch sign along with the time of the next tour at the ranger post. The eleven o'clock tour had just finished, and there wouldn't be another one until two, giving him just enough time to grab a sandwich from one of the nearby fast-food places.

Gravel crunched as the tour bus from the American Queen Steamboat pulled out of the large parking area. His gaze followed the colorful vehicle down the drive. It'd been a large crowd, something he enjoyed. More people meant more interaction, always a good thing. Then he frowned as a mint-green MINI Cooper pulled into the lot.

That could be no one but Sarah. He waited as she climbed out of the car and walked toward him, a white paper bag in her hand. "Have you eaten?" she asked.

"I was just going after something."

"Good. I picked up a couple of burgers from

the Camp Restaurant," she said. "Want one?"

"Is that a bribe?"

"Maybe."

He was hungry, and the Camp Restaurant had good burgers. If he didn't deal with Sarah now, she'd just come back. "Let's take them to the ranger station."

She followed him to the white building, where he grabbed a bottle of water.

"You didn't call," she said. "And neither has Ainsley."

Neither of them had told the reporter they would call. "Sorry. It's been a busy morning."

"You didn't answer your phone either."

He didn't remember hearing it ring. Linc checked his phone. He'd put it on "do not disturb" before the first tour and they'd been so busy, he forgot to take it off.

There were several alerts showing, but before he could check them, an older-model Toyota pickup pulled beside his Tahoe, and Emma Winters got out. "I need to see Emma," he said to Sarah.

"I wasn't expecting you here today," he said when he reached her.

"I heard what happened last night, and I figured you might want me to conduct the tours," she said. "I would have been here earlier, but I had a few things to do at Mount Locust this morning."

"Thanks." This would give him a chance to be

408

with Ainsley in whatever she had planned for the afternoon—if she wanted him to accompany her.

Emma smiled. "Glad to help. I think I'll go inside the house for now."

He jogged back to where Sarah waited. "You should've gone ahead and eaten."

"There's no fun in that," she said, handing him a burger. "Fill me in on what happened last night."

"I think you need to talk with Pete Nelson about that." He checked to see what was on the burger, prepared to get rid of anything that wasn't mustard and pickles. Linc almost did a double take and looked up.

"That is still the way you order your hamburgers?" she asked.

"I can't believe you remember that. How long has it been?"

"Ever since I was fifteen." Her gaze shot over his shoulder and briefly narrowed. "Ainsley."

He frowned and turned. Ainsley was walking toward them, holding a Subway bag.

"There you are! And I see you already have lunch."

"That's probably healthier, but I'm not trading," he said.

She eyed his hamburger. "I don't blame you. Can I join you?"

"Sure," he said.

"Yes, do," the reporter said.

Sarah's tone didn't match the smile on her lips. He scooted down on the bench, making room for Ainsley. Linc would ask how the session with the boys at the high school had gone if Sarah weren't there. Maybe she wouldn't linger long.

Very little was said as they ate lunch. The atmosphere wasn't hostile, but neither was it exactly warm and friendly. When they finished, Linc gathered the wrappers and tossed them in the trash.

Sarah took out her notebook and turned to Ainsley. "Can I get a statement from you about last night?"

Linc turned to face Sarah. "What did I tell you about that?"

"I'm not asking you, I'm asking Ainsley. I understand the man you shot was Ronald McClain. What was he doing in your aunt's house? Do you know what he was looking for?" Sarah asked.

"I'm afraid you'll have to ask him that."

"You haven't heard?" Sarah asked. "He slipped into a coma. They don't expect him to make it."

"What? Why wasn't I called?" She fumbled for her phone and stared at the screen. "I can't believe I forgot to turn it on after I finished at the school."

While she checked her missed voicemails, he did the same and listened to his message from the chief of police. McClain was in a coma and not expected to live. Evidently neither he nor Ainsley were firing on all cylinders today.

"I have to go to the hospital," Ainsley said.

"Wait," he said. "I want to go with you."

Ainsley hesitated as she glanced toward Sarah.

The reporter stood. "I guess that's my cue to leave," she said, a hard edge to her voice as she picked up her backpack. "See you Wednesday?"

"Yeah, and thanks for the burger," he said.

"Walk to my car with me?"

Sarah didn't wait for him, and short of being rude, he had no choice but to follow. He didn't miss the triumphant glance Sarah shot at Ainsley.

Maybe Wednesday he'd get a chance to talk to her about their nonrelationship.

His shoulders dropped. The anniversary of her brother's death wasn't the best day to disappoint her.

60

While Linc walked Sarah to her car, Ainsley called the chief. "Sorry I missed your calls. How is McClain?"

"I'm afraid he didn't make it. I'm sorry."

"Me too." Her heart sank. No need to go to the hospital now. "Did he regain consciousness?"

"No, but we found two more diaries at his apartment above the coffee shop."

"I'd like to look at them," she said. "Can I pick them up later today?"

"They're locked up in the evidence room. You'll have to sign for them, although with him dead, there's really no reason for you not to have them since they belong to Cora," Pete said.

"Cora will be glad to get them back," she said. "See you later today."

When Ainsley disconnected, she glanced toward the parking lot. Sarah had Linc cornered at her car, talking animatedly with her hands. A text came through on her phone from her supervisor, asking for another update. Ainsley took a minute to collect her thoughts before calling Brent.

She had reported what had happened last night, and now she had to report the man had died.

Ainsley hoped Brent didn't want to take her off the case. Reluctantly, she dialed her supervisor's number and filled him in.

"I don't have anyone else to send to Natchez or I would," he said. "Maybe I need to call in the FBI."

"I can handle this. Besides, Hugh Cortland, the FBI agent who would handle it, is tied up in a court case this week." Her gaze followed Linc as he broke away from Sarah and walked toward Melrose. She wished she had time for him to take her through the beautiful old mansion.

"They could send someone else. And you need to see the psychologist."

Ainsley brought her attention back to Brent. "But they wouldn't know anything about the case, and I believe I'm closing in on the murderer." She didn't think it was Colton, but he might have seen more than he'd told them. "I'm telling you, I can handle this, and I'll see the psychologist when the case is finished."

In the end, he agreed to wait, and she disconnected as Linc walked up.

"That woman has a serious crush on you," she said.

"I know," Linc replied. "Not sure what to do about it, but I have to talk to her."

"Won't do any good." With his rugged good looks, she could see why the reporter was so infatuated with him. Today Linc looked

413

especially appealing in the gray and green uniform that looked like it was tailored to fit his body.

She crossed her arms over her chest. Somehow, Linc had slowly but steadily inched his way past the shield she'd erected around her heart. And that would not do. For one thing, he was firmly entrenched in Natchez, and as soon as this case ended, she was out of here.

And the other . . . she may have forgiven him for siding with her dad about her music career, but she hadn't forgotten how his betrayal had hurt. Sure, he'd said it'd been for her own good. Well, he hadn't exactly said that, more like he'd been afraid she'd get hurt, but that had been her decision to make, not his, and not her dad's.

Linc nudged her. "Where'd you go?"

"Just thinking."

He smiled, looking as though he wanted to ask what she was thinking about, but then he sobered. "Any suggestions of how to handle this with Sarah?"

"Just tell her how you feel. It's up to her what she does with the information."

"I know, but it's not easy," he said.

"I'm sorry, but if you're not interested in her, the kindest thing you can do is to let her know."

"In other words, I can't protect her from hurt, even if it's coming from me?"

"No, you can't. You can let her down easy

though." She picked up her backpack. "I'm going to Rocky Springs. I'm afraid Colton snowed us."

"What do you mean?"

Linc listened as she filled him in, including that Peyton's parents had confirmed he was home. She finished with the information the boys gave her about Colton. "He gave Hannah the marijuana."

"You're kidding. He lied to us."

"I know it's hard to believe. I really felt sorry for him." She picked up her backpack. "I'm going to talk to him."

"I can go with you, that is, if you want me to," he said.

"Don't you have to work?" she asked.

"Emma's here. She'll take care of the tours. We can go in my Tahoe and on the way home check on your truck. And you can leave Cora's car here."

"That sounds like a winner. Driving that station wagon is like driving a tank." She would be happy to get her pickup back tomorrow.

Soon they were turning onto the Trace for the forty-five-minute drive. Neither of them spoke, but it was a comfortable silence. Her cell phone broke the quiet. "It's Sam." She swiped the answer button and put the call on speaker. "You got my message?"

"Yeah. I was by Rocky Springs an hour and a

half ago, and the Masons' camper was still there," he said.

"Good. We just left Natchez headed that way to talk to Colton. Can you meet us at Rocky Springs?"

"Sure. You'll get there before I do—I'm up near Jackson about fifty minutes away."

"We'll wait for you." Ainsley hung up and leaned against the seat. She was so tired.

"Did you talk to your dad today?"

"No. You?"

Linc was quiet a minute. "Your dad and I don't talk much."

"Really." Somehow, she'd just assumed they did. They sure used to talk a lot. "What happened?"

He shrugged one shoulder, but she noticed he gripped the steering wheel so tightly his knuckles turned white.

His Adam's apple bobbed. "I had no business telling you what you should do. I'm sorry."

Words she'd longed to hear for so many years. "What made you change your mind?"

"Maybe I've grown up. And maybe it's because I have enough trouble figuring out my own life without trying to run someone else's." He gave her a wry grin. "I never should have sided with your dad."

"Why did you?" The question was out of her mouth before she could stop it.

It lay between them like a grenade.

When Linc didn't answer right away, she glanced at him. He stared straight ahead at the road. A mile passed, and then another. "I'd really like to know."

He sagged against the seat and then lifted his shoulder in another half shrug. "Part of it was what I told you back then," he said. "I really was afraid the music business would chew you up and spit you out."

"You might have been right about that one."

"I take no pleasure in that."

"You said that was part of it. What was the other?"

"The rest of it is . . . The real reason was I . . ." He took in a deep breath and released it. "I thought if you went on the road, your feelings for me would change."

"You didn't trust me?"

"It wasn't you I didn't trust."

"You didn't trust yourself?"

"Me? No." He glanced at her. "It's just . . . I didn't trust the situation. Being on the road changes people. My parents had a happy marriage until my dad took a traveling job. I thought that might happen to us."

"I don't remember your folks splitting up."

"They didn't, but they came close after Dad cheated on Mom."

"What?" Linc's parents were rock solid. Things

like that didn't happen to families like theirs.

"I couldn't believe he'd do something like that. I always worshiped my dad." He glanced her way. "It happened my first year in high school, before we started dating. That whole year was a nightmare. Almost killed Mom. And if *he* could do it . . . ."

Maybe he was fooling himself, but what he was saying clearly pointed to him not trusting *her*.

"Okay, I understand how the affair could have devastated you, but I'm not your dad," she said slowly. "Just because he cheated didn't mean I would, but you painted me with the same brush. You didn't even give me a chance."

"I know that now, and I'm sorry. It's just that Dad had told me he was so lonely when he was gone, and there were so many temptations on the road." Linc rubbed his hand on his pants. "He quit the traveling job and they worked it out, but, I don't know, I guess it marked me. I hate that I ever gave you that ultimatum, but at that point, I didn't know a lot about trust."

She didn't know what to say. Ainsley turned and stared out the window, seeing only a blur of green. "I guess I understand what you're saying," she said slowly. "But I trusted you with my dreams . . . my heart." With a sigh, she turned back to him. "You destroyed my trust, and once trust is lost, it's hard to get back."

61

Ainsley's tone was so final. The hurt was still there.

Linc had to believe that if his parents could save their marriage, he and Ainsley could work things out. Only if she was willing, though. He glanced at the speedometer and eased off the gas pedal. "I'd like to try to regain your trust."

"Do you think that's possible?" she asked.

"If my parents can do it, I think we can too." He hoped she wouldn't shut him down.

She rubbed her eyes. "This is too deep a conversation to have on three hours of sleep."

"Just think about it."

Ainsley dipped her head. "I will."

That's all he could ask.

They passed the pullout for Mangum Mound. Ten miles to their destination. "Has Sam said anything about getting a report on the shoe prints?"

"No." She checked her phone. "You want to pull over and let me check with him while we have service?"

He turned into the Grindstone Ford pullout and tapped his fingers on the steering wheel while she quickly dialed the ranger's number and put the call on speaker. "Sam, Ainsley Beaumont. Just checking to see if you'd gotten a report back on the prints that were in the mud at the Dyson crime scene."

"Got an email right after you called. The shoe prints at the church were different from the ones in the mud. Those inside the church were Nike running shoes. The others were from a hiking boot. Lowas."

Linc exchanged a glance with Ainsley. "That's the kind of boots Jesse Mason wears," she said. "How far out are you?"

"Still a good half an hour out."

"We should be there in ten minutes, and we'll wait for you."

"Be there as soon as I can."

Linc pulled back onto the Trace. Backup was always good. Suddenly he became very aware of the semiautomatic strapped to his ankle. His pulse kicked up a notch. By the time he turned into the Rocky Springs campground, his mouth was like cotton.

"Watch out!" Ainsley cried.

Linc slammed on the brakes as a teenager darted in front of the Tahoe and kept running.

She leaned forward. "That was Colton! And he has a gun!"

They had no time to wait on Sam. Linc jumped out of the SUV. "Colton!" He scanned the trees. No sign of him. "I'm going after him."

"I'll check at the trailer. His mother may know where he's headed."

While Ainsley jogged toward the camper, Linc plunged into the woods. Colton was probably headed to the Old Trace . . . or the Methodist church. They were both in the same direction.

62

The camper looked deserted when Ainsley got there. What was the mother's name? She racked her brain for the name, but it was no use. She knocked on the trailer door. "Mrs. Mason! Are you here?" she called through the screen.

Ainsley strained to hear over her pounding heart. Nothing. *Alma.* That was her name. "Alma! Are you in there?"

Was that a groan? She jerked the screen door open and bounded into the trailer, scanning the small area. "Alma! Where are you?"

Another groan came from the back of the camper. Alma Mason lay trussed up like a roped calf.

Ainsley slid the gag off her mouth, wincing at the woman's swollen eye and ashen face. "Did your husband do this?"

"N-not this time."

She untied her and helped Alma to sit up. "Did Colton?"

"No! It was a man." She sucked in air. "Had a beard."

Maddox? "Where'd he go?"

"He . . . wanted money, and when we didn't

have any, he wanted Jesse's marijuana stash. That's where they've gone. Him and Jesse."

"Did your husband kill Hannah Dyson?"

Her eyes grew round, and she turned even paler. "He didn't mean to." Tears formed in her eyes. "Jesse found out Colton had given her a bag of marijuana. He just wanted it back, but she ran. Made him mad." Suddenly she clasped her hand over her mouth. "He'll kill me," she moaned. "You can't tell him I told . . ."

Ainsley squeezed her shoulder. "Don't worry. He won't hurt you again."

"You don't know him."

"Do you know where they're going?"

Alma stared wild-eyed at her, then she pressed her lips shut and shook her head.

She knew, all right, Ainsley was certain of it. "You've got to tell me, or Colton might die. I just saw him, and he had a gun."

"Colton? No . . . No!" She buried her face in her hands. "The marijuana is buried in the cemetery at the old Methodist church." She grabbed Ainsley's arm. "Please, you've got to help Colton. That man will kill him."

Ainsley raced to the Tahoe and hopped in on the driver's side. She pulled another magazine out of her backpack and slid it into her pants pocket. Wheeling the Tahoe around, she drove to the main road and hung a right, gunning the SUV forward.

Sam would never make it in time. She called him anyway. Even though he was rushing toward them, he was still fifteen minutes away. She quickly explained what was going on and where she was headed. Ainsley wasn't too worried about Linc—he didn't have a gun, so he would hold back, waiting for her to catch up. He better hold back. Linc didn't have a Kevlar vest on.

She stopped on the west side of the church and parked, quietly closing the Tahoe door. A quick scan of the woods didn't find Linc. *Where is he?* With her gun drawn, Ainsley skirted to the right of the old oak where Hannah had been found. That way, she could come up on the cemetery from the wooded section that bordered it and the church.

She reached the side of the church and peeked around the corner, zeroing in on Jesse and Colton on the ground with their hands and feet tied. He'd used their shirts to gag them. A shovel leaned against one of the tombstones. Their captor was nowhere to be seen.

Ainsley scanned again for Linc, and something moved in the woods near the far corner of the cemetery. She caught her breath as he crawled from the edge of the trees.

Something cold and hard pressed against the back of her neck.

"Well, well, well. Who do we have here? Drop your gun and join your friends."

He didn't try to disguise his voice this time, and Ainsley recognized it. "You won't get away with this," she said, dropping her weapon. "Backup is on the way."

"Yeah, I'm sure it is." He pushed her forward. "Move."

63

Linc raised up from his position on the ground. The man who had Ainsley fit the sketch of Maddox. He'd called 911, but help from Port Gibson was at least twenty minutes away. He didn't know how far away Sam was.

Saving Ainsley was up to Linc. A bead of sweat rolled into his eye, blurring his vision. He rubbed his face on his shirtsleeve and looked again. The Masons were bound and lying on the ground. Ainsley walked slowly toward the gate with the escaped convict behind her. Maddox pushed her through the enclosure, and she stumbled.

With Maddox distracted, Linc belly-crawled through the high weeds to a dead cedar, its bare branches covered in Spanish moss. Gnats buzzed his head.

The old church was to his right. To his left a shoulder-high crypt offered a hiding space and should get him close enough to hear their conversation.

He waited. Maddox turned his back to Linc as he tied Ainsley's hands. Where had he gotten the rope? He'd come prepared, but why? He couldn't have known she was coming here—her trip to

Rocky Springs this morning had been spur-of-the-moment. No, he'd come for another reason, and fate had put her in his hands.

Linc dashed to the low brick building and dropped down behind it. He worked his way around to the far side and peeked around the corner.

"Not so smart now, are you?" Maddox was saying. "Where's my wife?"

"I don't know."

Maddox backhanded her, the sound like the snap of a branch. Linc fisted his hands, pressure building in his chest. He reached for the pistol in his ankle holster, his fingers shaking so hard that they fumbled the snap.

"Leave her alone!"

He jerked his head toward them again.

Colton struggled to stand.

Maddox ignored the boy. "I'm asking you for the last time. Where is she?"

"I told you, I don't—"

Maddox backhanded her again.

Don't push him, Linc urged silently and risked another look. Maddox stood over Ainsley with his hand drawn back.

"Where's your boyfriend?"

"Don't know who you're talking about," she said.

"The ranger that's been sticking to you like glue."

"I came by myself." From his vantage point he could see Ainsley working her jaw. "But Sam Ryker will be here any minute."

"I'm shaking in my shoes." Maddox laughed. "You don't mind if I don't believe you? I'm only going to ask you one more time. Where's your boyfriend?"

"I don't care what you believe," she snapped.

Linc raised his gun, pointing it toward Maddox. It wavered in his hand. He couldn't do it. *Lord, help me.*

In his peripheral vision, Maddox jerked Ainsley to her feet and pressed the gun against her head.

"Nooo!" Linc rushed toward them.

Maddox jerked his head toward the sound. Ainsley broke free from his grasp as Maddox turned toward Linc and fired.

Linc barely felt the stinging in his leg until he went down. Still holding his Glock, he rolled, and a bullet kicked up dirt by his face. Muscle memory kicked in, and he raised his gun, aiming at the center of Maddox's chest. Linc squeezed the trigger.

Maddox went down, dropping his gun. He didn't get back up, and Ainsley kicked it away. Linc used a headstone to climb to his feet and then hobbled to her.

"Are you okay?" she asked as she felt Maddox's wrist for a pulse.

"Yeah. Is . . . is he dead?"

"I think so."

He raised his head at the faraway wail of a siren. "Help's on its way."

"I hear them, but we better make sure an ambulance is on its way too." She held up her hands to be cut loose. "You were great."

"I don't know about that." His head swam as he fished his pocketknife out and managed to cut her loose before darkness closed in.

64

"My mother—how is she?" Colton asked.

Ainsley looked up from where she was leaning over Linc. It was impossible to answer the boy without looking at Maddox. Death was never pretty, and no matter what kind of man he was, a human life had been lost. "She'll make it. I cut her loose from the restraints."

"She was trying to protect *him*," the boy said. "I don't know why."

Neither did Ainsley. She would never understand the dynamics of marriages like theirs. She turned her attention back to Linc. Judging from his pants leg, he'd lost a lot of blood.

Gingerly, she used his knife to slit the pants past the wound. It wasn't spurting, and Ainsley placed the pants material over the wound and pressed against it, hoping one of the sirens she heard was an ambulance.

"Cut us loose," Jesse Mason demanded.

She kept pressure on the wound as she glanced at him. Two long, angry scratches ran down his arm. Then she checked out his boots. Lowas. Just like she remembered. "I don't think so. While we're waiting, do you want to tell me what happened with Hannah Dyson when you ran her down?"

His eyes narrowed. "I don't know what you're talking about."

"Give it up, Mason. Your boots match the prints we found with Hannah's, and I figure the skin under her fingernails will match your DNA."

"You killed her?" Colton's voice shook.

"Shut up," his father snapped.

Ainsley kept the pressure on Linc's leg as the sirens grew closer. Sam was the first to arrive, quickly followed by the Claiborne County sheriff, and then an ambulance. While paramedics loaded Linc into the ambulance, the sheriff called the coroner to the scene for Maddox and then took Jesse Mason into custody.

"His wife told me that Hannah died after he chased her," she said as the ambulance pulled away from the church.

"How about the boy?" Sam glanced toward Colton.

"Yeah. What do you have on him?" Sheriff Randolph asked.

Once he was freed, Colton had stood off to the side, his hands in his pockets, looking as if he'd lost everything. She couldn't help feeling sorry for him.

"The only evidence I have on him is circumstantial," Ainsley said, glancing at Colton. She'd talked to the boy and learned he'd charged

431

Maddox, intending to make him pay for hurting his mom. Maddox had easily taken the gun away from him and bound him like he had Jesse.

"Where'd he get the gun?" Randolph asked.

"It belonged to Jesse, and as far as I can tell, it's legal. Colton used it to try to apprehend Maddox, and could've gotten killed for it," she said.

"I say we give him a break." The sheriff gave her a crooked grin. He thumbed toward two deputies taking packages from a hole in the ground. "Colton showed us the old well where Mason had stored his marijuana. Biggest score we've made this year."

"Thanks. Do you mind if I tell him he's free to go?" she asked.

"Go right ahead."

Ainsley walked toward Colton.

The boy looked up and glanced over her shoulder to the sheriff, who was walking away. "You gonna arrest me?"

"If I don't, will you make me a promise?"

Hope lit his eyes. "Maybe. What is it?"

She liked that he didn't grab at her offer without questioning it. "You'll finish school and take care of your mom."

"Not a problem," he said and took a deep breath and blew it out. "I thought I was a goner for sure after you found out—"

"I don't have any proof of wrongdoing on your part, so don't give me any. Okay?"

"Yes, ma'am. And you don't ever have to worry about me breaking the law a—" He swallowed. "At all."

"Good to hear. Why don't you go check on your mom? I don't think she was bad enough to go to the hospital, and I'm sure she's waiting for you at the camper."

He took off jogging, then stopped and turned around. "Thanks for everything."

Choking back tears, she waved him on. What was wrong with her, crying now? It was over. Finally over. Or it would be when she knew for sure how Linc was.

She found the sheriff and Sam together. "I'm going to the hospital, in case you two need me for anything. I'll send my reports later."

Randolph gave her a thumbs-up and Sam said, "I'll see you there."

Ainsley pulled the Kevlar vest off as she jogged to Linc's Tahoe. What a relief it was to know she wouldn't need it any longer. She called Brent Murphy while service was available and filled him in. He would take care of notifying the right people.

When she reached the hospital, a nurse stopped her from entering the ER patient area. "He's being prepared for surgery."

Her stomach sank to her knees. "Surgery? But the paramedic said it wasn't serious. That it was a through-and-through."

"They still have to go in and clean out the wound."

"You promise it isn't serious?" Of course it was serious. Anytime someone was taken to an operating room, bad things could happen. She stared at the nurse. Ainsley had to make her understand. "I have to see him. Just two seconds? I have to make sure he's all right."

"He's sedated and won't remember you were even here."

"I don't care. Come on . . ." When she hesitated, Ainsley said, "If it was someone you loved, you'd find a way to get back there."

The nurse pinched her lips together. "Oh, all right. Follow me."

True to what she'd said, Linc was sedated, but just seeing him gave Ainsley peace.

He stirred and his eyes half opened. "Ainsley?" he whispered. "I—"

His eyes closed again, and she leaned in closer and took his hand. "I'll be out in the waiting room."

"No!" Panic rode his voice as he gripped her hand. "Stay here."

She glanced at the nurse. "Just 'til they take him back?"

"Let me check. I'll tell them he's requesting it."

Ainsley bit her bottom lip. He'd taken a bullet for her. They had to let her stay. He opened his eyes again.

"Gotta tell you . . . know it . . . won't do much good . . . but . . ." He let go of her hand and touched her cheek. "I never stopped loving you. I—"

Footsteps approached. "Mr. Steele, I'll be your nurse in OR. Are you ready to go to surgery?"

His gaze held hers, then he took a deep breath and looked toward the OR nurse. "I'd rather go home," he said.

She chuckled. "I'm sure you would, and you will as soon as we get this wound cleaned out."

It couldn't be too serious if Linc could joke around. Ainsley walked with them as far as the OR doors. She leaned over and gave him a kiss on the cheek. "I'll be in the waiting room." Then she turned to the nurse. "How long will this take?"

"Not long." The nurse gave her a reassuring smile. "He'll go to a room in short-stay from recovery."

"How will I know when it's over?"

"Are you on his list of people the doctor can share information with?"

"No, but I'm his"—she almost stretched the truth with *fiancée*—"friend."

"Give me your phone number and I'll text you what room he's going to."

"Thank you!"

The nurse wrote her number on her arm and then pushed the bed through the double doors.

Sarah Tolliver was sitting in the waiting room when Ainsley walked through the doors. "How is he?" she demanded. "They wouldn't let me back there."

"He's okay. I talked to him, but he was sedated and barely coherent," Ainsley said. "How did you know?"

"Scanner. Didn't know who it was, just that they were taking someone to the hospital and I got over here just as they took Linc out of the ambulance." Sarah narrowed her eyes. "How did you get back to see him?"

"Stroke of luck, I guess," she said and glanced at her watch. There was still a little time left to visit Cora. "I think I'll check on my aunt."

"Wait! What happened? How did Linc get shot?"

Ainsley really didn't want to get into the details with her. "It was during a takedown."

"I need more than that. My videographer is on the way. Will you give me an interview?"

"I'm sure the Claiborne County sheriff can fill you in."

"But that's not an exclusive."

"I'll think about it. Right now, I'm going up to the second floor."

"I'll call you when Russ gets here."

"I'll see." Ainsley found the stairs and climbed them rather than take the elevator. Cora was in the recliner when she entered the room. The drain tube was gone, and Gran was getting her a cup of water. "Well, look at you," Ainsley said, crossing over to give her a kiss on the cheek. "You're looking much better."

"I'm ready to go home."

"And you will in due time." Gran handed Cora the cup. "At least you're moving out of ICU either this afternoon or tomorrow."

"Hmph."

"Cora Chamberlain! You know you don't want to leave here until you have physical therapy. What if you got home and fell again?"

"I did not fall. I was pushed!"

"What?" Ainsley stared at her aunt. "You remember what happened?"

Cora's eyes widened, and then her face fell. "Not really. It's just . . . for a second my mind . . . but now it's gone."

"You'll remember in time," Ainsley said. "And it doesn't matter. If you were pushed, we think it was Sonny."

"How is he?" Gran asked.

"I'm afraid he didn't make it."

A sheen covered Cora's eyes. "That poor boy."

That poor boy had tried to kill them both. "That's not all." Ainsley sat on the side of Cora's bed and filled them in about Maddox.

"Thank you, Lord," Gran murmured.

"Yes." Ainsley stood. "I'll be right back. I want to check on Drew Kingston."

When she looked into the boy's room, the bed was empty. A nurse passed by. "Do you know what happened to the patient in this room?" Ainsley asked.

"I'm happy to say he was discharged to a step-down unit," the nurse replied.

"So they brought him out of the coma?"

"Late yesterday. I expect he will go home in a day or so. Like your aunt. She's doing much better."

"Yes. I'm thankful for that. And thank you for the great care she got in here."

"She is a sweetheart."

Ainsley thanked her again and returned to Cora's room as a soft bell dinged overhead and a voice announced that ICU visiting time was over. "Drew's been moved," she said, "and we need to leave before they run us out."

Ainsley glanced at her phone as she and Gran walked out to the elevators. No message from Sarah, but there was one from the OR nurse with Linc's room number in short-stay. "I'm going to check on Linc. I'll see you at home."

"Aren't visiting hours over?"

"Just in ICU."

"You'll be staying at the house tonight?"

"Yes." While she hated that a man had died, it was a relief to not worry about someone trying to kill her.

"Give him my love," Gran said.

Ainsley found his room and knocked on the door. When he didn't answer, she pushed the door open and peeked inside. Linc lay sleeping, and she quietly entered the room and sat in a chair.

"I never stopped loving you." Would Linc remember what he'd said? If he did, how would she respond? Could they have a second chance at love? From the way she'd felt when he was shot, it was a real possibility. Time would tell.

Only they didn't have much time, depending on how long it took to find Drew's shooter. When she wrapped up that case, Ainsley would return to the Smokies. And Linc would stay in Natchez.

She stood and walked to the window that looked out over the parking lot. Not a great view, but he shouldn't be here long enough to notice. The nurse had said he'd probably be discharged this afternoon.

Her heart swelled with thankfulness. God had watched over them, and even though Linc had been shot, it was minor compared to what could have happened. The words to the song from Sunday came to her.

She began to hum. *His eye is on the sparrow, and I know he watches me.*

65

Light penetrated the darkness, beckoning Linc. He struggled against whatever held him back, and the light drew closer. Smells assaulted his nose . . . alcohol. And sounds . . . footsteps . . . a squeaky wheel . . . an angelic voice softly singing about a sparrow . . . and God.

He moved his leg and groaned. The singing ceased. "Don't stop," he murmured.

A cool hand brushed his forehead, and he blinked his eyes open. Ainsley stood beside the bed.

"I thought you were an angel."

"You're not bad enough to be delirious, but maybe I should call the nurse," she said, her tone teasing.

"No." Linc stayed her hand. He looked up into Ainsley's eyes that were the color of a clear October sky. He'd been such a fool fifteen years ago. "It's . . . beautiful. You should be singing on the stage."

"Now I know I need to call the nurse."

"No, really. I was so wrong to hold you back."

A shadow crossed her face, then she gave him a gentle smile. "Have you forgotten? I plowed right through yours and Dad's objections and claimed that dream. Only it turned out to be more of a nightmare."

"I'm sorry. Maybe if we'd been more—"

"Stop beating yourself up. I should have quit before I ruined my voice."

"I don't think you've ruined anything." He squeezed her hand. "From what I just heard, you—"

"It doesn't matter. Being on the stage isn't my calling." Ainsley gave a rueful chuckle. "Coming back to Natchez has driven that home to me. Evidently I'm supposed to be catching the bad guys."

His breath caught in his chest. Maddox holding a gun to Ainsley's head came flooding back. "So, Maddox is dead."

"He is." She pulled her hand away and rubbed her arms.

Relief mixed with regret settled in his heart. He'd killed a man. Knowing that was never easy. But Maddox would have killed Ainsley.

"You saved my life," she said. "And Colton's and his dad's. You're the hero in all of this."

He didn't feel like a hero. Then he realized he hadn't had a panic attack when he pulled his gun. "I wish we could've taken him alive."

"Me too. I have a lot of questions I wanted to ask him," she said. "And Jesse Mason has been arrested for Hannah's murder."

"I missed a lot. How . . . ?"

"When I rescued Alma, she told me Jesse confessed to her that Hannah died when he was chasing her. I don't think she knows yet that Hannah died because he covered her mouth, making her heart go out of rhythm."

"That means your job is finished here."

"Just about. I'd like to stick around long enough to make sure it was Maddox who shot Drew."

He had to tell her how he felt. "Glad you're not going back just yet."

Ainsley's shoulders stiffened as she skittered her gaze away, toward the window. "Do you remember what you told me before they took you to surgery?"

He didn't remember anything after Rocky Springs. "No, but I hope it was I love you."

She brought her gaze back to him. "It was, but . . ."

"But what? You can't say you don't love me, not after the way you kissed me."

"I wasn't going to, but I need time to process a few things."

The door opened, and her shoulders relaxed as a nurse bustled in. "I see you're awake now," she said and checked his IV line.

Linc willed the nurse to leave so he could finish what he'd started, but one look at Ainsley's face and the relief in it . . . the moment had passed. His head swam briefly as he raised the bed to a sitting position. "When can I get out of here?"

She patted him on the shoulder. "That'll be up to the doctor, and he's on the floor so you should have your answer soon."

Once the nurse left, Ainsley edged toward the door. "I better go. I have reports that need writing."

"I'd like to finish our conversation."

"Not now, Linc. I-I just can't."

"Okay." He clenched his jaw. "Do you have the keys to the Tahoe? I'll need wheels if the doctor releases me."

"You don't need to drive. Just call and I'll—"

"*I'll* see to it that he gets home," Sarah said from the doorway. "There's no need to bother you, Ainsley."

Linc hadn't heard Sarah arrive.

Ainsley hesitated, then gave him a half wave. "I'm leaving you in good hands."

"Don't go," he said. "We're not finished talking."

Ainsley glanced at Sarah. "We'll talk later."

The room felt empty when she left.

"You don't have to stay," Linc said.

"It's no problem," Sarah said. "Why don't you sleep until the doctor comes in?"

That wasn't a bad idea. That way he wouldn't have to make small talk with her. It seemed like he'd barely closed his eyes when the doctor came

443

into the room. After examining his leg, he gave Linc instructions on how to care for the wound and discharged him. Within an hour, a nurse was wheeling him out of the hospital while Sarah went to fetch her car.

Linc eyed the MINI Cooper and wished for his Tahoe.

"Here," Sarah said, sliding the passenger seat as far back as it would go. "You should fit now."

He gingerly slid across the seat and swung his injured leg around. Not too bad. "Do you have time to pick up the crutches the doctor ordered?"

"I'll get them for you tomorrow. They won't be open now."

That was right. He'd lost a whole afternoon. "I'm not sure how I'll get into my apartment."

"Before I came to the hospital, I ran by and grabbed my grandmother's walker. That should do the trick for tonight."

"Thanks." He looked up into her eyes as she closed the passenger door and wished he hadn't. Hope burned bright . . . and something else. Expectation.

Linc wished he knew what to say. It wasn't that he didn't care for Sarah, because he did. She was Blake's sister, but that's the only way he'd ever seen her or ever would. He blew out a breath. It was a conversation he wasn't up to right now.

Once Linc was settled in his apartment, he texted Ainsley he was home.

"She doesn't love you," Sarah said as she passed by him.

She'd read his text? "Sarah," he said. Might as well get this over with. "I—"

"I'm sorry. I shouldn't have looked over your shoulder. I just don't want you to get hurt. I know how that feels." She fluffed a pillow and put it under his leg. "Can I get you something to drink? And I guess I need to get us something to eat. What would you like?"

"I don't want anything to eat." The meds had nauseated him.

"You really need to put something in your stomach."

"How about a bowl of cereal if there's any milk."

"Cereal? What kind of supper is that?"

"The kind I want, and I'll fix it."

"No." She held her hand out as if to stop him. "If that's what you want, I'll do it."

When she brought him the cereal, he said, "Why don't you go on home."

"But—"

"No, really. I appreciate everything you've done, but I need to be alone."

Her shoulders drooped. "It's her, isn't it? Ainsley."

"No. I'm tired. I'm not used to anyone being here. That's all."

Her jaw hardened, then her whole face

445

changed, softening. "I'm sorry. I don't mean to be a pest." She laughed. "That's what Blake always called me."

"You're not a pest," he said. "And I really do appreciate what you've done today."

"All right, you win. But if you need me tonight, call any time. Okay?"

"Yes, ma'am," he said.

"I'll bring you breakfast, then pick up your crutches."

He couldn't win. "Thank you."

She stopped at the door and turned around. "I hope you sleep well."

The yearning in her face almost undid him.

66

When Ainsley woke the next morning, it took her a second to realize she wasn't at Cora's but in her own bedroom at Gran's. She threw the covers back, and a small leather-bound book fell to the floor. Ainsley picked it up and set it on the nightstand. Charlotte Elliott's diary from the time her husband died.

She'd gone to bed early, but it wasn't long before the flowing script blurred on the page and she'd fallen asleep. There were only ten or so pages left, and maybe she'd skim them and then take the diary to Cora later today.

Ainsley climbed back in bed and leaned against the headboard.

> *Sari found me unconscious and sent her husband, Mose, to fetch Robert. Before Mose left, he laid the pistol my father had given me on the floor beside me. I remember none of this and was informed of this later and only recall what follows in bits and pieces with Mose and Sari filling in the missing details.*
>
> *Sari tried to get me up, but being dead*

weight, I was too heavy for her to move. Smelling salts brought me to my senses. She pressed the gun in my hand just as Zachary returned to the house with a bullwhip. I remember his words and the fury in his face.

"I'll teach you to disobey me!"

When he drew back the whip in his hand, I barely remember firing the gun. And then, I remember nothing until the next day when Sari told me I'd shot Zachary dead when he attacked me again. By that time, it was too late to save my brother from my husband's murderous friends.

Sari and Mose convinced me to say nothing, that even though I was only trying to protect myself, the sheriff who was Zachary's friend might not believe me, and justice would not be served if I were arrested for killing him.

However, I do not know if I can live with this. It is eating away at me.

"Oh no." Ainsley lifted her hand to her lips as she read the last sentence. Poor Charlotte. But Cora would be so happy to learn the diary held the proof her great-grandfather hadn't killed Zachary.

The aroma of fresh-baked cinnamon rolls tickled her nose. She hadn't heard Gran in the kitchen. Ainsley slipped the book into the pocket of her cotton robe and padded down the hall to the kitchen, intending to show Gran the entry.

"Good morning, Sleeping Beauty," Gran said as she took the rolls from the oven. "I'd call that good timing."

"Me too." Ainsley poured a cup of coffee and took it to the table. Her mouth watered when Gran set a steaming hot roll in front of her.

"Wait until it cools."

She smiled. "How many times do you think you've said that to me?"

"At least once a day when you were growing up."

Ainsley cut the roll in fourths so it would cool quicker. As soon as it wouldn't take the skin off her tongue, she popped a bite into her mouth. "These are so good."

"Thank you. Your dad loves them too."

A shadow crossed her good mood. She hoped Gran didn't want to talk about him this morning.

"He's dropping by in a little while."

"Oh." That was the reason for the cinnamon rolls. "I'll try to be out of here before he arrives." Immediately her words shamed her. She sounded like a petulant ten-year-old. Besides that, she owed him an apology, one she'd successfully managed to avoid until this minute. "I'm sorry."

"I made them because you both love cinnamon rolls." Gran sat beside her at the table. "I'm praying you two can work out your problems."

"God did part the Red Sea," Ainsley muttered.

"I heard that." Gran squeezed her hand. "In the last year, he's changed."

She had noticed he wasn't as mercurial. "What caused it?"

"That's his story—"

"To tell, not mine," Ainsley finished the sentence she'd heard every time she'd asked her grandmother for information Gran deemed private.

A car door slammed. "You didn't tell me he'd be here this soon."

"You didn't ask. Just give him a chance." Gran stood as the back door opened. "Good morning, son."

"Morning, Mom," he replied, kissing her on the cheek.

"I'm going to get dressed while you two, uh, eat," Gran said.

The kitchen was quiet as her dad poured his coffee and then helped himself to a roll. She glanced toward the door, half tempted to leave.

"Stay," he said. "Please."

What? He had eyes in the back of his head now? "How—"

He turned around. "I knew what you were thinking. You always run when you don't want to deal with something. But today I want you to hear me out before you run."

A protest died on her lips. He was right about that. Best to get it over with. "I go first," she said.

He looked at her, a question in his eyes. "Okay . . ."

"I really am sorry for what I said Saturday night, and for thinking you'd broken in and tried to steal Cora's diaries. I had nothing to base my accusation on."

There. It was done. And now she stared at her clasped hands, waiting for the fallout.

"I accept your apology."

She held her breath, waiting for the *but*. When it didn't happen, Ainsley raised her gaze. Wait a minute. There was no accusation in his eyes. She rubbed her forehead, trying to gather her thoughts.

"I would like to know why you believed I would ever consider harming you or Cora."

Why had she been so quick to believe it? "You wanted the diary, and I wouldn't give it to you."

"And you thought I was willing to kill you to get it? Never mind." He raked his fingers through his hair. "Your expression says it all. When you caught Sonny in Cora's house, you were expecting it to be me."

Heat flamed her face. She couldn't deny it, but how could she have been so far off base? "Linc didn't expect you, and I shouldn't have jumped to conclusions without more evidence," she said. "Was Sonny blackmailing you?"

"Not blackmailing, but he was selling the diaries to the highest bidder, and there were only two bidders," he said. "I had no idea he'd stolen them from Cora. Said he found them in an out-of-the-way antique store between here and New Orleans. He made me believe Kingston wanted the diaries to use against me in the campaign, and I was trying to keep that from happening."

"That wasn't true?" she asked.

"Oh, it was true Kingston wanted the diaries, all right." He gave an ironic laugh and shook his head. "You know why Kingston wanted the diaries? Same reason as me. Pride."

Ainsley frowned. "I don't understand."

"His wife is involved in several women's groups that support minorities, president of one, and to Adele Kingston, perception is everything. She would be embarrassed if the diaries ever came to light. He was willing to pay whatever it took to get his hands on them."

Remembering the woman, Ainsley could believe it, but maybe there'd be a generation one day that wasn't fixated on pedigrees and family trees. "How did you find that out?"

"I picked up the phone Sunday afternoon and called Kingston."

"And he told you all that?"

"Not in so many words, but enough for me to read between the lines."

"I'm proud of you for calling him," she said.

His lips curved upward in a tentative smile. "I don't believe I've ever heard you say that before. Thank you."

She tilted her head, studying him. "You're different."

He nodded slowly as he wrapped his hands around the coffee cup. "Been going to church again . . . and listening to your grandmother. If I had a do-over, I'd do so many things differently, starting with our relationship. I hope it's not too late to mend it."

Was it? It would take time. "God did part the Red Sea," she said with a wry grin. "But it won't happen overnight like that did."

He laughed out loud. "You're right, but I want to be part of your life."

If God could change her dad's life, maybe he hadn't forgotten her. She'd been so close to him at one time. *He wasn't the one who moved.* Tears sprang to her eyes. Her dad wasn't the only one who needed to mend a relationship.

Ainsley reached for a tissue in her pocket, and her fingers brushed the diary. She pulled the leather-bound journal out and slid it across the table.

"Is this Charlotte Elliott's diary?" He opened it and gently thumbed through the pages.

She nodded. "It vindicates Cora's belief her great-grandfather didn't murder anyone."

"You're kidding!"

"No. Zachary had beaten Charlotte so badly she feared he would kill her. She shot him in self-defense. Robert arrived not long afterward and found his sister unconscious. He didn't tell the sheriff when he arrived that Charlotte had been the one who killed her husband.

"Robert was arrested, and you know what happened after that. Charlotte didn't know her brother had even been arrested until it was too late. She blamed herself for his death at the hands of her husband's friends, and I don't think she ever got over it."

Her dad closed the diary and slid it back to her. "I wonder what Cora will do with this."

"I don't know. Finish her book, I suppose, and then publish it. Might be a bestseller. Who knows?"

"She doesn't intend to offer it for sale," he said. "Her book is a historical record just for our family."

Ainsley should have known that. Cora wouldn't intentionally hurt anyone.

"I'm glad we've talked today." He blew out a breath. "Just wish it would've happened a long time ago."

She shrugged. "I don't think either of us is that easy to talk to. Gran says we're both just alike."

"You think?" he said with a laugh, then he pressed his lips together and looked up at the ceiling before he brought his gaze back to her. "Since we're being honest here, I owe you an apology too."

"For?"

"I was wrong to discourage you from your dream. You have a beautiful voice. Back then, all you lacked was confidence."

She pressed her hand to her lips. Ainsley never thought she'd hear him say those words. "Why did you?"

"I was afraid you'd get hurt—the music business is ruthless."

"I thought you believed I wasn't good enough."

His brows lowered into a frown. "No. I never thought that."

"But you called it a pipe dream. And you never *said* I was good."

"I didn't think I had to. I'm your father—you should have known I would've told you if your voice wasn't good."

"A little support every now and then would have gone a long way," Ainsley said.

"Maybe I didn't know how." He took a sip of coffee and made a face. "This is cold."

"I'll get you a fresh cup." All these years, she'd believed he doubted her singing ability. If she'd known the truth, would it have made any difference? Ainsley poured his coffee and set it on the table, then went back for hers. Not really.

Living what she thought was her dream had left her empty, not fulfilled like the job she was doing now.

When she sat down again, he said, "I'm glad you tried it, and I've never understood why you quit. You seemed to be doing well, and I thought you were headed for a solo career."

She felt like she was in la-la land.

"I never quite bought that story about you wanting to be a ranger, although you've done a great job there."

"I didn't quit because I wanted to. I'd strained my voice, and my agent and the recording studio didn't think I'd get it back." She waited for him to say I told you so.

"I'm sorry about that. It's been twelve years . . . is your voice better?"

Her voice hadn't cracked yesterday when she'd sung in Linc's hospital room, but that didn't mean anything. "I'm almost afraid to try."

"Maybe you should see a voice teacher."

"I'll think about it."

He pushed back from the table. "I think we're about done here. Let's not wait so long to talk again. Okay?"

"Good with me."

"Oh, and don't let Linc get away from you. He's a good man."

"Yes, he is, but I don't know if—"

"He's nothing like me," her dad said. "Even if he did side with me fifteen years ago, it was only because he was afraid of losing you."

67

Wednesday morning Linc used the crutches to maneuver around his kitchen. Occasionally, he tentatively tested his leg to see if the muscle was ready to bear weight yet. So far it wasn't.

The coffee machine gurgled one last time, and he set the cup on the countertop. Rather than risk spilling the hot liquid, he drank it standing while he checked his phone. He'd gotten one message from Ainsley saying she'd see him later this afternoon and five messages from Sarah.

Yesterday Ainsley had called him midmorning to see if he needed anything and to let him know she would be tied up in virtual meetings with her supervisor in East Tennessee and the FBI. Then she would be filling out reports. Then nothing until this morning.

His front doorbell rang just as he got a text from Sarah. *"At the front door with breakfast."*

He texted back. *"Come around to the back."*

In less than a minute, she opened the door and waved a tan paper sack, spreading the aroma of bacon through the kitchen. "I know how much you like these," Sarah said. "Let me take your coffee to the table."

While he hopped to his chair, she divided the biscuits, two for him and one for her, and then sat across from him. "Thanks for picking these up. You didn't have to."

"I knew if I didn't, you'd just have cold cereal again."

"You're probably right." The food was every bit as good as it smelled. "Not working today?" he asked, eyeing her tan-and-olive-green camo pants and an oversized T-shirt.

"No. Did you forget . . ." Disappointment rang in her voice. "You did. It's June sixteenth."

It hit him. Blake died two years ago today. His appetite gone, he set what was left of the second biscuit on the table. "I'm sorry . . . there's just been so much going on."

"We are still going on the picnic, right? I have a basket all packed." A note of panic raised her voice. "I really need to get away from everything for a few hours."

The truth was, Linc didn't feel up to going, but it had been his idea in the first place. What could a few hours hurt, especially after she'd helped him yesterday and today. He palmed his hands. "Sure."

She rewarded him with a brilliant smile. "Thank you. I just don't think I can do today by myself."

"How about your dad? Isn't he going?"

"I don't think he feels up to it," she said.

"I'd like to stop by and see how he is." Maybe he could persuade Mr. Tolliver to go with them. The picture of just the two of them in a cozy picnic setting was not the message he wanted to send Sarah.

"Okay, but don't forget your swimsuit."

He stared at her. "I have a gunshot wound to my leg, Sarah."

She looked stricken. "Of course, you can't get in the water. I don't know what I'm thinking. More proof I just need to get away for a few hours. If you're ready, we'll go."

"Now?"

"Yes. Didn't I tell you, I have to work this afternoon?"

"No. Why don't we wait until your day off?"

"It won't be the anniversary of the day Blake died. And besides, I already have a picnic lunch packed. We'll pick it up on the way."

He gave up. It was easier to go along with her than to argue. "Let me wash up and I'll be ready."

Linc slipped his phone in his back pocket and hopped to the bathroom. He should just tell Sarah he wasn't up to a picnic today. After he washed up, he texted Ainsley he would be out of pocket for a few hours with Sarah, and didn't get a response.

Fifteen minutes later they pulled into the

Tolliver drive. Linc had spent so many nights with Blake at this house when they were kids. He missed his old friend. "I'm glad you're staying here with your dad."

"He's really gone downhill since Blake's death. Want me to tell him to come to the car and save you from getting out?"

Mr. Tolliver had been feeble at Blake's funeral. "No. I'll go in while you're getting the basket." He climbed from her car and used the crutches to swing up on the two steps leading into the house.

"He's probably back in the den," Sarah said as she held the screen door open for him.

Linc hobbled down the hallway, passing Blake's old room. Maybe he'd peek in for old times' sake after he spoke to Mr. Tolliver. The older man sat in his cave-like den, focused on the Western playing on the TV.

"Hello, Mr. Tolliver." He leaned the crutches against a chair and sat down.

The older man switched on a lamp beside his recliner and turned toward Linc. He'd aged since Blake's death. His salt-and-pepper hair was snow-white, and creases lined his face. He couldn't be more than sixty-five but looked twenty years older. The weathered face broke into a smile. "Linc, haven't seen you since . . . that's right, you were at the funeral."

"How are you doing, sir?" he asked.

"Tolerable. It hasn't been the same with Blake gone."

"I agree. Are you going on the picnic with us?" Linc asked.

"Picnic?" His eyes lit with anticipation. "What picnic?"

Sarah entered the room. "You remember, Pop—I told you this morning. We're going to the cabin."

Mr. Tolliver sighed. "I imagine you did."

"Would you like to go with us, sir?"

Before he could answer, one of Linc's crutches slipped and fell to the floor. He leaned over to retrieve it, looking up just as Sarah gave her father a hard look.

The older man's shoulders drooped. "You two go on. I'd just be a bother."

"We're not going to force you," Sarah said and turned to Linc. "You ready?"

He nodded. "Go ahead. I'll catch up."

Once Sarah left, Linc shook hands with Mr. Tolliver. "I wish you'd reconsider."

"No, I better stay here."

"Well, if you ever need anything, give me a call," Linc said.

"I will." Mr. Tolliver paused for a moment. "I'm really worried about Sarah, though. She's taking his death very hard."

"I know. Anniversaries are always tough. Maybe it'll get better after today." Linc swung around on the crutches and hobbled back down the hall. When he came to Blake's old room, he opened the door and flipped on the light.

He caught his breath.

The room was a shrine to his friend. His photo hung on three walls and all Blake's trophies from high school and college lined the shelves under the photos. On the fourth wall was a rack with all of his guns. Linc counted them. Twelve. He'd often joked that Blake could start his own war.

Wait, there should be thirteen—he'd often teased Blake about the unlucky number. An empty space caught his eye, and Linc used the crutches to hobble in front of the guns.

"What are you doing in here?" Sarah demanded.

"Looking around for old times' sake." He turned around. Her face was flushed. "Which one of Blake's guns is missing?"

"Don't have a clue. I haven't been in this room in months. Are you ready? Don't want the potato salad to spoil."

With one last look, Linc followed her out of the room and to her car. As he settled himself in the passenger seat, he remembered one of the missing guns. "Blake's service pistol is missing," he said.

"You mean his Glock?" she asked. "Pop is probably cleaning it."

68

Ainsley swung into the hospital parking lot and found a parking space. Cora had been moved to a room in the step-down unit late yesterday and Gran had spent the night with her. She would probably be released in a day or two, barring an unforeseen complication.

As soon as she checked on Cora and Gran, Ainsley planned to interview Drew Kingston, who was on the floor. She wanted to get his statement and wrap up his part in the investigation. She'd tried to interview Drew yesterday, but his dad blocked her. Austin's argument was the boy needed his rest and didn't remember anything anyway.

Cora was in a chair by the window facing the wooded area.

"How's everyone today?" Ainsley asked.

"I'm ready to go home," Cora grumbled.

"What does the doctor say?"

Gran spoke up. "Maybe later this week, if all her blood work and CT scans are good."

"They'll find something wrong with it," Cora snapped back with a sniff.

Ainsley slipped three leather-bound diaries

from her backpack and presented them to Cora. "I believe you've been searching for these?"

Her aunt gasped. "Charlotte's diaries? How? When?"

Ainsley laughed. "One came from your safe—it's the one with the information you've been looking for. Sonny had the other two."

Her thin fingers caressed the leather. "Have you read them?"

Ainsley nodded. "They have all the information you need to prove Robert Chamberlain didn't kill his brother-in-law."

"You're not going to tell me what it says?"

She smiled. "No, ma'am. I might leave something out."

Cora turned to Gran. "You'll have to read to me since I don't have my glasses, and I can't see that well anyway since the surgery."

Ainsley walked to the door. "I need to check on someone. I'll see you two later."

Out in the hallway, she took out her phone to call Linc. She'd been meaning to check in with him to see what time she could stop by his house. Her heart thudded in her chest as thoughts of what she wanted to talk about crossed her mind. What if he'd changed his mind about them? After all, the way she'd left it between them hadn't been encouraging.

She opened her phone and frowned. He'd sent her a text. She hadn't heard it come in. After she read it, a shadow crossed her heart. It had only been two days since he'd been shot. What was he doing going on a picnic with Sarah Tolliver?

Ainsley was tempted to forget interviewing Drew. A sense of urgency told her to find Linc. No. She was here at the hospital. Get this done and then she could find him.

Drew's room was around the corner from Cora's, and she quickly walked to it. The door was partially open, and she knocked before she walked in. The boy was alone and looked as though he was sleeping. She cleared her throat.

His eyes popped open, and he shrank back when he saw someone was in the room.

"Drew, do you remember me? Ainsley Beaumont—I'm a law enforcement ranger."

"Oh yeah," he said, visibly relaxing. "I was afraid you were . . ."

"Who? The person who shot you?"

"M-maybe."

"Do you know who your assailant was?"

He didn't say anything.

"Don't you want the person who shot you to pay for what they did?"

He shrugged and raised the head of the bed. "I told my dad I didn't remember anything. He'll be mad if I talk to you."

She had to get him to tell her who the shooter was and tried a different tactic. "We caught the person responsible for Hannah's death."

"Really?" He licked his lips. "Could you hand me that cup of water?" When she gave it to him, he asked, "Was it Colton?"

Ainsley shook her head. "His dad. Seems he discovered Colton had given her a package of marijuana, and he wanted her to pay for it. Instead she ran, and they had an altercation and her heart got out of rhythm. That's why she died."

He was silent for a moment. "Thanks. Does her mom know?"

"Yes. Sam Ryker, the Natchez Trace ranger, told her," she said. "What were you going to tell us Saturday?"

He twisted a corner of the bedsheet. "She kept saying she was sorry. That I made her do it. That I shouldn't have been at Hannah's house that night."

"Who is she?"

He pressed his lips together and refused to look at Ainsley.

"You won't be safe as long as this person is running around loose."

"She came to the hospital . . . said she'd kill me if I talked."

"Whoever it is can't hurt you if she's in jail."

He closed his eyes, his lashes dark against his white face. "It was that reporter."

"What?" Her knees threatened to buckle. "S-Sarah Tolliver?"

He nodded. "She was going to shoot me again,

and suddenly it was like I was someone else. Somebody called Blake."

Ainsley's thoughts looped through her head like tangled fishing lines as she studied his face. Drew did resemble a teenaged Blake. Same blond hair and square jaw.

Suddenly Ainsley froze. *Linc.* He was with Sarah. Today was the anniversary of Blake's death . . . What if Sarah blamed Linc for his suicide and intended to hurt him?

"Thanks, Drew. And don't be afraid. I'll have security post a guard at your door," she said and rushed from the room.

Ainsley called for security outside Drew's door and then tried Linc's number. It went straight to voicemail. Was she already too late? No! She had to find him. Get him away from Sarah . . .

Where were they going on the picnic? Had he told her? *Think!*

If he had, she didn't remember the location. Who would know? She remembered Blake and Sarah's mother died when they were in grade school. Their dad. Tolliver . . . oh what was his first name? Ed, maybe?

She put his name in an app on her phone that provided addresses and background information. A few minutes later she was driving toward Mr. Edward Tolliver's house. What if he was with them? *Lord, I need help.*

When she lost her voice, God had been silent.

She had to believe he would answer her today.

Ainsley parked on the street and bounded up the steps to the front door. She pounded on it. Her heart felt like a hammer in her chest. She pounded again. "Mr. Tolliver! Are you in there?"

She raised her hand just as the door creaked open.

"My goodness, whatever is wrong? Do I know you?"

"It's Ainsley Beaumont. Can you tell me where Sarah is?"

"I remember you. Such a beautiful voice," he said.

"Sarah. Where is she?"

He smiled broadly. "She's on a picnic with my son's best friend. Do you remember Blake?"

"Yes, sir. Do you know where they went for their picnic?"

He rubbed above his eye. "She told me . . . if I can just remember. I think it was at Natchez Lake . . . no, she changed it . . ."

She clenched and unclenched her hands, waiting.

"Oh, of course. They went to my brother's cabin that borders Natchez Lake."

"Do you have an address?"

"Oh my . . . I suppose it has an address, but I have no idea what it is."

"How do I get to it?"

"You take the road like you were going to the

lake, but when you come to the turnoff, you go straight. Keep going until you come to a gravel crossroad and turn back toward the lake." He paused for her to type the directions into her phone. "When you get to the cabin, you'll see a wooden sign nailed to a post with the name Tolliver on it."

"Is the property in your brother's name?"

He nodded. "Kenneth Tolliver. But I don't understand why it's so important to reach her. She'll be back in a couple of hours."

"It just is. Thank you," she said and hurried to her car, then entered Kenneth Tolliver into the app. Just like she figured—no address for a cabin near Natchez Lake.

She put Natchez Lake in her GPS. She'd have to rely on Mr. Tolliver's directions once she reached the lake, and she hoped they were right. As she pulled away from the house, she phoned Sam Ryker and then added the sheriff to the call.

"I need your help," she said. "Sarah Tolliver is Drew Kingston's shooter, and I think she's going to kill Linc."

69

They passed the turnoff for Natchez Lake. "We're not going to the lake?" Linc asked.

Sarah shook her head. "I thought I told you. My uncle has a private lake and cabin on the other side. It's a much nicer spot to picnic, and there won't be a lot of people around to bother us."

After a few miles Sarah turned onto a gravel road. Private meant isolated, and he didn't like it that no one knew where they were. He took out his phone to text Ainsley. "No signal," he said. "Does anyone know where we'll be?"

"Oh, Dad does. Why?"

"I like to plan for contingencies."

"There won't be any, you'll see." She looked over at him and smiled.

"Watch the road," he said sharply.

"Oh, you're just like Blake. Bossy."

Linc gripped the armrest. "He was a good guy, and I didn't mean to be bossy."

"I haven't been out here since Blake and I came."

"I really miss him," he said. "I don't know how I kept from seeing the signals that he was thinking of ending his life."

Sarah didn't say anything, but her knuckles turned white on the steering wheel. After another mile, she turned onto a dirt road that wound back toward the lake. Soon a rustic cabin came into view. "Here we are," she said, a little too brightly.

She parked in front of the log cabin, and he looked around, taking in the dense woods and underbrush. The cabin didn't look as though anyone had stayed in it in years.

He crawled out of the car and balanced on the crutches. "How long has it been since you've been here?"

Sarah ducked her head as she locked the car doors and pocketed the key. Then she turned and faced the woods. "Isn't the lake beautiful? Blake always loved swimming in it."

Something was wrong. Bad wrong. Sarah had her hands in her pockets and stared past the cabin toward a wall of trees, smiling like she was watching a movie in her head.

"What do you see, Sarah?" he asked softly.

"The lake. Don't you see the sun shimmering off the water? Let's go down to the dock and join the others."

"I think we need to go home," he said. Sarah had totally lost it. He needed to get her back to Natchez where she could get help.

She whirled toward him, her eyes blazing. "No. We're not leaving."

"Yes, we are," he said firmly.

"No. We're staying here until Ainsley comes." She pulled a gun from her pocket.

Blake's service pistol. His heart slammed against his ribs. "She doesn't even know where we are."

"But I'll call her and she'll come, and this time I'll get rid of her."

"There's no cell phone signal . . ." he said. "What do you mean, you'll get rid of her?"

"Shut up!" She waved her free hand for him to stop, then yanked out her phone. "No! There has to be cell service!"

"I'm afraid there isn't. Why do you want her here?" Linc had a sick feeling he knew why.

Sarah turned on him. "It's your fault. You ruined everything. Blake is dead because of you. She has to come. You have to know what it feels like to lose someone you love."

If she came a little closer, he could use a crutch to knock her legs out from under her. "I know what it's like to lose someone I love. Blake was like a brother to me," he said.

"But he wasn't your brother. He was *mine!* It's your fault I had to kill him."

His breathing stilled. She'd killed Blake? "W-what? Why?"

"He was so miserable. I couldn't stand to see him suffer . . . so I gave him enough pills to give him relief forever."

"But he wasn't suffering," Linc said. "He was

going to a rehab place in Pennsylvania. He was putting his life back together."

"He was leaving me. Don't you understand? I did everything for him. Gave up my life for a whole year and just like that, he was going to leave."

Suddenly she rushed him, knocking the crutches away. Linc lost his balance and fell back, hitting his head on a post. He fought the darkness closing in.

70

Ainsley slowed at the road to the Natchez Lake campground. The chance of anyone knowing the location of the Tolliver cabin was slim. She kept going.

Nate and Sam were still at least fifteen minutes away, and according to Nate, there were houses that bordered lake property on the far side. Mr. Tolliver had said to stay on the gravel road and look for a sign.

Just ahead on the left it appeared there was a driveway, and she slowed. No sign. Ainsley gunned the motor. *Wait.* Was that a piece of wood nailed to a post? She stopped and backed up. Sure enough, "Tolliver" was written on a wooden sign almost covered with honeysuckle vines.

Ainsley parked just off the road in the drive so Nate and Sam could find the place. She eased the door shut and pulled her gun as she made her way silently to the cabin. There was no sound of anyone around. Maybe she was at the wrong place. She glanced at the ground. Grass flattened by a vehicle, probably Sarah's. But where were they?

Sweat ran down the side of her cheek, and she

wiped her face with her sleeve. Up ahead, the drive curved out of sight. When she had a clear view of the cabin, she saw a mint-green MINI Cooper parked out front.

Ainsley blinked. Linc was bound to the post on the porch, and he had a gag tied around his mouth. But at least he was still alive.

Ainsley started to charge forward and stopped. Where was Sarah?

She scanned the woods that had almost overtaken the small yard surrounding the cabin. Ainsley darted to the back of the MINI Cooper. Linc's eyes widened, and then he shook his head. She ignored him and dashed to the porch and pulled the gag down.

"Run!" he whispered.

"No. Where's Sarah?" She holstered her gun and fumbled with the knots on the rope binding his hands. She almost had the rope loose when she heard a sound behind her and looked over her shoulder. Sarah stood in the doorway, a gun in her hands. Ainsley reached for her Sig.

"Don't." Sarah waved the pistol in her hand. "Move away from him."

Ainsley hesitated, and Sarah turned the gun toward Linc. "Move away or I'll shoot him. Take your gun out and lay it on the porch."

She backed away from Linc. "Why are you doing this?"

"Someone has to pay for my brother's death.

Why not the one responsible? You're just icing on the cake. Your gun. Now."

"What do you mean?" Ainsley laid the pistol on the ground. She had to stall until Sam and Nate and their deputies could get here.

"This way he'll experience what it's like to lose someone he loves. Like I did."

"*You* killed Blake," Linc said.

She killed her brother? And let Linc believe it was his fault? In her peripheral vision, Ainsley saw Linc's arms move as he worked to get out of the rope. She had to keep Sarah's attention away from him. "It was you at Dad's political rally, wasn't it? Too bad you're such a bad shot. Not the shooter Blake was, are you?"

"Shut up."

"On top of that, you lost your brother's rifle. All for nothing."

"It wasn't my brother's rifle." Sarah's cheeks flushed and her lips flattened. "I told you to shut up."

"Is that the one you used on Connie Hanover?"

Sarah glared at her. "She wouldn't have been shot if she hadn't jumped up. And you would have been dead."

"But I'm not."

Linc's arms relaxed, and he gave her a slight nod. Ainsley sidestepped toward Linc, hoping to draw Sarah closer to him.

Almost automatically, Sarah moved with her, keeping the gun pointed toward Linc's head. "What are you doing?"

"The sun's in my eyes," she replied and took another step, and Sarah followed her.

"Enough talk. Time to say goodbye. And guess what, Linc? You get to watch." Sarah swung the gun around until it was pointed straight at Ainsley's chest.

Linc exploded into action, tackling Sarah just as she fired. Ainsley dove for the ground, feeling the heat of the bullet slice the air by her shoulder. She crawled to her gun and grabbed it, her fingers closing over the trigger.

Sarah broke loose from Linc and turned her gun toward his head.

Ainsley fired at Sarah. She still held her gun on Linc, and Ainsley's finger tightened on the trigger again.

Then the gun fell from Sarah's hand and she crumpled to the ground.

Ainsley dropped her gun to her side and rocked back on her heels, her gaze connecting with Linc's. Unexpectedly, tears filled her eyes and threatened to spill down her cheeks.

He wasn't hit.

Linc grabbed the crutch closest to him and hopped toward her. She met him halfway.

"Ainsley . . ." His voice broke. He pulled her into his embrace.

She leaned into him and laid her head on his chest.

"I love you," he murmured against her hair.

Her heart spiraled. "I love you too. When I thought she was going to kill you . . ."

He tilted her chin up. "But she didn't. Ainsley, I want to spend the rest of my life with you."

71

TWO WEEKS LATER

Ainsley stood with her dad on one side and Linc on the other, her palms sweaty as the congregation sang the first verse of "His Eye Is on the Sparrow."

Midway through the second verse, she joined in and soon was conscious of nothing but lifting her voice.

I sing because I'm happy,
I sing because I'm free,
For his eye is on the sparrow,
And I know he watches me.

It was on the last refrain that Ainsley realized hers was the only voice singing. Total silence filled the church when Ainsley finished. Then a thunderous applause broke out.

She was barely aware of sitting until Linc hugged her.

Her dad beamed at her. "I want you to know I thought that was beautiful," he whispered.

Peace filled her heart. She'd done it. Lifting her

eyes heavenward, she murmured, "Thank you."

The church service seemed to fly by, and they were soon leaving. "Ride to your grandmother's house with me?" Linc asked.

"I'd love to."

While he seemed happy for her, a somber frown creased his brow. "So," Linc said as he pulled away from the church, "we haven't talked about what your plans are."

No, they hadn't, because until this morning, she wasn't sure what she wanted to do. Not only that, she'd been so busy getting Cora settled in Gran's house after the sisters decided neither of them needed to live alone. Then she'd listed Cora's house with a Realtor and found someone to come in each day to help Gran and Cora after she left. If she left.

"Could we talk about that after we eat? Gran's expecting us in"—she checked her watch—"five minutes."

"You know you're killing me," he grumbled.

"Poor baby," she said and laughed. Linc had asked her about her plans at least once a day for the past two weeks, but she couldn't tell him something she didn't know. They hadn't talked about their relationship at all. She didn't know why Linc had skirted the subject, but Ainsley had because she feared he'd said he loved her while still caught up in the heat of the action.

And there was the matter of Sarah's death. It

was something they both had to live with. Ainsley had talked with the department's psychologist on an internet face-to-face and would have an in-person session before she returned to work.

Linc still had to come to terms with the fact that Sarah had killed her brother . . . his best friend. She feared he was still dealing with guilt over his hesitation when Blake was shot, but she did know he'd been visiting the gun range.

Maybe he didn't even remember saying he loved her.

Once Sunday dinner was over, Gran shooed them out of the kitchen. "You two have better things to do than help clean up, and besides, your dad will help me, right, son?"

"Sure," her dad replied.

Ainsley followed Linc out. "Where to?"

He cocked his head. "How about the river bluff? It would at least be cooler there."

"Your leg up to it?" While physical therapy had really helped him, she didn't want him to overdo it.

"I'm good."

They parked across from the Grand Hotel and climbed the steps to the River Walk and stood by the rail watching the mighty Mississippi flow by. She turned to him. "You've asked me what I'm going to do. How about you? Are you rejoining the FBI?"

He didn't hesitate. "No. I love what I'm doing.

Even though I can handle a gun again, it's not something I'd like to do regularly." Linc turned to her. "Last time, I'm asking what your plans are."

"It depends." She gave him a shaky smile and looked up into his eyes. What if he'd decided he'd spoken in haste that day?

"On?"

She licked her lips. "How you feel about us."

"Finally!" The word came out more a sigh than anything else.

"What do you mean?"

"I was so afraid you regretted what you said that day."

She stared at him wide-eyed. "I thought you—"

"I've never stopped loving you, but I didn't want to get hurt again if you'd changed your mind. Thought maybe if I gave you time, you'd bring it up."

"We're both crazy," she said.

He pulled a small box from his pocket and dropped to his knee. "Ainsley Beaumont." He opened the box, and a solitaire glittered against the black velvet. "Will you marry me?"

Tears spilled down her face, and she thought her heart would burst. "Yes, Lincoln Steele, I'll marry you!"

Acknowledgments

To my family and friends who believe in me and encourage me every day, thank you.

To my editors, Rachel McRae and Kristin Kornoelje, thank you for making my stories so much better.

To the art, editorial, marketing, and sales team at Revell, especially Michele Misiak and Karen Steele who have to deal with me directly—thank you for all your hard work. And to the ones behind the scenes, you're awesome!

To Julie Gwinn, thank you for your direction and for working so tirelessly with me and for being my friend.

To the rangers who have patiently answered my questions, thank you! Any mistakes I make are totally on me.

To Wesley Harris, thank you for answering my questions on police procedure so quickly when I shoot you an email! Again, any mistakes are mine.

To my readers . . . you are awesome! Thank you for reading my stories. Without you, my books wouldn't exist.

As always, to Jesus, who gives me the words.

About the Author

Patricia Bradley is the author of *Standoff* and *Obsession*, as well as the Memphis Cold Case Novels and Logan Point series. Bradley won an Inspirational Reader's Choice Award in Romantic Suspense, a Daphne du Maurier Award, and a Touched by Love Award; she was a Carol Award finalist; and three of her books were included in anthologies that debuted on the *USA Today* bestseller list. She is cofounder of Aiming for Healthy Families, Inc., and she is a member of American Christian Fiction Writers and Sisters in Crime. Bradley makes her home in Mississippi. Learn more at www.ptbradley.com.

Center Point Large Print
600 Brooks Road / PO Box 1
Thorndike, ME 04986-0001 USA

(207) 568-3717

US & Canada:
1 800 929-9108
www.centerpointlargeprint.com